He helped her down from the horse.

Buddy was waiting. Smith patted the dog's head and scooped up his hat. He wondered what Willa would do if he grabbed her and kissed her. She'd probably scream her head off. The dog would bite him and Charlie would come charging up the hill.

What the hell? He liked taking a risk when the odds were stacked against him.

With two quick steps he was beside her. His hands closed around her upper arms and dragged her up against him. He lowered his head, kissing her hard. The kiss left her stunned. She couldn't get her breath and for a minute she couldn't think. He held her, gave her a second softer kiss, his lips brushing back and forth across hers before he let her go.

"Why . . . why did you do that?" she whispered.

"To teach you a lesson. Don't trust a man to always play the gentleman. Especially . . . a drinking man. And . . . never, never go off alone with him."

"You want me to be afraid of you?"

"Why not? I'm sure as hell afraid of you."

"The undisputed grand master
of the frontier novel."
—*Romantic Times*

"The Louis L'Amour of the romance novelists."
—*Beverly Hills Courier*

A GENTLE GIVING

Dorothy Garlock

WARNER BOOKS

A Time Warner Company

WARNER BOOKS EDITION

Cover illustration by Donna Diamond
Hand lettering by Carl Dellacroce

Warner Books, Inc.
1271 Avenue of the Americas
New York, NY 10020

W A Time Warner Company

Printed in the United States of America

First Printing: January, 1993

10 9 8 7 6 5 4 3 2 1

This book is for my friend,
Mary T. Knibbe,
with fond memories
of
good conversation,
hot butter beans and cornbread.

A faithful friend is a strong defense.
A faithful friend is the medicine of life.
                              —Apocrypha

CHAPTER
* 1 *

Awakened by the heat beating against her face, Willa leaped from her bed. Flames enveloped the table and the bureau where she kept the pictures of her mother and the few mementos she had managed to save over the years. Suddenly the straw mattress on her bed erupted in a ball of fire.

Over the sound of crackling flames, a murmur of angry voices reached her.

She ran out the door as the fire blaze behind her roared angrily into the workroom where her stepfather made his beautiful clocks.

Was this a dream: the roof ablaze and flames dancing a queer rigadoon against the dark sky?

Willa Hammer faced the angry crowd. Why had they come to the edge of town to fire the little shack she had so lovingly made into a home? A clod of dirt struck her cheek. She cried out in surprise and terror and lifted her hand to shield her face.

"Slut! Spawn of the devil!" The woman who threw the clod had spoken to her just that morning when she had gone to post a letter. She had not been friendly but she had been civil. "It's because of you—"

"We don't want ya here!" yelled another.

"It's evil ya 'n' that deformed monster brought to this town," a man shouted. "Nothin's been right since ya come here."

"Get the hell out of Hublett or . . . we'll tar 'n' feather ya!"

A six-gun, fired into the air, made an unspoken threat clear to even Willa's befuddled mind.

Pelted with dirt clods, she raised her arm to protect her head and turned toward the road. A man with a hickory switch in his hand blocked her way.

"Uppity whore! Whelp of a thievin' murderin' hunchback," he shouted, his sneering face one she would never forget. Willa tried to edge around him, but he caught her nightdress at the neck and ripped it, leaving an arm and shoulder bare. Then he lifted his arm again.

Willa heard the breathy hiss of the switch slicing through the air just before it sent a serpent of flame writhing across her back.

"Ya ain't got no shotgun now."

Unremitting terror engulfed her. This was the man she had turned away a few nights ago when he had come pounding on their door, drunk, and showing off for his friends. He had wanted to know what she would charge for an hour in bed. She had endured the shouted insults until he had attempted to break down the door. Then she had flung it open and faced him with the shotgun. With fear making her stomach roil, though she had been through this many times before in so many towns that she had even forgotten the names, she had ordered him to leave.

"Bitch! Ever since ya come here ya've been lookin' down

yore nose at us decent folks.'' The switch came down on her back again.

In a daze of pain and confusion, she cried out, stumbled, regained her balance and tried to run. Again and again she felt the bite of the switch. The end of the pliable bough curled around her neck and stung her mouth.

Too numb to cry, too frightened to think, she ran to escape the agony of the switch and the clods and stones being thrown by the angry crowd. The light from the fire and the bright moon sent her shadow dancing crazily in front of her as she ran barefoot down the path. She reached the end of the lane to find it blocked by a canvas-covered, high-wheeled, heavily constructed wagon. Unsure what to do, she paused.

When a stone, thrown harder than any of the others, hit her in the middle of her back, the pain forced a scream from her lips. She staggered and grabbed the wagon wheel to keep from falling to her knees.

''Up here, girl! Quick!''

She had no idea who was on the other end of the hand that was extended to her. She grasped it gratefully, placed her foot on a thick spoke and was pulled up onto the seat. The instant she was in the wagon, a long whip snaked out and stung the backs of the mules.

''H'yaw! Hee-yaw!'' The driver shouted at the team as he cracked the whip over their backs. The wagon lurched forward. It made a wide loop and headed for open country

''Papa! Wait for Papa and Buddy—'' Willa cried.

''Too late fer yore pa, girl. They already hung 'em.''

''No! Oh, God—''

Then in the wavering light of a bonfire, she saw the body of Papa Igor hanging from a tree in a grove between their house and town. His shirt had been torn away. The white skin on the large hump on his back shone in the light from the fire. His head, oversized in proportion to the rest of his body and covered with thick dark hair, was tilted back as if he were looking at the heavens above.

There, abandoned and lifeless, was the only person in the world whom she loved and who loved her. The scene was burned into Willa's mind.

There is a time when a human being has taken all that can be endured, a time when strength and logic are burned away. This was that moment for Willa Hammer. The physical pain was so intense it was scarcely to be borne, but within her the awareness of her loss seared far more deeply.

She screamed, and screamed, and screamed.

It was the cry of a soul in agony, a sound most of the crowd would never forget. It pierced the cool night air, shattering the silence. Those who heard it said that it was not a human sound. It was as if a cold, desolate wind swept down from the mountains, raking the crowd with fingers of ice, chilling and awesome.

As the screams died away, a sorrowing voice spoke from among the hushed throng standing in front of the burning shack.

"Dear God. What possessed us to do such a terrible thing?"

But it was too late for regrets. The deed was done.

"What the . . . hell!"

To the west in the Bighorn Mountains, Smith Bowman, startled out of a half-sleep, dropped the empty whiskey bottle on the ground and leaped to his feet. Screams, wordless, terrified, unearthly screams blasted the silence. They filled every crevice of the mountains and sent a shiver of terror all through him.

The screams stopped suddenly and all was quiet again.

Smith shook his head to clear it and raked his fingers through his hair. He must be drunker than he thought. The cries he'd heard were only a cougar's mating call, but he would have sworn they were a woman's primal screams of grief.

An hour earlier he had awakened abruptly from a tortured sleep and reared up out of his bedroll, his eyes wide open, his face drenched with sweat, his hands reaching. A wave of sickness had washed over him, as it did each time the nightmare forced him to relive the horror of that dreadful day. Would he ever forget the pleading look in Oliver's eyes as he had reached for his hand just before . . . just before—

He had just coaxed sleep back again when the shrieking had begun. Smith's shaking fingers again combed through his thick blond hair before he pulled another whiskey bottle from his saddlebag. He took a long swallow, then cradled the bottle in his two hands. When he was a boy, he had yearned for nothing more than to have a horse of his own. When he had been left alone after his family had been lost in a flash flood, he had wanted nothing more than to see another human face. Then when he had gone to Eastwood, he had had a desperate desire to belong. Now, all he wanted was to be free of the invisible chains of guilt.

A tear slipped from the corner of Smith Bowman's eye and rolled slowly down his cheek.

Dear God, would it ever end? It had been six long years since Oliver's death—and guilt still clung to his back like a leech.

He drank from the bottle again. This was all the whiskey he had to last him until he reached Byers' Station. He would stop there and buy more before he crossed the river and headed for Eastwood Ranch.

He lay back down on his bedroll. Long ago he had developed an awed affection for the Bighorn Mountains, marveling at their trickery, their beauty, their valleys and their towering trees. Tonight they wore a crown of a million stars. Smith watched the shadows and listened to the sounds of the forest, wondering if there were another human being in the world who felt as desperately alone as he did.

In a few days he would cross the Powder River. Smith hated crossing a river, any river, even one he had crossed dozens of times. The damn river was a greedy bitch. If given half a chance, she would gobble him up.

Even after so many years, each and every time he came to a waterway, be it a creek or a river, he was a little boy again standing on the bank of a swollen, rolling river watching the wagon that had carried him whirl in an eddy, then crash against the rocks. He had been thrown out and had managed to cling to a boulder until he'd been pushed to the bank by his father, who then had rushed back into the relentless river in an attempt to pull his mother and sister from the wagon.

He would never forget the sight of the huge wall of water descending on his family like a great gray mountain. It rolled and thundered. Smith had seen his father swept up and carried to the top of the wall before it had crashed down on him, and he and the wagon had been lost from sight.

In a wild panic Smith had run along the bank for miles, searching, hoping, praying that his parents and sister were still alive. Then he had found the body of his little sister caught in the branches of a tree whose limbs protruded out over the water. Carrying her lifeless body, he had stumbled down along the river until he found the body of his mother and dragged her up onto the riverbank.

As fast as it had risen, the raging current had abated. It had narrowed to a river once again and then a stream. Smith had stood beside his mother and sister and sobbed.

"Papa! Papa!" He had called until he could call no more. He had staggered drunkenly along the riverbank straining to see a sign of his father. At last he had to give up and return to the lifeless bodies on the bank.

He had kept his vigil all night, all the next day, and through the following night, hoping his father had somehow saved himself. The following morning, weak from two days without food, he had scooped out a single shallow grave on the riverbank with a piece of birch bark and buried his mother and sister. A stolid sort of daze was on him. Sobbing without tears, he carried rocks and heaped them upon the grave.

While searching for stones, he found a fish flopping in a puddle where it had been stranded when the water went down. He killed it, skinned it with his pocketknife and, having no way to build a fire, ate it raw, gagging on the first few bites.

Smith had no clear remembrance of the next days. He had headed north along the riverbank until he had come to the dim trail his father had been aiming for when they had crossed the river. Doggedly he followed it. His all-consuming interest was in finding something to eat and shelter for the night.

Days passed with agonizing slowness. His stomach cramped with hunger pains. With his pocketknife he fashioned a crude bow and arrow, using his shoelaces for the bowstring. He sat for hours beside what he thought was a rabbit run. When he missed the first time, he sobbed with frustration. The second time he was successful. In later years he credited that small animal with saving his life.

One morning he awakened to the smell of meat cooking. He lay for a while wondering if he was dreaming. The tantalizing smell wafted over him again. Jumping to his feet, he ran staggering through the underbrush toward the delicious aroma. He had not seen a human being in weeks. He prayed that whoever had the means to build a fire and cook meat would not leave. Weakened by near starvation, he ran, stumbled, fell and picked himself up to run again, not caring whether he might be rushing to meet an Indian who would scalp him. At the edge of a clearing, Smith tried to stop, staggered again, and struggled to recover his balance by grabbing a branch. It broke with a loud crack.

Startled, the two men at the campfire turned quickly toward him. They stared in amazement at the lad, whose hollow eyes burned in a gaunt face. The clothes on the thin body hung in rags.

"Godamighty, Billy, it's a white boy!"

The man who spoke was big, taller than Smith's father. He had a head of thick white hair, a hawk nose and piercing blue eyes under heavy dark brows.

"Gee whillikers!" The husky, whispery sound came from the other man, who was small, bowlegged, and heavily whiskered.

"Son, what are you doing out here in the middle of nowhere? Where'd you come from?" The white-haired man asked in a deep, puzzled tone.

"Tennessee." Smith's voice was hoarse from disuse and sounded to him as if it were coming from someone else.

"Tennessee? That's a fair piece."

"It ain't no hoot 'n' a holler." The whiskered man leaned down to turn the meat sizzling in the skillet.

"Where's your folks?"

"D-dead. D-drowned."

Kindness and understanding warmed the man's eyes as he studied the worn boots, the ragged clothes and the thin, starved look on the boy's face.

"Are you hungry, son?"

"Yes, s-sir."

A look of sympathy came over the man's face. "What's your name?"

"Bowman. Smith Bowman." Again his voice sounded strange as did the other voices after his days of listening to crows and the screech of soaring hawks waiting to pounce on a careless rabbit or field mouse.

"Come on up to the fire, Smith Bowman. My name is Oliver Eastwood. This is Billy Coe. Most folks call him Billy Whiskers. Billy, dish up a plate of food for our guest."

"Howdy-do." Smith shook hands with each of the men before he squatted down beside the fire. "I'm obliged, but I don't want to run you short."

"We'll not run short. Coffee?"

"Yes . . . please."

Smith stared down at the plate of bacon, potatoes and eggs. Then he began to eat. Each bite brought on a ravenous desire for more. Before he realized it, the fork was making faster trips from the plate to his mouth.

"It's best to go slow if you haven't had much to eat lately," Oliver Eastwood suggested kindly. "How long have you been alone?"

"A week or two. Maybe three."

Smith put his fork down. Already what he had eaten was tormenting his stomach. Suddenly he was violently sick. He got up and stumbled into the bushes. Holding tightly to a small sapling, he bent over and retched. He cried, unable to stop the tears that flooded his eyes and washed down his cheeks. When he finished retching, Oliver Eastwood was there beside him offering comfort. He put his arm across the boy's shoulders and drew him to him. Smith turned his face into the man's shirt and sobbed his grief.

"Cry, son. You've earned it. Cry all you want, then we'll go home."

Smith remembered feeling safe for the first time in weeks as he stood within the shelter of the big man's arms. He was no longer alone in that vast emptiness. He was not made to feel ashamed for his tears. From that day forward he had devoted himself to Oliver Eastwood, a devotion that had lasted fifteen years.

As always, one thought brought forth others. He remembered the first time he had seen Oliver Eastwood's home. It looked like a fairy castle backed up to the green of the mountain. Large white pillars extended to the upper porch, long narrow windows reached to the floor, and a double glass door dominated the front of the house, the likes of which he had not seen since leaving Tennessee. It was a real Southern mansion with a tree-lined drive and a white picket fence. Behind it, instead of the slave cabins usually found behind such a house, was a network of corrals and a long bunkhouse attached to a variety of other buildings. Smith had been awed into silence, scarcely able to believe that Oliver Eastwood had said, "*We'll* go home." Did he mean that he could call this magnificent house his *home*?

That first night in the bunkhouse he had drifted off to sleep with a feeling of security, hearing the low voices of Billy Whiskers and the other men. But in the night he had had dreams of the rolling, muddy river and had awakened sweating and thrashing. Oliver Eastwood was standing over him and behind him was the figure of Billy Whiskers.

"You're all right, Smith. You're safe here. Billy will be close by. I came out to see how you were doing and heard you cry out. Go back to sleep. You're not out there in the night alone."

He had gone back to sleep and slept soundly the rest of the night, but when morning came the dream was still with him when Oliver came to take him to the house.

Smith would never forget standing beside the kitchen door and listening to Mrs. Eastwood's shrill, angry voice and Oliver Eastwood's quiet one trying to persuade his wife to let him be a part of the family.

"Get that little bastard out of my house. I'll not have him here."

"The boy has no place to go, Maud."

"This ain't no catch-all for every stray that comes down the pike."

"His folks were drowned—"

"What the hell do I care about that? Lots of folks drown. Get him out!"

"Maud—"

"Is this my house or not?"

"Of course, it's your house."

"I don't want him here."

"All right, Maud. He can stay in the bunkhouse with Billy."

"Why do you want him? Ain't me and Fanny good enough?"

"What a ridiculous thing to say. You're my wife. Fanny is your daughter—mine now. The boy being here won't change that."

"He'd better not be hanging around Fanny. I'll take a horsewhip to him."

"He'll not bother Fanny," Oliver said firmly. "And he'll not bother you. But I'll tell you this, Maud. That boy will have a home here as long as he wants to stay. You'd better understand that."

Tears had blinded him as he had listened to this unseen woman reject him. He hadn't seen that Oliver had returned until the big man had put his arm about his shoulders.

"I'm sorry you had to hear that, boy. Women folk get crazy notions sometimes."

As time went by, Smith and Oliver became constant companions. Oliver spent more and more time outside the house. Smith grew to be a man at Oliver's side, neither wanting nor needing anyone but Oliver and Billy Whiskers and the magical world that was Eastwood Ranch.

Smith had been at Eastwood a week before he even saw Fanny, Oliver's stepdaughter. The men in the bunkhouse had talked about her and Mrs. Eastwood, but the first sight of her was one he would never forget. She was about the age of his little sister. He thought she was the prettiest thing he had ever seen.

Fanny had been dressed in white with a pink sash tied about her waist, reddish-brown curls falling down about her shoulders and a face so white it looked as if it had never known sunshine. Fanny stood with her arm wrapped around a porch pillar, gazing off toward the mountains. When he passed near, as he had to do to pick up a shovel he had left behind, he raised the brim of the old felt hat Billy Whiskers had found for him. The girl stared at him with hostile eyes and poked out her tongue. Then she went back into the house and slammed the door.

Mrs. Eastwood, according to snatches of talk he heard in the bunkhouse, had lived on a homestead with her first husband. When Oliver Eastwood came west, he was as green as grass. When he wandered out into the Bighorn Mountains, he was thrown from his horse one day and would have died if not for Maud's husband, who found him and took him home. Maud set his broken leg and nursed him back to health. The nester died soon after and Oliver married Maud, who had no idea the greenhorn she married was a wealthy man.

Oliver built a fine home on his land for his wife and stepdaughter. Then he began to concentrate on building a herd of Texas longhorn cattle. The animals were of a nervous temperament and had pugnacious dispositions. They would run away from a horseman with the speed of the wind, but if a person were unhorsed, they would attack him in an instant.

Thinking back on it all, Smith took another drink from

the bottle and wondered for the thousandth time why Oliver Eastwood, an educated, kind man, had wanted to raise the wild, unpredictable cattle and why he had married a shrew like Maud, who over the years had become more belligerent, more unreasonable and more demanding.

Smith dragged his hand over his unshaven face. He was tired. It had been a long trip down to Denver, and although he had left the city days ago, he was still a long way from home. One thing was sure. Fanny, who now insisted on being called Francine, wouldn't be coming home. The damn bitch! He could wring her blasted neck. If she had answered her mother's letters, it would have saved him the trip. He wondered how the old lady would take it.

Smith felt old. He was caught by what he could never forget. He was sentenced to spend the rest of his life reliving the pleading look in Oliver's eyes, then the flash of mortal fear just before the end.

He reached for the bottle. Guilt ripped into his soul like a barb. He would give half his life for the chance to relive that one day.

CHAPTER

* 2 *

Willa lay on the pallet and listened to the creak and groan of the wagon, her heart shriveling within her. To the aching loneliness, the bitter sense of loss, was added the guilt of not having stayed to bury her loved one. Her grief had been wild and noisy before blessed blackness had enfolded her in its arms.

She felt calmer now; the storm of grief had abated for a little while, but the humiliation of being whipped and stoned was like a hungry dog gnawing at her pride. Words spoken by a preacher long ago came back to haunt her. He had said that when a sinner died, he would roast in everlasting hell—but he had failed to mention that the sinner's torment began in this world. It was *her* fault, someone had said. She had sinned. She must have sinned or God would not have punished her in such a cruel way.

What could have happened to stir the crowd to such a frenzy that they would strip Papa Igor of his dignity by exposing his deformed body to the crowd, then hang him? He was the kindest, gentlest man in the world. Well educated, he loved to visit and was able to converse on most any subject. She owed her love of books and history to his teachings. Why couldn't people see beyond his misshapen body and his features distorted by the large lumps that had appeared on his face the last few years?

At Willa's insistence they had moved six times in four years. When he had fixed all the clocks that needed repair in one town and sold all the clocks they were going to sell, they moved on. People tolerated the grotesque little man only as long as they needed his skills. And then the taunts would begin. Mothers would threaten their children with "be good or the clock man will get you."

Willa could scarcely remember life without Papa Igor. She did remember all those many years ago, standing with her mother beside the road in the Mississippi river town where she was born. They had been put out of the rooming house when they could no longer pay. Tired and hungry and with no place to sleep, they had welcomed the peddler wagon when it had stopped. The little man had jumped down and, after tossing their bundle of belongings into the wagon, lifted her up onto the seat and had helped her mother climb up to sit beside her. He had laughed at her shyness and thrust a stick of peppermint candy in her hand. From that moment on she had adored him and he had doted on her, loving her as if she were his own.

Papa Igor and her mother had never married because her mother had a husband. Willa's father had left them shortly after Willa was born. Her mother had told her he was an irresponsible boy with itchy feet. They used Papa Igor's name, and the townspeople assumed they were husband and wife. When she was older, Willa realized that her mother and Papa Igor had never shared a bed and that their relationship was more like that of a brother and sister. Her mother had been very fond of the little man and he of her.

It wasn't until after her mother died six years ago that the large lumps began to appear on Papa Igor's face. Willa had insisted he see a doctor. He had seen several, and they all had told him that there was no reasonable explanation and there was nothing they could do. Afterward they had moved frequently, coming to this town only four months ago.

"Are ya goin' to lay there all day?"

Willa felt something nudge her arm and opened her eyes. A girl sat on the flat top of a trunk, her bare feet inches from Willa's pallet.

"Well, are ya?" The pouting mouth was drawn down at the corners. An unbrushed tangle of thick dark curls hung about her face. The girl kicked the trunk with her heels to emphasize her words.

"Who are you? Where are we?" Willa whispered hoarsely.

"Jo Bell Frank. And I don't know where the hell we are."

If the girl thought to shock Willa with her swearing, she was disappointed. Willa merely gazed out the back of the wagon at the sky, brassy with sunlight. Had the mob killed Buddy too? she wondered. They must have or the dog would have warned her. Damn, damn! Oh, damn them!

"Papa said to give ya some clothes when ya woke up. Yore buck naked—almost."

The word naked caught Willa's attention and she realized that beneath the quilt covering her she wore only the torn nightdress. She sat up, holding the quilt up over her breast, and flexed her shoulders. Every bone in her body ached and her back felt as if it were on fire.

"They whipped ya good with that switch," Jo Bell commented, as though she were talking about the weather. "I put some salve on yore back—cause Pa told me to."

"Thank you."

"Ya ain't pretty, but ya ain't ugly either. Was that mud-ugly man really yore pa? You don't have no hump and no lumps. I didn't feel one when I was puttin' on the salve."

Willa was speechless; she sat staring at the young girl, her eyes dry and hot, her throat screaming for a drink of water. At first, observing Jo Bell's dress that came to mid-calf and her bare feet and legs, Willa had thought the girl to be ten or eleven years old. On closer examination Willa realized the girl was older, possibly fifteen or sixteen. The dress was loose, but not loose enough to hide her rounded breasts. The shapely calves were not the limbs of a child. She would be pretty, even beautiful, if not for the surly look on her face.

"Ya ain't as pretty as Starr was," Jo Bell was saying. "Yore eyes are a funny color. They're blue like the bluin' we used to put in the wash back home. Starr's hair was red 'n' her titties stuck out to here." Jo Bell held her fingers curled six inches from her own rounded breasts.

"Who is Starr?"

"A whore, I reckon. Papa picked her up in Aberdeen. She come with us almost all the way to Prairie City. Papa purely hates to sleep all by his ownself."

The girl's words sent a chill over Willa. She pressed her fingertips to her temples. Concern for her safety leaped into her mind.

"What happened to . . . Starr?"

"She took off with a mule-skinner. Papa was so mad he wouldn't let her take her trunk." Jo Bell lifted the trunk lid and carelessly threw out clothing. "She didn't care. She just climbed the wheel of that freight wagon and thumbed her nose at him." She giggled and slapped her hands against her thighs. "It was a sight. Papa shook his fist at her 'n' yelled she'd miss ah . . . you know what. Then he sulked all the way to Hublett."

Willa listened to Jo Bell's frank talk in stunned silence. The dresses the girl took from the trunk were large and gawdy. The undergarments, however, were of good quality and had drawstrings at the waist and neck. Holding the quilt around her, Willa searched the trunk for bloomers, but there was nothing but a teddy with a split crotch. She chose a black and white checked gingham dress and slipped it on over the teddy and the petticoat. She found an apron to tie about her waist.

Starr's shoes were many sizes too big for her, and when Jo Bell offered a pair of Indian moccasins, she accepted them gratefully.

"I hate Indians. I ain't wearin' nothin' made by no stinkin' redskin. What's yore name, anyhow?"

"Willa Hammer."

"I knowed the Hammer part. Well, ya ought to fix your hair so you'd look good when Papa gets back. Ya still won't be as pretty as Starr. Yore too skinny."

"Your father's not driving the wagon?" Willa glanced at the front of the wagon and the tied-down canvas curtain.

"Charlie is. He drives good. Papa tied down the canvas. He said it ain't decent for a boy Charlie's age to look on a buck-naked woman. Not yet anyhow. He'd get all excited and go off half-cocked, is what Papa said."

"How old is Charlie?"

"He's a year younger than me. He's big for his age. Anyhow Papa said his juices was up good and it was time he found him a woman."

The words coming out of the girl's mouth so matter-of-factly caused Willa's mind to freeze with shock. Dear God. What kind of a man would speak so frankly to his children? Had he rescued her from the mob thinking she would be a replacement for Starr? Willa stared out the back of the wagon until she recovered from the worst of the shock she had felt on hearing Jo Bell's words and the realization that she was out here in this vast emptiness with a man whose moral values were so lacking.

"Where did your father go?" she asked calmly while her fingers tried to bring order to her heavy hair. She twisted it in a roll, gathered it in a loose knot on the back of her neck and pinned it with long, wire hairpins from Starr's trunk.

"Yore hair's awful long. I sure do wish it was red like Starr's 'stead of that dry-grass color. I reckon it ain't too ugly, but it wouldn't melt no ice in no dancehall though."

"I reckon it wouldn't. Where did your father go?" Willa asked again.

"I don't know." Jo Bell shrugged. "He always goes off somewhere. He'll be back by supper time. Always does."

At sundown Charlie turned off the trail and stopped the wagon under a stand of ash trees and alongside a little branch that held a trickling of water. Jo Bell slid out the back of the wagon and Willa followed. Without a word to Willa or his sister, Charlie went about the business of unhitching the mules, watering and picketing them. He was a tall, slim, serious-faced boy and handled the animals as capably as a man would.

Jo Bell was small-boned and petite. From a distance she would easily pass for a child.

"Why do you dress like a little girl?" Willa asked.

"Papa wants folks to think I'm still little bitty. He says I'm so pretty that it'd take a army to keep the men away if they knowed I was full-grown." She giggled happily and preened. "He's savin' me for a rich rancher with lots of land. He says I'm like money in the bank."

There was nothing Willa could say to that. She merely shook her head in disbelief, a gesture totally lost on Jo Bell.

"Papa'll want supper to be ready," Jo Bell said, and lowered the front of a box attached to the side of the wagon. She pulled out a spider skillet, a wooden bowl and a coffeepot. "I hope ya make good biscuits. Papa sets quite a store by a woman what cooks good biscuits."

Apprehension gripped Willa. Here she was in the middle of nowhere with this strange family and no means to protect herself. She didn't remember anything about the man who had pulled her up into the wagon except that he had offered help when she needed it so badly. Deep in thought and ignoring both Jo Bell and Charlie, she walked behind a screen of bushes, relieved herself and went to the creek to wash. Life goes on, she thought dully. She would do what she had to do.

Charlie had started a fire and a slow finger of smoke was pointing upward. There was something so everlastingly normal about a campfire. Cooking in the open was nothing new to Willa.

Jo Bell sat on the end of the wagon swinging her legs.

"There 'tis," she said. "Ya better get started."

Jo Bell's tone as well as her words irritated Willa. So this is the way it's going to be, she thought. Well, not quite. She would do her share, but she'd not be relegated to the role of servant by this spoiled woman-child.

"I'll make biscuits. If you want meat fried, you'll fry it yourself." She took a cloth-wrapped slab of bacon from the supply box and smelled it to see if it was spoiled.

"What?" The word exploded from Jo Bell's pouting mouth. "Starr did *all* the cookin'."

"I'm not Starr. Slice and fry the meat. I'll make cream gravy. And, Jo Bell, go wash your hands before you handle the food."

"Well . . . horse turds! Ya sure got bossy in a hurry and ya ain't even slept with Papa yet."

"I'm not going to be *sleeping* with your father," Willa said sharply, pulling the flour tin toward her and peering inside. The flour looked to be free of weevils.

"He ain't goin' to like that none a'tall. What'a ya think he pulled ya outta that crowd for?'' Jo Bell tossed the words over her shoulder on her way to the creek.

Willa's back hurt and her mind whirled in confusion and fear. She worked automatically. When the biscuit dough was made, she pinched it into shapes and filled the dutch oven. With a stick she scattered the hot coals and placed the pot among them.

Charlie filled the water barrel. He was a nice-looking boy with straight dark brows and hair that hung down over his ears. He wore a battered felt hat with a snake skin wrapped around the crown. He caught Willa looking at him and looked away. So far he hadn't uttered a word. That was to change quickly, and she would learn that he had plenty to say when he thought there was something worth saying.

''Ma'am, your dog's comin'.'' The words were spoken to Willa's back.

She turned quickly and looked back along the trail. Her eyes glazed with tears when she saw the brown dog limping toward them. He broke into a painful lope, and by the time he reached them, his head was hanging and his tongue lolling out one side of his mouth.

''Buddy! Buddy!'' Willa ran to meet him, threw herself on her knees and encircled his big head with her arms. ''Oh, I'm so glad you're here. How did you find me?'' The bushy tail, full of cockleburrs, wagged; a wet tongue licked her face. ''Buddy, Buddy, I never thought I'd see you again.'' She knelt there with her arms about the dog and cried unashamedly until Charlie touched her arm.

''He's been hurt. Looky here. Somebody bashed him a good one.'' The boy's gentle fingers prodded the lump on the side of the dog's head.

''Damn, damn them! That's why he didn't come to the house.''

"The cut's still open. I can put some pine tar on it. It's what we do for the mules."

"Oh, Charlie, will you? I'd be so grateful." In her joy of seeing her dog, she failed to register the fact that Buddy, who never allowed anyone but her and Papa Igor to touch him, was accepting the gentle caresses of the young boy

"Yes, ma'am. He's wore out and hungry. Just think, ma'am. He followed the wagon tracks all this way. I was hopin' he would."

"You knew he was my dog?"

"Yes, ma'am. I saw him with you back in Hublett." He stroked the dog's shaggy head. "I always did want me a dog. Had one once, but he just went off and didn't come back."

"Pa ain't goin' to like it one little bit." Jo Bell came to stand with her hands on her hips.

Buddy looked at her and stiffened, instinctively knowing that the girl didn't like him. He turned to lick Willa's cheek.

"Are you hungry and thirsty, boy?" Willa asked.

"Pa ain't goin' to stand for ya givin' him none of *our* grub."

"Shut up, Jo Bell," Charlie snarled. "Shut your lyin' mouth."

"I ain't lyin' 'n' ya know it, Charlie Frank. Pa purely hates critters that ain't useful."

"He is too useful." Charlie stood over the dog protectively

"What's he good for? Just what's he good for, Mister Smarty?"

"He'd warn us if Indians or varmits come around."

"Ha, ha, ha! He didn't warn her. They hung that ugly, warty old man and fired the house right under her nose. That old dog didn't let out a squeak."

"He would've, but somebody knocked him in the head," Charlie shouted angrily.

"See there. All a body has to do is give him a little old tap on the noggin. Charlie . . . stop that," Jo Bell screeched when Charlie pushed her.

"Shut yore mouth about him."

"I'll tell Papa." Jo Bell flounced away.

Willa realized there was a certain amount of rivalry between siblings, but these two seemed to have an intense dislike for each other. Charlie appeared to be more mature than his sister even though he was younger.

"Don't pay her no mind, ma'am. Papa's spoiled her rotten."

"I can see that somebody has. Buddy won't be any trouble, Charlie. He'll hunt for his food. At the next town, I'll have to find work."

"Then what will you do, ma'am?"

"Well . . . I don't know. I have friends I could write to, but it would take time for an answer and I . . . well . . . I just don't know," she said again.

"We're going to my Uncle Oliver's. He's my mama's brother. We're goin' to live with him on his ranch. Him and Mama come into some money. Uncle Oliver took his part and come west. He'd always had a hankerin' to have a ranch." Charlie's serious young face creased with a smile. "Papa said he's got horses and cattle. He said I could be a cowboy. Uncle Oliver ain't got no boys that Pa knows of."

"You'll be a good cowboy. You have a way with animals. Buddy doesn't let many people touch him. He seems to know that you like him and want to help him."

"I like him a lot. I sure do wish he was my dog," Charlie said wistfully.

"While we're with you, I'd appreciate it if you'd help me look out for him. After he gets his strength back, he'll be able to look out for himself."

"I'll do that. I'll get the bucket we use for the mules and

get him some water. Look, ma'am, his paw is bleedin'. I'll put tar on it too."

"Thank you, Charlie." Willa begin to feel a strong liking for the boy as well as dislike for his sister.

"Papa's comin'," Jo Bell yelled. "Papa'll put a end to all this tomfoolery."

Willa stood. Buddy leaned against her legs as if sensing her distress and not wanting to be parted from her. She straightened her shoulders and held her head erect. Although grief, frustration and weariness were tearing her apart, she was determined to keep what dignity she had left and to make it clear to this man that she was not, as his daughter had hinted, a replacement for Starr.

Furthermore, she thought irrationally, if Buddy was not allowed to travel with them, the two of them would strike out on their own.

CHAPTER

* 3 *

The rider coming across the open prairie toward them rode a handsome sorrel horse and sat the saddle easily. He was a thin man and, according to the length of his stirrups, not very tall. He eyed Willa as he approached. When he stopped the horse within a few yards of her, she could see that he was not as old as she had expected. His eyes, so light a gray that they appeared to be almost colorless, studied her. Coal-black hair covered his ears. Dark sideburns framed his face and a neatly trimmed mustache drooped on either side of his mouth. He was smiling at her in open admiration.

Papa Igor would have called him a dandy. Willa did not like the smile on his face.

"Well, well, well—" he said and threw his leg over the saddle horn and continued his lazy inspection of her.

"My name is Willa Hammer. I want to thank you for helping me last night."

"I know who you are." Taking his time in an infuriating way, he ran his narrowed eyes over her face, down her slender figure and back up to the thick dark-blond hair that framed

25

her forehead and cheekbones. "Starr's dress don't suit ya at all."

As his eyes roamed, Willa begin to stiffen with indignation. She controlled her temper, took a quick breath and eyed him coolly.

"Nevertheless, I appreciate the use of it. I'll see that it is washed and mended when it's returned."

He laughed abruptly, showing a gold tooth that gleamed brightly beneath the black mustache.

"I knew it. I knew it."

Willa gave him a puzzled look. When he continued to stare at her, she asked, "Knew what?"

"That ya was proud as a peacock. I seen ya in Hublett actin' as if ya was a mile high above the common folks."

"I never—"

"Yes, ya did. I like it. Yore just the woman I need to teach my little Jo Bell how to be ladylike. She's got the looks, but she needs some polishin' up."

"I'll not be with you long enough to teach Jo Bell anything, Mr. Frank."

"Ya got book-learnin' too," he said, ignoring her words. "I watched ya. Ya walk with yore head high, a steppin' along like yore really somebody."

"What's wrong with that?" Willa's back stiffened even more and her temper took over, clouding her reason. "I am somebody. I'm a person with a reasonable amount of intelligence, equal to anyone."

"Pull in yore stinger, honey." He gave her a wicked, teasing smile. "Ya suit me just fine." He slid from the saddle and handed the reins to Charlie. Gil Frank was not much taller than Willa, and when their eyes met, they were on a level.

Until now he hadn't seemed to notice Buddy. He looked down at the dog pressing against her skirts. Her hand was fastened in the hair at the nape of the dog's neck. The man's eyes were hard when they met hers.

"The first time that dog makes a move against me or mine, I'll kill him."

"He'll attack only if he thinks I'm in danger."

"Don't worry about that, honey. I'm goin' to take good care of ya." He winked. Willa kept her lips pressed firmly together and glared at him. Then Jo Bell's giggle caused her temper to snap.

"I didn't ask for your help, Mr. Frank, although I'm grateful for it. I'll be with you only until we reach the next town. Meanwhile, I'll do my share of the work and I want to make it clearly understood that does not include *night* work!"

His roar of laughter was joined by Jo Bell's giggles. Willa's face flooded with color

"Ain't ya ever heard of nooners, honey?"

"No, I haven't and my name is Miss Hammer " Willa was shivering with suppressed agitation and fear She was certain that this man's intentions were less than honorable. He was bold as brass about that.

"My name is Gilbert. Ya can call me Gil, or honey, or sweetheart if yore a mind to." To Willa's relief he turned away from her and put his arm about his daughter's shoulder "Ya got supper ready, little pretty thin'?"

"It's ready but for the gravy *She* said she'd make it. I already done everythin' else."

"Ya done everythin'? Didn't Charlie help ya?"

"He unhitched—"

"—And watered the mules, staked them out, filled the water barrel and built the cookfire," Charlie said, coming up to the fire.

"Papa, he pushed me when I said you'd not let that stinkin old dog stay "

"Did he hurt you, lovey?"

"Not . . . much—"

"Son, I've told ya, 'n' told ya, real men don't manhandle their womenfolk. There's other ways a gettin' 'em to do what ya want." His eyes flashed to Willa. "Yore sister's just a little bitty girl. She's been cookin' 'n' doin' the camp chores."

"Starr did it while she was with us, now Jo Bell's pushin' it off on Miss Hammer."

"Watch yoreself, boy. Don't ya be gettin' sassy 'n' don't ya go gettin' sweet on Miss Hammer. She's a mite too old for ya."

Willa avoided looking at Charlie to save him further embarrassment. She waved Buddy away. The dog obediently went to lie in the grass beyond the wagon from where he could see her.

Working as she had done countless times when she and Papa Igor were on the road, Willa forked the meat from the skillet onto a graniteware plate and spooned flour into the fat. After it had browned, she added a dipper of water and a pinch of salt. When the gravy thickened, she pulled the skillet from the fire, stepped back to the end of the wagon and waited until the family had filled their plates before she helped herself.

Gilbert Frank and Jo Bell sat back away from the fire on a makeshift bench. Charlie squatted on his heels beside the wagon and attacked the meal with relish, emptied his plate, and went back for more.

Willa stood at the end of the wagon, her plate on the tailgate, and ate because she knew she must. Mr. Frank gave Jo Bell all his attention, for which Willa was grateful. Jo Bell plainly adored her father and he her. Charlie was more or less ignored by both of them.

While Mr. Frank was still eating, Willa concealed several biscuits in her dress pocket, picked up the water bucket and walked toward the stream. Buddy rose tiredly and followed.

When they were out of sight of the camp, she quickly fed him the biscuits.

"I'm sorry there isn't more. I know how tired and hungry you are." The sound of dry brush scraping on something brought her quickly to her feet. Relief flowed through her when she saw that it was Charlie.

"I brought him something to eat." The boy pulled biscuits and several strips of cooked sidepork from under his shirt and placed them on the ground. Buddy made no move toward them and Charlie frowned. "What's the matter, ma'am? Ain't he hungry?"

"Yes, he is, but he's waiting for you to tell him the offering is his. He'll not touch it otherwise."

Charlie knelt down. "Here, boy. This is for you." He held out a piece of the meat. Buddy went to him and took it gently from his hand. "You're just plumb tuckered out, ain't ya? I'll put some tar on that cut tonight. It'll keep them pesky flies from a botherin' you." The boy talked to the dog while he was eating and gently rubbed his head.

"Thank you, Charlie. Buddy will be a loyal friend."

"Ma'am." Charlie stood, looked at her and then away "Don't . . . don't be feared Pa'll . . . force ya to do anything ya don't want to. It ain't his way. He . . . ah . . . ain't never forced a woman that I know of."

"I'm glad to know that. I'm not that kind of woman, Charlie."

"I be knowin' that right off, ma'am. Just don't let him get ya off by yoreself. Stick with me or Jo Bell."

Willa dipped the water bucket in the creek. Charlie took it and started back toward the wagon. Her hand on his arm stopped him.

"Charlie, can you tell me why they hanged Papa Igor and burned our house?" Her pleading eyes sought those of the boy. Charlie set the bucket down.

"Ma'am, I don't know the whole of it."

"I do." Gil Frank appeared in front of them on the path. "Take the bucket back to the wagon, son. Go on," he said when Charlie hesitated.

Willa stepped around the bushes so that she would be in sight of the wagon, then turned back and faced Mr. Frank.

"What happened?" she demanded bluntly

"He shot two men."

"Shot two men? Why?"

"He was in the store. Brought in a clock he'd fixed. A couple of rowdies got to scufflin', knocked over the clock and broke the glass. He swore at 'em and made 'em mad. One thin' led to another. They yanked off his coat and tore his shirt. They started talkin' about you. One of 'em said he'd be in your drawers before the week was out. That made the ugly little bugger fightin' mad. He swung at one of 'em and bloodied his nose."

"Don't call him that! Don't you dare call him that!" Willa's eyes mirrored her anger.

Gil Frank laughed. "He warn't no *pretty* little bugger."

"He was a man. A human being the same as you or me."

"Anyhow, the boys pulled off his shirt to see the hump. They was just funnin' like some do when they're liquored up."

"Funning!" Her voice wasn't loud but angry and dripping with contempt. "You call stripping a man of his clothes in front of a crowd and making fun of his misshapen body . . . funning? He must have been so . . . humiliated!"

"He was hoppin' mad and the teasin' went on. Somebody said they'd ort to geld the freak. Well . . . dammed if the little bastard didn't pull out a derringer and shoot. Don't think he killed 'em, but they was bleedin' all over hell. Things turned ugly quick. Before you knowed it he was tossed in a wagon and took to the woods. Don't know why they fired your house or whipped ya. Once a crowd is worked up to a hangin', they're liable to do anythin'.''

Willa pressed her lips tightly together to keep from screaming at the injustice. She wanted to run; she wanted to lash out at Gil Frank, who was calmly building a smoke. Instead she turned and walked quickly toward the wagon, paused, then walked on.

Papa Igor had been pushed over the brink by the humiliation of having his humped back exposed. To him the horror of his grotesque body being displayed for ridicule was the final indignity. In the silent grove of a thick stand of oak trees, she wrapped her arms around a giant trunk and leaned her forehead against the rough bark. Tears gushed from her eyes and sobs from her throat.

''Bastards! Ignorant, insensitive bastards!''

Anger and grief tore at her heart. She slammed her fist against the tree trunk. How could they do that to him? How could they? Papa Igor had never hurt any living creature, man or beast. She cried bitterly, cried until her mind was drugged with grief and remorse. Covering her face with her hands, she shrank deeper into a pit of misery.

''Papa, Papa, I'll not forget you . . ever—''

She dropped to her knees, her face covered with her hands. When her storm of weeping was over, Willa looked around to see Charlie and Buddy sitting on the ground nearby The dog lay beside the boy. They were waiting. She peered at them from tear-swollen eyes.

''I put the pine-tar on Buddy's cuts.''

''Thank you.''

''Pa said leave ya be, ya'd get over it.''

''You never get *over* the death of a loved one.'' Willa went to sit in the grass beside them. ''Time sometimes dulls the grief.'' She burrowed her hand in the dog's thick fur. Buddy was all that was familiar in this tilting world into which she had dropped. "How long has your mother been dead?"

"Four or five years, I reckon."

"What part of the south are you from, Charlie?" Willa wanted to keep talking to keep tears at bay.

"Louisiana."

"Did you come up-river?"

"Part of the way. We been on the road for almost two years. Papa works a while and we go on. He says we'll be at the Powder River crossing in a few days. Uncle Oliver's ranch is on Clear Creek in the Bighorn Mountains."

"Did he say how far it was to the next town?"

"I don't think there is any towns. Pa says there's a stage station at the crossing. We might meet up with some folks travelin' west. Pa heard it ain't smart for a lone wagon to be goin' into that country even if Custer did clean out the Indians a few years back. Some are still killin' white people."

"Custer didn't clean out the Indians, Charlie. Crazy Horse out-maneuvered and out-fought Custer. In my estimation, Custer is not a man to be admired. He led his men to certain death even though his Crow scouts warned him against going into the Bighorns."

"He didn't whip the Indians?"

"No he did not. The Sioux won the battle. Custer was an egotistical little man trying to make a name for himself"

"If the Indians won why ain't they here?"

"They realize they are being overrun by the whites. They have scattered, but their spirit is not broken. It will be a long while before they lose their resentment of the white man. They are fighting for their land, their way of life, and who can blame them?"

"Pa heard they'd moved on west."

"Why would they stay? The buffalo is gone from here.

Their way of life is gone. White settlers are sweeping across the land, snapping and snarling at them like a pack of starving dogs. The Indians used this land for hundreds of years by taking only what they needed. Rawhiders came west and slaughtered thousands of buffalo just for the hides and left the meat to rot. When the Indians killed a buffalo, they ate the meat, used the hides for clothing and shelter, the bones for tools and utensils. The dung of the buffalo was used for fuel. Some tribes left the buffalo's heart behind believing that the mystical powers of the heart would help regenerate the depleted herd.''

Charlie looked at her with open-mouthed admiration. "Where did you learn all that?"

"From books."

"Can you read?"

"Yes. Papa Igor taught me to love books. He was a well-educated man and interested in many things. He has .   ah . . . had a wonderful library of . . . books. He called them his treasures, worth more than their weight in gold—'' Her voice faltered, then trailed.

"I sure do wish I could read. I can read my name and write it too," he said proudly.

"Did you go to school in Louisiana?"

"Not hardly any. Pa likes to move around." Charlie stood. "We'd better get closer to the wagon, ma'am."

The campsite was just as she had left it. Mr. Frank sat on the bench where he had eaten his supper. Jo Bell lounged on a quilt she had spread on the grass beside him. Glad to have work to do so she wouldn't have to talk with them, Willa washed the dishes and put them away, leaving the smoke-blackened coffeepot on the grate near the fire.

Occasionally she glanced at the man who had rescued her from the angry crowd. His hair was inky black and curly like Jo Bell's. To Willa's way of thinking, he was totally unsuited for this country. He reminded her of the riverboat gamblers she had seen on the Mississippi River.

As soon as the camp was tidy, she carried a washpan of warm water to the wagon, sat on the pallet and washed the best she could without removing her clothes. Using Starr's hairbrush, she brushed her hair with long sweeping strokes and braided it in one long, loose braid.

Jo Bell came to the end of the wagon.

"Ain't ya goin' to sit with me an Pa and tell us 'bout all the places ya been?"

"No. I'm very tired. I'm going to bed."

"Well, that ain't very nice after what Pa done for ya."

"I'm not in the mood to visit," Willa said bluntly

"Well, la-di-da. Go to bed then, but don't you get on the bunk, that's my sleepin' place."

Willa peered out the back of the wagon and saw that Charlie had spread his blankets on the grass and that Buddy had settled down beside him. It was a comfort knowing that Buddy was with her. Thank goodness Charlie wasn't like Jo Bell. The girl badly needed a lesson in manners.

Fully dressed, Willa lay on the pallet staring into the darkness. Every minute her despair and apprehension grew deeper. What was she going to do? She had no money to pay for a ticket to Deadwood when they reached the stage line. She couldn't go back to Hublett. Everything she owned was gone. She didn't even own the clothes that covered her nakedness. What choice did she have but to stay with Gil Frank? And he was taking her deeper and deeper into sparsely settled country. When they reached his brother-in-law's ranch, what then?

Until Jo Bell came to bed, Willa managed to keep her eyes open, feeling reasonably sure Gil Frank wouldn't come to her pallet with his daughter in the wagon.

A week and a half of days had passed so slowly that at times Willa felt as if she were suspended in time. The ranch houses they passed were so far off the road that they would only see the smoke from the chimneys. Buddy, sensing Jo Bell's and Gil's dislike, kept distance between them. He slept beside Charlie at night; and because of the extra food the boy was able to slip to him, the dog had regained his strength. During the day he trotted beside the wagon or hunted for food alongside the trail.

Riding beside Charlie on the wagon seat, Willa studied the country ahead. It was big, open and grassy as far as the eye could see. The prairie grass was a pale gold carpet that stretched to the low foothills. On the breeze that came from the south was the smell of the sun-ripened grass and cool river water.

It was lonesome country. Here the gigantic herds of buffalo had roamed for hundreds of years. Here the rawhiders had come to slaughter them by the thousands. Here the Indians had to give up their land and move west.

Somewhere ahead was the Powder River and the stage station.

Toward evening Gil rode back to the wagon.

"The station is ahead. I'll drive in, Charlie."

The boy stopped the team, jumped down and took his father's horse to the back of the wagon. When they were moving again, Gil looked over at Willa.

"Could be we'll run into a rough bunch here. It's best not to let 'em know you're a *loose*—I mean unattached woman." He grinned and winked.

Willa stared at him without a hint of amusement. She took a deep breath and controlled her temper.

"If I can get work at the stage station, I'll stay and earn my fare to Deadwood or Sheridan."

"Any work you'd get here would be flat on yore back. Better stick with me, Willa."

The familiar way in which he used her name made her temper flare. "You are a crude man, Mr. Frank."

"I'm tellin' ya like it is, sweetheart. Ya got no choice. Every stitch ya got on yore back belongs to me. I could dump ya off at that stage stark naked. That old torn up nightdress ya was wearin' didn't cover much."

Shocked speechless, Willa opened her mouth, then closed it. She breathed deeply and squared her shoulders.

"You . . . you'd take this dress? You're more despicable than I thought!"

He shrugged. "A man's got to do what he must, sweetheart."

"My gratitude doesn't extend to sleeping with you, Mr. Frank. I thought I had made that clear. Why do you insist on keeping me with you?"

"I need ya, honey. I want Oliver, my brother-in-law, to know his sister ain't the only highfalutin' woman I can get. Oliver sets store by manners 'n' all that. He's the kind that jumps to his feet when a woman comes in and puts his coat on for supper if'n it was hotter'n hell outdoors." Gil's laugh ended in a snort of disgust.

"That's the behavior of a gentleman, but I fail to see how that concerns me," Willa retorted with her chin tilted defiantly.

"Ya got airs, too, honey, just like Oliver. He'll set me up in a business in town cause it ain't fittin' fer a *lady* to be wanderin' around from pillar to post."

"You're going to let him think that we . . . that you and I—?"

"Ya guessed it, sweetheart. Yore my intended."

"You're out of your . . . mind!"

"It'll work. Wait 'n' see."

"I'll tell him as soon as we arrive that I've no intention of marrying you." His chuckle made her clench her teeth in suppressed fury.

"I got a week to change yore mind."

The station at Powder River had originally been built by soldiers sent to protect freighters carrying supplies to Fort Kearny. When it was abandoned by the army, it became first an outlaw hideout, then a stage station and post office on the route from the Black Hills to Sheridan. The wild and bloody history of the station was well known. At one time or another most of the noted outlaws and gunfighters had passed through.

Gil Frank stopped the team on a small rise and looked down at the long, low building with twin chimneys rising from each end. Striped with red clay that filled the chinks between the logs, it looked as if it had grown there along with the cottonwood trees that surrounded it. A weathered barn and a lean-to shed with a sagging roof stood amid a network of corrals.

Several unhitched freight wagons were parked outside the corrals. Mules inside the enclosure chomped on hay that had been tossed into a forked feeder. There were no horses tied to the hitching rail in front of the station, but more than a dozen horses were penned in one of the corrals, and others were staked out in a meadow nearby.

Smith Bowman had ridden in the day before. He liked the station manager. Byers ran a good place in this tough land of tough men. In his lifetime Smith had known a few good men, many more that were borderline and some that were downright bad. He had helped bury some of the reckless borderline type and had had to kill several of the bad or be killed himself.

As Byers prepared a meal, Smith sat in a far corner of the station room with his hat pulled low, listened to the rattle of dishes, and studied the occupants of the room. Four of the five men at the poker table were freighters. Several of the onlookers were cowhands he had seen before. The fifth man at the table was a notorious bounty hunter—one whom Smith would classify as risky. He'd stay shy of him. He had learned to trust his instincts.

CHAPTER

* 4 *

"We'll camp over yonder under those trees," Gil said, turning the wagon toward a grove a good distance from the station. "You 'n' Jo Bell stay out of sight. Charlie can do the camp chores. I'll go down there 'n' get the lay of the land."

"Do you expect trouble?"

"Women are always trouble if a man is hungry enough for 'em. Climb over the seat. Get in the back," he said sharply when a man came to loll in the doorway of the station.

Willa climbed into the back and tied the canvas down behind the wagonseat. She made her way to the end of the wagon and sat down. Charlie sat on the tailgate holding the reins of the sorrel horse. Jo Bell lay on her bunk.

"Just when there's somethin' to see, we can't see it," she complained.

The wagon bumped over rocky ground and came to a stop well out from a stand of oak trees, whose limbs grew too low to allow passage beneath them. The sun had gone behind the mountains. Long bars of red streaked the sky and pink-tinged clouds hung low on the western horizon. The air was cool as it can be on the prairie when no breeze is stirring. The smell of woodsmoke and cooked meat coming from the station hung in the air.

Gil came to the end of the wagon.

"Make camp, Charlie. I'm ridin' down to the station to see if it's a fittin' place for my women folk." He looked at Willa, grinned, and winked, a gesture that was becoming more and more irritating to her.

"Can I go, Pa?"

"Jo Bell, honey, mind yore papa 'n' stay out a sight. I ain't wantin' to have to worry none 'bout ya."

"I can't see nothin' way up here," she whined.

"Honey, if those horny roosters got a look at my little gal, they just might go outta their minds 'n' come a-stormin' out here. I'll be back soon as I can. Be a good girl, hear? It ain't goin' to be but a week or two now 'n' you'll be sleepin' on a featherbed at yore Uncle Oliver's."

"All right, Pa. But make Charlie go get a fresh bucket of water. I'm just so thirsty I could die."

Willa's desire to slap the girl was so strong that she clenched her fists and buried them in the pockets of her apron.

Gil Frank felt sudden excitement as he approached the squat log building. He had money in his pocket from his winnings in Hublett; and if he were lucky enough to sit in on a game, he would be well fixed by the time he left the station.

The mere prospect of playing cards with rough, unskilled men was exhilarating. Long hours of practice had made Gil a man who could do things with cards. While shuffling, he could load the top of the deck or the bottom and deal from either end. He knew all about slick aces, marked or trimmed cards, sleeve holdouts and finger rings for the purpose of marking cards. In short, he was a professional gambler and a good one. He usually played a fair game, but he was not above cheating in order to win.

He tied his horse to the rail and stepped into the smoke-filled room. The smell of cooking food and rank tobacco mingled with body odor and manure tracked in from outside. A red-faced man worked over a cookstove at one end of the room. At the other end five men sat around a table playing poker. Several onlookers straddled chairs. All eyes, including those of the man with his hat tipped over his forehead, turned to Gil when he entered. After a brief look the men went back to their game as if it were not at all unusual for an Easterner dressed in a dark suit and fancy vest suddenly to appear in the doorway of the station.

The station man wiped his hands on an apron tied about his ample waist and came forward. His face was extremely broad, his hair sparse, and he was clean shaven.

"Howdy." He held out his hand. "Figured you'd be here 'bout now."

"Ya was expectin' me?" Gil said after the big man had released his hand.

"Sure was. Knowed two, three days back ya was headed this way, 'n' ya had a lad 'n' a couple women folk. This is big country, but not much goes on out here that folks don't know about."

"Dog-gone. If that don't beat all? Name's Gil Frank."

"Byers. Station keeper and cook . . . now. Goddamn cook ran off a week back. Glad to know ya, Mr. Frank. I got a pot of chicken with tators and peas cookin'. Figure yore women'd be wantin' garden stuff along about now." The cook's face was flushed. He glanced quickly, guiltily around, then lowered his voice. "Course it ain't chicken. Pheasant is what it is, but there ain't much difference if ya don't know it."

"Well, now, ain't that good of ya? It's a shame, though, that ya went to all that trouble. My wife 'n' little girl are plumb tuckered out. Lordy, they're the bashfulest two you ever did see. It purely scares the daylights out of 'em to think of meetin' a room full of strangers. They're figurin' on washin' up, eatin' a bite, 'n' beddin' down.''

Byers studied the wiry, slender man with the insolent eyes. He'd seen a thousand men come and go. Something about this one didn't ring true.

"I'm plumb sorry to hear it."

"Tomorrow they just might be in a better frame of mind."

"If that's the way it is, I'll dish up a bait 'n' ya can carry it to 'em.''

The cook's attitude showed that he was disappointed at not having the females he had expected at his table for supper. Too bad. Gil studied the men in the room: freighters, cowboys, drifters, rough men who more than likely were as horny as a herd of billy goats. If he had Starr with him, he would set her up in the wagon and the two of them would pocket some easy money. He didn't have Starr so it was useless to think about that. But he had Willa, who would make him more money in the long run if he could keep her away from the freighters headed for Sheridan or back to Deadwood.

Gil eyed the whiskey bottles and glasses on the tables. The way the liquor was flowing, the card players would be primed for a good plucking by nightfall. It could not be said that Gil Frank was a man who missed an opportunity.

"What do I owe ya?" he asked when Byers handed him a pot with a rag wrapped around the bail.

"Nothin'. It's for the ladies 'n' the lad."

"They'll be obliged. They surely will. I'd like to come back and set in on supper. I ain't had a visit with nobody but women in a coon's age."

Byers stood in the doorway and watched Gil carry the pot up the hill to the wagon. "He ain't had a visit with nobody but women in a coon's age. Ain't that a downright shame?"

"He ain't goin' to let that woman come near." The comment came from a bug-eyed, slack-jawed man at the poker table.

"Reckon he thinks Rucker'd jump her like a ruttin' moose." The bearded man who spoke scraped the legs of his chair on the floor as he swiveled around to look out the door

"He ain't too far off. I ain't had me none in God knows when. Last I had was in Laramie. That was last March. Hellfire! It ain't no wonder I'm 'bout to bust my britches." The card player slammed his cards down and raked the chips in from the middle of the table.

"Hell, Rucker, I heared ya 'bout split that little whore in two down there in Laramie. Heard she's been a-walking spraddle-legged ever since."

Rucker grinned. "I give 'er one hell of a ride. She warn't complainin'. Nosiree! I left her a smilin' and a purrin' like a pussy cat."

"If she charged ya more'n two-bits she got stung."

"Good God man! Ain't ya heard? I don't pay whores. Whores pay *me*!"

"Haw! Haw! Haw!"

Smith, sitting with his feet up on a bench, his hat pulled low over his closed eyes and a whiskey bottle held between his thighs, sent a little puff of air rolling over his lips. He had heard the same boasts in a thousand way stations and saloons from Canada to Texas and from the Mississippi to California. He wasn't interested in their card game or how many whores they'd plowed. He wanted to get stinking drunk, sober up enough to saddle his horse and head out across the river Byers's place was one of the few places where he was reasonably sure he'd not get knifed in the back and robbed while he was in that sweet oblivion.

"Whata ya think, cowboy? Huh?" A whiskered freighter

nudged his booted feet. "By gum, I bet you played hob with a whore or two. Ain't ya got a story to tell?"

Eyes green as a cat's looked unblinkingly into the freighter's before they closed again. Smith refused to rise to the bait. With the ease of long practice he detached himself from the rowdy group, allowing them to see no expression at all on his face.

The freighter cussed himself for a suck-egged mule. His stomach muscles tightened as though he were in striking distance of a rattlesnake. That one had a devil riding him and wasn't to be messed with. He moved his chair to the other side of the table.

"If that woman comes down here, I ain't wantin' to hear no such nasty talk." Back at the cookstove, Byers vigorously stirred the contents of the boiling pot. "She ain't no painted up whore. Rusty saw her in the glass a ridin' on the seat by the kid. He said she looked like a fine, decent woman. Got blond hair too."

"How can he tell through a glass if she's fine and decent?"

"Christamighty! A woman travelin' with her man 'n' two kids ain't likely to be a whore."

"Musta been hard up, though, to hook up with that puny lookin' Easterner." Rucker snorted in disgust. "Betcha two bits he squats down to pee."

The dealer dealt the cards during the loud laughter that followed the remark. Orvis Rucker was a big, friendly man who liked to talk. Byers had never heard anything bad about him. He was a hell of a muleskinner. It was said he'd take a six-mule hitch pulling a double wagon places where no other driver dared to go.

"If old Rusty saw a stump with a skirt on he'd think it fine and decent. Haw! Haw! Haw!"

"A woman is a woman. Good, bad, ugly, skinny or fat, they all have a glory hole." All eyes turned to the man who

sat across the table from Rucker. He was a cold-eyed man
with a long, narrow face filled with potential viciousness.

"Ain't nobody arguin' that," Rucker said gruffly and shuffled the cards.

"I like 'em skinny. The closer the bone the sweeter the
meat. And . . decent. There's something about being on top
a fighting woman that gets me big as a fence post and hard
as a rock. Come to think on it, I ain't had me a *decent* woman
for quite a spell."

The silence that followed was drawn out, broken only by
the scraping of heavy boots on the plank floor and the snores
of the man sleeping on a bench. Good women and kids were
something to be cherished in this rough, sparsely populated
land, and few men would risk molesting one. Outlaws had
been known to turn on one of their own for doing the unpar-
donable.

"Where you from, mister?" Byers asked.

"Kansas, and the name's Fuller. George Fuller." He said
his name slowly and looked directly into the eyes of each
man gathered around the poker table.

"I don't know 'bout Kansas, but up here a man better keep
his hands off a woman less she invites it."

"And if he don't?"

"He'll ride lookin' over his shoulder . . . that is if he
makes it to his horse."

Byers hadn't recognized the name, but the man was with
Abel Coyle, who was a known gunman, a bounty hunter who
operated just inside the law. Coyle was a dangerous man who
used intimidation first, and, if that didn't work, he used his
gun. He and Fuller had ridden in about noon and asked for a
night's lodging. After a few minutes of friendly conversation,
Coyle had been invited to sit in the card game with the
freighters, who were waiting until morning to cross the river.
Byers did not like having Fuller and Coyle here, did not like

it at all. He was sure there would be trouble before the night was over.

Smith Bowman took a long draw from the whiskey bottle, then slammed the cork in place. Dammit to hell. Between that slack-jawed drifter with the shifty eye, Abel Coyle, and the Eastern dude with a woman in his wagon, there was bound to be trouble of some kind before morning. He wanted no part of it. If he had any brains he'd push on. He hadn't stopped here because old Pete couldn't swim the river, swollen due to the rains up north. He'd stopped because he wanted to get dead drunk. Hell, he'd take himself and his bottle out to the barn and be well out of it.

"Ain't ya stayin' to eat, Smith?" Byers asked as the green-eyed man headed for the back door.

"No, thanks."

"Drinkin' when ya ain't et for a day or two'll rot yore guts, sure as shootin'."

"Let 'em rot."

Byers shook his head and watched Smith walk out to the barn, still as steady on his feet as a mountain goat, clutching an almost empty bottle of whiskey in one hand, a full one in the other. He was determined to get pissy-eyed drunk. There would be no help from him if trouble started.

"Come 'n' get it," Byers bellowed. "Come belly up to the table. Y'awl got all night to finish yore game."

"Now hush up yore fussin', Jo Bell. That ain't no fit place for a pretty little thin' like you. Tomorrow, when some of them toughs are gone, we'll stop in to say howdy to Mr. Byers."

"But, Papa, it ain't no fun settin' a way off up here."

"Mind me, now. I got to be gettin' back 'n' seein' if we can trail along behind one of them freighters when they head out. I'm thinkin' Mr. Byers might know where your Uncle Oliver's ranch is. He might know somebody to take us there.''

"Charlie and Willa won't talk to me," Jo Bell whined. "They go off with that old dog and talk so I can't hear."

"Pay them no mind, honeybunch. Charlie, keep a eye out. If anybody comes nosin' around, shoot off the gun. I'll come a hot-footin' it out here." Gil moved over close to Willa. "Stay by the wagon," he murmured in a conspiratorial tone. "There's a bunch a horny bastards down there that'd be between yore legs before ya hit the ground."

Willa let his words wash over her knowing full well he was trying to frighten her into staying away from the station. He needn't worry about that tonight. She wasn't foolish enough to go into a place where men were drinking. Tomorrow would be soon enough. Her mind was racing ahead. She would talk to the station keeper and, if he was a decent sort, ask him to help her.

She watched Gil hug Jo Bell and whisper something to her. The night swallowed him as soon as he stepped out of the light from the campfire. Willa looked toward the station. Light streamed from the open doorway and the front window. The evening was cool and alive with the sounds of masculine voices, crickets, and the occasional hoot of an owl.

"Don't be scared, ma'am," Charlie said. "I've got the rifle and I can shoot."

"I'm only scared of the future, Charlie."

Willa needed to touch someone; needed the contact with a warm, caring human being. She clasped the boy's hand tightly with hers.

"Things has got a way of workin' out, ma'am."

"Charlie, if I ever have a boy, I want him to be just like you," Willa said suddenly. "You're sweet, gentle, caring, and dependable. I pray that you don't change. Don't let this land make you hard and unfeeling like the people back at

Hublett.'' She stopped herself before she added—and conniving like your father.

"Ma'am . . . ma'am—''

A great tenderness welled in her for the boy who was so thunderstruck by her words of praise.

"What'er ya butterin' *him* up for, *ma'am*?'' Jo Bell, sulking as usual, sat on the end of the wagon. "You'd better be butterin' up Papa or he'll tie a can to yore tail like he's done a few others.''

Charlie turned on her. "Shut yore mouth, Jo Bell,'' he said threateningly. Then to Willa, "Pay her no mind. Sometimes I think she's rotten clear through.''

"She's spoiled, but not rotten . . . yet. Do you have another gun, Charlie?''

"We have an old shotgun. You expectin' trouble?''

"Papa Igor and I traveled a lot. We always had weapons close at hand. A time or two we needed them.''

"Didn't that mean old dog warn ya?'' Jo Bell asked hatefully.

"One time we had a thief try to make off with our horses,'' Willa said, ignoring the girl. "Buddy got him down and took a bite out of the seat of his britches. He'll let us know if anyone comes near.''

"The shotgun is under the wagonseat. I'll douse the fire a bit,'' Charlie said kicking dirt onto one side of it. "Me'n Buddy'll bed down here under the wagon. If he growls, I'll tap on the bottom with the rifle butt.''

"Jo Bell,'' Willa called from the end of the wagon. "Do you want to go to the bushes with me?''

"I can go by myself.'' The surly voice came out of the darkness.

"Suit yourself ''

Willa walked a short distance into the trees. Buddy padded along silently behind her. After she had relieved herself and straighted her clothes she knelt down and put her arms around the shaggy dog.

"Oh, Buddy, what are we going to do? We're alone in wild new country—dangerous country. We don't have Papa Igor to put things in perspective for us. But I think he would tell us not to let ourselves be pushed into anything, to wait and see what happens. Tomorrow, after I meet Mr Byers, I'll decide if I should seek his help. If he's a decent man, he'll not let Mr. Frank strip me of Starr's clothes as he threatened to do."

Back at the wagon, Willa sat on her pallet and took the pins out of her hair. She looked out the end of the wagon, staring into the shadows. A poignant longing for her mother and Papa Igor surged through her. Thinking of her mother's life, Willa smoothed her hair from her cheeks and hooked it over her ears. Words her mother had said came back to her *There may come a time in your life when you think you can't go on, but you will.* Tears trickled from Willa's eyes as she recalled the forlorn look on her mother's face when she spoke of the man who had deserted her and their child.

Willa removed her dress and pulled on the nightgown she had carefully mended over her underclothes. Not since the night the mob burned the house had she completely undressed, and not a night passed that she didn't wake up suddenly, her heart thudding wildly in her breast.

She sat for a long while looking out the back of the wagon, thinking about her former life and worrying about what lay ahead. Finally she lay down and pulled a blanket over her Life goes on and so does heartache and uncertainty Filled with tension, she listened to the leaves whispering through the cottonwood trees and the occasional loud guffaw of laughter coming from the station. Soon the tiredness of her body overcame her restless mind and she slept.

CHAPTER
* 5 *

Willa awakened suddenly and sat up. The wind had come up. A fierce gust rocked the wagon, but that was not what had awakened her An urgent tapping on the bottom of the wagon sent her slipping out the back to stand against the tailgate. Charlie crawled out and stood beside her.

"I heard two shots."

"Something woke me, but I didn't know what it was."

The campfire had died. It was pitch dark. Willa and Charlie stood close together, the dog beside them. A bright ribbon of light shone from the doorway and window of the station house.

"They musta lit every lamp they got. It wasn't that light a while ago. Whata ya think happened, Willa?"

"Someone got drunk and shot off their gun. There doesn't seem to be a fight going on. I don't even hear any loud talking." The cold night air caused her to shiver.

"You're cold. Go back to bed. Me'n Buddy'll stay up and watch."

"What time is it?"

50

"It's between midnight and mornin', but the birds ain't makin' a racket yet."

"I think I'll put my dress on and stay out here with you. I'd never get back to sleep now."

Willa dressed quickly, and when she stepped from the wagon, she had an old leather jacket which she handed to Charlie and a blanket which she draped about her shoulders.

"What do you know about your Uncle Oliver, Charlie?" Willa asked after they had sat down on the ground cloth Charlie pulled from beneath the wagon.

"Not much."

"Your father said he was refined, very much a gentleman."

"I guess my mother was too. Folks said she was quality Real pretty. Prettier than Jo Bell and nicer."

"Life will be hard for Jo Bell unless she marries a man who spoils her like her father does. After a while a man will get tired of her sulks no matter how pretty she is."

"Papa's just always doted on her " There was a wistful note in Charlie's voice she hadn't heard before. So he does care, she thought. He cares that his father ignores him.

"Look, ma'am. Someone's comin' with a lantern. Is it Pa?"

Willa got to her feet and grasped the thick hair on back of Buddy's head. "I don't know," she said as she watched the bobbing, swaying light come toward them.

A dozen yards from the wagon the light stopped moving and a voice came out of the darkness.

"Hail the camp."

"Whata you want?" Charlie replied.

"I'm Byers, the station keeper. I want to speak to Mrs. Frank."

Charlie hesitated. "Is somethin' wrong?"

"I mean no harm." The lantern started moving again.

"We got a gun and a dog that'll tear ya up if ya ain't what ya say ya are."

"It's all right, Buddy " Willa patted the dog's head when he began to growl.

"Whata ya want, mister? Where's Pa?" Charlie demanded.

"Mrs. Frank?" Byers held the lantern out at arm's length and looked at the pretty young woman with the blond hair hanging down about her shoulders.

"I'm Willa Hammer I'm traveling with Mr Frank and his children."

"Will you wake Mrs. Frank?"

"My ma passed on," Charlie said. "Pa ain't got no wife."

"May be that I mistook the man," Byers murmured and took a deep breath.

"What you want, mister?"

"There just ain't no easy way to say it, folks. Mr. Frank got hisself shot . . . killed."

It took a dozen heartbeats for the import of his words to sink in. Willa had suspected the station keeper was bringing bad news, but she had not dreamed it would be so bad, so . . . final.

"Oh! Oh, my goodness." She reached for Charlie's hand. The boy stood stone-still, staring at Mr. Byers.

"What happened?" Charlie asked in a strangled voice.

"Your pa'd been playin' cards and winnin'. I reckon he wasn't as slick a card-sharp as he thought. Feller by the name of Abel Coyle caught him dealin' hisself aces off the bottom of the deck. It might not've come down to a killin', but yore pa palmed a derringer that slid down his sleeve. He missed. The other feller didn't."

Charlie made a big to-do about leaning the rifle against the wagon. "You sure?"

"I'm sure, son. Lordy. I hate that it happened at my place. But it was fair. Yore pa shot first."

"Don't reckon it's yore fault, mister. Where is . . . he? I'll bring him home . . . ah . . . back here. My sister'll take it mighty hard."

Byers's hand came down on Charlie's shoulder and gripped. "Wake yore sister, boy. We'll bring him here if that's what ya want."

"I'd be obliged."

Byers turned to go, then turned back. "I'll see that ya get what yore pa won fair 'n' square."

When they were alone, Willa put her arms around the boy He pressed his cheek tightly to hers.

"I gotta tell . . . Jo Bell." There were tears in his voice.

"Would you rather I do it, Charlie?"

"Guess it's my place. Will ya come with me?"

"Of course."

Charlie knelt down beside the bunk where his sister lay sleeping. Her back was to him. The blanket was pulled up over her ears. He gently shook her shoulder.

"Jo Bell, wake up." When she didn't move he shook her shoulder a little harder. "Wake up."

"Get away!" She lashed out with her elbow.

"Jo Bell, I've got somethin' to tell ya."

"Get away and let me be, or I'll tell Papa."

"Turn over and listen—"

"I ain't gettin' up. So there!" She flipped the blanket up over her head.

"Jo Bell! Papa's been killed," Charlie yelled with a sob. "Get up or   or I'll slap ya!"

"Don't you dare—" Jo Bell rolled over and pulled the cover off her face. "What'd you say?"

"Papa's been . . . killed."

Jo Bell sprang up from the bunk swinging her fists. The blows landed on Charlie's cheeks.

"Liar! You mean old liar! I always did know you were a mean old liar"

Charlie caught his sister's wrist when she drew back to hit him again.

"Stop it! Papa is dead. Mr Byers said so."

"He is not! You're makin' it up."

"Get dressed, Jo Bell," Willa said gently "They're bringing him here—"

"I ain't believin' anythin' *you* say, *ma'am*."

"It's true. Mr Byers was just here and told us."

"Nooo . ."

"Come on. I'll help you—"

"Get away!" She kicked out at Willa. "Papa! Pa   pa!"

When she made for the back of the wagon, Charlie caught her around the waist and wrestled her down on the bunk.

"Please, Jo Bell—"

"I ain't listenin' I ain't listenin' "

"What'll I do, Willa?" Charlie pleaded.

Willa sat down on the bunk and tried to put her arms around the distraught girl. Jo Bell struck out at her and Willa backed away.

"Leave her alone, Charlie. You've done all you can do."

"I hate ya." Jo Bell pounded on her brother with her fists. 'I h-hate ya!"

Charlie stood and looked down at his sister "Hate me all you want. But Papa is still dead and I'm all ya got."

Willa followed Charlie out of the wagon. Jo Bell had thrown herself back down on her bunk.

"I don't know what I ever did to make her hate me so much," Charlie said with so much sadness in his voice that Willa wanted to cry for the young boy "Guess it don't matter now "

"She didn't mean it." Willa said the words although she was not sure she believed them. "She's hurting and lashing out at the person who brought the bad news."

"Pa . . . pa— Pa . . pa— Pa . . . pa—" A wail like that of a wounded animal came from inside the wagon, followed by hysterical sobbing.

In a small plot set aside by the army when the station was an outpost of Fort Kearny, Gilbert Frank was buried alongside drifters, soldiers, outlaws and pioneers who had died on their way west to settle the new land. Willa, Charlie and Jo Bell followed the two freighters who carried the blanket-wrapped body to the secluded area. Mr. Byers and his stock-tender, a whiskered old man named Rusty, were the only others present when Gil Frank was laid to rest. Willa recited *The Lord's Prayer* and then led Charlie and Jo Bell away while their father's grave was filled, making him a part of this wild country forever.

Her father's death had left Jo Bell in a strange state of shock. She had meekly put on the dark dress Willa found in her trunk: a dress that no doubt had belonged to her mother. She let Willa pin up her hair and put a black straw hat on her head. Her eyes were swollen, her face pale, but for once she looked more woman than child.

Charlie had not tried to talk to his sister. He had shown surprising maturity when his father's body had been brought back to the wagon and placed on the ground cloth. With Willa beside him, he had gone through his father's pockets, placed the contents in a small cloth sack, then folded his father's hands across his chest. He and Willa had sat beside the body until Mr. Byers had come an hour after sunrise to tell them the grave was ready.

After the service Jo Bell climbed inside the wagon and lay

down on her bunk. It was clear to Willa and Charlie that any decisions regarding the future would be made without her.

For the graveside service, Willa had dressed herself as modestly as was possible in one of Starr's dark dresses. She removed it now and put on the checked gingham dress. Overnight her situation had changed. She couldn't abandon Gil Frank's children after what he had done for her, even if his motives had been selfish. She would have to stay with them until they reached their uncle's ranch.

She found Charlie sitting on a log, his back to the camp, Buddy sitting between his knees. His hands were buried in the dog's fur. He sniffed and blinked away tears when Willa sat down beside him. She reached for his hand.

"Don't be ashamed of crying, Charlie."

"Papa said . . . men don't cry."

"Sometimes they do. If they don't cry on the outside, they cry on the inside. Papa Igor said that tears had a way of building up inside you and making you bitter if you didn't let them out."

"Are you goin' to . . . leave us?" Charlie blurted, trying to keep his voice from cracking.

"I had planned to ask Mr. Byers for work, but if you want me to stay with you and Jo Bell, I will."

"Please, Willa. Please . . . stay. I don't know what to do. Jo Bell ain't goin' to be no help at all."

"The only thing you can do is go on to your uncle's ranch."

"I don't even know where it is. Papa didn't talk to me . . . much."

"Your father told me it would take about a week to get there. The station is a post office. Maybe Mr. Byers knows. He may even know someone who can take you there."

"I'm so glad you're here, Willa—you and Buddy. Stay with us until we get to Uncle Oliver's. He might not want us there without Pa."

"He will! You and Jo Bell are his sister's children. Remember what you told me the other night? You said things have a way of working out."

"Jo Bell is actin' strange—for her."

"I know. She needs time to come to terms with what has happened. We can leave Buddy with her while we go down and talk to Mr. Byers."

"I'll take Pa's rifle. We're alone now, Willa. You'd better put that little derringer in your pocket. Do you know how to shoot?"

"Papa Igor taught me to load and shoot a rifle and a pistol. I've never shot at anything but a target. He told me never to take a gun in hand unless I meant to use it. So far I've not had to, but I know I could."

Only one freight wagon remained at the station. The teamsters, swearing viciously, were harnessing the mules and backing them into the traces. Chickens picked, scratched in the dirt, and fought each other over a morsel. A mule brayed, a mare in the corral nickered softly. This day was like any other day, yet overnight a man had lost his life here.

Charlie looked back to see Buddy sitting at the end of the wagon watching them. "Buddy didn't want to stay."

"No, but he will. If anyone goes near the wagon, he'll let us know."

Mr. Byers came out the door as they approached the station and came to meet them.

"I'd just as soon ya didn't go inside, miss. There's a couple of fellers in there that ain't fit company fer a lady." He motioned them toward the corner of the building. "I thought they'd be gone by now, but they ain't."

"Sir," Charlie said. "We wanted to talk to ya . . . if ya've the time."

"What's on yore mind?"

"Did my Pa ask ya if ya knew the whereabouts of my Uncle Oliver's place up on Clear Creek?"

"No." Byers scratched his nearly bald head. "He et 'n' seemed anxious to get in on a poker game. I had chores to do. Never paid him no mind till the trouble started."

"Pa was figurin' on trailin' along behind a freighter goin' into the Bighorns—"

"I ain't heard of any Franks in these parts."

"Name ain't Frank. It's Eastwood. Oliver Eastwood."

"Eastwood. Well, I'll be doggone."

"Ya know him?"

"Did. Oliver Eastwood died six, seven years ago."

Willa saw Charlie's shoulders slump. He looked off toward the wagon where his sister slept and tried hard not to show his disappointment.

"Mr. Byers," Willa said. "Do you know if Gil Frank's children would be made welcome at the Eastwood Ranch?"

"I not be knowin', ma'am. Mrs. Eastwood lives there. They had a girl, but she ain't been around for a long time."

"Is Mrs. Eastwood alone?"

"Well . . . not exactly. She's got hired hands."

"How far is the ranch from here?"

"Maybe seventy miles. That ain't far in this country."

"Sir, could ya draw us a map?"

"Well, now, son—" Mr. Byers scratched his head. "You ain't ort to be strikin' out on yore own—two women and a boy."

"We won't do anything foolish, will we, Charlie? We'll wait here, if you don't mind, until we find someone to guide us."

"Well, now—" Byers scratched his head again. "Course

ya can wait here. But happens there's a feller here now that knows the way like the back of his hand.''

"See there, Charlie. I told you things would work out.''

Charlie's serious young face didn't return Willa's smile. "Is he a man we can trust?''

"Son, this man's straight as a string 'bout women folk. His word's as good as gold. If he says he'll do somethin', he'd do it come hell or high water. Thin' is, he's in bad shape right now. He's on a drinkin' spree—has been fer a couple a days.''

"A drunkard!'' Willa remembered the many times she had seen families on the verge of starvation because of drink. Papa Igor had explained that some men had such a craving for liquor that they could not help themselves. She had no such compassion for a man who drank until he was senseless. "Charlie, we'd be better off going alone than with a fall-down drunk. Mr. Byers, could we follow the freighters?''

"Ya'd not be on the same trail but a day. Then ya'd be wanderin' round out there by yoreself. Don't think I'd do it, ma'am. Them two fellers in there''—he jerked his head toward the station door—"know ya ain't got no man now.''

"They might get a surprise.'' Willa smiled proudly at the boy. "What do you think, Charlie? Shall we chance it alone or with the drunk?''

"Hold on, ma'am. I ain't sure Smith'll take ya. He's a touchy bast—feller. At times he's meaner than a steer with a crooked horn. Ain't no man I know'll take him on in a fight if he can't stand up a'tall. He don't fight by no rules and he ain't got no quit in him oncet he gets wound up.''

"We ort ta talk ta him, Willa.''

"It's up to you, Charlie. I've never known a man who drinks himself senseless to be dependable. From what Mr Byers says, he's not only a drunk, but a brawler ''

"Don't reckon I meant that, ma'am. Man's got to stand up for hisself out here."

"Where is he?" Charlie asked.

"Sleepin' it off in the barn. If yore bound to talk to him, come on. Don't be surprised if'n he comes up outta that hay a fightin' 'n' swearin' a blue streak."

Willa and Charlie followed Mr. Byers toward the barn. They passed the teamsters who had carried Gil Frank to his grave and who now tipped their hats politely to Willa. The double doors of the barn stood open. A whiskered old man with a pitchfork came out of one of the stalls when they entered.

"Howdy, ma'am," he said hastily and snatched off his battered hat.

"Hello, Mr. Rusty. Charlie and I want to thank you for coming to the burial."

The old man's mouth worked up and down. Without teeth his lips almost touched his nose.

"It warn't nothin'. Nothin' a'tall."

Willa smiled at him. "Yes, it was. We appreciate your taking the time."

"Where's Smith, Rusty?"

"Smith? He's back thar in a stall a sleepin' it off. He ain't going' to like bein' waked up," Rusty said when Byers started down the aisle between the stalls. "Ya know how he gets. He's liable to come up shootin'."

They came to a stall where a powerful Appaloosa stood, ears peaked, nostrils flaring. He snorted and pawed the ground when they stopped to look over the rails of the opposite stall.

"Even his goddamn horse is meaner'n all get out," Byers grumbled.

Smith lay on his side, his head resting on his bent arm. His hat was over his face, but Willa could see a thatch of thick blond hair long enough to curl down over his ears. He was tall and on the lanky side. He wore a faded flannel shirt, britches so ragged that you could see the skin on his knees, and what were commonly called well-worn—down-at-the-heel—boots. Nestled close to his chest, with his fingers curled around the butt, was a six-gun.

CHAPTER
* 6 *

"Smith, wake up."

Byers lifted the bars holding the stall gate and folded it back. When Smith didn't stir, he yelled again and kicked the bottom of his boots.

Quick as a striking snake, Smith came up out of the hay with the gun in his hand. The growth of dark beard on his face was in sharp contrast to his hair. His eyes squinted against the light and his lips drew back in a snarl. He looked dangerous. Willa was reminded of a vicious cornered animal. She and Charlie sprang back.

"Goddammit, Byers. You wantin' to get your blasted head blowed off?"

"There's some folks here that want to talk to ya."

"Goddamn! I ain't carin' if Jesus Christ is wantin' to talk to me. Get the hell out and leave me be."

"Watch yoreself," Byers warned. "There's a lady here."

"Lady? Hell! Now ain't that somthin'?"

"Are ya sober enough to talk, Smith?" Byers asked.

"Sober enough to know I ain't needing a whore." Green eyes shot with red glared at Willa. "You're outta luck, hon.

I couldn't do ya any good if I wanted to. Come back tonight. I might be able to get it up. Goddamn! My heads bustin' wide open—''

Willa was shocked speechless but only for a moment. She took a deep breath and when she released it, anger boiled up.

"You . . . crude, pitiful excuse for a human being! It would serve you right if the top of your filthy head blew off!"

"Get out."

"Come on, ma'am. He ain't fit company for a warthog much less a lady."

Byers nudged Willa gently toward the aisle, but she resisted and stood looking down at Smith, her face rigid with impatience and anger

"Get the hell out!" Smith yelled again and moaned at the sound of his own voice.

"Whiskey-soaked sot! Just look at you—wallowing in filth like a hog!" Willa focused on what irritated her the most.

"Get her outta here, Byers, unless she wants to stay and watch me take a piss."

"Smith! For God's sake. What's got into you?"

"I don't need a nasty-nice little heifer tellin' me what I am!" Smith yelled and held his hand to his head. "Get the hell away from me."

"Gladly! You stink like a   like a privy!" Willa jerked her chin up and stalked out of the stall, muttering something under her breath that sounded like a string of cuss words.

She rounded the corner and ran into a water barrel. A bucket floated on the top. Too angry to think about what she was doing, she grabbed the bucket, filled it with water, whirled, and flung it in the face of the man still sitting on the straw

"That's water in case you don't know what it is!"

He jumped to his feet. "Goddamn whore! Damn you to hell—''

Willa glared at him with deep-rooted dislike showing on her face. She had never done such an outrageous thing in her life. She took a deep breath to steady herself and spoke in a low, controlled voice as she drew back the empty bucket.

"Call me that name again and I'll . . . smash your face!"

"Jesus! Get her outta here before I hurt her "

Charlie flung himself in front of Willa. "Touch her and I'll shoot yore blamed head off."

"Good lord! She's got a cub!"

"Come on, ma'am. He's in no mood to talk now "

"—Or ever .   to her!" Smith yelled, wiping water from his face.

With her back ramrod straight, indignation in every line of her face, Willa led the way back down the aisle to the door, where the old man leaned on the pitchfork.

"Reckon he won't be in no shape a'tall till 'bout noon," Rusty said.

"If then," Byers growled as he passed.

The freighters were ready to pull out. One was already on the wagon seat. The other stood beside the wheel.

"Hey, Byers. Speak to ya a minute."

"Yo. Beg pardon, ma'am." Byers excused himself and headed for the wagon. The man waiting for him was a head taller and built like an ox: broad and strong. His feet were planted firmly on the ground. His face was rugged but pleasant.

"Wanted to tell ya to keep a eye out. Heard Coyle and Fuller talkin' 'bout Frank's women folk. Fuller likes 'em young. Younger the better. He got a peek at the girl and liked what he saw." Orvis Rucker ran blunt fingers through tight black curls that clung to his head like a cap. "Hell, if I didn't have to get this load to Sheridan, I'd stick around."

"Low-down bastard! I'm obliged to ya, Rucker. I'll get

out my old buffalo gun and keep it handy. Smith Bowman's in the barn, but he's in bad shape."

"Sober him up 'n' he's worth any three men ya can find. Drunk, he ain't worth shit. Sorry I can't stay and lend a hand."

"So long, Rucker. See ya next week."

As soon as the man climbed the wheel and grabbed the reins, the whip sang out over the backs of the mules. The big wagon rolled. Both men nodded to Willa as they passed. She smiled and waved.

"What do we do now, Willa?" Charlie asked.

"Wait until someone else stops by, I guess."

"Son, I'm thinkin' it'd be a good idey if ya moved yore wagon on down here and parked it there where the freight wagon was. Put yore mules in the corral. I'd feel better if I could keep a eye on ya till ya move on."

"That's mighty thoughtful, Mister—"

The sound of a barking dog cut off Charlie's words. He looked quickly at Willa. Without the slightest hesitation she began to run. She knew when Buddy's bark was urgent. Another minute or two and he would go after whatever it was that was upsetting him.

She rounded the building with Charlie sprinting ahead of her, Mr. Byers behind. A man with a wide brimmed, high-crowned hat stood beside the Frank wagon. Buddy was hunkered down ready to spring if he took a step.

"Get away from that wagon," Byers shouted.

Willa watched in horror as the man pulled a gun from his holster.

"Shoot that dog and ya'll get it in the back," Charlie yelled. He stopped, cocked the rifle and aimed.

"Back off! Back off, or by God, I'll shoot ya myself." Byers was huffing from the short, fast run.

The man lifted his hands. "I ain't turnin' my back on this dog."

Willa went ahead and called to Buddy. The man shoved his gun back into the holster and turned.

"What the hell is all the ruckus, Byers? I was just paying a call on a grieving family."

"Like hell ya was. Get the hell away from here, Fuller."

"Listen good, Byers. You're not telling me what to do or who to call on."

"While yore at my station, ya do as I say. It's time for ya to ride on." Mr. Byers stood on spread legs and looked the man in the eye.

"If I don't?"

"Word'll be passed 'n' ya'll not find bed or board in a station in the territory."

Willa looked at the man and shivered. He was a short weak-jawed man with bulging eyes—a man who needed to prove he stood tall. She'd seen such a man as this lord it over Papa Igor a hundred times. The frog-like eyes turned on her.

"I beg your pardon, ma'am. Seemed proper to me to call and pay my respects."

"You could have done that at the burial service," Willa said frostily.

"That dog will get a bullet between his eyes if he comes at me again."

"Then you'll get one between yours," Charlie said.

"You're talking pretty big, boy. You ain't dry behind the ears yet."

"I don't have to be to pull a trigger."

Willa couldn't have been prouder of Charlie if he had been her own son.

"What's goin' on?" Jo Bell climbed out of the wagon and stood with her hands clasped in front of her. "Answer me, now, Charlie Frank. What's that man talkin' about?"

"Nothin'." Charlie moved over beside his sister. "He's goin'."

"Watch the end of that rifle, boy. Somebody might draw on you thinking you're about to shoot." Fuller pulled a cigar from his pocket, struck a match on the iron rim of the wagon wheel, and lit it. He stared down at Jo Bell. "Howdy, miss." He spoke in a soft, intimate voice.

"Get in the wagon, Jo Bell." Charlie gave his sister a gentle push.

"Don't push me!"

"Name's Fuller, Miss Frank. George Fuller. I'm sure sorry about your pa."

Jo Bell looked at Fuller with large, violet eyes, the surly expression gone from her heart-shaped face. Inky black curls tumbled about her shoulders. She was lovely. Willa realized suddenly that Jo Bell Frank was one of the most beautiful girls she had ever seen. Fuller was looking at her as if he was a cat and she a dish of cream.

"No, you ain't. You ain't sorry a'tall." Jo Bell said in a voice Willa had seldom heard her use. The whine was gone. "You come to get a look at me. Well, look yore fill."

"You're sure enough somethin' to look at."

"I know that too. I'll tell ya straight out. I ain't havin' no talk with a buggy-eyed old man. So get yoreself away from here."

The silence that followed was filled with tension. Then Fuller laughed.

"You need some of the sass taken out of you, honey, and I know just how to do it."

"I ain't yore . . . h-honey—" The word was a seductive whisper.

Fuller stared. Jo Bell tilted her head and stared back with her mouth tilted at the corners. She lowered her lids, then lifted them to give him a wide-eyed innocent look. Willa could have slapped her. She was practicing flirtation on this horrible man.

"You will be," Fuller said breathlessly and walked away.

Mr. Byers watched him leave. "That man's trouble. Keep a eye out. Hitch up, Charlie. Move to where I told ya. Ladies, it'd be best if ya stayed outta sight till them fellers ride out. I'll see if I can hurry them along."

"Move?" Jo Bell said. "I ain't goin' to leave . . . Papa—"

"We're moving down closer to the station." Willa began to clear the campsite.

"Ain't you leavin' on the stage?"

"Charlie asked me to stay with you until you get to your uncle's."

"Why? You don't like me."

"You've not given me much of a reason to like you, Jo Bell."

"I don't care. 'Cause I don't like you anyhow. I w-want Papa—"

"I know you do," Willa said gently. "I miss my Papa too."

"That ugly, little old warty thin'?" Jo Bell screeched. "He wasn't like my Papa. My Papa was handsome."

It clearly required all Willa's self-restraint to refrain from grabbing the girl and shaking her.

"Papa Igor was beautiful on the inside—where it counts," she replied softly. "He was intelligent, compassionate . . . loving. There was not a better father in the whole world."

Jo Bell burst into tears and climbed into the wagon.

By telling herself the girl was grieving, Willa tried not to let Jo Bell's words hurt. Absently Willa lifted an iron pot from the campfire. Jo Bell was going to be a handful. Poor Charlie. It wasn't his fault that his sister was a selfish little chit. A burning ache seared Willa's throat when she thought of the nights Gil Frank had spent laughing and talking to his daughter while Charlie sat alone with Buddy. Charlie would not desert the sister who held him in such contempt. But what would become of them if Mrs. Eastwood refused to put up with her?

She hung the kettle on a hook beneath the wagon.

Jo Bell was still crying.

Willa sighed. She would stay and tolerate the girl   for Charlie's sake.

The station manager suggested to Willa that she and Jo Bell stay inside the wagon until Abel Coyle and George Fuller rode out and crossed the river. The girl lay on the bunk with her eyes closed, but Willa made good use of the time. Charlie had said she was to use what she wanted from Starr's trunk because it was unlikely they would see her again.

The dress Willa had worn every day since she had joined the Franks was badly in need of washing. Having been taught to be fastidious with her person and her clothing, she felt uncomfortable being unclean. She had washed the dress only one time. More than a week ago, feeling reasonably sure of some privacy, she had bathed in the creek, washed her clothing and put them on wet until she could get back to the wagon. She had hung them up and they had dried overnight.

As far as she knew, Jo Bell had not bathed and had washed her face and hands only after being told to do so.

As the hours slipped away, Willa ripped the ruffles and lace from several dresses. She filled in the neckline of one of them and added a white collar. With the material from the ruffles she made a sash for a better fit at the waist. Out of a floppy straw hat she made a poke bonnet by removing the faded satin flowers and adding streamers to the brim which she tied under her chin.

"What're you doin'?" Jo Bell sat up on the bunk. Her eyes were swollen, her face streaked with tears.

"Making over these dresses," Willa said calmly.

"They ain't yours. Starr'll be back."

"Charlie said she left with a teamster headed for Canada. If she returns, I'll pay her for the dresses."

"With what? You ain't got nothin' but that old dog."

"That old dog may have saved you from that man today."

"Well poop-de-do! I ain't seen the man yet I can't wrap round my little finger."

"The men out here are a different breed. They take what they want—if they can. We're fortunate to have Charlie and Buddy with us."

"Men are the same the world over. Papa said so. He said they mostly wanted *one* thing, and if I'd give it to 'em they'd buy me fine silk dresses or anything else I want. He said they'd keep me like a pretty doll and show me off."

"I'm sure your father believed that," Willa said kindly. "Things have changed now. He's gone and can't protect you. You have to depend on Charlie and . . . Buddy."

"And . . . and yore g-glad he's . . . d-dead—" Sobs bubbled from Jo Bell's lips.

"How can you say that? I'm not glad. I'm terribly sorry."

"Yore not. Ya didn't even c-cry."

"That doesn't mean I wasn't sorry."

"I don't want ya in *my* wagon—"

"I'm sorry about that too. Nevertheless, I'm staying until you get to your uncle's ranch."

"I don't want ya to stay and I ain't goin' to no old ranch. I'll make Charlie take me to a town. I'll get a job in a dance hall till I find me a rich man."

"I promised Charlie I would stay and I will."

"Charlie ain't boss. I'm sixteen. He ain't but fifteen."

Willa made no reply. She knew that it was useless to try to reason with the girl.

"What'll you do when we get to Uncle Oliver's? Ya ain't kinfolk. He won't want *you* hangin' around."

"Your uncle is dead, Jo Bell. His wife, Mrs. Eastwood, lives on the ranch."

"Uncle Oliver is dead? Papa didn't tell me."

"Maybe your father didn't know."

"He did so. Papa knew e-everything—" Her words ended in a wail and she threw herself back down on the bunk.

Later, when Charlie came to tell them the men had left the station, Willa was wearing the pink dress she had made over. Her hair had been brushed and coiled at the nape of her neck, and although she still wore Jo Bell's moccasins, she felt she looked presentable. The weight of the Derringer in her pocket was reassuring.

"Jo Bell, do you want to go with me to the outhouse?"

"I guess so."

The girl's mouth was drawn down at the corners. She looked like a pouty child as she followed along behind Willa to the small building in back of the station. Almost new, the outhouse had been built for the convenience of the stage passengers. It was a luxury to be able to sit down instead of squatting in the bushes, even though the odor was overpowering. Men didn't seem to notice such things, but a woman would insist on a layer of lime every so often. These thoughts passed through Willa's mind as she waited outside the door for Jo Bell.

"Come on in 'n' have a bite to eat," Mr. Byers called from the doorway of the station as they approached it. "It ain't much. I got to be cookin' up a mess for tonight. The stage comes in about sundown."

"I'll be glad to help you with that," Willa said as she stepped into the long, dim room.

"Don't ya be sayin' that too loud, ma'am. I jist might hear ya. Come and sit down."

"We need to wash."

He indicated the shelf on the wall just around the corner from the door. There was a tin wash basin, a bucket of water, a slab of soap and a roller towel that looked as if it had been hanging there a week. Willa ladled water into the basin and handed Jo Bell the soap before the girl could move away without washing.

Smith Bowman was sitting at the table with a mug of coffee between his hands. His face was gaunt. Small cuts on his chin were proof that his hands had not been quite steady when he had shaved. His hair was wet, but combed. His eyes passed over Willa and went to Jo Bell.

A feeling of apprehension stirred restlessly in Willa as she observed the green-eyed man looking at the girl. His eyes flicked to hers, and suddenly she was so nervous that she felt as if her heart would choke her. Why would a young, strong man want to drink himself into oblivion? Did he have a wife and children waiting for him at home? And what had made her act so impulsively as to throw the water on him? She usually just walked away from an unpleasant situation. A queer little shock went through her when she thought about how much she had changed in just a few weeks.

"Have a seat, ladies." Mr. Byers placed two graniteware plates on the table. "Baking powder biscuits, butter and honey. We've got fresh buttermilk, too."

"I hate buttermilk." Jo Bell's voice was pouty and her lips turned down at the corners.

"I'd like some, please. But let me help—"

"—Sit right there, ma'am. I'll get it. Miss," he said to Jo Bell, "would ya like a cup of tea?"

"Black tea or green tea?"

"Green is all we get here."

"I'll take it if it's got sugar in it." Jo Bell sat with her elbows on the table, her chin on her laced fingers, and spoke as if she were doing the man a favor by accepting the tea.

Willa decided she couldn't do anything about Jo Bell's manners and refused to be embarrassed. The girl was impossibly rude. Charlie cast Mr. Byers an apologetic look. The station keeper seemed to be unaffected by Jo Bell's rudeness. He placed the biscuits, a crock of butter and a jar of honey on the table.

"Help yoreselves, folks. There's plenty a what I got. The buttermilk is in the cellar."

As soon as he left the room, Charlie glared across the table at his sister. "Where's yore manners? Mr. Byers don't have to get ya anythin'. He's tryin' to be nice."

"Shut up," Jo Bell hissed. "Stop tellin' me what to do."

Willa's eyes went automatically to Smith to see how he was taking this exchange between brother and sister. His head was turned, and she could see his profile. He was younger than she had at first thought. His face, darkened by sun and wind, was still, remote, lonely. It was the face of a hard man.

Slowly his head moved, and before she realized it, her eyes were locked with a pair of startling green ones that looked at her with total dislike. She turned her face quickly, conscious that she was a little breathless. Something in the lazy negligence of him as he lounged there, the cigarette between his lips, his eyes upon hers, went beyond dislike. It was as if he thought she was unworthy of even his appraisal. She had a sudden fear that he would reach across the table and swat her as he would a fly. The impression was so definite that she cringed away.

Mr. Byers returned with the buttermilk. He poured a cup

for Willa. She saw Smith turn his eyes away from it. Angered by the way his look had affected her, she couldn't resist taunting him.

"Buttermilk, Mr. Smith? Perhaps it would settle your stomach."

Her contempt washed over him like a chilling torrent. He got up from the table and went to the stove. After refilling his cup from the smoke-blackened coffeepot, he stomped past the eating table, went to the far side of the room and sat down.

CHAPTER
* 7 *

"**M**r. Smith," Charlie followed and stood behind one of the chairs at the poker table.

"What do you want now?"

"Willa didn't mean to rile ya." Charlie murmured the words as if not wanting the others to hear.

"Ah, hell!" Smith spat disgustedly. "It takes more'n a know-it-all woman to rile me." He spoke so that his voice carried the length of the room.

Mr. Byers came to the table, hooked out a chair with his foot and sat down. "I'll swear, Smith, I never knowed ya to be so down right cantankerous."

Smith ignored the station keeper for a moment and wiped the sweat from his forehead with his kerchief.

"I'm not one for parlor chit-chat, Byers. You know that."

"Ya ain't one for manners either or ya'd not said what ya did in front of that woman."

"I'm not caring what I said. I told you I'd stay until Coyle and Fuller were gone. Rusty tailed them. When he gets back, I'm riding out."

"I was hopin' they'd head for Deadwood."

"They crossed the river and went north."

"These folks ain't got nowhere to go but to the Eastwood Ranch, Smith. If ya don't take 'em, they'll strike out on their own."

"Dammit to hell! That's no skin off my back."

"Mister," Charlie said and straddled the chair he was leaning on. "My pa never talked to me much. He never said nothin' about what to do if somethin' happened to him. The only thin' I know to do now is take my sister on to Uncle Oliver's. I ain't askin' nobody for a free handout. I'll work for our keep."

Smith turned cold green eyes on Charlie. "Take your sister and that nasty-nice woman to Buffalo, Sheridan or back to Deadwood. They've got no business at Eastwood. That old woman will eat 'em alive."

"But, sir—"

"Don't sir me, either, boy. Name's Smith."

"We got no money. I thought Pa had more, but guess he lost it in the poker game 'n' got desperate enough to cheat. Uncle Oliver was my ma's brother. My ma was quality folk 'n' I'm thinkin' Uncle Oliver was too. Quality folks take care of their kin at least until they get on their feet."

"What was your ma's name?"

"Regina."

"He talked of her some."

"You knew him? You knew Uncle Oliver?"

"Yeah, I knew him."

"I wish I could of knowed him. I was hopin' he'd teach me to be a cowboy, and maybe I could stay there after Pa got a rich husband for Jo Bell."

"Jesus!" Smith swore and plopped his feet up on a chair

"I know I'm not full-growed yet, but I'm strong," Charlie continued doggedly. "I'll work hard if Mrs. Eastwood will take my sister. I can take care of myself and I think Willa can too, but Jo Bell—She's just too dang pretty for her own good. I can't turn her loose in a town, mister. She don't know beans when it comes right down to it.''

Something that may have been amusement flickered in Smith's green eyes. "Where does the other woman fit in?"

"Willa? She's a . . . friend of the family."

"Your pa's woman, huh?"

"Not like yore thinkin', mister. Miss Hammer ain't that kind." Charlie lowered his voice. "She's stayin' with us till I get Jo Bell settled. Then . . . me 'n' her'll move on."

"I heard what you said, Charlie Frank. You ain't goin' off no place with *her*!" Jo Bell marched across the room and stood facing her brother with her hands on her hips.

"Stay out of this," Charlie snarled.

"She ain't no kin to us. She ain't nothin' but a down-n-outer a ridin' in our wagon and eatin' our food cause Papa felt sorry for her. She could be a whore for all we know."

"She's no such thing! Shut up your mouth! Hear?" Charlie yelled so loud Smith winced.

"I don't have to and you can't make me." Jo Bell stamped her foot like a stubborn child.

"Go to the wagon," Charlie shouted.

Smith pressed the heels of his hands to his temples, wishing he had saddled his horse and ridden out as soon as Byers kicked him awake. Right now he could be lying in the cool shade where there was peace and quiet.

"Folks back at Hublett hung her pa," Jo Bell blurted with a defiant look at her brother. "He was mud-ugly with lumps on his face and a hump on his back. He looked like . . . like the boogy man. They hanged him cause he shot a man. Deny that, Charlie Frank. Folks were after her with stones and switches. Said she'd brought bad luck to the town."

Charlie grabbed Jo Bell's shoulders. "You don't have a

brain in yore stupid head!'' Even while he shook her, the girl babbled on, her voice shrill.

''They burned her out, hit her with dirt clods, tore off her clothes 'n' called her a whore. Pa pulled her up on the wagon or they'd a hung her, too.''

''It wasn't her fault—'' Charlie looked beseechingly at the two men.

''Papa helped her get away and she wouldn't even sleep with him after all he done for her. She told him right out, bold as brass, she didn't do *night* work.''

''That proves she ain't no whore,'' Charlie shouted.

''Papa had Starr to give him comfort till she run off with a freighter. Papa said a man needs comfort from a woman—'' Jo Bell watched the men to see their reaction. ''Now . . . he's gone—'' When neither spoke, she did what she usually did to gain sympathy: she collapsed on the floor in a storm of weeping.

In the moment after the girl's outburst, Smith looked over his shoulder. The blond-haired woman's chair was empty. His head had been fuzzy when he first had awakened, but after getting a good look at her, he realized that she had that scarcely definable something that Oliver called breeding. It was harder to recognize in people than it was in a wild horse that was the offspring of a thoroughbred, but it was there if you looked close enough. The woman had it. He wasn't surprised that she'd refused to be Gil Frank's whore. She would aim for bigger game than a two-bit gambler.

The boy seemed to be a level-headed kid. He wouldn't mind having him around for a while. Too bad he was saddled with a pea-brained sister. The old woman wouldn't want any part of her. Then what would they do? Dammit to hell! He didn't want the sister or the nasty-nice woman hanging on his coattail. He didn't want to look out for anyone but himself and . . Billy.

Smith looked dispassionately at the bawling girl. She needed someone to take a stick to her behind. Goddamn! She made more noise than a calf stuck in a mud hole.

Gradually the import of the girl's words sank into Smith's mind. Gil Frank wanted to sleep with the blond woman and she refused him. Good Lord! What kind of man would discuss a thing like that with his daughter?

"Come on, Jo Bell. Yore makin' a show of yoreself." Charlie lifted his sister off the floor. "I'm down right sorry she kicked up such a to-do. She just got it in her head she don't like Miss Hammer. Starr petted her along like Papa did, but Miss Hammer—Jo Bell, stop that!" he said as the girl tried to hit him. "I'll take her out to the wagon."

"Well, Smith?" Byers said when they were alone.

"Well, what? The boy ought to take a belt to that girl."

"Are you goin' to take them to Eastwood?"

"Old Maud'll slam the door in their face. She wouldn't take in Jesus Christ if he come riding in on a mule."

"They've got to find that out for themselves. If you don't take 'em, they'll strike out alone. I ain't likin' to think of Coyle 'n' Fuller waitin' up the trail."

"Why in hell don't they go back where they came from?"

"Hell, I dunno that. I want 'em on their way. Take 'em to Mrs. Eastwood. It's her problem, not ours."

"Ah . . . shit!" Smith stood and glared down at Byers. "Tell 'em I'm leaving in an hour. They can tag along behind if they can get across the river."

"Now ain't that big of ya? How'n hell will that boy get the wagon across the river?"

"If you want 'em out, get 'em across the river." He stepped out the door, took the cigarette from his mouth in one quick, impatient gesture, and threw it down.

* * *

It was the stock-tender, Rusty, who drove the wagon to the river crossing with Willa and Buddy sitting beside him on the wagon seat. Jo Bell, after raising a fuss about leaving her father's grave, had cried herself to sleep. Willa looked back at the station. She could scarcely believe that less than twenty-four hours had passed since they had come over the rise and had seen it for the first time. So much had happened in the short time they had been in this forsaken place.

Riding Rusty's horse and leading his father's, Charlie was to cross the river first.

"Jist sit back'n let that old bangtail take ya across, son. He knows the way 'n' don't cotton to nobody tellin' him what to do. We be comin' right behind ya."

When the boy reached the middle of the river, Rusty coaxed the team into the muddy water. The frightened animals fought for purchase on the slick river bottom, but they obeyed the old man's signals on the reins and his shouts of encouragement. Willa tried not to look at the water swirling around the wagon. She had read that more people drowned in river crossings on the way west than were killed by Indians. Why did she have to think of that now? A cry of fear escaped her when the wagon fishtailed in the water.

"Don't be sceered, ma'am. Ya be as safe as if yore sleepin' in a featherbed. Many a wagon has crossed here a dodgin' floatin' logs 'n' I ain't seen nary a one." Rusty grinned at Willa showing toothless gums. "This ain't bad a'tall. This be good rock bottom. Ain't no quicksand. H'Yaw! Get on up that thar bank, purrty critters," he sang out to the mules. "Yore a fine team, is what ya are."

Rusty urged the mules up the bank and guided them to the track worn deep into the grassland by the freight wagons. Willa searched the landscape ahead and saw no sign of Smith. Had he gone on and left them? Rusty answered her unspoken question before she could ask it.

"He'll not be far off, ma'am. That boy's got him a devil ridin' his back. He'd a never spoke so if'n he was sober. He only be half-bad."

"That's the part I'm worried about."

"Tell ya one thin', ma'am, yore better off with Smith than any ten men I know, includin' me. He told Byers he'd see ya to Eastwood Ranch. It's good as done."

"That's comforting to know." The touch of sarcasm in Willa's voice didn't escape the old man.

"Gets yore back up, don't he?" Rusty's laugh was like dry corn shucks rubbing together. Willa couldn't keep the smile off her face.

"I guess he does. You like him, don't you?"

"Ya betcha. He's hickory. Ain't nobody else like Smith."

"Thank goodness for that."

Charlie came to the wagon mounted on his father's horse.

"Are you sure you want to drive, Willa?"

"Of course." She pulled a pair of Starr's gloves from her pocket and put them on before she took the reins. The dog settled on the floor at her feet.

"Behave nice, fellers," Rusty said to the mules, and stroked their noses. "'Tis a lady ya'll be pullin' fer." Their ears stood, then flopped as if they understood the old man's words.

"Thank you, Mr. Rusty. Thank you for being so kind."

"'Twarn't nothin', ma'am. 'Twarn't nothin' a'tall." Rusty mounted his horse. "Yore water barrels is full, young feller. Smith'll get ya to water before they run dry. Keep yore eye peeled 'n' move right along. There be a good camp spot up the ways a piece. Ya'll know it when ya come to it." The old man reached over, shook hands with Charlie, and turned back toward the river.

"I've not seen Mr. Smith," Charlie called out nervously

"Smith'll be around somewheres." Rusty flung the words over his shoulder and urged his horse into the river.

Smith spurred his horse into a run until they reached an overhang where he could look down on the track below. The boy, Charlie, was riding ahead of the wagon. The blond woman, with the dog beside her, was driving. Somehow that didn't surprise him. The woman appeared to be fragile, but his guess was that she would be no pushover if it came right down to it. The boy and the dog were devoted to her He snorted with disgust. She was pretty, no denying that. The boy reminded him of himself when he had been a callow lad and enamored of a woman.

Smith rode along the ridge and watched the wagon until it reached a campsite alongside a small trickle of water that came down out of the foothills. He was relieved that the boy recognized it as the logical place to spend the night. He sure as hell didn't want to ride down and turn them back. When he saw the woman pull the mules to a halt and climb wearily down from the wagon, Smith turned away and headed for a place where he could cook some supper and bed down for the night.

Willa felt as if her arms had pulled her shoulders into a permanently rounded position. The mules were harder to handle than the pair of horses Papa Igor hitched to his wagon, but she supposed she would get used to it. When Charlie dismounted, she took the reins of the horse, unsaddled him and led him to the water before she staked him out to crop the grass that grew alongside the stream. While Charlie unhitched and picketed the mules, she started a fire within a circle of stones that appeared to have been used many times.

While she worked, Willa felt strangely exultant. It suddenly occurred to her that she had fallen in love with the country, her heart lost to it forever. She gazed across a waving sea of grass and the rolling aspen-cloaked hills toward the Bighorns. It was wild, beautiful, untouched. She drew in a deep breath.

There was every chance that she would not be made welcome at Eastwood Ranch, Willa thought now as she brought her attention back to the small flame she had kindled amid the dry leaves. She flapped her skirt to spread the fire and vowed that she would never go back east. She had no ties now. Surely there was a place for her in this lonely, beautiful land.

"I ain't seen no sign of Mr. Smith." Charlie dropped an arm full of dry wood beside the fire.

"His name is Mr. Bowman. But I don't suppose it makes any difference what we call him." Willa fed the sticks to the fire. "Rusty said not to worry, he'd be close by. All we can do is trust that Rusty knew what he was talking about."

"Well,"—Charlie looked nervously around—"I'd feel better if I knew where he was. Mr. Byers said Fuller and that other feller had headed this way."

"We've got Buddy. He'll warn us if anyone tries to sneak up on us."

The boy sighed heavily. "I sure am glad we got Buddy. Ma'am, Jo Bell ought to be out helpin' ya. Is she still sleepin'?"

"I don't know, but I'll see."

Willa pulled back the flap at the end of the wagon. Jo Bell was sitting on her bunk brushing her hair. Willa stared at her in open-mouthed amazement. The girl tilted her chin and looked back defiantly.

The white dress she had taken from her mother's trunk had at one time been modest, but not anymore. Rough seams showed where Jo Bell had ripped out the sleeves. With the scissors she had cut the neckline down until it just barely covered her breasts. A red sash was wrapped tightly about her waist from just beneath her breasts to her hip bones. And the skirt . . . good Lord! The skirt came to just below her knees, showing a length of bare legs. Her cheeks and lips were rouged, something she had no doubt learned from Starr, and dangling from her ears were a pair of Starr's red earrings.

"My goodness gracious me!" It was all Willa could say.

"How do I look, *ma'am*?" The last word was emphasized to put Willa in the category of an older woman.

"Jo Bell, ya get on out now and help Willa. Jo Bell! Good godamighty—"

Jo Bell shoved her brother aside and climbed down out of the wagon.

"Whata ya think?" She preened, walked a few steps swaying her hips, turned and came back.

"Ya . . . ya . . . look like a t-tart!" Charlie almost choked. "Get back in that wagon 'n' put on some decent clothes," he shouted.

Jo Bell ignored him. "I'm pretty, ain't I?" Her eyes gleamed as she looked at Willa. "Don't ya wish ya was as pretty as me? You're old, ain't ya? Bet that man back at the station didn't give ya a second look."

"Yes, you're very pretty," Willa said calmly. "I am four years older than you are. Old enough to be glad a man like that didn't give me a second look."

"Yore twenty? Shitfire! And ya ain't found a man that'd have ya?"

"I haven't been looking. Jo Bell, I agree with Charlie. You look like a . . . tart. Dressed like that you're sending a signal that you're . . . you're loose."

"What do you know about it? Starr said I was shit-stompin' pretty."

"What's that suppose to mean?" Charlie yelled. "Starr was nothin' but a whore."

"Don't you ever talk to each other in a normal tone of voice?" Willa asked, then realized she hadn't even been heard by the two glaring at each other

"Don't ya talk bad about Starr," Jo Bell screeched.

"Stop yelling," Willa said firmly "Voices carry We don't know who is within hearing distance."

"I'm hungry. Ya best get to fixin' supper, *ma'am*." Jo Bell jerked a stool out of the back of the wagon, walked a distance and sat down.

Willa looked at Charlie and shook her head.

"I'm making coffee. Mr. Byers gave us some smoked deer meat, biscuits, and a jar of buttermilk."

"I hate buttermilk. Ain't ya cookin' eggs? Mr. Byers gave us some."

"No."

"I want eggs."

"Charlie, I noticed that worn leather collar has made a sore spot on the grey mule."

"I saw it. I figure to put somethin' on it after supper."

"I want eggs," Jo Bell said in a shrill voice. "Where's that Mr. Smith? Ain't he comin' for supper?"

"I'm kind of sore," Charlie said, turning his back on his sister. "I ain't used to ridin' five, six hours straight."

"Ya ain't ridin' Papa's horse no more. Papa'd want me to have that horse. I'm sellin' him for cash money."

Willa glanced quickly at the boy to see if his sister's words had provoked another shouting match. To her surprise, he looked at her and winked.

"We'll be in the foothills tomorrow " Grasping the handle of the coffeepot with the end of her apron, Willa pushed it over the flame, then stood.

"Damn you! Listen to me! When I tell ya to do somethin',

do it. I said I want eggs!'' Jo Bell grasped Willa's arm and spun her around.

Willa reacted instinctively as she had done in the past when she had been grabbed by rough hands. Jo Bell had scarely time to blink her eyes before Willa's balled fist landed squarely on her jaw. The girl staggered back a few steps and fell heavily to the ground. Willa stood over her, anger making her breathless when she spoke.

''Don't ever put your hands on me again. Understand?''

''Why . . . why—''

''Do you understand?''

''Charlie! Charlie!'' Jo Bell's eyes found her brother leaning against the side of the wagon, his hand in the fur on Buddy's neck. The dog's fangs were bared. ''She   . she hit me!''

''Yeah. She packs quite a wallop. Ya had it comin' ''

Jo Bell looked at him with disbelief. ''Ya'd let her beat me?'' She turned, buried her face in her bent arm and burst into tears. She rolled in the dirt, racking sobs shaking her shoulders.

Anger left Willa as quickly as it had come. She looked down at the girl, then at Charlie. The boy was looking off toward the foothills, whistling through his teeth in order to appear unconcerned. Willa went to him.

''I'm sorry I hit her. It's just that I've been grabbed so many times in so many different towns that I just reacted—''

Charlie looked directly into her eyes. ''Don't be sorry She needed it lots a times, but I didn't dare. Fact is I'm shamed that she acts so.''

''Don't be. It's not your fault.''

''I don't know what to do.'' Something in his voice and the sad look on his face caught at Willa's heartstrings.

''Just do the best you can. It's all any of us can do.''

* * *

High on the ridge overlooking the campsite, Smith looked down on the scene. In spite of a splitting headache, his lips twitched in a grin. The nasty-nice woman wasn't so nasty-nice after all. She'd knocked the spoiled brat on her ass. Something, in his judgment, that should have been done long ago.

Smith tried to remember the woman's face, but all he could conjure up was blond hair, a funny color of blue eyes and a boyishly thin body with small pointed breasts. He chuckled out loud. It was a strange sound, one he hadn't heard for a long time. He had thought the woman fragile. She was about as fragile as a string of barbed wire. Hell, she had exploded into action like a cat with its tail on fire.

He went back to his campfire, where the blackened pot was sending up a plume of steam. A grin still crinkled the corners of his eyes.

CHAPTER
* 8 *

I t seemed to Willa she had just closed her eyes when she felt a hand on her ankle and heard Charlie's whisper "Willa. Wake up."

"What is it?" She sat up quickly and crawled to the end of the wagon.

"Somebody's prowlin' around out there. Buddy keeps looking off toward the creek. Look at his tail. It's standing straight out."

"It could be a coon or skunk."

"I heard a horse whinny a while ago. At first I thought it was ours, but it didn't come from the right direction."

"I'll wake Jo Bell. If it's those men, I don't want to get cornered in the wagon. Jo Bell,"—she shook the girl— "Jo Bell, wake up. We need to get out of here and hide."

"What?"

Willa explained quickly, surprised that for once the girl didn't argue. They dressed and climbed out of the wagon. Willa felt the comforting weight of the Derringer in her pocket. As they passed the side of the wagon, she lifted the heavy iron skillet from the hook. Holding it close to her side, she and Jo Bell followed Charlie and Buddy into a dense stand of sumac that grew along the bank of the stream.

"Stay here," Charlie said. "I'm goin' to the other side of the road."

"Be careful," Willa whispered. "Go with Charlie, Buddy."

"He'd better stay with you."

"No, he'll warn you if he hears anything."

Behind the screen of scrub and brush, Willa strained her ears for a foreign sound. The night was so black she could barely see her hand in front of her face. Her heart was whamming, but it didn't seem to be pumping enough air into her lungs. She grimaced in self-disgust at the frightened fluttering of her heart and waited while the minutes went slowly by.

Behind her Jo Bell was breathing heavily. Willa hoped and prayed the girl wouldn't burst into tears and give away their hiding place.

Down the creek an owl hooted and was answered from nearby. *Indians!* Didn't they use bird calls to signal one another? Frogs croaked nearby, then far, far away a coyote lifted its nose to the sky and howled for a mate. The lonely cry sent a chill shimmering down Willa's spine. Jo Bell moved so close to her back she could feel the girl's breath on her neck.

"Why'd Charlie—?"

"Shhh . . ."

Willa's keen ears had heard a faint sound. She cocked her head to the left and heard it again. With her left arm she swept Jo Bell farther behind her. Her right hand gripped the handle of the iron skillet while her eyes tried to penetrate the darkness around them.

Suddenly, without a sound, a man was beside them. Seeing him and acting was simultaneous. She swung the skillet. The man's hand went up to ward off the blow. *Ping!* She heard the sound of iron striking metal. Before she could draw a breath she was wrestled to the ground. Rough hands jerked the skillet from her grasp. Then a string of obscenities spewed forth that would have made a bartender blush.

"Damn you! I ought to break your neck," he hissed.

Break your neck! The words registered in Willa's mind. *He was going to kill her!*

"Hel . . . lp! Bud . dy!" Willa kicked and tried to get her fingers in position to scratch his face.

"Shit! You crazy damn woman!"

"Char . . lie! Bud . . . dy! Run . . Jo Bell! Run!"

"Grrr . . " Suddenly the dog was there. He sprang onto the man's back. Ferocious growls came from his throat. "Grrr—"

"Call off the goddamn d—" Willa's fist connected with the man's mouth. "Shit! Yeeow! Charlie! Son of a bitch!" he cursed. "If the damn dog don't kill me she will."

"Mr Smith?" Charlie grabbed Buddy at the scruff of the neck and pulled him away

"Stupid, featherheaded, brainless woman! Of course, it's me. She broke my hand and drove my ring right into my head. Jesus, deliver me from hair-brained females."

"Oh, Lord. We're sorry. Buddy heard something and—"

"He probably heard me. I was keeping an eye out for Coyle and Fuller." Smith got to his feet waving his injured hand. "It isn't safe to be within ten feet of this this wildcat. She ought to be in a cage."

Willa stood as fear left her and anger blossomed into full bloom. "You got just what you deserved. You had no business sneaking up on us."

"Sneaking! Sneaking!" he shouted.

"Yes, sneaking," she shouted back trembling so violently that she could hardly stand. "Too bad your hand got in the way. Nothing could hurt that hard, stupid . . . pickled head of yours."

"What the hell were you doing out here, anyhow?"

"We were   hiding—not that it's any business of yours!"

"Hiding! Ha! A blind man could've spotted you in those light clothes. You stood out like a shithouse in a fog."

"Can't you carry on a *decent* conversation?" Willa asked haughtily

"If I want to," he answered back, his tone mocking hers.

"Are you all right?" Charlie asked anxiously, still holding onto the growling dog.

"Yes, but no thanks to your   Mr Pickled-brain Smith," she said scathingly as she brushed the dirt and leaves from her shoulders and arms.

"Be thankful you're a woman," Smith growled menacingly "If you'd been a man, I'd have shot you."

Willa produced the Derringer and pointed it at him. "And I'd have shot you right back."

"Godamighty! Put that thing away If I'd a shot you, woman, you'd a been dead before you hit the ground."

"Well, you didn't, so that's that." Her voice was calm, but her stomach was threatening to revolt, and her heart was racing like a wild mustang. She returned the Derringer to her pocket. "Come on, Jo Bell. There's no need to let him ruin the rest of the night. I'm thinking he wants to get back to his bottle and drown his sorrows."

"You hurt him, ma'am." Jo Bell's voice was soft, caressing, intimate. She moved to stand between Willa and Smith. "Don't mind her, Mr Bowman. She's just a fussy old maid. Come to the wagon. Let me bandage your hand."

"Get away from me, you little brat," Smith snarled. "I'll take care of myself " He stomped off into the darkness, leaving them to look at the spot where he disappeared.

"Well—" Jo Bell tossed her head, angry at being rebuffed. "I hope yore old hand rots and   falls off!" she yelled.

"I sure do hate it that we've made him mad at us," Charlie said on the way back to the wagon.

"I'm not one bit sorry I hit him." Willa suddenly burst into laughter "Ping! I'll never forget the sound of that skillet hitting his ring."

"Buddy was going for his throat." Charlie spoke quietly and Willa sobered. "He could have killed him."

"I suppose that'd be all right with you, ma'am," Jo Bell's voice was laced with sarcasm. "You think that old dog is so grand."

"No, it wouldn't have been all right. I hate to see any living creature killed. The time may come, Jo Bell, when you'll be glad to have Buddy's protection."

"I doubt that. I just doubt that."

The next afternoon, when the heat of the day was making itself known, Jo Bell climbed into the back of the wagon to rest in the shade.

"I'm just not goin' to sit out here and let the sun cook my face. Heavens! I'll have freckles all over my nose."

Willa was glad to be relieved of the girl's senseless egotistical chatter She removed her hat and placed it on the seat beside her and wished that all she had to worry about was a few freckles on her nose. Her level brows drew together in a puzzled frown, and once again she tried to think of what she was going to do after she had fulfilled her promise to Charlie to stay with them until they reached Oliver Eastwood's ranch.

Emotion began to infiltrate the barrier with which she had protected herself when she thought of the days and weeks ahead. A wave of fear rolled over her at the thought of going off alone, penniless, in an almost lawless land where only the strongest survived. She was utterly alone without a person in the world other than Charlie who cared what happened to her Charlie and Buddy.

She was sick to death of stupid, ignorant people. The "good" people of Hublett thought Papa Igor evil because of the affliction that distorted his features and the hump on his back. They had not even tried to know him for what he was, a kind, highly intelligent human being. They had thought she brought bad luck to their town because she was his daughter Heaven only knows what they would have done had they known her mother had lived with him all those years without benefit of marriage. Well, if she were a witch, she would snap her fingers and the whole town would go up in flames for what they had done to her papa.

Oh, my God! What was she thinking? Papa Igor wouldn't want what happened to leave her a bitter, empty shell.

Feeling more desolate than she had in weeks, Willa was trying to blink the tears from her eyes when suddenly Smith appeared in the trail ahead. He and his horse were standing motionless, watching the wagon approach.

A long quiet settled over the area, broken only by the jingle of the harnesses and the clump of the iron-clad hooves on the hard-packed trail. Even the wind seemed to rest for a while and the puffy clouds stood still. Willa couldn't take her eyes off the man and the horse silhouetted against the sky.

Smith's eyes were on the woman on the wagon seat. She was pretty and proud, plucky beyond reason. This was his first look at her when his head was not feeling as if someone were pounding on it with a hammer. If it were true about her papa being hanged, her house burned and her being run out of town, she'd had more trouble during the last few weeks than most women have in a lifetime.

Her face was tanned from the sun, her hair sun-bleached. She was capable, a hard-working woman, despite her fragile appearance that made a man want to protect her. She had demonstrated *that* well enough when she had thrown the water on him and later when she had attacked him with the skillet. Smith didn't know much about women, but something about this one interested him. He couldn't remember the last time he had been curious about a woman. These thoughts went through his head as the space between them grew shorter until the wagon was alongside.

Her head turned. Her great eyes held him.

He nodded.

She answered with a scarcely perceptible dip of her head.

"Where's Charlie?"

"He went on ahead."

"Go on to where you see a cut off to the left. Wait there."

He was off before Willa could reply and he quickly disappeared over the rise.

"What'd Smith want Charlie for?" Jo Bell climbed back over the wagon seat and sat down after tossing Willa's hat on the floor. Willa moved it back under the seat to keep it safe from the girl's feet.

"I think we'll be turning west soon."

"Right into the sun?" Jo Bell complained.

Charlie came racing toward them, his face red with embarrassment. "I went right past the turnoff."

Shortly after, Charlie led the wagon into a dense stand of aspen and onto a little-used track that headed straight for the foothills. As soon as the turn was made, he came back to the wagon.

"We're headin' cross-country. I think I'll ride ahead and see what's up there."

Willa laughed. "Go ahead. We'll be all right."

"I don't like him ridin' Papa's horse." Jo Bell was holding a cardboard fan in front of her face to shield it from the sun.

Willa ignored her. She was watching Buddy, who suddenly

took off in hot and hopeless pursuit of a jackrabbit that had appeared on the edge of the road. It had twitched its long ears to emphasize its disapproval of this invasion of its domain and then whirled back through the trees. Willa laughed. The chase would end, she knew, as all such similar ones had ended—with victory for the pursued. Buddy would enjoy the chase and return.

"It ain't *his* horse," Jo Bell said spitefully

Willa looked at the girl. It was characteristic of her to not let go of a subject until someone responded to her complaint. The corners of her mouth were turned down and her lips were puffed in a pout. Poor Charlie. She was afraid Jo Bell was beyond redemption.

"It's as much his horse as yours." Willa tried to keep the irritation out of her voice. "I think your father would be proud of Charlie for taking charge and doing all he can to see you safely to your uncle's ranch."

"He'd not be proud of Charlie lordin' it over me. He'd be mad as the day is long. He'd want me to take charge. He's told me a hundred times that Charlie isn't near as smart as me. He said I learned to write my name twice as fast as Charlie did. He said Charlie'd not fit in with quality folk and he'd never amount to a hill a beans. Papa knew all about manners and things like that."

Willa sighed. It was too bad he didn't teach some to his daughter She searched for a way to reach the girl and convince her that her father was a stupid fool to fill his daughter's head with such nonsense. Jo Bell would have a tough row to hoe if she didn't change her ways. At least today she had put on a decent dress. She no longer dressed like a child. She was a lovely young woman with her mass of dark, unbrushed curls tumbling around her face and down her back.

"Ain't there no towns? Why'd Uncle Oliver want to live out here for? There ain't nothin' but trees and grass."

"There's the blue sky, the clear sharp air, and yonder are the Bighorn Mountains."

"Why'er they called that?"

"Because of bighorn sheep, I suppose."

"Ain't there a town?" Jo Bell asked again, a whine in her voice.

"They talked about a town named Buffalo. I understand that it's just a little one-horse town—not much there."

"How far to Sheridan? That's where the freight wagons were goin' "

"I don't know "

"Ya don't know much a'tall, do ya, ma'am?"

Willa refused to let Jo Bell draw her into an argument. She whistled a tune Papa Igor had taught her when she was a child, and surveyed the beauty around her

In the stillness of the woods there was only the muffled sounds of the wagon wheels and the mule's hooves. The ground was padded with years of dried pine needles. There was no undergrowth beneath the thick foliage that at times intermeshed. The tree trunks were so close together that you could see no more than twenty feet into the forest.

It was dim and quiet and peaceful.

CHAPTER

* 9 *

When the horseman darted out from among the trees, Willa thought at first it was Charlie. Then a hand was grasping the mule's cheek strap.

"Whoa—"

Shocked out of her reverie, Willa pulled on the reins, then, recognizing Fuller, the man who had come to the wagon after the burial, she slapped the reins against the backs of the mules to urge them on. He held fast to the bridle and the confused team danced in place.

"Let go!" Willa reached for the whip.

"Don't do that. I'll put a bullet in the head of this mule. I waited all day for Smith and that kid to go on ahead."

"What do you want?"

"To finish the little visit I had yesterday with the young lady." He rode up to the side of the wagon and tipped his hat to Jo Bell. "Howdy, miss. You're about the prettiest thing I ever laid eyes on."

"You ain't sayin' nothin' I ain't heard a hundred times before."

"What are you wantin' to hide yourself out here in the sticks for? In town men would line up just to get a look at you."

"What' a ya mean?"

"I'd like to take you to Sheridan and show you off."

Fuller smiled. His protruding eyes, showing white all around the iris, were fastened on Jo Bell's face. He inched his horse closer

"You'd better leave. Charlie and Smith will be back soon." The mules had calmed. Only the fear that he would shoot one kept Willa from putting them in motion.

Fuller ignored her, his eyes on Jo Bell. "I ain't thought a nothin' but you since I saw you. You liked me too, didn't you? Yeah, I could tell you did. You ain't got no pa now You need to be took care of Come with me and I'll show you the sights."

"I didn't either like ya. You ain't young and handsome. Bet you ain't rich either " Jo Bell tilted her head and straightened her shoulders to push her small breasts out. She looked at him, her smile saying that she was teasing him. He caught the message and his nostrils flared like a bull after a heifer in heat.

Willa's heart leaped with fear *The stupid girl was flirting with this dangerous man.*

Delighted with her, Fuller laughed. "Ya could name yore price in Sheridan, honey "

"Doin' what?" Jo Bell asked in a low breathless whisper

"Somethin' I could teach ya to be real good at."

"I don't know what yore talkin' about, sir·"

"Yes, ya do. Ya was born for it."

"I was born to be took care of by a rich man. My papa said so."

"Yore papa was right, honey " He held out his hand. "Come on, sweet thing. I'll take care of ya real good.

Jo Bell cringed back against Willa as she suddenly realized the dangerous game she was playing.

"No! Get away. Go on. Get!"

Fuller's face turned ugly. Then, with the speed of a striking snake his hand lashed out and grabbed Jo Bell's arm. He would have pulled her off the seat and onto his horse if Willa had not dropped the reins and thrown herself across the girl's lap. She held onto the wagon frame with one hand and beat at the man with her fist.

"Let go of her!" She clawed at the hand holding the girl's arm.

A thin, shrill frightened scream tore itself from Jo Bell's throat.

Fuller pulled on Jo Bell and hit at Willa with the ends of his reins. Even when the leather slashed across her face, she hung onto the girl. Ducking her head, she sank her teeth in the man's hairy wrist and hung on like a bulldog.

"Shit! You damned bitch!" Fuller yelled and let go of Jo Bell's arm. He righted himself in the saddle. "I ought to split yore goddamn skull—"

Desperately Willa tried to get her feet back under her so that she could reach for the Derringer in her pocket. In a panic, Jo Bell was lashing out with both her arms and feet, causing them both to fall from the seat.

As Fuller's frightened horse shied, he spotted a shaggy brown apparition advancing on him. The hair on the dog's back stood stiff; his upper lips curled away from gleaming fangs in a blood-chilling wolfish grin. Angry growls came from his throat.

"Christ—" Fuller drew his gun and fired as Buddy sprang. The shot blasted the stillness. Buddy dropped. "I told ya I'd shoot that goddamn dog. I'll fix you later." His eyes spit pure hatred at Willa. He wheeled his horse, spurred him into a run and headed back down the track.

"Buddy!" Willa grabbed the reins and wrapped them around the brake handle. Jo Bell burst into a fit of hysterical sobbing. Numbed with shock and fear, Willa climbed down and ran to her dog.

"Buddy! Oh, Lord—" She threw herself on her knees beside the faithful animal. The dry leaves were red with the dog's blood. He whined and tried to raise his head to see the owner of the dear and beloved voice. "You're alive! Oh, thank God! Lie still! Buddy, oh, Buddy—" She had to stop the blood. There was nothing but her apron. She whipped it off and held it against his side. "Don't die, Buddy. Please . . . don't die. You're the dearest thing in the world to me."

Over the roaring noise in her ears and the sobs coming from her throat, Willa heard the hoofbeats of a running horse. She dropped the apron and fumbled in her skirt pocket for the Derringer. Crouched over Buddy, the gun in her hand, she waited. Her mind refused to think beyond the fact that Buddy was still alive and if the bastard that shot him was coming back, she would kill him.

To her relief, Smith rode toward her at a fast pace, and right behind him, Charlie. They reined their horses to a stop and jumped off.

"Put that damn thing away before you shoot yourself," Smith growled. "What happened here?"

"A man tried to jerk Jo Bell off the wagon seat. Then he shot B-Buddy." Willa's heart was pounding so hard she could scarcely hear her own voice. She dropped to her knees again, tears flooding her eyes and streaming down her cheeks. "Buddy—" She stroked the dog's head.

"Who?"

"Fuller. Oh, please . . . help Buddy—"

Smith knelt on the other side of the dog and brushed her

hand away. A growl came from deep in the Buddy's throat and he bared his fangs.

"I'm not going to hurt you, boy." Smith spoke in a soft, coaxing voice and caressed the dog's nose with his fingertips. "I want to see if we can help you. Get scissors to cut away the hair " He spoke without looking up.

"I'll get 'em," Charlie said. "For crying out loud, Jo Bell. Hush up yore damn bawlin' Ya ain't hurt, are ya?"

"A lot you'd care. Ya care more for a   a old dog than yore s-sister "

"Thunderation!" Charlie stalked to the back of the wagon and climbed in.

"Take his feet, Willa, and roll him onto his back," Smith commanded. The dog whined and tried to reach his mistress. "That's a good boy " Smith talked to the dog in a calm soft voice. "We don't have to worry about the bullet. It went in and out." He stroked Buddy's head. The dog licked his hand.

"Will he live?" Willa asked fearfully The fact that he had used her first name had failed to register in her troubled mind.

"I don't know The bullet went in along his ribs." Smith reached for the scissors when Charlie returned to squat down beside the dog. "Be still, boy I got to see what we can do." He quickly clipped the hair down to the skin around the wound on the underside as well as where the bullet had come out along the shoulder leaving a gaping hole.

"Does it need stitchin'?" Charlie asked.

"Got anything to stitch it with?"

"White sewing thread."

"Get it."

With a knife Smith drew from his belt, he picked out the hair that had been driven into the wound by the bullet.

"It isn't as bad as I thought it was, old man. You're lucky this time." He spoke to the dog, ignoring Willa hovering on the other side. "You'll not be chasing any rabbits for a while. Do you have any ointment, Charlie?" he asked, and took the needle and thread.

"Got pine tar."

"It'll have to do. Get the whiskey out of my saddlebag."

For the first time it registered in Willa's worried mind that Smith's left hand was badly bruised, the fingers and knuckles swollen. He held one finger out as if he were unable to bend it. *She had done that with the skillet!* She looked up. His head was bent over Buddy and all she could see was the brim of his hat and his chin.

Charlie returned with the bottle. Smith took it with his right hand, lifted the bottle to his mouth and pulled the cork with his teeth. He cupped the needle and thread in his injured hand and spilled the whiskey over it.

"A waste of good whiskey," he murmured. Suddenly his green eyes were looking directly into hers. His brows were tilted in mocking amusement. "Hold him," he said.

After he doused the wounds with the fiery liquid, he re-corked the bottle, placed it on the ground beside him, and quickly pulled the jagged edges of the wound together with the thread. Charlie held out a tin of dark ointment. Using a corner of Willa's apron, he coated the wounds generously then stood.

"What's this thing?"

"An apron. What do you need?"

"Something to bind him with. He may have a broken rib."

"Use it."

"You and Charlie will have to do it. I   ah injured my hand."

Willa's eyes met eyes that mocked her His eyes were as green as oak leaves in the spring, and as he moved his head the sunlight glinted on them, causing them to glisten like brilliant emeralds. His nose was straight and arrogant. Her eyes flicked to his mouth but did not linger. She did not like the faint amused smile it wore as he watched her.

When she said nothing, Smith took the apron from her hand and knelt down. "Lift him, Charlie, so I can get this under him."

"Tell me what to do." Willa went down on her knees beside the dog.

"When Charlie lifts him, slip this under. It should go around him twice. Wrap him tight and tie the binding in place with the sashes."

Charlie lifted the dog's upper body. With his one good hand Smith lifted the back part. Buddy whined, then yelped. Willa worked quickly.

"Pull it tighter," Smith said. And when she did, "That's good. Tie it." He stroked Buddy's head. "Get him some water. He'll have to drink often; he lost a lot of blood."

Smith took the bottle back to his horse and shoved it in his saddlebags. Willa followed him, thinking that he was going to mount and ride out without giving her the opportunity to thank him.

"I'm sorry about . . . your hand."

Taking his time, he ran his narrowed eyes over her face, down her slender figure in the dark cotton dress, and back up to the blond hair that framed her forehead and cheekbones. She was pretty, real pretty, but not beautiful as was the spoiled little twit still bawling on the wagon seat. An angry red welt started at her temple and reached almost to her mouth.

"What's that on your face?"

Willa's hand went to her cheek. Her skin was hot.

"I guess it's where Fuller hit me with the end of his reins."

"He hit you?"

"—Before I bit him."

Smith's frown was replaced with a sudden smile that crinkled the corners of his eyes and brightened a dirt-streaked face that needed a shave. Their eyes met and held. Color tinged her cheeks as his gaze traveled over her face, taking in the freckles on her nose, the wisps of curly hair that had escaped her braid. She stared at him, her blue eyes holding a definite shimmer of defiance.

"It was all I could do. I couldn't let go of Jo Bell to get my gun."

"Christ! If you'd pulled out that pea-shooter, he'd have shot you quicker'n a loose goose sh—" He cut off his words abruptly.

Her lips tightened grimly. "If I have to use the gun, I'll shoot while it's still in my pocket. It's what Papa Igor told me to do."

Smith watched her. He was aware of two things. She was not a woman to be backed into a corner, and she wasn't one of those females who were all ruffles and flutters. Life had given her some hard knocks. Instead of making her weak, they had made her strong. She knew who she was and was coping the best she knew how with the hand fate had dealt her.

"I'm sorry I hit you with the skillet."

"You should've used it on Fuller." His eyes were wicked, teasing, and jarred her heartbeat to a quicker pace.

"Did I ruin your ring?"

"It wasn't much of a ring. I won it in a poker game."

"Thank you for helping with Buddy. He's been with me a long time."

"I like dogs," he said simply and fumbled in his shirt pocket for a tobacco pouch. "Animals got more gumption than some people."

"Let me build your smoke." She reached for the pouch and papers. "It's the least I can do after hurting your hand. I used to do this for my papa." She continued to talk, hoping to cover her nervousness. "I've never seen a woman smoke cigarettes. Papa Igor said that down in the Ozark hill country women smoke a pipe, dip snuff, and chew tobacco."

"I saw a woman smokin' a cigar in Denver." He didn't tell her the woman had been in a fancy bordello where he had treated himself to a few hours of female company.

Feeling foolish now for offering to build his cigarette, she poured the shredded tobacco into the paper, licked the edge to seal it and rolled it neatly. After twisting the end, she handed it to him.

Smith's hands shook as he put the open end of the cigarette between his lips, struck a match on the sole of his boot and held the flame to the end. He dropped the match and ground it with the toe of his boot before he spoke.

"Tell me what happened." He spoke softly, but his eyes were hard. They looked searchingly at each other.

His hard eyes were a brilliant, jeweled green. Willa looked away and folded her arms across her chest in an attempt to calm the fluttering she felt in his presence. The man was as alert as a wild stag. She could feel his unrest and it made her nervous. He radiated energy, strength. Sober, he was the most confident person she had ever met.

"I think he'd been following us, waiting until you and Charlie went on ahead." To ease her own nervousness, Willa rushed into speech. "He came out of the woods and said he'd shoot the mules if I didn't stop. He wanted to take Jo Bell to Sheridan. He said she could . . . name her price. When he tried to jerk her off the seat and onto his horse, I hung onto her. He hit me, but when I bit his wrist, he turned her loose. That's when Buddy got there. He sprang at Fuller and he shot him. Then thinking you'd come when you heard the shot, he took off."

"The low-down dirty bastard!" Smith spoke around the cigarette hanging from the corner of his mouth. He drew smoke deep into his lungs and let it out slowly

He cursed himself. When had he been so damn careless? That morning he had watched Abel and Fuller head north. He should have waited to make sure Fuller didn't double back. Only a damn fool would take a woman against her will and leave a witness. Fuller had acted alone. Abel Coyle was too smart to get mixed up in killing a woman.

Smith wondered if the little flirt had been leading Fuller on and he was counting on her going with him willingly. If that was the case, sooner or later, she'd get that brother of hers killed.

"You don't know much about men like Fuller, do you? If he had taken her, he would have killed you. He couldn't afford to leave a witness."

Willa's mouth opened in surprise. "He wouldn't have."

Smith snorted in disgust.

"I couldn't let him take Jo Bell. She's only a child. A spoiled one, I admit, but—"

"How old is she?"

"Sixteen."

Smith snorted again. "Some are born to end up bad. She's one of them."

"How do you know? Perhaps Mrs. Eastwood can straighten her out."

"Don't count on it. I'd bet ten years of my life that Old Maud wouldn't let her put a foot inside the door if she was freezing to death."

"Then maybe we should bypass Eastwood Ranch and go on to Buffalo . . . or Sheridan. I owe it to her father to do what I can to help her and Charlie."

"Why?"

"Because he saved my life."

"He didn't appear to be the kind of man who did anything out of the goodness of his heart," Smith said dryly. "Did you sleep with him?"

Willa's face flamed. "I did not!"

The long searching look he gave her said he didn't believe her There was a curious stillness between them—a waiting, uneasy silence that deepened as the seconds went by Her cobalt-blue, thick-lashed eyes and the color that lay across her cheeks betrayed the fact that she was mortified. He thought she was a whore! He had called her that—in the barn. His opinion of her should not matter in the least. Yet for some reason unknown to her, her heart sank like a rock.

CHAPTER

* 10 *

Suddenly irritated at himself because of his curiosity about her, Smith walked back to Buddy and hunkered down.

"How'er you feeling, boy?" He stroked the dog's head. "Feel like riding a little way? Let the tailgate down, Charlie. We'll get out of these woods and make camp."

Willa felt a strange tenseness come over her and fought it with a sudden desperation. She could feel Smith watching her. It made her uneasy. She worked swiftly to make a bed for Buddy out of her blankets. When she finished, she covered it with a ground sheet and Charlie carried Buddy to it.

"Don't know why yore makin' such a fuss over that old cur dog for," Jo Bell said when Charlie elbowed her out of the way. "Ain't ya carin' that that awful old bug-eyed man almost stole me away?"

"But he didn't—thanks to Willa and that 'old cur dog.' "

Jo Bell put her hands on her hips and stuck her tongue out at her brother. "That old man thought I was the prettiest thin' he'd ever did set his eyes on. He told me so."

"You ain't been makin' eyes at him have ya, Jo Bell? Papa warned you about doin' that."

"Papa would'a gone after him and shot him down like a . . . a sidewinder for what he done."

"Maybe he would've and then maybe he wouldn't've," Charlie shouted, his temper flaring. Then in a softer tone, "Sit back here with Buddy, Willa. I'll tie my horse on behind and drive."

"It ain't *yore* horse," Jo Bell yelled.

Charlie glanced at Smith. He was standing at the end of the wagon, his narrowed eyes on Jo Bell. Charlie watched his sister as she became aware of the man's observation. Her sulky expression changed in an instant. She looked at Smith out of the corners of her violet eyes and smiled shyly up at him, a trick her papa had taught her.

Charlie felt disappointment tighten his stomach. His new friend continued to gaze at his sister. His eyes rested on her face for a long time without movement, without any discernible emotion except for the flaring of his nostrils. Charlie felt an emotion close to hatred. Jo Bell had always come first with everyone except their mother and Willa. Couldn't Smith see anything but her pretty face?

Willa was also watching the play between Smith and Jo Bell. She saw the disappointment on Charlie's face. Puzzled and troubled by conflicting emotions, she stepped up into the wagon and sat down beside Buddy.

Smith turned abruptly as if Willa's movements had jarred him back to reality. "Let's get moving."

With a pleased smile on her face, Jo Bell jumped up onto the tailgate and sat with her legs hanging down.

"He's not bad to look at. He's young, too. But he don't have no money, leastways he don't look like he does. He was sure givin' me the eagle eye. Did ya see it, ma'am? He was likin' what he saw. I can tell. Did ya ever have a man look at you like that? Like he just wanted to eat ya up?''

Charlie called out to the mules and the wagon lurched forward. Willa bit back harsh words and instead patted the dog's head, her throat choked with bitterness. Jo Bell Frank was the most selfish person she'd ever met. She had not offered one word of thanks to her or to Buddy for saving her from being taken by that terrible man. She had not a thought in her head but for herself.

They camped in a grassy field. Charlie unhitched and watered the mules from the barrels tied to the wagon. Willa pulled grass to make a soft bed under the wagon for Buddy, and she and Charlie carried him to it. After pouring water in a shallow pan and placing it beside him, Willa found a place to build a cook fire and started it with dry grass and small sticks while Charlie searched for firewood.

Jo Bell stayed in the wagon until the meal was ready. She climbed down as Willa was filling Charlie's plate with fried potatoes and scrambled eggs.

''Where's Smith? Ain't he comin' to supper?'' Jo Bell went to the front of the wagon and looked around, her hands on her hips. ''Why'd you camp here for?'' she asked when she came to the fire to fill a plate.

''Because *he* told me to.'' Charlie sank cross-legged on the ground and began to eat.

Willa's heart ached for Charlie. He was sure that Smith was smitten by Jo Bell and would fawn over her like all the other men that met her. Well, it didn't matter to her if he did. He was a man, and her mother used to say that most men thought with their reproductive organs. Why would Smith be any different?

She served herself from the skillet and sat down beside

Charlie. She had cooked more than she ordinarily would have for the three of them in case Smith did show up for supper. She was thankful that for once the brother and sister did not bicker and that they would eat in peace and quiet.

After the meal Jo Bell walked up and down, pausing ever so often to look up the trail. She was waiting, Willa realized, for Smith to come to the camp. Her heart pounding with anger, she wondered if she should insist on the girl helping with the cleanup. She decided that she was not in the mood to argue with her and went about the work swiftly and efficiently. Afterward she fed bits of the leftover food to Buddy

As darkness fell, Charlie shoveled dirt on the fire.

"Smith told me to," he said when Willa looked askance.

"Does he expect trouble?"

"He didn't say, but if there is we'll be out in the open and nobody can sneak up on us."

"We may have a heavy dew tonight. I'm glad Buddy's under the wagon." Willa watched the boy cover the dog with a blanket.

"Where did Smith go?" Jo Bell stood at the end of the wagon and peered at Buddy

"How would I know," Charlie growled.

"That old dog will die and I don't care," Jo Bell said as she straightened up and crawled into the back of the wagon.

"Damn ya! Ya got a mean streak in ya a mile wide. He got shot tryin' to help ya."

Willa shook her head at Charlie. "Please. Not tonight. You can't change her mind." She wrapped a blanket around her shoulders and walked a distance from the wagon. Soon Charlie was beside her

"She just makes me so mad."

"I know she does. She makes me angry too. She knows just what to say to start a fight. You can't win an argument with her, so why try?"

"I don't know what'll become of her." There was genuine regret in the boy's voice. "If it warn't for Ma I'd let her go. But I promised I'd look out for her. Ma knew Pa was spoilin' her rotten."

"You can only do so much. I'm sorry to speak of the dead this way, but your father put the wrong ideas in her head. She's selfish and self-centered."

"And I can't help her. Not that she wants me too," the boy added.

"Smith doesn't think that Mrs. Eastwood will welcome her, Charlie. He's so sure that he said he'd bet ten years of his life on it."

"Yeah. He told me. Aunt Maud must be a bear-cat. Smith's closed-mouthed. He don't tell me much about the place." Charlie was silent for a while, then he said, "He says I can work there. The work will be hard, but it's a way for me to learn."

"Then you should. You wanted to be a cowboy. This is your chance."

"If Mrs. Eastwood won't have you and Jo Bell, I won't stay." He stopped and put his hand on Willa's arm, his young face filled with worry. "I wish we could stay there."

"Stay, Charlie. I'll go on to Sheridan and find work. I'm a good cook, more than good with a needle and I can fix clocks. I'll take Jo Bell with me and look out for her the best I can."

"I ain't stayin' if you don't. I thought that . that if Jo Bell found a man who'd marry her, you and I could well, I ain't never had a friend like you before. It's just comfortin' to have someone to talk to. I wish *you* was my sister."

"Why, thank you, Charlie. That's the nicest thing anyone ever said to me." Willa's voice was husky with emotion.

"But I'm not your sister and Jo Bell is. Even if Mrs. Eastwood takes her in, there's nothing I could do there to earn my keep. Maybe Smith or one of the other men will take me to Sheridan."

"I'm not stayin' if you don't," Charlie said firmly "I already told Smith."

"And what did he say to that?"

"Said he'd put us on the track to Sheridan and it was pert near a hundred miles."

In the stillness that enclosed them after Charlie's words, Willa swallowed her disappointment and her fear It made her realize just how much she had been hoping to stay at Eastwood Ranch.

Smith had a good idea where Fuller and Coyle would camp. The place was a hollow among the rock and brush, invisible from the road. He rode to within a half-mile and dismounted. From his saddlebag he took a pair of Indian moccasins, slipped them on, tied his boots together, and slung them over his saddle. After poking his hat under the straps that held his pack, he unhooked a cloth bag of biscuits and jerky from his saddlehorn and sat down with his back to a boulder to eat and to wait until it was pitch-dark before he approached the camp.

His stomach was crying for hot food. It beat all how this country could be hot in the daytime and could chill your bones at night. He wished he was back at the wagon where Willa would be cooking supper He would give his new boots in the bundle tied behind his saddle for a skillet of fried potatoes and a cup of hot coffee.

Six years. It had been a long time since he had returned to Eastwood for what he thought would be a brief visit with Oliver and Billy Whiskers. He had been on the place for only a week or two when the event happened that would keep him at Eastwood until Oliver's wife died. She had always hated him, had been jealous of the time Oliver spent with him. When he was nineteen, he had taken off for Texas, thinking it would make life easier for Oliver if he weren't around. For the next three years he had punched cows, fought Indians, driven a team over the mountains to California, and lived the hand-to-mouth existence of a drifter It was a hard life, a bitter, lonely life.

When he was a youngster everything had seemed easy He had settled in at Eastwood, learned from Billy and Oliver, and life had seemed forever He had dreamed about girls. At first it was Fanny He dreamed she would grow up and fall in love with him. Only it never happened. She despised him every bit as much as her mother did.

He'd had dealings with other women. There had been a girl in Buffalo, only when he returned, she was married and already had a baby That was just as well. He realized now that they wouldn't have hitched together The longing for a home and a family of his own had never left him, but for now the possibility seemed more remote than ever

These thoughts went through his mind as he ate the jerky and dry biscuits. The trouble with him, he was thinking, was that the kind of woman he fancied was hard to come by Willa Hammer was a rare woman. He liked her fragility, her toughness, even her bitchy side. She had courage of a rare kind. She had survived a terrible ordeal and didn't whine about it. There was iron in her and she was all woman, too.

He was crazy for thinking about a woman when his life was up in the air He had heard about love and commitment, read about it; it was an elusive thing. Why was he thinking about it now?

Smith crammed the last bite of biscuit in his mouth and got to his feet. Pete nuzzled his shoulder

"You wouldn't like that biscuit, boy. It was so hard I could crack a nut with it." He stroked the horse's neck. "Stay here, but if I whistle, come on the run."

Smith checked the gun in his holster, picked up his rifle and took off in a slow lope toward Fuller's camp. When he arrived five minutes later, he wasn't even breathing hard. Two horses were picketed back from the camp in a grassy patch. He approached them slowly They raised their heads and peaked their ears. Unlike Pete, who was a mountain-bred horse with strong survival instincts, they were unafraid. Smith went to the horses with a handful of grass. He waited until they started cropping grass again before he moved closer to the camp and the two men who sat beside the small smokeless fire.

Why had a man as smart as Abel Coyle teamed up with a second-rate crook like Fuller? Not that he had any liking for Coyle, but he'd not heard of him going outside the law Smith backed away from the camp and circled until he could approach without having to look across the fire. Fuller sat on a bedroll nursing a cup of coffee and Coyle lounged against his saddle. Smith made sure of his cover before he spoke.

"Howdy, gents."

When the voice came out of the darkness, both men grabbed for their guns and sprang to their feet.

Smith moved ten feet to the right, then laughed. "Kind of spooked, aren't you?"

"Who are you? Where are you?" Fuller demanded, turning his head in a half circle to scan the bushes.

Smith moved again. "I'm the feller who's come to beat your brains out, Fuller. But first I need to know where Coyle stands in this."

"Who are you?" Coyle asked.

"Smith Bowman."

"I fight for no man unless there's money in it."

"That don't tell me a damn thing."

"Count me out of your fight with Fuller. He ain't no special friend of mine."

"I hear you're a man of your word, Coyle. Holster your gun. Throw yours to the left, Fuller " When he hesitated, Smith snapped impatiently, "Now, or I'll blow your damn hand off "

Fuller tossed his gun and Smith came out of the brush behind them.

"Here I am." Both men spun around to face the end of the rifle Smith held waist-high against his side.

Coyle sat back down. With his hands in plain sight, he lifted and stacked them behind his head. "I'll just watch the show." He leaned casually against his saddle.

"What the hell's eatin' you, Bowman?" Fuller's eyes darted toward the gun he had tossed to the ground.

Quick as a striking snake, Smith's hand moved and the end of a narrow leather quirt bit into Fuller's cheek.

"Ye . . . ow! What the hell—"

"Does that tell you what's eating me? How does it feel? Hurts like hell, don't it? It would hurt a woman twice as much. Am I right, Fuller? Maybe another will help you decide if I'm right or not." The quirt struck Fuller across the face again.

"Ya gawddammed shit-eatin'—"

"Watch your mouth." Smith spoke calmly. Then suddenly and viciously he swung his foot and kicked Fuller in the crotch. Stunned, the man staggered back, his mouth opened as breath left him; his eyes crossed as the pain became excruciating. He screamed in agony, grabbed his injured parts with both hands and fell to his knees.

"It seems to me that's where you carry your brains—right there between your legs. I want you to remember how that hurts. The next time you try to drag a young girl off a wagon seat, I'm going to cut off your   brains.''

Smith glanced at Coyle. He was still sitting with his hands behind his head, a lopsided grin on his face.

"Ya   b-bastard! I'll k-kill   ya—'' Fuller gasped as he swayed back and forth on his knees.

Smith stuffed the quirt inside his shirt and drew his six gun. "Be still, damn you. I owe you a bullet for what you did to the dog. Move again and you'll get it in the belly instead of the butt.''

"Gawd! Coyle, do s-somethin' I'm not a-armed.''

"Neither was the dog,'' Smith said quietly and fired.

The bullet tore a path through the fleshy part of Fuller's bottom and on out into the brush. He bellowed with rage and pain, fell flat on his stomach, one hand between his legs protecting his privates, the other frantically searching to find where the blood poured from the wound on his backside

"You won't die, you horny sonofabitch, but you'll be standing in the stirrups all the way to Sheridan. If you get within a mile of those women again, I'll strip the hide off you inch by inch.''

"Comanche fashion?'' Coyle asked in a conversational tone.

Smith nodded. "A warrior down in Indian Territory showed me how to do it so a man would stay alive until he was nothing but a piece of raw meat.''

"I've heard of it.''

"You got anything more to say, Coyle?'' Smith started backing out of the clearing.

"Can't think of a thing, Bowman. Nice cool evenin ain't it?''

"Sure is. Makes a body glad to be alive.'

"See ya sometime, Bowman.''

"Yeah. Evenin' to you."

Smith went into the brush surrounding the camp as silent as a shadow, then moved quickly in a half circle. He could see Fuller writhing on his blankets.

"Why the hell didn't ya do somethin'?" Fuller shouted, attempting to lessen his pain with anger at Coyle. "Ya had yore gun."

"I'm not about to get myself shot to hell cause yore pecker's up. Ya stupid son of a bitch. Ya went back there and bothered those women." Coyle spoke with disbelief in his voice. "Are ya crazy? Ya heard Byers say they were going with Bowman. Ya got what ya had comin' "

"Damn you. You talked about humpin' one."

"Are you sayin' you did it for me, Fuller? Bullshit. You've had a stick in your britches ever since you set eyes on that young gal. When my urge for a woman gets to eatin' on me, I'll get one myself I'll not send a two-bit, bug-eyed, bung-head like you out to get one for me."

"Gawddamn that Bowman. I'm goin' to kill him!"

"I'd not bet on it. He's one mean sonofabitch when he's riled. He don't back off I saw him take on three of the toughest, meanest drovers that ever came up the trail. They beat the shit out of him, but he fixed two of them so they'd be gumming their grub from now on and the other'n was carryin' his pecker in a sling when he left town."

"Oh, Gawd! Oh, Lordy me!" Fuller moaned, stood, unbuttoned his pants and pulled them down. The seat of his longjohns was red with blood. He opened the front and looked at his privates, reached in and touched them gently "That bastard pert near ruint me."

"They're still there, ain't they? Haw! Haw!" Coyle bellowed with laughter

"By Gawd! You'd not think it so damn funny if yore balls

felt like they'd been smashed with a hammer I ain't forgettin' this.''

"You shouldn't've messed with his women. What'd y do? Take a quirt to one of 'em?''

"I didn't hurt her none. I shot the gawddamn dog that wa tryin' to eat me up.''

"Did you think Bowman would let you get away with that?''

"They ain't his, goddammit!''

"He kicks like a mule, don't he? Haw! Haw! Haw! If he'd a had on his boots you'd a been walking spraddle-legged till the end of your days.''

"Jesus! It hurts to even touch 'em.''

"Beats me that you're more worried about them little nuggets than that there gunshot in the ass or how you're going to stay clear of Bowman.''

"Well? Are ya goin' to help me or not?'' Fuller whined.

"No. Tie a bandage round your ass and one round your balls. Haw! Haw! Haw! You're lucky you got something left to tie a rag on.''

Smith drifted away grinning.

CHAPTER
* 11 *

Willa saw very little of Smith during the three days following Fuller's visit. He appeared in the morning and once again at night to ask about Buddy. He would speak briefly to Charlie, pointing the way he should go the next morning, then ride away without a word to her or Jo Bell. One night he brought two rabbits, skinned and ready for the frying pan.

"One is for the dog," he said curtly and dropped them in the grass at Willa's feet. Before she could even thank him, he wheeled his horse and rode away.

Another night he brought a mess of fish. Willa asked him to stay for the evening meal. He acted as if he hadn't heard the invitation. Jo Bell hastily climbed out of the wagon when he rode in. He ignored her attempts to talk to him. After he examined Buddy's wound, he patted the dog's head and left.

Each day Willa became more and more fascinated with the country through which they traveled. It was a land of splendid green forests and meadows that faded into the purple mountains. If only she could, she would build a little cabin in a

120

lonely valley where the trail ran up to the sky. She would be perfectly content to live out her days there without ever seeing another town. She felt her stomach drop away when she thought of what she and Papa Igor had endured at the hands of "civilized" people.

She knew what she wanted. She wanted isolation, yet she wanted a home and someone who needed her as much as she needed him. She wanted to love and be loved. She wanted . . . roots, something she had never had. But she wasn't a fool, and a woman was foolish to wish for things she couldn't have.

Buddy gained strength each day, but he wasn't yet strong enough to hunt his own food or walk for long stretches beside the wagon. Willa made sure she made enough biscuits and pan gravy each night to furnish a meal for him as well as for Smith if he decided to stay.

Jo Bell was unbearably cross. Part of it was because Smith ignored her. She couldn't understand why he preferred Charlie's company to hers. Charlie bore the brunt of her displeasure. When she failed to pick a yelling fight with him, she would turn on Willa, reminding her that she didn't even own the dress on her back and that she had no cause to act so high and mighty. When she did this, Willa held her head high, her back stiff and refused to give the girl the satisfaction of knowing how she hated being the recipient of charity. She silently vowed never to be beholden to anyone again.

One evening, unable to get a rise out of Charlie or Willa, Jo Bell stalked to the wagon and stumbled over Buddy, who moved too slowly to get out of her way.

"Ya . . . nasty old thin'! Yore tryin' to trip me." She drew back her foot and kicked the dog in the side. Buddy yipped, his hind legs collapsing as he dragged himself under the wagon. Long hurtful yipping sounds continued to come from him.

Jo Bell stood defiantly with her hands on her hips when Willa and Charlie ran to the dog and knelt down.

"How could you do that?" Willa stood when the yipping ceased and looked into the girl's sullen face. Unable to hold back her anger, she stiffened her arm and shoved the girl back. "You're a hateful, mean girl and I'm sick to death at the sight of you."

"Don't ya dare talk to me like that, ya . . . ya ragtag bobtail. Ya ain't nothin'. Yore pa was a . . . f-freak." Jo Bell drew back her hand to strike Willa.

"Don't," Willa said calmly and grabbed her wrist. "Don't kick that dog again and don't hit me or I'll mop the ground with you. I swear it!"

"Char . . . lie!"

The boy looked at his sister and shook his head. "I'm just so ashamed of ya I could die. Why'd ya go and kick that dog? He got shot tryin' to help ya."

"I didn't ask him for no help. I could'a took care of myself. Ya don't care 'bout me. Ya care 'bout her! Smith won't come to the wagon cause of her, but ya don't care."

"Yore sick in the head, Jo Bell. There ain't a decent bone in ya."

"She's cozyin' up to ya and yore wantin' to diddle with her, ain't ya?" she screeched. "She's too old for ya. Papa said so."

"Hush yore filthy mouth! I won't have ya talkin' about Willa like that. Hear?"

"I'll talk 'bout her any way I please. Ya ain't the boss of me, Charlie Frank."

"I'm sick a hearin' ya say that!" he shouted.

"I ain't stayin' out here either. I'm leavin'. I'll get Smith to take me to a town. Ya can have yore . . . old maid. She's ugly, anyhow."

"Ya got bad blood, Jo Bell. And it didn't come from Mama."

"Don't you say anythin' bad about Papa. Oh, I hate ya, Charlie Frank. I hate, hate, hate ya."

Willa turned to kneel beside Buddy. Tears flooded her eyes when she saw blood oozing from his wound. He whimpered and tried to lick her hand. She was tired and wanted desperately to go off somewhere and cry. It was as if her heart and her emotions had been pounded to a pulp.

"Can you get up, old friend? Come on, let's you and me get away from here for a while."

Buddy got slowly and painfully to his feet. Willa threw a shawl over her shoulders and they headed for a grassy knoll above the campsite where there was a clear view of the valley below.

The night was beginning to lower. It was the time of day that Longfellow wrote about. Willa sat down and leaned against a giant oak that had stood watch over the valley for a hundred years. Buddy lay down beside her and rested his head on her thigh. She stroked his shaggy head.

Alone except for the dog, Willa let the tears she had been holding at bay for weeks slowly fill her eyes and slide down her cheeks. She deserved it, she told herself. She deserved to cry. It wasn't a luxury, Papa Igor had said. It was necessary to wash misery from the soul. He had always been there for her. Now she was alone. She felt sick and empty and frightened and tired of pretending she wasn't.

"What are we going to do, Buddy? I don't think I can stand being saddled with that awful girl, and I promised Charlie I'd take her with me if Mrs. Eastwood won't let her stay at the ranch. How can I take care of her when I don't even know how I'm going to take care of myself?"

"I would suggest that if you must talk to your dog, you be

sure his are the only ears present." The cool masculine voice came from behind her.

Buddy's ears peaked and his tail scooted back and forth on the grass. Willa recognized the voice instantly, straightened her shoulders quickly and made a hasty swipe at her cheeks with the back of her hand.

"How was I to know you'd come sneaking up on me?"

"Does the dog answer you?"

"He knows what I say. He's smarter than some people I know."

"I'll agree with that." Smith came around the tree and knelt down beside Buddy. The dog's tail continued to wag halfheartedly. "What happened to you, boy? I heard you yipping."

"He . . . got in Jo Bell's way. She stumbled over him."

"She kicked him."

"If you saw what happened, why did you ask?"

Smith sat down cross-legged on the grass and Buddy crawled to him. "I brought you a tough old jackrabbit leg. The old boy must have been a hundred years old." He unwrapped the meat from a large maple leaf. Buddy sniffed it but didn't eat until Smith said, "Go ahead. It's yours."

Willa realized that she was seeing a glimpse of the real Smith Bowman. There was no way she could completely dislike a man who had such love for animals, even if he was a fall-down drunk.

He placed his hat on the ground beside him. In the growing darkness, she could see that his hair was damp and she could smell strong lye soap.

"Are we near a river?"

"No. But we're near several creeks."

"Did you bathe in the creek?"

"You noticed, huh? I must have smelled like a goat before."

"I noticed your hair is wet."

"There's a warm spring a few miles from here."

"A warm spring," she repeated. "I've heard of springs that were warm year around, but I've never seen one."

"This is the only one I know in these parts. There's several more on west of here."

"It seems a lifetime ago that I had a warm bath."

"That long, huh? You'll be at Eastwood before noon tomorrow. Maybe Maud will let you bathe before she runs you off."

"That would be good of her," she replied drily.

Unaware of the forlorn look on her face, she listened to the sounds Buddy made cracking the rabbit bone with his powerful jaws and kept her eyes on the sky that seemed to go on forever. Far down the valley an owl hooted a lonely cry and was answered by another owl farther away. Birds getting settled for the night fluttered in the branches overhead. The silence between them stretched into frozen moments in time—two people sitting on a grassy hill with a dog lying on the grass between them.

"I'll take you to the spring," Smith said suddenly, breaking the silence.

"It's nice of you to offer, but I can't."

"Why not?"

"I can't leave Charlie and Jo Bell. Fuller or some other varmint might try to sneak up on them."

"And you'd protect them?"

"I'd try."

"Christamighty! You'd get yourself killed over that feather-brained kid."

"Charlie is a good boy."

"I'm not talking about Charlie."

"I know, but like I said, I owe it to their father to try and get them to Mrs. Eastwood." The silence dragged on for several minutes before she spoke again. "Will Fuller come back?"

"Not likely. If he's smart, he's in Sheridan by now. I've kept a close watch on our back trail. No one's following."

"He said he'd be back."

"His kind has to brag."

"He should be turned over to the law."

"There's not much law out here, lady. Be satisfied if he leaves you alone." He stood. "If you don't want to go to the spring I'll get on back to my camp."

"How far is the spring?"

"Not far. Three or four miles."

It had been weeks since she'd had a full bath and washed her hair. The logical part of her mind argued that she was taking a risk to go with a man she knew so little about. All of life is a risk, the other part argued. Rarely did she throw caution to the wind and do anything against her better judgement. Besides the luxury of a bath, the thought of being away from Jo Bell for a while was tempting. She looked at the man looming over her. If he was going to harm her, he would have done so before now, wouldn't he?

"I'll tell Charlie."

"You'll not be gone long. I doubt they'll even miss you, especially if they get to fighting. Will Buddy stay here until we get back?"

"He'd be sitting here this time next week if I told him to stay."

"Tell him." He gave a low whistle and his horse came to him.

"Can't we walk?"

"We can get there faster on Pete."

"Stay here, Buddy," she said when the dog started to get up. "Stay." She put her palm against his nose and the dog lay back down.

"Now, Pete, as far as I know you've not had a lady on your back." Smith spoke softly to the horse as if he were talking to a human. "Pay no mind to her skirt flopping about. It's just something a man has to put up with when he's around a woman." He mounted and held out his hand. "Put your foot in the stirrup and I'll pull you up," he instructed.

Willa tried, but the stirrup was too high.

Smith let go of her hand. Before she realized his intentions, he had grasped her beneath her arms, hauled her up and plunked her down on his lap. It seemed to her she was a mile off the ground.

"Oh! Oh! I'll fall."

"You won't fall." He settled her snugly between the saddlehorn and his chest. She grabbed him around the waist. When his arms encircled her, she felt closed in. Seized by inexplicable panic, she reared back and attempted to slide off his lap. He held her locked to him.

"Dammit, sit still," he said sharply. "Pete doesn't know what to think about your skirt flopping and you kicking him in the side." The horse danced and tossed his head. "Settle down, Pete. Where's your manners?"

"I want to get off."

"For Christ sake! I just got you up here. I'm not wasting all that effort for nothing. Let's go, Pete."

The nearness of him was something she hadn't anticipated. She could feel him in every nerve in her body. She was unprepared for the warm hardness of his body, for the strength in the arms around her. She sat as if her backbone were an iron rod, her face turned away from him, her unseeing eyes straight ahead.

Willa Hammer, you've lost your senses. What possessed you to ride off into the night with this strange man?

She is scared to death, Smith thought. Well, she should be. It's foolish of her to trust a man she knows nothing about, nothing except that the first time she'd seen him he had been stinking drunk. Godamighty, he had thought her smarter than the little tart back at the wagon. He didn't know why he'd offered to take her to the spring. She had looked sad and lonely sitting there under the tree with the dog. He reckoned she'd had a rough time. But hell, she'd better wise up if she was going to last in this country.

"It was dumb of you to come with me," he blurted almost angrily.

"I know." The words were so low he scarcely heard them. She faced the breeze and wisps of her hair blew back in his face, catching on the rough stubble on his cheek.

"Don't ever go off alone with a man you don't know. Hear?"

"I hear."

"I could stop this horse right now and have my way with you. There'd be nothing you could do."

"I'd fight you."

"Bull hockey!" he snorted.

"Why are you scaring me?"

"You're already scared stiff. Why did you come with me? I'm nothing but a worthless, no-good drunk. Remember?"

"You're not drunk now. And . . . and Buddy likes you. You can't be too mean if you like animals and they like you."

"Good Lord. That's the stupidest thing I've ever heard. The dog likes me because I feed him."

"He does not. He's smarter than that. He'd know it if you were just making up to him. Besides, Mr. Byers said you were reliable in spite of—"

"—Being a drunk."

"Yes, that's what he said. And . . . the thought of a bath and the chance to wash my hair just overcame my common sense. I don't know what I was thinking about. I don't have soap or a towel. Take me back, please."

"Are you always so polite—a pleasin' and thankin' every-body in sight?"

"I try to be," she said coolly. "Take me back . . . please."

"No. I have soap and you can use one of my shirts for a towel."

"No, really. I'd rather go back."

"Tomorrow you'll meet Maud. She won't let you stay, but at least you'll be clean when you head out for Sheridan."

In spite of her fear and the absolute idiocy of the situation she was in, a soft giggle blew from her lips. She wasn't sure if it was caused by hysteria or nerves. It was impossible to have coherent thoughts while every step the horse took caused her to feel the hard thighs against her bottom and her shoulder against his chest. Yet unknowingly her fear began to recede and she relaxed . . . a little.

"Spunky and foolish—" he murmured against her hair.

"How much farther?" One of her hands gripped the saddle cantle behind him, the other held tightly to the horn. "This poor horse will be worn out."

"He doesn't even know you're up here except for your skirt flapping against him."

"He must feel the extra weight."

"He's used to it. I find a woman every night who needs a bath."

Willa turned her head toward him. The moon had just crested the mountain. His face was so close . . . far too close. He had left his hat back with Buddy. His hair, stirred by the breeze, curled down onto his forehead. She could feel his gaze, hot and questing, on her face and was grateful for the darkness that hid the blush that crept up her throat to her cheeks.

His arms held her. She had never been this close to a man other than ones who had grabbed her and held her against her will. This hard, warm body against hers sent a tide of excitement through her. She could feel the warmth of his breath on the side of her face and wondered if he could feel the thumping of her heart.

Smith stopped the horse amid low-growing willows and chokecherry bushes. He sat still for a short while and listened. Caution was bred deep in Smith. The habit of years was hard to break. His sharp ears heard the flapping of wings, then the squeal of a small animal caught in the powerful claws of an owl. It was a natural sound. Still he listened a while longer with all his senses attuned to the night sounds before he lifted Willa down and dismounted.

"Stay here with Pete while I have a look around." He spoke in hushed tones, and then the darkness swallowed him.

In this secluded place Willa could see only the outlines of the trees and bushes. She stood close beside the horse, holding onto the stirrup. Pete made no move, but he was as alert as any wild animal would be. Anxiety caused her breath to catch in her throat. Her hand sought her pocket. The only weapon she had was a pocketknife. She gripped it and waited.

Smith appeared on the other side of the horse. Without a sound he was there, his light hair a glow in the darkness.

"You scared me!"

"Pete would have let you know if it had been anyone but me. His eyesight and hearing are far better than ours. His ears will swivel and twitch, he'll lift his head and sniff into the wind and become restless if something unfamiliar to him is near." He talked while delving into his saddlebag.

"Why did you have to look around?"

"Some wild thing might have come down to drink even though they don't usually drink from the warm pool. Come on. Stay here, Pete."

When Willa stumbled after him on the uneven ground, he

reached around and took hold of her wrist and led her through the willows to a small pool that gleamed in the moonlight.

"Five, six feet out it will be over your head." He placed a bar of soap on a flat rock beside the pool and took off his shirt.

"What are you doing?"

Mentally he swore when he heard the anxiety in her voice.

"Leaving you my shirt. I'll get another out of my bedroll while I'm waiting for you."

"Maybe this wasn't such a good idea—"

"Suit yourself. I'll be back there with Pete when you want to go. Don't call out—whistle. Voices carry."

He dropped his shirt on the rock where he had placed the soap. Willa's breath was a vibrant pressure in her throat. His bare shoulders and chest had a silky sheen to them. The moon cast a pale light on the blond hair that framed a face darkened by hours in the sun. Her eyes flicked over him and away. When she looked back, he was gone.

A velvety silence followed. Willa took a shaky breath, looked at the inviting pool, knelt down and tested the water with her hand. Warm. Wonderfully warm. Why was she hesitating? *This was what she wanted, wasn't it?* She pulled the shawl from her shoulders and became aware that it was warmer here in this magical place. Minutes later after removing her dress and mocassins, she slipped into the pool and sat down.

It was heavenly. The warm, almost hot water caressed her skin. She let herself sink into the water's embrace, and slowly the tension left her. She stood to soap herself. After lathering every part of her body, she let down her hair, holding the hairpins in her mouth. She soaped her hair with Smith's harsh-smelling lye soap without even thinking about the scented soap left behind when she had escaped the burning house.

It was so pleasant in the water. She didn't want to leave it but knew it was not wise to linger. When she thought about it later, she was surprised that she had not been afraid that Smith was standing in the shadows watching her when she came out of the pool. She reached for his shirt and dried her face. For a moment she reveled in the male smell. It was as if he were stroking her face. A sudden charge of sexual desire flowed through her. She clutched the shirt to her breasts and pondered the reason for the soaring feeling before she dropped it as if it were burning her fingers and drew her clothes on over her wet body.

When she was dressed, she whistled one short and one long blast. No more than a minute passed, when she saw the gleam of Smith's light hair at the edge of the clearing.

"That didn't take long," he said, coming toward her. "Where did you learn to whistle like a bobwhite?"

"How did you know it wasn't an Indian?"

"An Indian would have done a better job. Your hair is still dripping." He took the shirt from her hand, stepped behind her and lifted the wet hair from her back. "Good Lord, it's so long you could sit on it. Why do women bother with it?"

"Back East women are bobbing their hair. I think it's a good idea."

"I don't," he said gruffly; he squeezed the water from the long rope of hair and wrapped it in the shirt. He pulled the sleeves up and tied them on top of her head.

"Is this pool warm even when the snow is on the ground?"

"Yeah. You can see the steam a mile away."

"It would be wonderful to have a house right here beside the pool." She spoke to his back. He was already leading the way back to the horse.

The ride back to where they had left Buddy went quickly. The horse's movements brought Willa into rhythmic contact with Smith's chest. There was no way she could escape his closeness and she didn't even try. She was very aware that something loud and determined thumped between them. Was it his heart or hers? His, of course. The exertion of lifting her to sit across his lap would cause even a strong man's heart to pump faster.

"Thank you for taking me to the pool. And, I'd like to apologize for the things I said to you that day in the barn."

"Why? They were true."

"Even so, it was none of my business."

"Forget it. I have."

After that, not a word was said until they reached the knoll overlooking the valley and he helped her down from the horse. Buddy was waiting. Smith patted the dog's head and scooped up his hat. He wondered what she would do if he grabbed her and kissed her. She'd probably scream her head off. The dog would bite him and Charlie would come charging up the hill.

What the hell? He liked taking a risk when the odds were stacked against him.

With two quick steps he was beside her. His hands closed around her upper arms and dragged her up against him. He lowered his head and fastened his lips to hers, kissing her hard. The kiss lasted only a few seconds, but it left her stunned. She couldn't get her breath and for a moment she couldn't think. A full ten seconds passed before her heart began to thump and her mind cleared. Shock evaporated and she tried to pull back. He held her and gave her a second, softer kiss, his lips brushing back and forth across hers, before he let her go.

"Why . . . why did you do that?" she whispered, the back of her hand against her mouth.

"To teach you a lesson. Don't trust a man to always play the gentleman. Especially . . . a drinking man. And . . . never, never go off alone with him." He really didn't know why he had kissed her, he certainly hadn't planned it; but he had to tell her something.

"You want me to be afraid of you?"

"Why not? I'm sure as hell afraid of you."

"Because of the skillet?"

"And . . . other things. Go on. I'll watch until you reach the wagon." He told himself that he was ten times a fool. The touch of her soft lips had melted something inside of him, leaving a dark, aching vacancy.

"Thank you for the lesson," she said primly. With chin tilted and back straight, she started down the hill, but she turned back and thrust his shirt in his hands. "Will we see you tomorrow?"

"Maybe."

"Do you have any suggestions on how I can approach Mrs. Eastwood to get her to let Charlie and Jo Bell stay on at the ranch?"

"Not one." His answer was curt.

"You don't want them to stay, do you?"

"It doesn't make a damn bit of difference to me."

They looked steadily at each other. Even though it was dark, the force of his eyes held her as firmly as he had held her with his hands. He was a hard, ruthless man. She had been a thick-headed fool to go with him. Yet it had been pleasant. She had felt safe even in the pool with only her shift covering her. The kiss had been pleasant too. She had not felt in the least threatened. Thoughts of the kiss brought a flush of embarrassment that tinged her cheeks. She turned away.

Smith watched her go down the hill, keeping pace with the slow-moving dog. She had clung to his mind like a burr during the last few days, a disturbing presence. It had been a mistake to take her to the spring, a bigger mistake to kiss her. What had possessed him to do it?

Hellfire and damnation! He knew why he had done it. He had liked holding her in his arms. She had seemed fragile, but she was wiry, like a cat that would fight if cornered. It was something about the way she moved that made him think this; a mixture of caution and alertness. She would be a fit mate for a man, that is if he were looking for a mate.

Smith wheeled his horse and rode back toward his camp. He didn't want to care what happened to her after she left the ranch, but dammit it to hell, he did.

CHAPTER

* 12 *

Maud Eastwood opened her eyes and found herself lying flat on her back on the floor. Fearful that she would be plunged into that terrible blackness again, she lay perfectly still. Soon pain in her shoulder and in the back of her head made itself known to her. She tried to focus her eyes on the iron spider that hung on the wall behind the cookstove. It swayed back and forth like the pendulum on a clock.

"Stay still, damn you!"

When her mind cleared enough to know that she had hurt her head when she fell, she lifted a hand to feel the lump. Her arm felt as if it weighed a hundred pounds. She rolled her head to the side and saw that the kitchen door stood wide open.

"Ah . . . dammit!" If that whiskered old busybody came up onto the porch he would see her. Afraid to get to her feet because of the dizziness, she rolled slowly and painfully across the floor until she was close enough to kick the door shut with her foot.

Exhausted, she lay with her forearm over her eyes. What

had she been doing when she blacked out? *Think. Think.* Oh, yes, she had just finished eating her breakfast. What was it? What was it? Oh, God, what was it? *Milk and mush.* Thank heavens, she remembered. Sometimes she couldn't remember what she had been doing before she had what Fanny had called a "fit." She would waken with her mind a total blank. Not this time. Maybe she was getting better.

"You have fits, Mamma." Fanny had said those hateful words long ago—before Oliver died.

"No. They're sinkin' spells. Oliver said so."

"A girl in my school had a fit. She fell down and twitched and slobbered. Oliver is being kind."

"No! No!"

"Yes, he is. Do you think he wants people to know his wife has fits?"

That very day, Fanny, her little girl, had left for Denver, and she had not come back.

Maud wished she could remember how long it had been since she'd had one of her spells. A week? Two weeks? A month? This was the first one since Smith left. She had marked that date on the calendar. Damn his hide. He owed her that trip to Denver to see Fanny and tell her that her mother needed her to come home. She had sent letters, but they must not have reached Fanny because there had been no answer.

When Fanny got here, she was going to tell Smith once again to get the hell off her ranch. And if he didn't, she'd have Fanny get the marshal down from Sheridan. She didn't want him around. She had never wanted him around. The no-good bastard had come here with only the clothes on his back. He'd sucked up to Oliver, wormed his way into Oliver's good graces, thinking to get the land and the house. He'd not get it. It was hers and Fanny's.

When Fanny came home, the house would be bright and

shiny again. Fanny's friends would come up from Denver. They would have a picnic on the veranda, and in the evening they would sit in the glider swing. Oliver had built this grand home for her and Fanny. It was just as Oliver left it, Maud thought drowsily. She had lived right here in the kitchen and had not even gone into the other rooms unless absolutely necessary. She had not been upstairs since Oliver's funeral. Fanny would be pleased that she had kept it so nice.

Maud pulled herself up and sank down in a chair at the kitchen table. She would rest awhile. She'd clean the kitchen before Fanny got here.

With the sun behind him, Smith rode up the lane to the ranch buildings. Long ago, when he was a kid, he had thought of this place as home. Home had been where Oliver and Billy were. Now Oliver was gone and there was just Billy. The old man was the only family he had, and each time Smith left him he was fearful Billy wouldn't be here when he returned. Billy was fond of him, too. The cantankerous old man wouldn't admit it to him, but he showed it in a hundred different ways. Smith grinned a lopsided grin in anticipation of seeing him.

He supposed he could call Plenty Mad sort of family. The Indian had been at the ranch longer than he had. He was another stray Oliver had picked up. Plenty Mad and his mother, who had been used by a member of a wandering tribe and therefore was unfit for marriage, had lived in a lone little tepee at the edge of a Sioux village, hangers-on, dependent upon the meat and hides divided among those without a man to hunt for them. After his mother died, Plenty Mad had roamed, following the herds, until Oliver had found him, sick and half-starved.

Smith chuckled when he thought of the first time he had

seen Plenty Mad. He had been scared to death of him. The Indian delighted in making an Eastern tenderfoot think he was a bloodthirsty savage. He had hopped around on first one foot and then the other, brandishing a stick with a stone tied to the end of it and chanting in gibberish until Billy had come out and put a stop to it.

Now, scanning the area, Smith noted that nothing had changed during the four weeks he had been away. This morning, before dawn, he had rolled out of his blankets in order to reach the ranch before Willa and the Franks arrived. Two of his mares ran along the fence nickering a greeting to Pete. The stallion pranced, his ears peaked and his nostrils flared.

Smith laughed.

"You got a treat coming, boy. I think both of these ladies are waiting to welcome you."

Smoke came from the cookshack attached to the end of the bunkhouse. No smoke came from the two chimneys on the big house Smith observed as he rode up to the corral gate. After he unsaddled Pete, he turned him into the pasture with the two mares. With his tail in the air the stallion raced to join them. Smith watched as one of the females wheeled and kicked at him playfully. Pete nipped her on the flank and let out a shrill blast to let her know he was not in a courting mood and intended to get right down to the serious business of mating.

"Go to it, Pete. You've had a long trip and deserve some fun." Smith shouldered his saddle and headed for the barn.

"How-do, Smith. You back, damn you." Plenty Mad came from the side of the barn with a pitchfork in his hand.

The Sioux had a permanent grin on his face due to the deformity of his upper lip. The wide space between his two front teeth and his small pug nose added to his unusual appearance. Smith was used to his ugly features and didn't even notice them anymore, but he never doubted that Plenty Mad's mother had been *plenty mad* when she had seen her son for the first time.

"Howdy, Plenty. How's things here?" Smith went into the barn and flung his saddle over a rail.

"Bad. Plenty damn bad here. Plenty glad you back, Smith."

Everything with Plenty Mad was *plenty*. He picked up every cuss word he heard and was the most pessimistic person Smith had ever known. Plenty Mad was happiest when he was utterly miserable.

"How's Billy?"

"Mean. Plenty damn mean."

"What's he done now?"

"What's he done now?" he repeated. "He done all things. He done plenty bad things."

"Couldn't've been too bad. You two haven't killed each other." Smith's hand came down heavy on the Indian's shoulder.

"You laugh, Smith. You see. Hell damn kiss my ass." He continued to grumble as he followed Smith out of the barn. "Things is plenty damn bad. Bad grass. No water. No game. Big fire come like big herd a buffer. Take all away. Big smoke cover sun. You see plenty damn quick."

Smith looked up. There wasn't a cloud or a wisp of smoke in the sky. "I'm glad to know things are going good."

"Good, my bare damn you ass." Plenty hopped around on his short, permanently bowed legs. His shoulder-length hair danced on his shoulders. "You ask. You don't hear. I say plenty bad smoke come. I tell Billy. Damn Billy tell Plenty Mad go pitch horse shit. Billy don't pitch horse shit. Plenty Mad pitch horse shit. All day rake and pitch horse shit. Plenty Mad tired rakin' and pitchin' horse shit."

"Don't get in a sweat. Stop raking the horse shit and oil my saddle. Where's Billy?"

"How I know where Billy is? God the hell damn. He don't tell me. You hear?"

Carrying his bedroll, Smith chuckled as he went through the bunkhouse to reach the cookshack. The long narrow room was neat as bunkhouses go. Before it became a habit for Smith to keep both himself and his sleeping place clean, Billy had insisted upon it. Even with a full crew of men living here, there had been no spitting on the floor in this bunkhouse. Cigarette butts were in a can, bunks were spread with a blanket, floors were swept every Saturday.

A familiar, worn, sheep-lined duck coat hung from a peg on the wall. Sant was back.

Smith's lips spread into a broad smile. Sant Rudy was the man who had taught him how to defend himself when he had been just a stripling. He was the only man beside Billy that Smith would trust with his life.

As far as Smith was concerned, Sant Rudy had done about all a man could do. He had scouted for the army, ridden shotgun on the stage, led wagon trains to California, mined for gold and lived with the Indians. It was said he had killed a dozen men. Smith never doubted that every one of them needed killing.

The only thing in the world that Sant loved was wild horses. He shared that love with Smith. The two of them had spent weeks trailing a wild herd and driving them into a blind canyon where there was plenty of grass and water. It will be damn good to see Sant, Smith thought, as he dropped his bedroll and his hat on the floor beside the door and entered the cooking and eating room of the bunkhouse.

"Saw ya ride in." Billy was standing at the iron cookstove raking ashes and cinders out of the firebox into a tin bucket. He kept his head bowed to hide the welcoming grin. It would have been impossible to see, however, because his face was covered with a white beard that extended to his chest.

"Howdy to you too, Billy."

"Coffee's hot. I baked ya a couple apples."

"How did you know I was coming today?"

"Bird told me."

"Humpt!" Smith snorted. "Probably a buzzard."

There was no hiding the pride in Billy's eyes when he straightened and looked at the tall, lean man still standing in the doorway. Love was there too. The boy who had stumbled into his and Oliver's camp that morning had grown to be a man any father would be proud of—not that he would admit it to Smith.

He had baked the apples, Smith's favorite, every morning for the past week. Course, he wasn't going to tell him that or how much he had missed him.

"You made good time. Denver's a fer piece."

"Yeah, it is." Smith rubbed his hand over the stubble on his cheeks. "How long has Sant been here?"

" 'Bout a week. He's out south with a couple fellers he rode in with. Said they'd drive Eastwood cattle cross Crazy Woman Creek then go on down to Horseshoe Canyon. He wanted to show them fellers those wild horses ya got bottled up."

"Were they horse buyers for the army?"

"Don't rightly know. One might a'been. The other'n was a know-it-all kid with a itchy finger." Billy snorted. "He won't last long."

"Sant going to stay awhile?"

"Didn't say. Ya know how close-mouthed he is. He rode in and went to work like it ain't been half a year since he left." Billy looped his thumbs in the wide suspenders that held up his britches. "Boomy came in for supplies. They're pushing a couple hundred head onto Bison Flats. Said they'd be in in three, four days if'n they don't have to go on down towards Little Fork. Says it's mighty dry up that away."

"Had any trouble?"

"Didn't mention any."

"Seen much of the old woman?"

"Some. I put milk to the porch every mornin'. Once it set there two days and I threw it to the hogs. She comes out once in a while and goes to the outhouse. Smells like she empties her chamber pot off the end of the porch. Did ya see Fanny?"

"I saw her. Maud isn't going to like what I found out if I tell her." Smith sat at the table with his coffee. Billy brought the baked apples to him, a fork stuck in the top of one. Smith smacked his lips and grinned. "That's prettier than a woman dancing bare-ass naked on top a barroom table. I've eaten so damn many rabbits I'm beginning to hop."

Billy eased himself down into a chair. "I take it the trip went sour."

"Trip went all right. What I found in Denver was enough to make a dog puke."

"She ain't comin'. I ain't sure if I'm glad or not. Course if she did, it'd mean we could get the hell outta here."

"She's not coming. Ever." Smith looked steadily at his friend. "She's an uppity bitch, Billy. At first she refused to see me. I kicked up such a fuss, she agreed to meet me in the garden at the back of the house. She wasn't the slightest bit interested in what I had to tell her about Maud. She's cut herself loose from everything. She doesn't want any part of Eastwood Ranch or her mother. I nosed around and found out that she's put out the story that her mother and stepfather drowned at sea. She's burned her bridges."

"At sea! You couldn't drag Maud a hundred miles from this place with a team of mules. That's the biggest cock 'n' bull tale I ever heared of. Fanny was a snotty, uppity kid. Guess she's worse'n I thought."

"She's called Francine now, Billy. All she cares about is her position as Mrs. Nathan Brockford. They're leaving Denver within a month to go to England. *Mr. Brockford* is in line for a title and they plan to live there.''

''Now if that ain't a lick. Fanny a dooches, or somethin'. *Francine's* come a long way from that dugout on the prairie.''

Smith finished the apples, pushed the dish back and cupped the coffee mug in his two hands. ''That's the best eatin' I've had in weeks, Billy.''

''Knowed ya'd be pert near starved,'' Billy said gruffly to keep Smith from seeing how pleased he was. ''I'll put on beef 'n' dumplin's for supper.''

''I've got to decide what to tell Maud.''

Billy scratched his head. ''Ya can always tell her how it was, that *Francine* don't care no more for her than fer a old hound dog.''

''It'd be like pulling a rug out from under her.''

''What'a ya care 'bout that for? She hates yore guts.''

''I know that, and I care about as much for her as she does for me, but I owe Oliver, dammit.''

''I ain't forgot how she'd not let ya in the house not even when ya was just a little ol' youngun who'd lost yore folks. She was meaner than a rained-on hen. Down right ugly-mean. That old woman wouldn't walk on you if ya was dirt.''

''I know that. Still I've got to leave her a little something to hope for. It's what Oliver would do. He was the kindest man I've ever known.''

''Yeah.'' Billy got up shaking his head. ''I ain't never goin' to figure out why he done it if I live to be a hundred.''

Smith drained his cup. ''Done what?''

''Married up with her.''

''We'll never know, will we? There's something else, Billy. Remember Oliver talking about his sister, Regina, who married a gambler named Gilbert Frank?''

''Yeah. Said she was pretty as a picture 'n' real ladylike too. It set sorely with him that she married that bird.''

"Well, her boy and her girl and a woman traveling with them will be here in about an hour."

"Be *here*? What'n hell for?"

"They were on their way here with their pa who hadn't heard about Oliver being gone. Guess he was coming to leech off his wife's brother. Anyway he got shot down at the stage station—drew a gun on Abel Coyle when Coyle accused him of cheating at cards."

"Abel Coyle? Jumpin' catfish. He must not'a had no sense a'tall. Air the kids younguns?"

"Guess you'd call them half-grown. The boy is fifteen, a good kid, but his sister is spoiled rotten and dumber than a fence post. She should of been named Trouble." Smith purposely left out mentioning Willa and was glad Billy didn't ask about the woman traveling with the Franks.

"'Tis the drizzlin' shits, is what it is. It'll rain silver dollars before that old woman takes anybody in, even shirttail kin. Hell, she ain't got one ounce of charity in 'er a'tall. Ya ought to be knowin' that."

"I know it and I told them. They were determined to come here and find out for themselves. Maybe I can get Sant to take them on up to Sheridan in a day or two."

"Are ya feelin' obliged to help 'em cause they're Oliver's kin?" Billy stood in the doorway of the cookshack.

"Something like that," Smith said absently. He was looking toward the mountains, but he was seeing a blond-haired woman with big sad eyes sitting under a tree. Her dog was beside her and she was wiping tears from her cheeks with the back of her hand. "Maud probably saw me ride in. I'd best get on up to the house and get it over with."

Smith ran his fingers through his hair as he passed through the gate that enclosed the yard surrounding the house. The gate swung easily on the hinges, but it was badly in need of paint. Maud wasn't about to turn loose any money for anything as unnecessary as paint or whitewash. He and Billy had kept the place in as good repair as possible with what they had to work with.

By the time he reached the porch, Smith had about made up his mind to tell Maud the truth—that Fanny wanted nothing to do with her or the ranch. Then when Maud flung open the door, and he saw her ravaged face, he couldn't do it.

"Well, it took ya long enough to get up here. I saw ya ride in. Ya didn't bring her," she said accusingly.

"Come on out on the porch and I'll tell you about it."

Maud slid out the door. Staying close to the wall, she inched over and sank down on a bench beside two empty washtubs. It was plain to Smith the woman was sick. Hair had come loose from the usually tight knot at the back of her head and strands hung down on her neck. Her eyes were dull, her cheeks hollow, her legs so trembly they could hardly hold her thin body. The severe black widow's dress she wore accentuated the pallor of her skin.

"When's she comin'?" she demanded.

"I didn't see her. She's in London."

"London? Is that in California?"

"No. It's across the ocean. Someone over there left her husband some money and they went to collect it."

"Why'd she go way over there for? This place is worth a lot of money. It'll be hers when I'm gone."

"I guess her husband wanted her with him."

"When's she comin' back?"

"Mr. Brockford's people told me they'd be back in six or eight months and that they would be sure and tell her to come right on up here."

"Liar!" Maud's thin lips barely moved. "You always was a liar," she hissed, staring at Smith with hate-filled eyes. "You didn't go to Denver."

"I rode to Laramie and took the stage to Denver when I

had more important work to do right here. I talked to Fanny's in-laws. Now dammit, I don't care a hell of a lot if you believe me. I did what I said I'd do.''

"You didn't go there. You've been off drinkin' and whorin'. I told Oliver the day he brought you here that you were a no-good leechin' little bastard some whore had dumped in the scrub.'' Maud's eyes took on a strange, feverish shine and the words gushed from her mouth in gasped whispers. "You think if you keep Fanny away you'll get this ranch. You won't get a stick. I'll burn it to the ground first.'' Her legs were trembling violently when she stood and stumbled to the door.

"Are you sick, Mrs. Eastwood? Do you want me to get a doctor?''

"*You* make me sick! Get off my land! Don't take one thin' with you or I'll have the law on you, hear? You come here piss-poor. You leave piss-poor.'' Maud's heart was pumping madly and her insides were quivering from the effort it took to keep her legs under her.

"I'd like nothing better than to ride out of here, but I can't do it and you know why. No one else would put up with you, and this place would go to rack and ruin in no time at all. Then what would you do?''

Smith's control was slipping. He knew he had to get away from her before he said something he would regret. The door slammed, leaving him to stare at it and wonder why he had taken the trouble to lie to save her grief.

Maud leaned against the other side of the door and held her clasped hands to her flat bosom. Tears of weakness and despair filled her eyes and rolled down her cheeks. He was lying. He had made up the story about Fanny being across the sea. If she had the strength she would kill him. She had hated him since the day he had come here riding in front of Oliver just as pretty as you please. Oliver had fawned over him like he was somebody. He had paid more attention to that homeless by-blow of some whore than he had to Fanny.

Sobbing with anger and frustration, Maud stumbled around the table toward the couch. She stepped on a spot made slick by food she had dropped on the floor. When her foot slipped sideways, she tried to grab the back of a chair, missed, and hit the floor hard.

Pain like a hot flame enveloped her leg and hip in a sheet of agony.

CHAPTER
* 13 *

*I*t was almost noon.

The knot of dread Willa had felt when she had awakened was now a sick feeling in the pit of her stomach. Her throat felt as if a hand were squeezing it; her eyes burned from lack of sleep. She had lain awake most of the night after an unusually nasty scene with Jo Bell. The girl had been furious when she had learned that Smith had taken Willa to a warm spring to bathe and had accused her of every ugly thing she could think of.

"Yore wastin' yore time, *ma'am*. Ya can take him off in the dark every night and give him what ya wouldn't give Papa, but it still won't matter none. I can have him if I want him. All I got to do is snap my fingers and he'll take me to a town and look after me till I can find a man with lots of money."

Jo Bell's words rang in Willa's ears long after the girl had flounced off to bed. What really hurt was the disappointed look she had seen in Charlie's eyes and the fact that he hadn't tried to defend her against his sister's harsh words. Had he seen Smith kiss her? Did he think she was a loose woman after all?

Why *had* Smith kissed her? It had not been an insulting, cruel kiss—of that she was sure. She had experienced *that* kind. If his intention had been to teach her a lesson, he had gone about it gently. His mouth had been soft, the kiss sweet. Not that she had liked it, she hastened to tell herself. She had been vulnerable at that moment. Her mind had been muddled with worry or she would have screamed her head off.

Oh, shoot, she wished she could stop thinking about it, but she had never felt quite so alive, so feminine, so protected, as she had while sitting across his lap, his arms around her. But not even being really clean for the first time in weeks could untie nerves tied up as tight as a fiddle string.

This morning she had taken special care when she dressed, telling herself that it was important that she look her best when she met Mrs. Eastwood. Wearing the light blue dress with the white collar, she brushed her hair until it shone and wound it in a neat coil at the nape of her neck. Of course, she would feel more confident meeting the strange woman if only she had shoes on her feet instead of Jo Bell's moccasins.

Jo Bell was still in her bunk when they broke camp. Charlie tied the horse to the back of the wagon, climbed up on the seat beside Willa and took the reins. When he spoke, it was for the first time that morning.

"In a little while I'll stop and put Buddy in the wagon." He cracked the whip over the backs of the team. They strained at the harnesses and the wagon began to roll.

Willa was silent for a while. She felt a desperate need to make things right with Charlie. It was all she could do not to squirm. When she looked at him, he averted his eyes.

"Charlie," she said when she could stand the silence no longer. "I want you to know that nothing happened last night between me and Mr. Bowman. He said he had been to a warm spring and offered to take me there if I wanted a bath. I wanted to go—it had been so long since I'd had a full bath. Maybe it was foolish to go off alone with him, but Mr. Byers seemed to have complete trust in him. He took me there and brought me back. He didn't do anything improper.'' The last wasn't exactly true, but how could she explain the kiss to Charlie?

''Why didn't ya take Jo Bell with ya? Didn't ya think 'bout her wantin' a bath?''

''To tell you the truth one of the reasons I went was to get away from her for a while. Jo Bell hasn't been exactly friendly. I'm not a saint, Charlie. There's a limit to my patience.''

''I know ya don't like her . . . and I can't say I blame ya.'' Charlie's voice was low, heavy, tired.

''She makes it hard for me to like her. Regardless of whether I do or not, if you can stay at Eastwood, I'll take her on to Sheridan with me and do the best I can for her.''

''Why'd ya do that?''

''Your father saved me from that mob. They might have killed me if he had not taken me up on this wagon.''

''I'm not pushin' Jo Bell off on ya. Besides Eastwood probably ain't no place I'd want to stay nohow.'' His voice was imbued with defeat. He stopped the wagon, climbed down and lifted Buddy up onto the seat.

An hour passed, then another. The day had grown warmer, but the air was surprisingly cool. Willa squinted her eyes and studied the terrain, trying to put thoughts of what Smith had said about Mrs. Eastwood from her mind, trying not to think of him at all.

The trail ran alongside a stand of pine and cedar. The faint breeze carried their scent and the song of the birds in their branches. To the left was a meadow that stretched to the purple mountains. Two deer, knee-deep in grass, stood stone-still watching the wagon. Suddenly they lifted their tails and sped away. Willa watched them, marveling at their grace and speed.

At the top of a rise Charlie pulled the team to a halt.

"Well, looky there."

The slopes on either side of the shallow valley were blanketed with stately pines, and beneath their branches was an abundance of green grass and wildflowers. The green was a startling contrast to the white mansion that nestled in the valley. It stood like a perfect jewel in its mounting. Willa laughed with sheer pleasure. The scene was breathtakingly beautiful and beyond anything she could have imagined Eastwood Ranch to be.

"Do you reckon that's Uncle Oliver's ranch?"

Willa turned quickly, sharply and looked at Charlie's puzzled face.

"It's . . . got to be. My, what a lovely place. And that big house. Oh, Charlie, Mrs. Eastwood has got to have more rooms than she knows what to do with. How can she not welcome her husband's kinfolk?"

"I never expected anything so grand. Uncle Oliver must a been rich."

"It's grand all right. It's as pretty as a picture."

"What is it yawl are talkin' about?" Jo Bell opened the canvas to peer over their shoulders. "Is that it? Is that Uncle Oliver's?"

"Reckon it is. The trail leads right to it."

"By whoopee damn!" Jo Bell yelled happily. "It won't be bad a'tall stayin' there for a while. I thought it'd be like some of those old ranches we passed. Ya know, like where poor whites live in back home."

"It seems strange that we're here without Pa," Charlie said.

"I bet Aunt Maud knows lots of rich men."

"Get some clothes on," Charlie said crossly and started the team moving. "And dress decent to meet Aunt Maud."

"Don't ya be tellin' me what to do, Mr. Know-it-all. Ya ain't nothin' but a snot-nosed kid." Jo Bell waited to see if her brother was going to reply, and when he didn't, she yanked down the canvas between them.

Willa noticed the anxious look on Charlie's face. She put her hand on his arm.

"Don't worry. It won't be the end of the world if your aunt won't let Jo Bell stay here. We'll just leave. The supplies we got from Mr. Byers will last for another week or two."

The serious look on his face made him appear far older than his fifteen years.

"I told ya I ain't stayin' if you don't."

"You must be practical, Charlie. You can work here. I can't live on charity for the rest of my life. I've got to make a place for myself. I'll be all right. This may come as a surprise to you, but I can fix clocks and it pays well. What do you think about that?"

"I ain't never heard of a woman doin' that."

"Papa taught me. Of course, people are a little put off at first. Women are just as smart as men, Charlie. It doesn't take muscles to work on clocks. Once folks get used to the idea, they'll only be interested in getting their clocks fixed."

"I ain't stayin' at Eastwood without ya and that's that." Charlie turned away, but not before she saw the look of yearning in his eyes.

An awareness of what that look meant slowly penetrated her already troubled mind. My goodness gracious me! Charlie was *almost* a man. Did he have man-to-woman feelings for her? Feelings deeper than friendship? She wished it were not so but was afraid that it was. How could she have been so blind not to have seen it coming? Now she understood why he had been so cool toward her last night and again this morning.

He was jealous of Smith.

She must be careful, very careful, not to give him any hope for anything more than friendship between them. She was more than five years older, but to a boy starved for affection, the age difference wouldn't matter. She couldn't worry about how she was going to rectify the situation now, she thought, and pressed her fist against the knot forming in her stomach. The immediate problem lay just ahead.

As they drew near the ranch, Willa could see what distance had prevented her from seeing before. The house badly needed scraping and painting. Sun-faded draperies were drawn over the windows. A sheet or a blanket hung over the glass of the double doors. Veranda chairs were stacked against the wall and a swing with a broken chain swayed crazily. What appeared to be a magnificent house when they were a half a mile away now looked shabby . . . deserted.

Behind the house, several low buildings fanned out from the barn. A spiral of smoke came from one of them. Willa's gaze came to rest on two men standing beside a huge pile of cut wood. One had white hair and a long white beard. The other was Smith. His blond hair shone in the sun. He stood with one booted foot resting on a thick stump beside an axe embedded in the wood, his elbow on his thigh, his face turned to watch them approach.

Willa felt discomfort aplenty. What had happened between them last night had awakened her to the fact that there was more to the man than he allowed people to see. He had a compassionate side where animals were concerned. And, according to Mr. Byers, he was completely dependable . . . when he was sober. It had been totally out of line with his previous disagreeable behavior to go out of his way to accommodate her and take her to the pool. Yet he had not made a threatening move even when she had sat on his lap, her shoulder pressed to his chest, his arms around her.

After being chivalrous, he had grabbed her and kissed her. Had he felt the need to preserve the image of being a hell-raiser? She wondered if he had created the image to use as a shield between himself and others to avoid a close relationship. He had been forced to take on the job of leading them to the Eastwood Ranch. He certainly hadn't wanted to be bothered with them. He had made that clear enough.

There was only one conclusion to be drawn: he had kissed her to see how she would react, and she hadn't protested at all. Thinking about it, she felt her cheeks grow hot with shame. He must have laughed all the way back to his camp, thinking about how he had given the "old maid" a treat.

Willa pulled her eyes away from him. She must not give him or the kiss another thought. She couldn't waste time thinking about a man who was such an enigma when she didn't know how she was going to survive until she could find work. Heavens! Her head ached from all the confused thoughts that floated through it.

Smith watched the wagon approach while only half-listening to what Billy was saying.

"—And old Maud'll go up in smoke is what she'll do. Jehoshaphat! There ain't been no younguns on this place in a coon's age."

"They're not younguns, Billy. Charlie's about the age I was when Oliver put me in charge of a crew. He's a damn good boy. I like him. The girl is another matter. She's the stuff that gets men killed."

"What ya mean by that?"

"You'll see."

"Zat her on the seat?"

"Naw, that's the woman traveling with them."

Billy turned to look at Smith, but he was looking straight at the approaching wagon. "Ya never said she was a young, fine-lookin' woman."

"You never asked me."

"Well, thunderation! Ya could'a told me the woman was sightly. What'er ya goin' to do with two females?"

"Nothing," Smith said absently. His eyes were on Willa. She wore the blue dress she had worn the day at Byers' Station. He wished she would take off the damn bonnet so the sun could shine on her hair.

She was pretty as a bluebird and proud as a peacock. Her rounded bottom had sat on his thighs and her soft breasts had been crushed against his chest when he had kissed her. She had trusted him—because her dog liked him. Gawd! Now wasn't that a harebrained reason to trust a man? With reasoning like that she'd not last a month in a town like Buffalo or Sheridan.

His stomach knotted with frustration. What had she called him that day in the barn? *A whiskey-soaked swine, wallowing in filth like a hog.* A woman like her would never understand that at times he needed, had to have, relief from the pain, the bitter loneliness.

His logic told him that he should be putting up barriers between him and this woman. They were as different as day and night. She would bring him nothing but misery. He muttered a curse. It was too late. Somehow she had seeped into the secret recesses of his being, and it was going to be difficult, if not impossible, to get her out.

Dammit, he didn't want to care about her. Right now he needed to be tied to a woman like he needed a hole in his head. Hell, women like Willa meant marriage . . . a noose like the one Maud had used to make Oliver's life miserable.

These thoughts were going through Smith's head as the wagon stopped, and his feet were carrying him toward it so that he could help her down.

Willa lowered her eyes as she accepted his help. She placed her hands on his shoulders, his hands spanned her waist and he easily lowered her to the ground.

"Thank you," she murmured, and stepped away as soon as her feet touched the solid earth.

"Smith," Jo Bell called from the back of the wagon. "Will ya help me down?"

"How come of a sudden she can't get down by herself?" Charlie growled so low that only Willa could hear. "She's been a doin' it all the time."

Jo Bell was wearing a pink dress with a low rounded neckline. The bodice fit over her young breasts like a glove. Her hair was fluffed around her face and caught at the nape with a ribbon, making her look soft and pretty. She clasped Smith's upper arm with her two hands, pressed her breasts against him, and smiled up at him in such an obvious flirtatious manner that Willa wanted to slap her.

Irritated by Jo Bell's blatant pursuit of Smith, Willa turned her attention to the white-haired man. He was watching Smith trying to extract himself from Jo Bell's hands. The eyes he turned to Willa were bright blue and twinkled with amusement.

"Howdy, ma'am."

"Hello." Willa held out her hand. "I'm Willa Hammer."

"Billy Coe. Glad to meet ya."

Willa waited for Smith to introduce Charlie and Jo Bell. When he didn't, she said, "This is Charlie and Jo Bell Frank, Mr. Eastwood's niece and nephew—his late sister's children."

"Howdy, son, young lady."

Charlie shook hands with the old man.

"Hello," Jo Bell murmured, looking off toward the house. "Sure does look dead 'round here."

Smith lifted Buddy down from the wagon. The dog whined a greeting and licked his hand.

"Is it all right to leave the wagon here till we know what we're goin' to be doin'?" Charlie spoke to Smith, who was paying more attention to Buddy than to the rest of them.

"I'll take care of the team." Smith stroked the dog's head for a minute before he looked up. "You might as well go on up to the house and talk to the old lady." He climbed up onto the wagon seat.

"Where's he takin' it?" Charlie asked.

"I 'spect he'll park it there back of the bunkhouse." Billy's eyes went from Charlie to his sister, then to Willa. It had been a mighty long time since there had been a woman on the place. He didn't know what to say to them. He scratched his head. "I reckon Mrs. Eastwood saw you come in."

"You and Jo Bell go on, Charlie. I'll wait here," Willa said.

"Ain't ya comin' with us?"

"No. She's your aunt—"

"—But what'll we say?"

"Just tell her who you are and the circumstances."

"What'er ya askin' her for?" Jo Bell said crossly. "It ain't nothin' to her what we say to *our* aunt."

"She's right, Charlie. You and Jo Bell should talk to her alone."

"But what about you, Willa?"

The smile she gave him was affectionate and . . . sad. "We already discussed that. Your first obligation is to your sister."

"That's what I've been tellin' the dumb cluck all the time." Jo Bell jerked on her brother's arm. "Are ya comin' or do I have to go by myself?"

"I'm comin'." Charlie jerked his arm free of her hands. "I still mean what I said," he spoke over his shoulder to Willa, and started up the path to the back of the house. Jo Bell grabbed his arm again, holding him back so that she could walk in front of him.

"Will Mrs. Eastwood let them stay, Mr. Coe?" Willa asked softly. There was defeat in her voice and on her delicate features.

"There ain't much chance a'tall, ma'am."

"That's what Smith said." Her shoulders sagged slightly under the weight of her despair.

"Mrs. Eastwood ain't got no kindness in her. It all drained out a long time ago."

"She's got such a big house. Surely she will feel some obligation toward them and let them stay when she realizes they have no other place to go."

Billy lifted bushy white brows and looked at her closely. "Don't ya be countin' on it, lass."

Willa was still for a time, gnawing on her lower lip as she watched the brother and sister.

"Charlie was looking forward to being with his uncle and working here on the ranch. He's a good boy, Mr. Coe. A dependable boy. He's a fast learner and willing worker."

"Smith said as much."

Willa watched anxiously as Charlie and Jo Bell stepped up onto the porch. Charlie moved past his sister, rapped on the door and stepped back.

"Mr. Bowman told him he could stay here and work with him."

Willa watched Charlie rap again.

"I ain't surprised at Smith sayin' that."

The door remained closed and Charlie rapped a third time. He walked to the edge of the porch and looked back at Willa. A minute or two passed. Jo Bell stood impatiently with her hands on her hips. Finally she knocked. When there was no answer, she flounced off the porch and headed back to where Willa and Billy waited beside the wood pile.

Willa turned worried eyes to the old man. "If Mrs. Eastwood is home why doesn't she answer the door?"

Billy shook his gray head slowly. "I be guessin' she don't want company, ma'am."

"Does she live in that big place alone?"

"Yup. Ain't nobody stepped foot inside for more'n six years."

"Maybe Smith will talk to her."

"He ain't likely to do that. They don't cotton to each other none a'tall."

"For goodness sake—"

"Horse turds!" Jo Bell reached them several strides ahead of her brother. "Ain't no use hangin' round here. Me and Charlie are goin' on to a town."

"Just hold on," Charlie said. "I'm not takin' ya anywhere yet. We got to get the lay of the land, 'n' decide what's best to do."

"If you won't take me, Smith will. And it ain't none of your business where I go and what I do. You can't do anythin' right anyhow. Papa said ya was dumb as a cow-pie 'n' would never amount to anythin'. He was right 'bout that." Jo Bell's face was a reflection of her contempt for her brother. "Go get Smith right now, Charlie Frank. I want to talk to him."

Willa saw the hurt look on Charlie's face. She thought he would be immune to Jo Bell's nasty remarks by now. But it still hurt him to hear that his father had thought so little of him. Willa placed a hand on his arm.

"Do you want me to try and talk to your aunt?"

"How? She won't come to the door."

"If this don't beat all." Jo Bell turned on Willa. "Yore just the limit is what ya are. Yore wastin' time, ma'am. I'm leaving with or without Charlie. Ya can stay at this old run-down place, 'cause I don't want ya comin' with me.''

Both Willa and Charlie ignored the girl.

"Charlie, if I can get her to open the door, I'll explain that you were on the way to visit your uncle when you heard of his passing. She may agree to let you stay through the winter.''

"I . . . ain't . . . stayin' . . . here.'' Jo Bell yelled shrilly. "Ain't ya hearin' anythin' I said? Yore not payin' no attention to what I want a'tall. Charlie, ya stop talkin' to *her* right now and listen to *me*.''

Charlie's patience finally snapped and he turned on his sister with a raised hand.

"Shut up, Jo Bell, or I'll . . . I'll slap your jaws.''

"Ya wouldn't dare! Smith won't let ya hurt me. He'll hitch *our* mules to the wagon and take me to town. I want to leave here 'n' I want to leave *now* and ya can't stop me.'' She stomped off toward the barn.

Willa glanced at Billy, a flush of embarrassment on her cheeks. He was watching the play between brother and sister as if he doubted what he was seeing and hearing. When his twinkling eyes met hers, he shook his shaggy head in disbelief.

"Maybe ya *had* better try and talk to Aunt Maud, Willa.'' Charlie's voice held a note of defeat. "Ask her if ya and Jo Bell can stay with her for just a little while. Just till we can get somethin' figured out. *Ask*, mind ya. We ain't beggars. If she don't want us here, we'll hitch up and go.''

Willa's almost twenty years had brought her a better than average acquaintance with many different kinds of people. Charlie was top-notch. Charlie had pride. Charlie deserved to stay here and learn ranching if that's what he wanted to do. It was unfair that he felt obligated to look after such a spoiled, ungrateful sister.

"All right. I'll go talk to your aunt."

Willa's shoulders went straighter, giving a regal look to her slight frame. She slicked the hair back from her temples with her palms and straightened her collar. She didn't have the slightest idea of what to say to this hard-hearted woman, but she was determined to try to persuade her at least to take Jo Bell for a while.

She had gone less than halfway to the house when she heard a woman's terrified screams coming from the barn. The sounds sent tiny hairs at the back of Willa's neck erect as she recognized Jo Bell's voice locked somewhere in the scream. She whirled about. Charlie and Billy were running. Fear put her feet in motion and she ran after them.

Smith heard the screams, too. He had unharnessed the mules and turned them into the corral. It took only a split second for him to determine where they were coming from. He vaulted a fence and raced to the barn. He reached it and heard a familiar Indian chant mixed with hysterical shrieks.

"Heya . . . a . . . a . . . heya!" Plenty Mad was dancing around the terrified girl, waving his war club. A feather was stuck in his headband and his face was streaked with red paint.

"Heya . . . a . . . a . . . heya! Me scalp um white squaw."

On her knees, her arms wrapped around her head, Jo Bell continued to screech.

Smith swore viciously.

"Goddammit, Plenty!" he shouted to make himself heard over the noise. "Shut up that damn sing-song and get the hell out of here."

"No sing-song. War chant. Heya . . . a . . . a . . . heya!"

"War chant my hind foot. What the hell do you think you're doing?"

"Silly damn white squaw want to see savage Indian."

"You've had your fun. Get out before *I* scalp *you*."

"Why you mad, Smith? Plenty Mad show silly damn white squaw savage Sioux warrior," the Indian grumbled. His ugly face looked more grotesque than ever decorated with smears of red paint.

"You've scared the hell out of her." Smith strode to where Jo Bell knelt on the hard-packed dirt.

"I did? That plenty damn good, huh, Smith? You know hell what? Damn white woman think Plenty Mad damn fierce warrior. Think Plenty Mad take hair, boil her in pot."

"If you pull this stunt again, I'm going to be mighty tempted to take *your* hair and boil *you* in a pot." Smith's face was a dark mask of harshness.

Plenty shrugged indifferently and shoved the handle of his tomahawk in his belt. "No like black hair nohow," he grumbled.

Smith grasped Jo Bell's arms and pulled her to her feet. "You're all right. Plenty is harmless. He's just showing off. He won't hurt you."

"Smith! Oh, Smith!" Jo Bell threw her arms about his neck. "That . . . savage! That . . . filthy, ugly savage attacked me. He was . . . he was goin' to kill me."

"No. It's a game he plays. He just likes to scare city folk."

"He was going to s-scalp me! Shoot him, Smith! Shoot the ugly old thin'."

"He wasn't going to hurt you," Smith said firmly. "This is his idea of having fun."

"Ha! Ha! Ha!" Plenty Mad's laugh was a cackling sound. He doubled over, laughed and slapped his thighs. "Stupid damn white squaw think savage Indian scalp her. Ha! Ha! Ha! She plenty scared? Huh, Smith?"

Billy and Charlie came hurrying down the lane between the stalls.

"I figured that ya was up to yore tricks, ya dal-burned mud-ugly mule's ass," Billy yelled at Plenty Mad. "Ya ain't got brains enough to spit downwind. I been tellin' ya to cut that out. Ya'll try it on the wrong tenderfoot and get that hatchet buried in yore ugly head."

When Plenty Mad saw Charlie, he lifted the tomahawk in a threatening gesture. He tried to look fierce, but he was laughing so hard he had to give up. Holding his sides, he fell back in the hay and laughed with unrestrained delight.

CHAPTER
* 14 *

"What'd he do to Jo Bell?" Charlie moved past Billy to where his sobbing sister stood clinging to Smith.

"She's all right. He just scared her."

"He was goin' to k-kill m-me! Take me away from this scary old lonesome place. Just you and me, Smith. We can take my wagon and go find S-Starr. P-please. I'll be . . . real nice to ya." Jo Bell wrapped her arms tighter about his neck and snuggled against him.

Over Jo Bell's head Smith caught sight of Willa standing quietly beside Billy. Her back was straight, her hands clasped in front of her. Eyes so astonishing blue and luminous looked directly into his. He saw pain there before she blinked it away. In the dim light her pale face appeared infinitely soft and beautiful. Her delicate features seemed to stand out with additional clarity that he had not noticed before.

She looked as if the strength had been drained out of her.

An unexpected twinge of yearning stirred deep inside of him. This weepy, stupid girl disgusted him. He wanted to shove her away from him. Instead he reached up and gently pulled the clinging arms from around his neck.

A storm of emotions flooded Willa when she saw Smith with his arms around Jo Bell, her arms wound about his neck, his chin in her hair. The entire length of her body was pressed to his and he bent over her protectively. The breeze sweeping through the barn wrapped the girl's skirts intimately about his legs. *I can have him if I want him. All I've got to do is snap my fingers.* Jo Bell had believed the words when she had said them. She was young, beautiful; and although her beauty was only on the outside, it was enough for a man like Fuller. Was it enough for Smith?

Willa's heart thumped against her ribs with a feeling of incredible sadness. Tears welled up inside her, threatening to burst free. She choked them back as she left the barn. Standing in the warm sunshine, she tried to put her thoughts in perspective. If Smith took Jo Bell away, would Charlie stay here? It would be a blessing for the boy to be rid of the thoughtless sister who took such delight in hurting him.

So why was she feeling such keen disappointment? Smith was not the kind of man she wanted to spend her life with. He was a drunkard, a hellion, a man who would keep a woman at arm's length and never reveal his true feelings. Willa sighed, closed her eyes, and let her shoulders slump wearily.

"I'll see that you get to Sheridan, if that's where you want to go. I told you the old woman wouldn't let them stay."

Smith's voice coming from close behind her caused Willa's eyes to fly open, but she didn't turn.

"They haven't talked to her yet. She wouldn't come to the door."

"There's a cabin out behind the bunkhouse. You and the girl can stay there for the time being. I'll find someone to take you to Buffalo and you can take the stage to Sheridan."

Willa turned and met his eyes evenly. "You're not taking her to Sheridan?"

"Her?" An unpleasant smile crossed his features. "Did you think I would?"

She shrugged. "She's very . . . pretty."

"So is a bear cub, but I don't want to sleep with one."

Willa fought to convey a calm she was far from feeling. She wondered what thoughts lay behind the half-shuttered green eyes that looked into hers. Her gaze was drawn to his mouth. Remembering the kiss, her face flooded with color.

"Charlie asked me to talk to Mrs. Eastwood," she said quickly, controlling her voice with effort.

"Good idea. Then maybe you'll see what you're up against."

"I've got to try—for Charlie."

"I doubt she'll come to the door. So open it, go on in, and get it over with."

Smith's eyes were fixed unwaveringly on hers. There was a terrible intensity in his gaze, as if what she was saying was a matter of life or death to him. Seconds passed. Smith felt that something totally unexpected was happening to him. He was softening toward her, and he didn't like it, didn't like it at all.

"Don't expect the old lady to be nice and polite," he said gruffly, turning on his heel and walking away.

"All right." She breathed a sigh and watched him until he went through the door at the end of the bunkhouse.

Willa rapped on the door for the third time. While she waited, she tucked the loose hair blowing about her face into the knot at the back of her head. The smoothing of her hair was not due to vanity but to nervousness. The breeze behind her billowed the skirt of her blue dress and lifted strands of her hair from the top of her head.

She looked back at the long narrow building that fanned out from the barn. Was Smith watching with that I-told-you-so look on his face? Did he expect her to slink off the porch because this rude, inconsiderate woman refused to come to the door? He had said for her to go on in, and, by golly, she would.

"Mrs. Eastwood?" Willa called out while opening the door. "Mrs. Eastwood? May I come in?"

It took a minute for her eyes to become accustomed to the dim light, but her sense of smell told her immediately that the room had not been aired for quite some time. Wrinkling her nose at the offensive odor of soured milk and a variety of other unpleasant scents she could not identify, she stood just inside the door and gazed at the disorder. The cookstove, the kitchen cabinet and the work counter were covered with soiled pans and dishes. The table was littered with everything from dirty clothes to crystal glasses. The floor, constructed of wide, smooth slabs of oak, was littered with grease and food scraps. In the light coming through the open doorway she saw cobwebs floating from the ceiling beams.

As she hesitated, Willa heard a low moan coming from the far corner of the room. Peering around the table and the high-backed chairs, she saw a large overstuffed couch, and lying on the floor beside it, a thin, gray-haired woman in a heavy black dress. Her forearm was over her eyes.

"Mrs. Eastwood? Oh, my goodness! Are you hurt?"

The moaning sound came again. Willa moved around and peered down at the woman. Even in the dim light she could see that her face was ashen gray. Her mouth was open and with each breath she made the moaning sound, as if she were in pain.

"Mrs. Eastwood—"

Silence except for the moaning.

"Mrs. Eastwood, are you hurt? Do you want me to get help?"

The arm came down and black eyes stared up at Willa.

"What'er ya . . . doin' in my house?"

"Are you ill?"

"I'm not sick. I fell down and hurt my hip is all. Who the hell are ya?"

"My name is Willa Hammer. I came here with Mr. Eastwood's niece and nephew. They came for a visit not knowing their uncle had passed on."

"Liar! He ain't got no kin. Ohh-h—" Maud was suddenly sick. She turned her head and vomit spewed out onto the floor at Willa's feet.

"Mercy me!" Willa found a towel on the counter beside the hand pump, wet it and brought it back to the woman. "Let me wipe your face. Then we'll get you up on the couch."

"Don't . . . touch me—"

Willa's anxious eyes searched the woman's face and saw that her eyes were not focused. She was slipping into unconsciousness.

"Fanny. My little girl. I knew you'd come." Maud's hand went out to Willa. "Fanny, I feel so . . . strange—"

She was out of her head!

Willa was frozen for a second before she took the thin, cold hand in hers. The woman's eyes, black as midnight, were drifting shut. Deep creases in the skin on her face and her sunken eyes spoke of a recent weight loss. Willa tried to keep from breathing because the woman's breath was so putrid.

"Oh, my. You need a doctor—"

With a sudden rush of horror, Willa saw that Mrs. Eastwood's leg was twisted beneath her at a ghastly angle. She hadn't noticed it before because of the heavy black skirt.

"Mrs. Eastwood! Mrs. Eastwood!"

Oh, sweet mother of God! The woman was not only sick, she had a broken leg and possibly a broken hip.

Unaware that her heart was racing like a runaway prairie fire, Willa ran out the door and onto the porch. Her eyes searched frantically for someone, but no one was in sight. She ran toward the bunkhouse.

"Smith!" she yelled. "Smith! Come quick!" She sucked air into her lungs and yelled again. "Smith!"

Smith came out the bunkhouse door on the run. Billy and Charlie were right behind him.

"What is it?" His long stride quickly ate up the distance between them.

"Mrs. East . . . wood," Willa gasped. "She's . . . broken her leg and maybe her hip. And . . . she's sick—"

"She what?" His hands went to her shoulders.

"She fell down. Her leg is bent under her. She's sick too." She grabbed his hand and pulled him toward the house. "Come. We've got to do something—"

"She'd not want me there, Willa. I'll get Charlie and the girl—"

"No! Jo Bell would be useless. Smith, please. Help me. I know a little about nursing."

"Maud hates me. She'll have a fit if I go in the house." They were at the porch. Smith held back.

"She'll just have to have it. I can't get her up off the floor by myself," Willa said crossly.

Smith reluctantly followed Willa into the kitchen and to the corner where Maud lay beside the couch. Her eyes were closed. She was breathing through her half-opened mouth.

"She was out of her head. She thought I was someone called Fanny." Willa pulled up Maud's skirt to show the black-stockinged leg bent beneath her.

Smith snorted an obscenity. "Fanny is her daughter. Good God! It sure as hell is broke."

"It's so dark in here. Will you take the blankets off the windows so we can see?"

"She won't like it."

"That can't be helped. We can't help her if we can't see."

While Smith removed the blankets from the three tall windows; Willa pumped water into a basin and wet a cloth. She bathed Maud's face before she placed the folded wet cloth on her forehead. Smith stood in the middle of the room gazing with disbelief at the filth.

"Godamighty! I knew it was bad, but not this bad."

"Didn't anyone ever come in to see about her?" Willa asked frostily.

His face froze into lines of resentment. "Hold on a damn minute. I'm not welcome here. I don't make a habit of going where I'm not wanted," he said in a tone as frosty as hers had been.

"I'm sorry. Whatever is between you and Mrs. Eastwood is your affair. She needs help now."

"What do you suggest?"

"The obvious. Straighten her leg out and get her up off the floor and onto a bed. She's fainted. Let's do it before she comes to."

A few minutes later Smith sat back on his heels and wiped the sweat from his brow with the back of his hand. Maud had screamed when he had moved her leg. It had unnerved him.

"I think her hip is broken too."

"How long will it take to get a doctor here?"

"Tomorrow, if the one in Buffalo is sober enough to ride. I'll send Plenty to fetch him. But you'll have to write something down on paper for Plenty to give the doctor or he won't come."

"Where can I find pen and paper?"

"Here? You'd have to hunt for it. I'll get some from Billy."

"Smith," she called as he headed for the door. "We've got to get Mrs. Eastwood in a bed. She can't stay here in the kitchen."

"Why not? She's stayed in here for six years."

"She slept in here? Well, for goodness sake. She needs to be in a bed," Willa insisted. "She needs quiet."

"She's had plenty of that." Smith threw up his hands. "Are you staying on?" he asked begrudgingly, as if it pained him to ask.

"Is there anyone else to take care of her?" Willa raised her brows in a gesture of impatience. "I just can't go off and leave her even if *you* don't want me here."

Smith looked at her steadily. "She won't thank you."

"I don't need thanks. I'll do it for myself as much as for her."

Smith's eyes examined her from head to foot. Finally he went out the door.

Willa didn't stop to think that fate had stepped in and provided her with a roof over her head and work to earn her keep. She pushed open the swinging door that led to the other parts of the house. The foyer was as dim as the kitchen had been. A cloth covered the glass on the double front doors. She yanked hard on it and dust settled in a cloud around her as the faded blanket hit the floor.

At the end of the foyer a magnificent clock stood silent and lonely. Its glass door was dust-covered, its brass pendulum dull. Spiders had wrapped it in a webby embrace.

Sliding panel doors on the right of the entry opened to reveal a parlor, tastefully furnished but dust-coated. Mice had chewed holes in the upholstery of the loveseat and built nests in the cotton among the springs. Leaving the doors open,

Willa crossed the hall. The room was a small library. The walls were lined with row after row of books. She gasped with pleasure as she ventured inside to run her fingertips over leather-bound volumes of Longfellow, Nathaniel Hawthorne, and James Fenimore Cooper—a treasure covered with dust. Mice droppings were thick on the library table behind the upholstered sofa that faced a stone fireplace.

Next to the library was a study and between the kitchen and the parlor, a stately dining room. Above the table that seated twelve hung a chandelier with hundreds of dull, dusty prisms encased in cobwebs.

Squares of once colorful Persian carpets covered the floors. At the windows, heavy draperies of thick tapestry decorated with long tassels hung from round wooden poles with fancy corrugated ball ends.

Willa had once seen such an elegant home in a picture book. She shivered. The house was quiet as a tomb; quiet and cold and lonely. She had to shake off the feeling that ghosts wandered up and down the foyer before she could force herself to go up the open stairway to the rooms above.

The second floor consisted of a wide hallway, four richly furnished bedrooms, a small unfurnished room and a water closet with a claw-foot bathing tub. A narrow door opened onto a stairway that led to the attic.

At the front of the house was the main bedroom. After opening the draperies to let in some light, Willa immediately realized that it was strictly a masculine room. The furniture was heavy walnut. A shaving cabinet sat beside a wardrobe that contained only men's clothing. Nothing here indicated that Mrs. Eastwood had ever shared the room with her husband. It was neat as a pin except for years of accumulated dust and cobwebs.

The room across the hall was the one used by Mrs. Eastwood. It was cluttered with a variety of clothing, some items still in their original boxes. Old newspapers and several animal pelts lay scattered; and an unfinished, poorly done piece of embroidery secured in round wooden hoops sat on the table. A set of quilting frames leaned against the wall. Willa instinctively knew that this was where Mrs. Eastwood had once spent most of her time. It would be familiar to her.

Working quickly, Willa cleared the bed by rolling up the covers with the clutter and tossing them into the hall. The mattress was in good condition, and she began a search for bed linens. She found sheets and pillow covers in a chest at the end of the hall. They had a musty smell as did everything else in the chest, but they were clean and there was no evidence of mice. Willa made up the bed and hurried back down to the kitchen.

After rewetting the cloth, she knelt beside the still unconscious woman and placed it on her forehead.

"I've had some nursing experience, Mrs. Eastwood, and the doctor will be here tomorrow. I'll be here. You'll not be alone. Can you hear me, Mrs. Eastwood?"

No response.

Smith came in with a tablet and a stub of a pencil. Jo Bell was with him. She stood just inside the door with her mouth turned down in what Willa recognized as her sulky expression.

"Write what you're going to and Plenty will be on his way."

Willa sat down at the table. After a few minutes she tore the sheet from the tablet and handed it to Smith.

"I told the doctor she has a broken leg and possibly a broken hip and that she is also sick with a fever. Do you think he'll come?"

"He'll come. I don't know what good he'll be, but he'll come. This place needs a cleaning. Jo Bell will help you."

"I ain't doin' no nigger work, and that's that," Jo Bell sputtered. "Phew! It stinks in here."

"If you don't work, you won't eat." Smith said the words flatly, leaving no room for argument, and walked out.

"Hear that? Don't that beat all? He's sure gettin' high 'n' mighty all of a sudden. He's only a hired hand here. He don't own nothin' 'n' he ain't bossin' me." Jo Bell looked around, took a deep breath, then continued. "Papa said Uncle Oliver was rich. But things is so run down he must'a run out of money."

"Jo Bell . . . hush," Willa whispered. "If Mrs. Eastwood comes to she'll hear you."

"I don't care."

"She's your aunt and she's very sick."

"She ain't no blood kin. Charlie can help if you're bent on cleanin' up this place. Papa said he didn't raise me to do nigger work."

"Things will go more smoothly and be more pleasant if you do your share, Jo Bell."

"Papa said ugly girls work 'n' pretty girls like me was to be looked at. Charlie knows that he's suppose—"

Jo Bell stopped speaking when Smith stepped into the kitchen carrying a slab of wood, obviously a door he'd removed. He placed it on the floor beside Maud.

"Your papa was mighty wrong about a lot of things," he said curtly to Jo Bell. "Charlie will not do *your* work. He has his own work to do. You *will* help here in the house or you will leave."

"Me 'n' Charlie are goin' anyhow."

"Not Charlie. You."

"All by myself?"

"All by yourself. Charlie is staying and so is Willa."

"Charlie will go if I tell him to."

"He won't. I've hired him on to work here. Here's the coal hod and the shovel. Clean the ashes out of the cookstove so I can build a fire. Willa will need hot water."

Jo Bell stared at him as if he had lost his mind. "It's dirty. I can't do that." Her eyes began to fill with self-pitying tears.

"You can and you will. Goddammit, you will!"

"I won't 'n' ya can't make me." She sniffed prettily.

"I think I can."

"Why'er ya bein' m-mean to me?"

"You'll not be petted here like you were a young virgin being groomed for a harem. You pull your weight or get out of the harness and go it alone."

"What's a . . . harem?"

"How are we going to get Mrs. Eastwood upstairs?" Willa asked quickly in order to prevent what was sure to be a nasty scene between Smith and Jo Bell. "I've made up a bed—"

"Billy and Charlie will be here in a minute."

"Moving her will be terribly painful. Let's lift her onto the door before she comes to."

Smith's eyes went from Willa to the woman on the floor and back again. He closed them for an instant and clenched his jaws. Willa saw pure agony on his face.

"Smith?" Willa went to him and placed her hand on his arm and looked up into his face. "What is it?"

"You can't know how I hate to touch her."

"Try not to think about anything that happened between you in the past. Think of her as someone you don't know. She needs our help or she will die. She may die anyway," she finished softly.

"She despises me."

Willa's heart contracted painfully at the sight of misery on his face. Her mind groped for something comforting to say. The man was a curious mixture of compassion and bitterness. As she looked into his eyes, she had the feeling that he was allowing her to see a glimpse of the real man beneath the rough exterior.

"There are times when we have to do things that go against the grain. But if we don't do them, we show ourselves to be small and petty. You're strong, Smith. You're strong and she's weak."

"What 'er yawl whisperin' about?" Jo Bell's pouting voice broke the spell. "What 'er yawl sayin' that ya don't want me to hear?"

Smith's hand moved to cover Willa's. Realization filtered through his mind slowly at first, and then burst upon his consciousness. This small lovely woman was completely without guile. She could become very important to him. *He must not allow that to happen.* He sensed a mystery, a loneliness about her, but whatever it was, it inspired confidence. Even while thinking these thoughts, he bent his head until his lips were close to her ear.

"I . . . can't overcome years of bitterness in five minutes. I'll do this because you ask me. Let's get it over with."

It was one of the hardest things Smith had ever had to do. Until today he had not touched Maud Eastwood in all the fifteen years he had known her. Although she was as limp as a rag doll, when he scooped one arm beneath her buttocks and the other under her legs, she screamed as if he were torturing her. Willa took her shoulders and they eased her over onto the door.

In order to keep from thinking of how the bitter, contrary woman continued to make his life miserable, Smith kept his thoughts on Willa. In spite of all she had endured the last few weeks, she had kept her pride, her dignity.

What would he have done if she had not been here? Unable to summon help, Maud would have died. Not that he cared a wit for the old witch, but he had promised Oliver—

CHAPTER
* 15 *

Maud was carried up the broad stairway with Willa walking alongside to be sure she didn't roll off the slab of wood. Still in a swoon, Maud screamed again when Smith and Billy lifted her onto the bed.

Billy and Charlie hurried back down the stairs as if they had stumbled into a private sanctuary. Smith paused in the hallway and drew in a deep quivering breath. In spite of his desire to get out of the house, his curiosity forced him to look around. He had never been in any room except the kitchen and yet the house seemed familiar to him.

Oliver had talked about it many times. The plan was the same as that of his home in West Virginia, which had been destroyed during the first few months of the War. When Oliver and his sister had inherited money from their grandparents in England, Oliver had invested his in a gold strike, taken his profits, bought land and built a replica of his old home. He would be sick to the depth of his soul, Smith thought now, if he could see the state it was in. Oliver had loved every stick and stone in the house and had taken great pride in maintaining it.

The door to the room across from Maud's was open. Smith looked in. A pair of Oliver's boots were sitting beside a wardrobe and his shaving tools were on a shelf beneath the hanging mirror. The big leather chair still had the shape of Oliver's robust body imprinted in it. A pain so fierce that he almost reeled stabbed Smith's heart. He leaned against the door frame for a long moment before he stomped down the stairs two at a time.

He needed a drink!

When he entered the kitchen, Jo Bell was sitting at the table, her face buried in her folded arms. From beneath a cascade of shiny dark curls came the sound of dainty, pitiful sobs. Smith had to suppress the desire to kick the chair out from under her. Instead he grasped her arm and yanked her to her feet.

"You worthless little . . . man-teaser!"

"I . . . I can't get the door . . . o-open." Her violet eyes sparkled with tears and her lips trembled. She tried to get close to Smith to lean against him, but his hands on her arms pushed her away from him.

Smith turned and kicked the handle on the cookstove with his booted foot. The door to the fire box swung open.

"It's open. Have it cleaned out by the time I get back with wood to start a fire." At the door he turned to glare at her. "I meant what I said. As long as you're on this ranch, you'll pull your weight."

"It ain't *yore* ranch," she muttered under her breath.

Smith passed the woodshed without a word or a nod to Charlie and Billy, who had resumed the work they had been doing when they had been called to the house. He shoved open the door and went into the bunkhouse. On his way to the kitchen he pulled off his shirt. After washing himself with warm water and Billy's strong lye soap, he rummaged in the cupboard beside the stove until he found a bottle of whiskey.

He uncorked it and took a long drink. When he thought of taking another, the image of a woman with big sad eyes made him change his mind and put the cork back in the bottle.

"Is she gonna die?" Billy asked when Smith came out again, allowing the screen door to slam shut behind him. He was stacking the wood he and Charlie had cut with a two-man saw.

"How'n hell do I know? I know it'll about kill her to have someone in the house using what's hers." Smith shoved his arms into a clean shirt, buttoned it and stuffed the tail into his breeches.

"I guess Jo Bell and Willa can stay if they're goin' to take care of her," Charlie said with relief.

"Willa is taking care of her. Your sister is a worthless little twit who thinks she's something that should be set on a shelf and looked at. How did she get to be so spoiled?"

"Papa," Charlie said with a shamed face. "He just always doted on her."

"No one is going to wait on her here, Charlie, and that includes you."

"She's never had to do anythin' and she don't know how."

Smith had to suppress the vile language that rushed to his lips. "Then it's time she learned. Willa will have her hands full taking care of Maud. She lived in the kitchen, Billy. Slept there. It smells like a privy."

"Now ain't this a fine kettle a fish." Billy snorted a word Charlie didn't know the meaning of. "Pity she didn't die right off. We'd a been shed of her."

"Did you ever know Maud to do anything to accommodate anyone?"

"Well, now that I think on it—no."

"There's a couch in the kitchen that's got to be hauled out and burned. It's beyond cleaning up." Smith loaded his arm with kindling, then sat back on his heels and looked up at Billy. "I'll need you and Charlie to help me carry it out."

"Why shore."

Smith stood. "Cook up enough grub for the women, Billy. It'll be a while before they can cook a meal in the house."

Billy and Charlie followed Smith into the kitchen. Jo Bell had half-filled the coal hod with ashes. She held her skirt back away from the stove with one hand and with the shovel at arm's length was taking small amounts of ashes from the fire box and dumping them in the hod. She was still crying. Smith ignored her and gave Charlie a warning frown.

"Jehoshaphat! Ain't she never cleaned in here? If Oliver knowed, he'd have him a pure-dee old—" The rest of his words were lost in the noise made by the kindling being dumped into the woodbox.

"Let's get the couch out," Smith said irritably.

Billy walked over and looked at it. "Phew! It's e'nuff to gag a maggot. Turn it up on the side. We'll slide it out."

After grunting, pushing and swearing, the three men got the couch through the door. Charlie was the last to go out. Jo Bell tugged on his sleeve.

"C-Charlie, help me. Smith is so m-mean—"

"Leave him alone," Smith snarled, coming to the door. "Go on, Charlie."

"I . . . I hate you! I'm gettin' all dirty—" she wailed.

"I'll take this end," Smith said, ignoring her. "Both of you take the other end."

Upstairs Willa wished for a cloth to tie over her nose as she bent over the woman on the bed. While she lay on the floor, Mrs. Eastwood had lost control of her bowels. That combined with her sour stomach and the odor of her unwashed body made Willa's stomach turn. Her main concern was to get Maud clean and comfortable. She was forced to use the shears from the sewing basket and cut up the front of the heavy black dress before she could remove it. After covering Maud's naked body with a sheet, she rolled the dress and the soiled undergarments in a tight roll and carried them downstairs.

She reached the kitchen as Smith was coming in the back door.

"I need a tub of water to soak her clothes."

"We're burning the couch. Throw them on the fire. You don't have to wash that mess."

"Oh, but——"

Smith snatched the bundle from her hand and threw it out onto the back porch.

"He thinks he . . . knows ever'thin'," Jo Bell whined in a low tone. She wiped her tear-stained face with her hand and left dark smears on her cheeks. "I don't like him, none a'tall."

Willa worked the pump handle to fill the bucket she found beneath the counter.

"Didn't you hear me, ma'am?" Jo Bell snapped.

"I heard you. Have you seen any soap?"

Smith answered. "Good God! There should be some here somewhere." He yanked open a drawer and found a box containing bars of soap from Sears Roebuck. "What else do you need?"

"She hasn't eaten in a while. She'll need something. But first I've got to clean her up."

"Do you need the girl to help you?"

Willa glanced at Jo Bell standing beside the coal hod full of ashes. Her face was mutinous.

"No. I can manage. Later . . . there will be piles of washing."

"There's a wash house, but Maud hasn't used it for a long time."

"She's in terrible pain. Is there any laudanum?"

"Billy usually keeps some around. He's making splints to go on her leg."

"Is she goin' to die?" Jo Bell asked belligerently.

"Not if I can help it." Willa picked up the bucket of water and started for the door.

"Why do ya care, ma'am? She ain't yore aunt. She don't want ya here anymore'n she wants me 'n' Charlie." Jo Bell's voice reached into the hall.

"She's a human being. I'd even do the same for you, Jo Bell," Willa said irritably over her shoulder.

Maud came to while Willa was washing her body.

"What . . . what'er ya doin'? Get away! Oh . . . my Gawd . . . Oh, Lordy—" She tried to push Willa's hands away.

"Shhh— Be still, Mrs. Eastwood. I'm washing you. You had an accident and didn't make it to the chamber pot," she said matter-of-factly.

"Liar!" Maud shouted, her face twisted with pain. "Cover me up, damn you! Get out!"

"No," Willa said firmly. "You can't be alone, Mrs. Eastwood."

"How'd I get up here?"

"Smith Bowman, Mr. Coe and your nephew, Charlie, carried you up here."

"No!" The strangled cry brust from her throat. "Noooo . . ." she whispered hoarsely, and the word was a sob in her throat. She rolled her head from side to side. The eyes that clung to Willa's face were wild and bright. "That . . . that bastard come in my h-house! I gotta get up. Fanny'll come. Fanny'll . . . run him off—"

"Don't move!" Willa said quickly. "We've got your leg

laid out straight. Mr. Coe is making splints to keep it still until the doctor gets here.''

''I ain't . . . havin' no dad-blasted butcher—'' Maud almost choked on the words.

''Calm down. Please lie quietly. It'll not hurt nearly as much if you stay still. Mr. Coe has some laudanum. It'll help you rest until the doctor gets here.''

''No!'' Maud's claw-like hand clutched at Willa. ''Noooo . . .'' she screeched. ''He'll kill me!''

''No,'' Willa said soothingly. ''I'll be here. He'll set your leg and look at your hip. He'll tell me how to take care of you.''

''He'll kill m-me—'' Maud began to cry.

''Doctors take an oath to help people—''

''Not the doctor, ya stupid fool! Smith! Smith will . . . kill me!''

''Smith? You're wrong. He helped me get you up here. He has sent someone to fetch the doctor.''

''He'll kill me!'' Maud tried to rear up, but Willa held her down.

''Don't distress yourself, Mrs. Eastwood. Mr. Bowman won't harm you. I would bet my life on it.''

''But . . . but . . . he killed Oliver!'' Maud began to cry in earnest.

Willa looked down at the woman in open-mouthed amazement. Why would she say such a thing unless it were true? Willa tried not to think of it as she washed as much of Maud as she could without disturbing her leg and her hip and then worked a nightdress over her head. The dresser drawers were full of gowns, stockings and underclothing that had never been worn. When she finished dressing Maud she found a hairbrush and brushed her hair and plaited it.

''Don't worry about anything but staying still. I'll be right here with you. No one will hurt you. I promise. I've had some experience in nursing, Mrs. Eastwood. My mother was a good nurse and she taught me a lot. You need to eat something, then rest as much as you can. I know you're in pain, but don't you feel better now that you're clean?''

It was hard to gauge Maud's reaction to what was being done for her. After her storm of weeping she lay as limp as a rag, her eyes closed. She continued to breathe steadily.

Willa carried the pail of water to the water closet at the end of the hall. She wondered if she could dump the water in the closet bowl, but decided against it because it looked as if it hadn't been used for years.

She paused unnoticed in the doorway of the kitchen when she reached it. Smith was scraping the inside of an iron skillet. Water on the cookstove was sending up a cloud of steam. A washtub had been brought in and placed on two facing kitchen chairs. It was full of dirty dishes and hot soapy water. Jo Bell, with her arms in dishwater up to her elbows, was washing the dishes and putting them in another tub of hot water. Her eyes were swollen from crying. She sniffed and every so often she sobbed.

"Hush up your dammed snivelling and scald the dishes. Godamighty! You make more noise than a dying calf." The hard tone in Smith's voice left no room for argument.

Willa was sure that no man had ever talked to Jo Bell in that tone of voice and that she was finding it hard to come to terms with the fact that she hadn't charmed Smith as she had charmed other men.

The kitchen now looked and smelled like a different room. The cabinet had been washed; its doors and drawers hung open to allow it to dry. The tin flour bin and sifter had been washed. The table, chairs, and even the cookstove had been scrubbed. Cobwebs had been swept from the walls and ceiling and the floor was still wet with soapsuds. The rank offensive odor had been replaced with the scent of wet wood and strong lye soap.

Smith turned to face Willa. Neither spoke while they studied each other. His blond hair was damp with sweat and curled close to his head. He was tall and broad and, she supposed, handsome in a completely masculine way. Willa seemed to lose herself in the depth of his green eyes. He appeared to be less dangerous here than he had been at Byers' Station, but Maud's words continued to pound in her head. *He killed Oliver*. She wanted to ask him if it were true; and if he had done such a terrible deed, why was he still here.

The curious stillness between them, the waiting uneasy silence that deepened, seemed to push them apart. Only Willa's thick-lashed eyes and the faint color that lay across her cheeks betrayed the fact that she was not completely at ease.

"You've done a lot in a short time," she said, feeling the need to break the terrible silence.

"Billy and Charlie helped." Smith continued to study her thoughtfully. Damp hair stuck to her forehead and she looked tired enough to drop. "Maud still alive?" he asked bluntly.

"Of course, or I'd have told you. It's hard to tell if she's sleeping or if she's just ignoring me."

"Billy will be in to help you put the splints on her leg."

"I'd like to do that before I try to feed her something. Afterwards I'll give her a few drops of the laudanum. She's in a lot of pain." Willa crossed the room to the door and threw the water out into the yard. "Where is Buddy?"

"He's all right. He's with Charlie."

"I . . . wish I was—"

Willa glanced at Jo Bell and away. Embarrassed, she didn't think the girl's comment worthy of a response. She glanced quickly at Smith and saw the frown on his face deepen.

"Mrs. Eastwood's room is so full I hardly have room to move around. Will it be all right if I take some of the things out and put them in the storage room at the end of the hall?"

Smith shrugged. "Do what you want if you can stand her yelling about it." His voice was brisk.

"There are quilting frames, coats and dresses, and stacks of catalogs. There's even a stereopticon still in the box. Other boxes with views of Norway, Sweden and Denmark look as if they've never been opened. I'll need help getting that stuff out of there."

"Charlie will help you."

"How come Charlie can help her 'n' he can't help me?" Jo Bell broke into a fresh spat of sobbing.

Shocked by the intensity of her disgust with the girl, Willa hurriedly left the room.

Smith watched her go. Willa Hammer was unlike any woman he had ever met—soft, pretty as a wild rose, calm, sensible, and compassionate. He wondered for a brief instant about this awful physical attraction he felt for her. He needed a woman, he decided, any woman to whisper sexy words in his ear, to look at him with a lustful look in her eyes.

He scowled. Hell, he didn't need a woman who would tie him down. He swore to himself. He'd sure made a mess of things. He'd give a farm in Georgia, if he had one, if he hadn't kissed her and started all these fanciful wonderings.

By evening Willa was so tired she felt dull and dim-witted. Maud's room was clean and she slept, her leg held in the splints and wrapped with soft cloth. Fresh air came in through the partly opened window. The room was neat; and although it was not as clean as Willa wanted it to be, it would have to do. A china pitcher and bowl sat on the commode and clean towels hung on the rack above. A lamp with a clean chimney sat on the bedside table and cast a rosy light over the room.

Charlie had been wonderful help. After carrying out the boxes and quilting frames, he had found a rocking chair in one of the other rooms, cleaned off the dust and cobwebs and set it beside Maud's bed. It had been his idea to ask Billy for a bucket with a lid for the soiled pads Willa took from between Maud's legs.

Maud had become increasingly more difficult. When Willa tried to feed her the beef stew, she raved that Smith was going to poison her and refused to open her mouth. Willa reassured her by eating from the bowl and managed to get her to accept a few bites of food. After the meal Willa slipped a few drops of the laudanum in Maud's drinking water and soon after that she was asleep.

Willa dropped wearily down in the chair beside the bed, leaned her head against the high back and watched the shadows created by the flickering lamplight play on the walls. She'd had nothing to eat since breakfast. The full day of hard work had taken a toll on her strength. She was so tired that she had no desire to stir from where she sat. Closing her eyes, she gave herself up to the dreamless state between repose and wakefulness. One second she was awake and the next she was asleep.

"Willa."

From far away she heard someone speak her name. She opened her eyes, and as her vision cleared, she saw the tall man standing in the doorway. It was Smith. His intense green eyes were on her face. She looked at him dully for a moment, dark circles emphasizing the blueness of her eyes.

"Flitter! I must have fallen asleep." Her voice was barely above a whisper.

"Come on down and eat your supper."

She stood and looked down at Maud to be sure she was

still sleeping, then rounded the end of the bed and headed for the door. Smith moved out of the way and she passed through. A lamp had been lit at the top of the stairs and another in the hallway below. The house was as quiet as a tomb.

"It's a lovely house," Willa said as they descended the stairs. "Lovely and sad. It should be lived in."

"Only the kitchen has been lived in for the last six years."

"Was it ever a happy place?"

"I wouldn't know. It was off-limits to me."

"Mice are happy here," she said in an attempt at humor.

"They've got the run of the place. I've a notion to bring in a couple of barn cats. They'd clean them out in a hurry."

"I hope the mice don't chew up the books."

"You like books?" They were at the kitchen door.

She paused and looked up at him. "I love books. If you have books and like to read, you'll never be lonely."

"I never had much time for it."

"There's a wonderful library here—"

"I know, but I've not seen it."

Willa walked ahead of him into the well-lighted kitchen. It was spotlessly clean. A cloth covered the table. The lamp chimneys glistened and the copper teakettle sent up a plume of steam. A lamp sat on the table, another in a wall bracket over the work counter. A delicious aroma came from the pot bubbling on the stove.

"A good cleaning does wonders," Willa said softly, then smiled, causing her eyes to glow. "It smells different, too."

"Amen to that. Billy sent in a pot of stew and fresh bread."

"I didn't realize it, but I'm starved."

"Sit down and dig in," Smith took a bowl from the shelf above the work counter and filled it from the pot on the stove.

"I can do that. I'm not used to being waited on." Willa was at the wash basin washing her hands.

"I'm not used to waiting on anyone, so we're even. Sit."

She did, and helped herself to a slice of sourdough bread and spread it with butter.

"Has everyone else had supper?"

"All but the little twit. She was so put out because she had to work that she refused supper, thinking to make her brother feel guilty."

"Does he? Feel guilty, I mean."

"I suppose so. Habits of years are seldom broken in a day. He keeps making excuses for her."

Smith placed the bowl and a spoon on the table, then returned to the stove and poured coffee into two heavy china cups.

"Where is she?"

"In the wagon." He sat down across from Willa and fastened his hands around his cup.

"She can't stay out there by herself."

"She can tonight. Later when the men come in she'll have to stay in here. She'd start a war among that wild bunch."

"How many men work here?"

"Six beside me, Plenty and Billy. Sant Rudy, a friend of mine, comes and goes as it suits him."

"This is beautiful country. I wish I knew more about ranching."

"Planning to take up land?" His eyes teased her.

"No." She laughed lightly. "I plan to make my living fixing clocks."

"Good Lord. I never heard of a woman clock-fixer."

"You have now. I'm good at it, too."

"Old Maud must have a couple around here that need fixing."

"Why do you call her *old* Maud?" Willa wished immediately that she hadn't asked the question when she saw the smile leave his eyes. A crimson tide flooded her face. "I'm sorry. That was rude of me. Papa Igor told me repeatedly that it was not polite to pry into a person's private affairs.''

Smith shrugged. ''If that's the case, I shouldn't ask you about yours.''

''No, you shouldn't. Jo Bell told you how I came to be with them. She took great delight in the telling.''

''I remember.''

Willa placed the spoon beside the bowl. Her eyes were bright with unshed tears when she looked at the man sitting across from her.

''Papa Igor did not deserve to be hanged,'' she said quietly and with great dignity. ''He did nothing any other man would not have done in his place. I don't know why they burned our house and ran me out of town unless it was ignorant superstition. They might have killed me if Mr. Frank hadn't come along and pulled me up in his wagon. I'll tell you about it if you like. I have nothing to hide.''

Smith's eyes searched hers for a long silent moment. He swallowed dryly as he realized she was refusing to humiliate herself by letting tears fill her eyes. A well of protectiveness surged up within him. He could see the heaving of her breasts even though the dress she wore was loose, and the thought of the sweet softness he had felt when he had held her, caused his own heart to lurch suddenly.

He reached across the table and covered her hand with his.

CHAPTER

* 16 *

"I have no right to ask you anything," Smith said.

"I want to tell you. I don't want you to think that Papa was a bad man. His appearance would lead one to think that he was, but he went out of his way to be kind. I'll never forgive myself for not going into town with him that night to deliver the clock he had fixed. Papa always tried to shield me from anything unpleasant. He told me to go on to bed and I did. If I had gone with him, I might have been able to prevent what happened."

She suddenly became aware that his hand was covering hers and slowly pulled it free.

"I only know what Mr. Frank told me. He said that Papa shot two men, but he didn't think that he had killed them. He said the men had taunted Papa, made insulting remarks about me, and then stripped off Papa's shirt and bared the hump on his back." Willa's throat clogged and she swallowed repeatedly before she could go on. "It was probably just more humiliation than Papa could bear . . . at the moment."

"They hanged him for protecting himself?"

"You see, Papa was a hunchback, and about five years

ago big lumps grew on his face, distorting his features. It didn't matter to me that he was not . . . pleasant to look at. He . . . was dear to me. I loved him for what he was on the inside. And . . . he loved me. Some people are not tolerant of someone who is different. Papa and I learned to keep to ourselves. As a result, some thought I was uppity. It wasn't that at all.

"When I was younger, I wanted to be included in parties and picnics and other social gatherings. Unfortunately mothers were afraid their sons would want to court me and girls didn't want to associate with the daughter of a hunchback. Now I realize they were waiting for me to grow a hump. It was ridiculous, of course. There was no danger of that even if I had been Papa Igor's real daughter."

The shadow of hurt he saw in her eyes cut him to the quick. His hand on the table formed a fist.

"Do you have other kin?" he asked.

"Not that I know of. My real father left me and my mother when I was a baby. My mother called him an irresponsible boy."

Willa told him about how she and her mother had come to be with Igor Hammer and about the schools she had attended.

"At times, due to Papa's teachings, I knew more than the teacher and, of course, that rankled the teacher and made a wider gap between me and my classmates." She tried a weak little laugh that didn't quite come off. "I soon learned to keep my knowledge to myself."

"I take it you didn't stay very long in one place."

"No. We traveled from town to town selling and fixing clocks, and Papa and I continued to do that after Mama died."

Smith listened intently.

"Life was painful for Papa and becoming more so." A terrible sadness was reflected in her eyes. "In a way, it's better that he no longer has to suffer, but the way he died was so unfair. He should have been allowed to die with some dignity.''

Die with dignity. The words knifed through Smith. He looked away from her and gritted his teeth against the pain of remembering Oliver's broken, bloody body lying in the dirt. When he looked back at Willa, she was gazing intently at her laced fingers resting on the table.

''I'd like to stay here for a while and take care of Mrs. Eastwood. I'm a good nurse. She needs someone and I need a place to stay.''

''Can you put up with her meanness? I doubt if you'll ever do anything to please her.''

''You would be suprised at what I've put up with in my lifetime. Are you sure Mrs. Eastwood isn't blood kin to Jo Bell?'' She lifted her eyes to his, a smile tilted the corner of her lips.

Smith smiled back, not only with his lips, but with his eyes. It made him look young—handsome.

''That wasn't nice of me,'' Willa said quickly. ''I don't know Mrs. Eastwood.''

''You will.'' His smile faded. ''You'll earn your money.''

''I don't expect . . . much. I'd not take any, but I don't even own the clothes on my back. They belong to someone named Starr who left her trunk with the Franks.''

''I heard about her from Charlie.''

''Shouldn't Mrs. Eastwood's daughter be notified?''

He snorted an obscenity. ''Forget her. She wants nothing to do with Maud or this place. She's hooked a big fish and Maud would only cramp her style.''

''It's hard to believe a girl would feel that way about her mother.'' Willa carried her empty bowl to the work bench and dipped it into the pan of dishwater.

''Believe it. She and Maud are cut from the same cloth.''

Smith turned his head so that he could watch her. How could a woman who had worked as hard as she had today still look so faultlessly clean? She had braided her hair in one long rope. It hung down her back to her waist. She looked more child than woman. But this was no empty-headed girl. He had known that from the start. She wasn't feeling sorry for herself or expecting anything for nothing.

Willa washed her soup bowl and coffee cup and dried them on the cloth that hung on the oven door.

"If Maud's hip is broken, she may never get out of that bed." Smith's words dropped into the silence.

"You don't like her, do you?" Willa turned to look at him, knowing that her question was ridiculous.

"No, I don't."

"Then why do you stay on here? You're a man. You're free. You could go anywhere you want."

"You think I'm here because I hope to get this place when she's gone." He drew in a ragged breath. "Yeah, I can see that's what's in your mind."

"I didn't think that at all. But I did wonder why you stay. Especially after Mrs. Eastwood said that—"

"—I'd killed Oliver. Is that what she said?" He smiled cruelly. "Let me tell you one thing, lady. The minute that old woman up there breathes her last, I'll high-tail it off this place like I was propelled from a slingshot and I'll never come back."

"What will happen to this house?"

"I don't give a damn what happens to it. No. I take that back. I hope it burns to the ground. I'd rather see that happen than have it sit here and decay like a rotten old pumpkin left in the garden patch."

His coldness mangled her nerves. She walked to the door, aware that he was watching her.

"What time do you think the doctor will be here? I don't

want to give Mrs. Eastwood too much laudanum. She should be awake to talk to him.''

"I won't know until Plenty gets back. That should be any time now." Smith's eyes clung to her. It had been damn pleasant talking with her. She was so confident, so calm, and so damn pretty. "Willa—I'll be down here if you need anything. Billy will be in later to sit with Maud so you can get some sleep."

"I'm glad you'll be here. This house is kind of . . . spooky." The words rolled off her tongue easily and she smiled. A dimple he hadn't noticed before appeared in her cheek.

"Yeah, it is."

Willa's head whirled in a quickening eddy of confused thoughts as she went up the stairs. She had told Smith more about herself than she had ever told another person. Why? Her mind argued that it was madness to think of him as anything but a hellion who was staying on here for reasons of his own.

He hadn't denied that he had killed Oliver Eastwood.

He thoroughly disliked Mrs. Eastwood. But he hadn't abandoned her. He seemed concerned for her welfare. The man was a puzzle. Papa Igor would say that Smith was fighting a war with himself.

When Willa entered the room, Maud was still sleeping, but not peacefully. She was moaning and rolling her head. Willa lifted the covers and moved her good leg well away from the one encased in the splint. She pulled on the sheet she had placed under Maud to change her position and take some weight off her hip. After a few minutes Maud stopped fidgeting and breathed more evenly.

Willa sank down in the chair and looked at the woman on the bed. She might have been pretty at one time. Her hair would have been dark brown. Now it was thin and streaked with gray. Her missing jaw teeth would have filled out her cheeks. The hands that lay on her chest were long and bony, almost claw-like. Willa guessed Maud's age to be somewhat older than her own mother would be had she lived. Bitterness had taken a toll, not only on this beautiful house, but on its mistress.

With the lamp wick turned down until only a faint glow lighted the room, Willa slipped her feet out of the moccasins and rested them on the edge of the mattress. Bending over the bed was hard on her back. Tomorrow she would ask Smith if they could put blocks under the legs to raise it.

The moment she closed her lids she saw his face; green eyes, smooth cheeks, wide firm lips and shaggy blond hair. He had a look of loneliness about him. Willa's eyes flew open. She had to stop thinking about him and any problems he might have connected with the Eastwoods. She had plenty of problems of her own. Thank God one had been solved for the moment. Because of Mrs. Eastwood's misfortune, she could stay here for a few weeks, maybe even months.

In spite of her resolve not to think about him, her thoughts moved determinedly back to the man downstairs. Was it her imagination, or was he more relaxed in her presence than he had been before? He certainly wasn't as explosive as he had been back at Byers' Station. Did he drink like that often? Mr. Byers seemed to be under the impression that he did.

Willa was sure Jo Bell had been most surprised that Smith hadn't fallen under her spell as she had expected him to. Willa smiled when that thought floated through her mind. She continued to smile when she remembered Jo Bell with her arms in dishwater up to her elbows.

Willa woke from a sound sleep. Her first instinct was to scratch her ankles. When she reached for them, her terror-filled eyes focused on a large rat on the bed beside her feet. Its sharp claws had awakened her when it had walked across her ankles toward Maud's face. Now it sat perfectly still, its beady eyes on her. Its hairy body was almost a foot long; an even longer tail stretched out behind it.

A scream tore from her throat as her feet hit the floor. The rat scampered across Maud's still form and jumped from the bed. Instead of heading for the door, it turned to face Willa. It appeared to be unafraid and moved back toward the bed. Fearing that it would come under the bed and attack her bare feet, Willa jumped up into the rocking chair.

"Smith! S-Sm . . . ith!" Willa's terror gave strength to her voice. She looked for something to throw, but there was nothing within reach and she was too terrified to move. "Sm . . . ith!" Cold sweat was on her body, cold fear in her heart.

Suddenly the rat turned and ran out the door. A second later Smith was there. Barefoot and shirtless, he paused in the doorway, his eyes on her face.

"A . . . rat! A big . . . one—"

"I saw it. It's gone. Ran out just as I got here."

"It was . . . on the bed—" Willa trembled so that she could barely talk.

"Did it bite you? Or Maud?" Quick strides brought Smith around the bed to her side.

"No. Oh . . . Smith—" Words failed her after she cried out his name. The eyes that looked at him were large and fearful.

He reached for her. She launched herself into his arms. He hugged her against his chest and stroked her back. Her arms went around his neck. She clung, her teeth clamped against chattering. She was trembling violently.

Smith felt the pounding of her heart against his chest. His need to soothe and protect her was far greater than his need to gratify the physical desire the touch of her soft, woman's body demanded. He wanted to hold her, calm her with gentle words, tell her not to be afraid. He would protect her with his life.

By God, he would!

"You're all right. Don't be afraid. It's gone," he consoled in a whisper.

His lips caressed her hair, his hand cupped the back of her head, holding her securely to him. He held a treasure here in his arms. The thought struck him with a soul-jarring force. Suddenly aware that he was holding her off the floor, he allowed her to slide down his body until her bare feet reached the tops of his.

"Willa." He drew her name out into a long, soft caress. "You're all right now. It won't come back."

She shuddered with revulsion. "If there's one . . . there's more—"

"You're shaking. Are you still afraid?"

"I'm not afraid . . . now. It's nerves, I expect," she managed shakily and drew in a deep breath.

"You scared the living hell out of me," he whispered hoarsely—his breath warm against her ear.

"I'm sorry, but . . . please— Don't leave me alone up here."

"I won't. I won't."

Fear had drained Willa of all reason. She hadn't been held so tenderly since she was a little girl. It was wonderful to be wrapped in his arms, to feel safe, to realize that he cared that she was frightened.

"I'm so glad you're here—"

"Ah . . . Willa—" Smith hoarsely whispered her name, his lips against her brow.

Willa didn't know she had moved her head until his mouth closed over hers and moved with supplicant precision until, unknowingly, her lips parted, yielded, and accepted the wandering of his. Her trembling increased and unfamiliar sensations prickled her body.

Their lips met in joint seeking. She needed the strength and security of his warm, male body. He needed her gentle touch to heal the wounds in his soul. Her mouth was wonderfully warm, sweet beyond his wildest imagination. He moved his head and kissed the soft skin of her temples, then took her lips again. It was a hungry, almost desperate kiss, an eager, primitive seeking, but Smith was wise enough not to spoil the mood by demanding more than the instant of sharing.

He looked down at her, his lips just inches from hers, his breath on her mouth, shaken by the almost heart-stopping realization that he had lost some part of his heart to her.

Willa was pressed so tightly to his naked chest that she could feel his heart beating against her breast. His skin smelled of soap and she liked it. His mouth had tasted of tobacco and she liked that, too. She tilted her head. They looked into each other's eyes.

His face was different. A warm light shone from his eyes. It was hard to believe this man who watched her with such tenderness in his eyes and who held her so protectively was the uncaring, arrogant, demanding person she had met in Mr. Byers' barn.

He hadn't kissed her for any reason other than he wanted to.

She drew in a deep, quivering breath and began to smile. The kiss had shaken her to her toes and sent her thoughts flying in every direction. Her insides felt jittery and she unashamedly admitted to herself that she hungered for more.

The dimple in her cheek flirted with him. Looking down into her wide, clear eyes Smith saw no anger, no disgust at what they had shared. Joyous relief washed over him.

"Are you all right now?" Still holding her securely to him, his fingers brushed the hair back over her ear.

"I think so. Rats and snakes scare me to death."

"I'll put out some bait and get rid of them. Would you feel better if I brought Buddy in here to stay with you?"

"Oh, yes. Do you think Mrs. Eastwood will mind?"

"We'll not ask her. I'd think that she'd rather have a dog under her bed than a rat on it."

Willa's hands slid from around his neck, down over his shoulders to his chest. She felt no self-consciousness about being close to him, but she did feel the steady thrum of his heart beneath her palm, his breath in her hair, and she was acutely aware of the smooth warm flesh of his body.

"I'm not usually so easily frightened—"

"—Yeah. I remember—"

"I couldn't reach anything to throw at it."

"I should have armed you with a skillet." His eyes teased her. His smile spread charm all over his face.

She grinned back at him. Neither seemed to be in a hurry to separate from the other. Her bare feet were on top of his, his knees against her thighs, his arms about her waist, her palms against his bare chest. They just stood there, looking at each other as if they were the only two people left in the world.

"I thought you'd never get here."

"I took the stairs three at a time."

"Were you asleep?"

"No. But I put down a bedroll."

"In the kitchen?"

"It's clean."

"It's the only clean place in the house. The beds up here need airing."

"We'll fix one for you tomorrow. Buddy can stay with you."

Babbling from Maud brought Willa back to the present.

"She's about to wake up. I'll give her just a drop or two of the laudanum."

"I'll leave. She'll get riled up if she sees me."

"She thinks you want to kill her."

"I know. What do you think?"

"If you had that in mind, you would have had plenty of opportunity before now."

"Precisely. Now, I'll get Buddy. Don't worry," he said quickly when he saw the fear on her face. "The rat can't get in with the door shut. It must have come from that privy room at the end of the hall."

She stepped down off his feet. His hands squeezed her upper arms before he released her, and he moved reluctantly to the door.

Without him beside her, Willa felt suddenly terribly alone. She stood there, hardly knowing what she was thinking, but fully aware that she wanted to be with him, talk to him, see him smile, hear the sound of his voice and his laughter. She wanted to know what he was thinking and what he dreamed about. She wanted to know why he was so hard on the outside when just beneath the surface there was so much gentleness.

Smith paused at the door and looked back. Green eyes met blue ones and held. This calm, beautiful woman in the borrowed dress of a whore would bring so much warmth and pride to a home with her loving, womanly ways. Her coming had given his world a new brightness. His heart cried out that he didn't want to love this woman, but he doubted if he could endure the gut-crushing pain of not having her here.

"Smith?"

He grunted a sound.

"What do you want out of life?"

He seemed dumbfounded by the question. His hand came up to move restlessly over his bare chest.

"What any man wants, I guess," he said quietly. "Peace, contentment . . . someone who cares if I live or die."

Willa nodded.

He went out the door and closed it behind him.

When Smith returned with Buddy, Charlie was with him.

"Charlie will sit for a while, then Billy will be in to finish the night."

Willa hugged Buddy's shaggy head. The dog was glad to see her. He wiggled his tail so hard his back feet almost went out from under him.

"If you'd been here, Buddy, that rat wouldn't have dared come in." When she looked at Smith, she was suddenly self-conscious. Her cheeks turned pink and she looked away. "I should be here in case Mrs. Eastwood wakes."

"You won't be far. Charlie can get you if he needs you. Tell him what to do."

"When she wakes up, call me. I give her a couple drops of the laudanum. Other than that when she's restless, I move her a little by pulling on the sheet under her to take the pressure off her hip."

"Got that, Charlie? If she wakes, call Willa. She'll be in the kitchen. Buddy will stay here with you and discourage any visitors."

Before Willa could utter a protest, Smith's hand in the middle of her back was urging her from the room and down the stairs. When they reached the kitchen, he moved away from her and cleared the kitchen table down to the wooden surface. She watched him, wondering what in the world he was doing. He quickly unrolled a bedroll atop the table.

"Your bed," he said. "I knew you'd not like sleeping on the floor."

"Is this your bedroll?"

"Got any objections to that? No lice. No bedbugs."

"I . . . don't want to put you out."

"Don't worry about that. I'll stretch out on the floor. Need help getting up there?"

"No. It's just that I've not slept on a table before."

"I have. On 'em and under 'em in every jug saloon from Laredo to Virginia City." He bit off his words sharply. His expression showed none of the warmth she'd seen earlier in the room upstairs.

Willa nodded her understanding of his meaning. He was putting up a barrier. He didn't want her to make too much of what had happened between them. He wasn't a man who would let a woman get close to him. He wasn't the kind of man to give his heart. She had to be careful or he would take hers and smash it into little pieces.

Her mother had said that someday a man would come into her life and fill it with his presence. He would cherish her. She would love him and she would give him children. She had cautioned Willa not to allow what had happened between her parents to influence her when she chose a man to share her life. For a brief moment, Willa had thought Smith was that man.

Thinking of the bleak, lonely future ahead, her heart felt old and heavy. Her eyes moved away from his face, but not before she saw bleakness in his eyes and he saw utter disillusionment in hers.

After she was settled, Smith blew out the lamp. The hall lamp still burned and a faint ribbon of light came through the door. He lay down on his blanket, staring at the ceiling, assembling and sorting out his thoughts. He had not meant for the intimate, soul-stirring experience he'd shared with her upstairs to happen.

Dammit! *When he was close to her, he lost his head.* He

begrudgingly admitted that every night since he'd met her he had fantasized about holding her, warm and naked, in his arms. Hell, what man in his right mind *wouldn't* want to hold her. He had a hunger that tore at his groin like any other man. It was that age-old male urge. That's all it was.

Why had she allowed him to kiss her? She had participated openly, completely. Had she been carried away by the novelty of a romantic interlude with a whiskey-soaked sot? She had called him that and also a crude, pitiful excuse for a human being. When she found out more about him, she would look at him with contempt in her beautiful eyes. He didn't know if he could endure that.

In the quiet of the night, Smith reached the conclusion that this was a woman he could give his heart to, but with whom he could not share his life. Being with her would be like living with a keg of powder that could erupt at any moment. When she found out how Oliver had died, she would despise him, leave him, and his life would be shattered.

Willa lay on her side, her head resting on her bent arm. She had made a complete fool of herself, and tempestuous feelings of embarrassment were threatening to overpower her. She held her lips tightly between her teeth and swallowed the lumps clogging her throat. She was bone-weary, she told herself, so tired she was not thinking straight and that was the reason why she felt so weepy and alone. She turned her face into Smith's blankets. The scent of his body was there.

To stave off the sweet memory of being held close against his naked chest, and the warm comfort of his arms, she reminded herself of when she first saw him lying in the hay at Byers' Station. That was the real Smith Bowman: gunman, hell-raiser, and, according to Mrs. Eastwood . . . murderer.

The full weight of her wretchedness hit her, sending her into the black pit of despair that not even tears could reach.

CHAPTER
* 17 *

"Ma'am, I hate like sin to wake ya."
Willa awakened instantly as she had done each time Charlie had needed her. This time Billy Coe's face hovered over hers.

"It's all right." As she crawled down off the table, she glanced at the corner where Smith had spread his blanket. He was gone.

"She's a blabbin' and buckin' somethin' awful. She ain't makin' no sense a'tall."

"She's in terrible pain. What time is it?"

"It's dawn, ma'am. Roosters is crowin'."

"I'll have to give her a few drops of the laudanum and hope it'll carry her over until the doctor gets here."

"She don't like the look of my face none a'tall. I left the boy holdin' her on the bed," Billy said as they went up the stairs.

"Charlie's still here?"

"I tol' him to go on back to the bunkhouse, but he curled up on the floor with the dog."

Maud was out of her head with the fever and was uttering

every obscenity Willa had ever heard and some she hadn't. The woman must have been raised in a saloon, Willa thought as she forced water with the laudanum down her throat. When Maud calmed, Willa asked Billy and Charlie to leave the room. As soon as they were alone, she bared the woman's body and bathed her with cold water in hopes of bringing her fever down.

Maud muttered about Fanny and Oliver, but mostly about Smith.

"He'll kill me." She looked into Willa's eyes and spoke as calmly as if she were in her right mind. "He killed Oliver, you know. He ain't got no right to be in my house after what he done."

"He's not in the house. Don't worry. He won't hurt you. I'll stay with you and take care of you." Willa spoke soothingly as if she were talking to a child.

After Maud fell asleep, Willa continued to lay the cool wet towels on her forehead, arms and chest. She worked until sunup. Then, realizing she had done all she could do, she covered the woman and sank down in the chair. Buddy, lying at her feet, whined and licked her ankle.

"You need to go outside, don't you, old friend?" She stroked the dog's head before she got wearily to her feet.

Willa closed the bedroom door behind her and blew out the hall lamp. Buddy followed her down the stairs to the kitchen.

Charlie was pouring cold water into the coffeepot to settle the grounds, and Jo Bell, her curly hair wild about her sullen face, sat at the table.

"Well, ma'am, I hope yore satisfied."

Willa looked blankly at Jo Bell and then turned her head. She didn't know what the girl was talking about and had no desire to find out.

"Good morning, Charlie."

"Mornin'. Coffee's ready. Billy said to come down for bacon and biscuits when you've a mind to."

Willa followed Buddy out the back door and stood for a moment on the porch. It was a warm, cloudless morning. There was not a whisper of a breeze to turn the blades on the windmill. Chickens scattered when Buddy walked out into the yard, even though he paid them not the slightest attention. Smith's horse stood saddled and waiting in front of the cookshack at the end of the bunkhouse. In the distance jagged mountain peaks were muted by a soft purple haze.

She stepped off the porch and went down the path toward the outhouse that sat back amid bridal wreath bushes. She had used the chamber pot in Mrs. Eastwood's room sparingly knowing that she would have to empty it, and now her bladder ached for relief. She expected a facility equal to if not worse than the one at the stage station and was pleasantly surprised that, although it was not entirely odor-free, it was clean, and sheets of newspaper had been provided.

Buddy came to meet her as she walked back up the path to the house. Smith's horse was gone. Plenty Mad, the Indian who had scared Jo Bell, sat at a grindstone sharpening an ax. Stacked between posts that had been driven into the ground was neatly cut firewood. There was so much of it, Willa was reminded of the long, cold winter ahead. Where would she be when the north wind brought ice and snow to the Bighorns?

Back in the kitchen, she washed her hands and splashed water on her face. She glanced at herself in the mirror as she dried with the linen towel. Deep, dark circles rounded her eyes. The hard work and sleepless night had taken its toll.

"There's coffee in the pot," Charlie said.

He and his sister sat at the end of the long table. Smith's bedroll had been removed and the tablecloth once again covered the top, although it hung lower on one side than it did on the other.

"I'd better see if Mrs. Eastwood is still asleep."

"I'll look in on her."

"Thanks, Charlie. Be sure to close the door."

"You ain't wantin' to kill the goose what lays the golden egg, are ya, ma'am?" Jo Bell spoke as Willa filled her cup.

"What do you mean by that?"

"If she dies, ya ain't got no reason to be here."

Willa didn't answer. Behind the calm facade, her thoughts were filled with turmoil. She didn't know how much longer she would be able to endure this girl. She stared at her while several minutes went by, then calmly looked away from her as if what she said was of no consequence. That, more than any words she could say, infuriated Jo Bell.

"Did ya hear me? If she dies ya'll be throwed off this place faster than a goose shittin' apple seeds."

Willa studied Jo Bell's face for a moment, then shrugged. The girl was eager to quarrel. Willa clenched her teeth to hold back a retort. However, her silence did nothing to discourage Jo Bell.

"Yore just a hanger-on here, 'n' don't ya forget it. It ain't yore kin that owns this place. Me 'n' Charlie is next kin to Uncle Oliver. Papa had done figured that out. He said we got a claim here. I figure with Uncle Oliver dead, we got more claim. It stands to reason that when that old woman dies, it'll be ours. I hope it's today. By God, I do. Ya can bet yore bottom dollar I'll send that Smith packin'. Then what'll ya do, *ma'am*?"

Willa looked up to see Charlie standing in the doorway. He was looking at his sister as if she had lost her mind.

"I'll swear, Jo Bell. I told you to get that notion outta yore head."

"If ya wasn't so thick-headed, ya'd figure out a few things 'n' stop tryin' to keep that old woman alive." Her lips curled in contempt when she looked at her brother.

"I don't think you should count on getting this ranch when Mrs. Eastwood passes on," Willa said. "She has a daughter who will inherit."

"Ya don't know nothin' about it. So . . . shut up!" Jo Bell jumped to her feet, braced her arms against the table and glared at Willa. "I'm sick of ya puttin' yore nose in my business."

"I'm not. I'm just telling you—"

"Ya are, too. And . . . ya ain't nobody to be tellin' me or my brother a dad-blamed thin'. Yore a . . . slut, is what ya are. Starr said whores got paid. Sluts don't."

Shock and anger drew Willa to her feet.

"Hush yore dirty mouth!" Charlie shouted at his sister.

"Don't tell me to hush tellin' what's true. She was in here all night with Smith, wasn't she? Whata ya think they was doin', dumb-head? Holdin' hands?" She turned the full force of her angry violet eyes on Willa. "What'd he pay ya, Miss Nasty Nice? Or did ya give him a ride on this here table for nothin'? If ya did, it proves yore a dumb slut just like Starr said."

For the first time in her life Willa felt an almost uncontrollable rage. It propelled her feet around the end of the table, her eyes never leaving Jo Bell's sneering features.

"I've . . . taken all the abuse I'm going to take from you."

Willa's voice trembled with the effort not to scream. She drew back her hand and slapped the girl across the face so hard that it knocked Jo Bell back down in the chair.

"Ohh . . . !" Jo Bell's hands went to her cheeks, her eyes widened with disbelief.

"Out of respect for Charlie and for what your father did for me, I have put up with your mean mouth. No more. If you ever call me one of those names again, I'll pull every hair out of your head, or at least make an attempt to do so. Do you understand me? You are hateful and spoiled and think the world revolves around you and what you want.'' Willa grabbed a handful of black curls and tilted Jo Bell's head so that she could look down into her face.

''Ya'll be . . . sorry—'' Violet eyes blazed with hatred. ''Ya'll be sorry,'' she whispered again.

''You're selfish and insensitive. I'm sick to death of you.''

''Yore jealous cause yore old and ugly and . . . men don't look at ya when I'm around,'' Jo Bell spat out venomously.

''I'd ten times rather be ugly on the outside than ugly and evil on the inside like you.''

Practically smoking with rage, Willa released the hold she had on Jo Bell's hair and walked out onto the porch. Leaning against the support post, she felt small and weak. The hand she lifted to brush hair off her brow was shaking with anger and humiliation.

''Willa—''

''I'm not sorry, Charlie. She pushed me to the limit.'' Willa turned to look at the tall, serious-faced boy. ''I've been taught to look for some good in everyone. I can't seem to find any in your sister.''

''I . . . thought she'd straighten out—''

''She isn't going to change. The more you try the more she rebels. You'll have to let go, Charlie. She'll drag you down with her or get you killed.''

''Somehow she's got it in her head that we'd get this place if Aunt Maud dies—''

''That's wishful thinking. Mrs. Eastwood has a daughter and maybe grandchildren for all I know.'' Willa's shoulders slumped wearily. ''Would you mind bringing me something to eat, Charlie? I don't want to leave Mrs. Eastwood alone.''

''I'll make Jo Bell watch her—''

''No,'' Willa said quickly. ''I'd rather do it.''

Charlie stepped off the porch, then turned back, his young face troubled.

"Smith said Jo Bell would have to stay in here from now on. The men are comin' back today and he don't want her stirrin' them up."

"That's up to Smith. My job is to take care of Mrs. Eastwood."

Willa watched the boy walk toward the cookhouse with Buddy close to his heels. At that moment Smith rode into the yard, dismounted and came toward the house.

"The doctor will be here in about half an hour." he said without a greeting. "I spotted his buggy down on the flats."

"Mrs. Eastwood was still asleep a few minutes ago." Willa looked away from him as she spoke. Jo Bell's words had somehow dirtied what had happened between them. "I'll go see about her," she said, as she opened the door to go back inside.

"Willa—" Smith waited until she turned back to look at him. "I set up a rat trap in that privy room at the end of the hall. Keep the door shut. You may have a few mice, but I don't think you'll be bothered with anymore rats."

"—A *few* mice," she broke in scathingly. "I would say there's more than a few."

"I'll send Plenty to Buffalo to buy some mouse traps."

"He was just there yesterday. How far is it?"

"A couple hours if you cut across the foothills. About three hours if you come on the road."

"The doctor must have left before daylight."

"Plenty says he's new. Old Doc's dead. I suppose he drank himself to death. Actually it's not a bad way to go. You'd feel no pain." After he spoke, he stood motionless, studying her with cold, hard eyes. It was a scrutiny that made Willa exceedingly uncomfortable.

"I wouldn't know about that as I've never drunk myself senseless." She looked at the remote expression on his face and her heart sank, but she kept her voice level. "If a man is too much of a coward to face life, I suppose that it's as good a way as any to duck it.''

She continued to stare at him. There was not a trace of the Smith who had held her so protectively and who had told her not to be afraid. She could see no hint at all of the Smith who had kissed her so tenderly and awakened in her a hunger to love and be loved.

"Keep the girl in the house today—''

"—I have enough to do taking care of Mrs. Eastwood—''

"I don't want her in the bunkhouse.''

"Let her stay in the cabin behind it.''

"That's my cabin and I don't want her in it.''

"Well, for crying out loud! I have no control over her. Tell her yourself.''

Willa met Smith's green stare with all the poise and self-control she could muster. She was more scared of his effect on her than she wanted to admit. He kept staring at her as if he were deliberately trying to read her mind. She would be damned if she would give him the satisfaction of letting him know that the kisses they had exchanged were of any importance to her at all. She waited impassively for his answer.

"I will,'' he said and swallowed, his mouth unaccountably dry.

Stop thinking about it, he commanded himself. It should have never happened. But he couldn't stop thinking about how perfectly she had fit into his arms. He couldn't look away from her glossy thick hair, her large, round, clear blue eyes, and her mouth. Lord! Her lips were pink and soft, and they had tasted sweeter than anything he had ever tasted before. He glanced at her hands clasped in front of her. They were small, her wrists fragile, and they had caressed his naked chest.

She was everything that was beautiful and good. He wasn't fit to hold her hand, and yet he had pressed her softness against him and kissed her mouth again and again. What in the world had he been thinking of? If by some miracle she had special feelings for him, he would only cause her unhappiness and disillusionment.

The silence between them was broken by the squeaking of the screen door. Willa stepped into the kitchen. Her eyes swept the room. Jo Bell was not there. The door leading to the other part of the house was closed. She remembered Charlie leaving it open so they could hear Mrs. Eastwood if she called.

Small hairs prickled on the back of her neck. An acute feeling of urgency caused her to hurry across the room, barely aware that Smith had come into the kitchen behind her. When she reached the stairs, she lifted her skirt with her two hands and ran up the steps to the second floor, not pausing until she flung open the door to Maud's room.

Jo Bell stood beside the bed looking down at the woman on the bed. She turned her head slowly. A mysterious smile twisted her mouth, her eyes glittered brightly.

"She's pig ugly, ain't she?"

"Who'er you?" Maud demanded.

"I'm Jo Bell Frank. Uncle Oliver is . . . was my mother's only brother. Me and my brother came a visitin'."

"Get out!"

With her heart pounding so hard that she drew air into her open mouth, Willa moved around the end of the bed to stand close to Maud's head.

"The doctor will be here in a few minutes. I need to get her ready."

"So . . . get her ready. It's what yore gettin' paid for."

"I would rather you'd go—"

"—I got more right here than you."

Smith stood in the doorway behind Jo Bell. Willa glanced

at him and then wrung out the cloth in the washbowl and placed it on Maud's head.

"Do you need her help?" Smith's voice was soft but with a sharp edge.

"Murderer! Bastard! Get . . . outta my house!" Maud shouted.

"No." Willa yelled to make herself heard.

Jo Bell whirled around, a practiced smile lighting her face. "Mornin', Smith."

"Get out of here." The edge in his voice had grown sharper. "Now!"

"Well, fiddle-faddle. I just wanted to help my . . . aunty." The words rolled off Jo Bell's tongue in a heavily accented southern brogue. She fluttered her lashes as she looked up at the tall man.

"Come on." He jerked her out into the hall and closed the door. With a hand wrapped about her upper arm, he pulled her down the hall to a room at the end.

"What—? Let go of me." Jo Bell struggled to free herself from his grip.

"This is where you'll stay." Smith opened a door and shoved her inside. "You can clean it or you can stay in it as it is."

"I ain't stayin' here! It's all . . . cobwebs and dirt."

"You will stay here, and if I hear of you giving Willa any more sass I'm going to turn you up and tan your hide."

Jo Bell wheeled on him. "If ya lay a hand on me, I'll . . . I'll . . . have you shot."

"You scare me to death, sweetheart. Who'll you get to do it? Charlie? Lord, but I feel sorry for that kid. Saddled with a blister like you will deal him nothing but grief." Smith turned his back on her and went silently back down the hall, his moccasined feet making no sound on the hall runner.

"Ya . . . ya mean old thin'." Jo Bell called after him. "Ya ain't the boss of me."

Too bad Fuller didn't get her, Smith thought, unaware that he was grinning. The two of them deserved each other.

When the doctor drove into the yard, Smith went to the horse's head, unhooked the tie rope from the harness and looped it over a rail.

The doctor stepped from the buggy, removed his canvas duster and placed it on the seat. He was a plain-looking man in his mid-twenties, solid and stocky. His cheeks were ruddy, his eyes bright brown, and he wore a bushy mustache.

"Howdy," Smith said. "You must have left Buffalo before daylight."

"Actually I spent the night at a ranch halfway between here and Buffalo." The doctor lifted a black bag from the floor of the buggy. "The Mathews children are down with chicken pox."

"I'm Smith Bowman."

"I figured you were. I'm Doctor Hendricks—John Hendricks. I've taken over Doctor Goodman's practice."

"Yeah. Plenty, the Indian who brought you the note, told me old Doc had died."

Smith looked the man straight in the eye and waited for him to extend his hand. When he didn't, a wave of the old sickness washed over him. It made him angry—but at himself. He thought he had gotten used to being ostracized by the community and that he no longer gave a damn.

The tinhorn doctor had heard about him and judged him unworthy of a handshake. *To hell with him.* How the hell did he know what he would have done under the same circumstances? Smith backed away and jerked his head toward the house. When he spoke, he clipped his words and his voice was tinged with hostility.

"Go on in. Upstairs. The first door on the left."

Smith made no move to lead the way.

The doctor appeared to be surprised by Smith's sudden coldness. The silence between them became awkward. He looked up at the big house, then back to Smith.

"This is quite a place."

"Yeah. Ain't it?" Smith never took his cold gaze from the doctor's face. "Give your instructions to Miss Hammer. When you finish, your pay will be on the kitchen table."

John Hendricks, usually the most patient of men, felt a sharp prickle of irritation that goaded him to say:

"You don't know my fee."

"Don't worry. It'll be enough."

"Why should I be worried?"

The doctor waited for a reply and when none came, he lifted a brow and headed for the house. He had been warned that Smith Bowman was as touchy as a snake with a knot in its tail. He must have said something to get his dander up. Damned if he knew what it was and damned if he cared.

John Hendricks had no more than hit town when he had heard about Eastwood Ranch and the woman who lived there. He had been told that she hadn't left the house since her husband had been killed. Bowman, the man's foster son, had been with him at the time. He hadn't paid enough attention to get all the details straight; but after meeting Bowman and seeing this place, it was a story he'd like to hear.

CHAPTER

* 18 *

Suffering the woman's verbal abuse in silence, Willa hurried to make Maud ready for the doctor.

When the doctor came in, he listened attentively as Willa explained Maud's injury. Maud resisted every move he made to examine her, and the words she used to berate him embarrassed Willa to the extent that she could not look at the man, although he didn't seem to be the least bit disturbed by the obscenities coming from the elderly woman.

"Give her another dose of laudanum," he said after Maud began to get hysterical and thrash about on the bed. "How much has she had?"

"This much." Willa held up the small vial. "It was full at noon yesterday."

"This is the last she'll get," he said firmly. "But she must be relaxed while I set her leg."

While waiting for the laudanum to take effect, he asked Willa to make up a pot of thick starch.

"You'll find starch as well as a bag of powdered glue in the back of my buggy. Add a cup of the glue powder to the starch after it has cooled."

Willa tore strips from sheets and rolled them into bandages while she waited for the water to heat. She then located a soft flannel nightgown to tear and use as padding between Maud's leg and the starch and glue cast.

"Whoever put the leg in the splints did a good job," the doctor said, while wrapping the flannel strips around Maud's leg. "The ends of the bones were placed nicely together."

"Mr. Bowman did it. Because we thought her hip was broken too, we were very careful when we lifted her to the board to bring her up here to her bed."

"She's lucky. It isn't broken. She wrenched it. Only rest and time will heal it. She'll not be an easy patient to take care of, but I guess you've already discovered that."

"She has a very colorful vocabulary," Willa said with a half smile. "I don't mind. She's frightened and hides her feelings behind her bluster."

The doctor looked up. His sharp brown eyes met Willa's. "Are you kinfolk?"

"No. Heavens, no. I'm . . . I'm just passing through on my way to Sheridan and happened to be here yesterday shortly after she fell."

After that the doctor worked silently, wrapping the limb with the strips of cloth. He applied the starch and glue mixture with his hands after each layer of cloth until Maud's leg was encased in a thick bandage.

"It will take about twelve hours for this to dry," he said, washing his hands in the china bowl. "She must not move."

"Her fever ran high last night. I sponged her to bring it down."

Doctor Hendricks dried his hands. Miss Hammer was worn out although she tried not to show it. The dark circles beneath her beautiful blue eyes and the tired lines around her mouth told him it had been days since she'd had sufficient rest. He had heard her stomach growl. That told him that she hadn't taken the time to eat.

"Have you had nursing experience?"

"Some."

"I thought so. You appear to be handy in the sickroom."

"Thank you."

"I'll leave some quinine. Give her one powder mixed in water every four hours."

"That's for the fever. What about the pain?"

"She can have laudanum no more than twice a week or she'll become addicted. There's not much I can give her for the pain. She'll have to tough it out for a few days." He looked down at Maud. "She needs some good food in her. A breeze would blow her away."

"She's lived in this house by herself for six years. I don't think she did much cooking."

"Are you staying with her until she's on her feet?"

"Mr. Bowman seems to be in charge here. He asked me to stay and take care of her."

The doctor looked long and carefully at the woman standing beside the bed. Her back was straight in spite of the fact that she was so tired she was about to drop. The dress she wore was too big for her and had seen better days. She wore no stockings. It was plain to him that she had fallen on hard times. What was her connection with Bowman?

"You could use a rest and I could use a cup of coffee. Mrs. Eastwood will sleep for two or three hours."

"I don't know if I should leave her alone." The thought of Jo Bell standing beside Maud's bed flashed through Willa's mind. Another thought followed immediately. The girl wouldn't do anything while the doctor was here. Besides, the malice she saw on Jo Bell's face could have been her imagination.

"She'll be all right." Doctor Hendricks snapped his bag

shut and set it up on the bureau. "I'll stay until she wakes. I want to talk to her again."

"Well . . ." Willa smiled. "She's quite . . . salty, as my stepfather used to say."

"A tough old bird." The doctor flashed her a grin and followed her out of the room and down the stairs.

If he noticed the unkempt condition of the house he never let on. Willa glanced at him; he seemed to be lost in his own thoughts.

John Hendricks had suddenly and unexpectedly felt the stab of loneliness and pain tearing at his insides again.

Bertha!

Bertha had died horribly and alone, attacked while he was away tending a patient. Bertha, who was beautiful and tender and thoughtful, who could not bear to see anything suffer, had died in their Missouri home at the hands of a man crazed with pain in his head.

Dr. Hendricks had stayed in Missouri for as long as he could, trying to live with the awful rage that burned within him. Finally he had turned his face toward the west. Bertha was gone, and the thought of life without her, even after two years, was at times almost more than he could cope with.

This silent, proud, shabbily dressed woman reminded him of his Bertha in the way she moved and quickly obeyed his instructions. Bertha's hands had been almost an extension of his own hands. They had worked as a team. Somehow he thought it could be so with this woman, but she or no other woman would ever take Bertha's place in his heart.

Willa was not sure if she felt relief or irritation that Jo Bell was not in the kitchen when they reached it. Coffee was simmering on the stove, put there, she was sure, by Charlie or Smith. The doctor should be offered a meal, but Willa wasn't sure that it was her place to do so.

Charlie came in as she carried the coffee cups to the table. He placed a small kettle on the cookstove before he spoke.

"Howdy, sir. I'm Charlie Frank." The boy stepped forward and shook the doctor's hand. "Smith said for ya to come on down to the cookhouse for the noonin'."

"Thank you. Do I have time to finish my coffee?"

"Shucks, yes. Billy'll keep it hot."

"I hope you brought a meal for the lady. She could use one."

"Oh, Lordy, Willa! Ya didn't get no breakfast, did ya? Smith'll have my head. He tol' me to brin' ya some flapjacks and I done forgot."

"Don't worry about it. We won't tell him."

"There's chicken and dumplin's in the pot. Billy thought it'd do Aunt Maud good too."

"Mrs. Eastwood is your aunt?"

Willa sat silently while Charlie explained. He was careful to leave out the circumstances that had brought Willa to them.

"You plan to stay on?" Dr. Hendricks asked, his curiosity pricked by the unusual condition of the house and the boy's story.

"For a while. At least until Aunt Maud is on her feet."

"That might be a while."

"Charlie! Damn yore rotten hide!" Jo Bell came storming into the kitchen, her hands on her hips. She ignored the doctor and Willa and thumped her fist against her brother's chest. "Why'd ya take Starr's trunk outta the wagon? Them's Starr's things."

Charlie grabbed his sister's wrists and forceably backed her toward the door. He didn't speak until they were on the porch, but his voice carried into the kitchen.

"Because I wanted to. Ain't you got no manners? Now stop makin' a show of yoreself. I'm takin' the food stuff out, too. There ain't no use them settin' out there spoilin'. We ain't goin' to use 'em.''

"Don't strip down that wagon. I'm goin' to Sheridan as soon as I find a man to take me.''

"Jo Bell, I'll swear. You don't have the brains God gave a goose. You're not takin' that wagon 'n' goin' off with the first man that comes along. Now, dammit. Listen to me.''

"That's what ya think, ya flitter-headed ninny. I'm not stayin' here and takin' crumbs throwed out by that crazy old woman 'n' kowtowin' to Smith. I'm goin' to Sheridan 'n' see one of them lawyers. It's what Papa'd done.''

"Is she giving you trouble?'' Smith's voice. "It seems I told you to stay in that room and stay away from the bunk-house.''

"You ain't the boss of me,'' Jo Bell's voice rose to a screech. "This ain't yore uncle's place. Yore just a hired hand. I ain't doin' what you say.''

"No?''

"Ye . . . ow. Put me down! Damn you to hell!''

Smith came through the door with Jo Bell slung over his shoulder, his arm locked about her thighs. She was kicking and beating his back with her fists. Smith crossed the room to the door leading to the hallway.

"Open it, Charlie. I told her to stay in that room, and for once in her life she's going to do what she's told. Stop it, you little she-cat.''

"All ya 'n' Charlie care 'bout is that . . . slut. I hate her! I hate her!''

"Hush up!'' The flat of Smith's hand came down hard on Jo Bell's bottom. She yelled and burst into tears.

With a half smile on his face, Charlie opened the door, waited for Smith to pass through, then followed him and his sister up the stairs.

Staring into her cup, Willa blinked rapidly. She would not cry. She would not let the embarrassing scene make her cry.

Dr. Hendricks pushed his chair back and stood. "I think I'll amble on down to the cookhouse and get a bite to eat. You'd better eat too, Miss Hammer. Your stomach probably thinks you've deserted it." He looked down and saw two tears slip from Willa's eyes and roll down her cheeks. "You're tired . . . and weak," he said gently.

"I'm . . . embarrassed," she said so low he just barely caught the words.

"Why? Do you think Bowman is abusing her?"

"No! She's . . . impossible to reason with."

"Her brother seemed to approve."

"Smith is afraid she'll cause trouble among the men. She's very . . . pretty."

"Is she? I didn't notice. Buck up, now." He placed his hand on her shoulder. "You'll have your hands full taking care of Mrs. Eastwood. The others can sort out their own problems."

Willa, pale and wrung out, with a kind of downtrodden stoicism, wiped her eyes with the heels of her hands. It was humiliating to sit here and be unable to control her emotions. She longed to crawl into a dark hole and cry to her heart's content.

"You're a good nurse." The doctor squeezed her shoulder gently. "But you must take care of yourself or you'll be unable to take care of your patient. Conserve your strength. Eat and rest."

"I know. And I beg your pardon for . . . letting down."

"If you need work when you've finished here, look me up in Buffalo. I need someone to carry on in the office while I'm away. You'd get your fill of taking out splinters, lancing boils and passing out sugar pills."

"Thank you. I'll keep it in mind."

Smith paused in the doorway when he saw the doctor's hand on Willa's shoulder and listened to the quiet conversation. He felt a surge of primitive jealousy, shocking in its intensity. He wanted to punch the doctor in the face for putting his hand on her, for realizing how tired she was, and trying to comfort her. *He* should be the one to do that, by God!

Smith hid his feelings when the doctor looked at him, but that didn't make them go away. He knew what was the matter with him, but it didn't make it any easier to tolerate. This light-haired, blue-eyed woman was in his blood, in his thoughts during every waking moment. She haunted his dreams at night. He wanted her for his own. The want, the need to have her, was burning a hole deep in his gut. But it was impossible to have her—he knew that. He would never ask her to share his miserable life. Knowing this, why did it hurt so much to see her with another man?

Charlie was behind him, forcing him to step into the kitchen. Willa's eyes, bright with tears, met his. By God— if that man has hurt her—

"The doctor says Mrs. Eastwood didn't break her hip; she wrenched it. Isn't that good news? She'll be in bed, though, for quite a while."

"Good news," Smith repeated, his mind not absorbing the import of her words, only that she had spoken. Who had made her cry? *Jo Bell's foul mouth!* Hard green eyes shifted to the doctor. "What's your fee, Doc?"

"Four dollars."

Smith tossed some silver on the table. "Here's five. We may need you to come back."

John Hendricks picked up four silver dollars. "Send for me if you need me. Now, I think I'll accept your invitation to . . . ah dinner."

"Take him down to the cookshack, Charlie."

Smith waited until Charlie and the doctor stepped off the

porch, then went to the stove and dished up a plate of the chicken and dumplings. He carried it to the table and set it in front of Willa. He returned with eating utensils and a glass of buttermilk. Still not a word passed between them. Willa spoke when he came to the table with a cup of coffee and sat down in the chair opposite her.

"You don't have to wait on me."

"I know that."

"Then why did you?"

"Because I wanted to. Why were you crying?"

"Oh, I don't know. I guess . . . I'm tired."

"Was it because of what that little bitch said?" His voice was rough as if he was having difficulty swallowing.

"Partly."

She fervently wished she could hide her suddenly flushed face from his knowing eyes. She couldn't tell him that her monthly flow was due and that sometimes she got weepy at that time.

"She'll get more than a swat on the butt if she don't shape up . . . and shut up!"

"What can you do? Beat her?" Willa looked into his eyes and smiled. "I can't see that happening."

"I'd like to." His tone of voice revealed his frustration.

They were silent for a while before Willa spoke again.

"You were rude to the doctor. Why?"

"I wasn't rude. What did you want me to do? Bow and scrape? He's only a saw-bones in a one-horse town."

"You deliberately set out to make people dislike you."

"Eat your meal. You look like you're going to bawl again."

"I won't . . . bawl."

"You can't take care of Maud day and night. If I know you, you'll be cleaning on this mausoleum every spare minute."

"You don't know me. I don't know you. Sometimes I think I do, then you switch into someone I don't know." Her eyes were shadowed with sadness.

Smith stirred uneasily and turn his head to stare up at the ceiling. He drew in a deep, shaky breath. When he looked back at Willa, the look on his face was the look of a man who has seen too much of life's miserable side.

"Are you going to work for him?"

Willa took a bite, chewed and swallowed before she answered. "I thought I had a job. Am I fired already?"

"You know damn well you're not fired," he said irritably. She could see a muscle tighten in his jaw.

Willa continued to eat slowly, not really tasting the food, but knowing she had to eat. The buttermilk was deliciously cold. She drank, leaving a white ring on her upper lip.

"How do you keep the milk cold?"

"There's a spring in the well-house. The windmill draws water from deeper down for the horse tanks and general use. More milk?"

"No, thank you."

Willa could feel his eyes each time he looked at her and then away. When she had eaten all she could of the food he had heaped on her plate, she carried the plate to the kitchen cabinet.

"Where's Buddy? I'll give him what I can't eat."

"You needn't have left it so he'd have something to eat. Billy will see to it that he's fed."

"Buddy will get spoiled, He's always had to scrounge for part of his food."

"I know a woman who will come help you," Smith said, abruptly changing the subject. "She's part Mexican. As long as Maud is tied to the bed it might work."

"I don't think you should have anyone here Mrs. Eastwood objects to."

"I tried not having anyone here she objects to and you see what happened. It's for her own good. You can't be with her all the time. She could have one of her fits."

"Fits?" Willa turned to look at him. "What in the world are you talking about?"

"Oliver told me a long time ago that Maud has some sort of fits. She falls down and twitches. It doesn't happen often. I'm wondering if she had one, fell and broke her leg."

"Well, for goodness sake. Did you tell the doctor?"

"I didn't tell him anything. I'm not someone he wants to chew the fat with."

The pained look on his face caused her to laugh shortly, without humor.

"I swear, Smith. You're the limit," she said in a brittle little voice. "What gave you that idea? Never mind. I'll tell the doctor. He should know." She picked up the silver dollar Dr. Hendricks had left on the table and dropped it in Smith's shirt pocket. Standing close to him, she looked up into his face. The concern in her eyes almost shattered his control. "You're so afraid that someone will get the impression that you're a decent man, that you go out of your way to make them think you're an ill-tempered reprobate." She smiled and lifted her brows. "Know something, Smith? You've not convinced me."

He frowned down at her, shifted from one foot to the other, not liking the feeling that she was looking into his very soul and seeing the coward there.

"Do you want Inez or not?" he asked gruffly, wanting more than anything to put his hands on her shoulders and pull her against him.

"Inez? The Mexican woman?"

"Part Mexican, part she-wolf, but she cooks a damn good pot of chili." He grinned wickedly.

"It isn't for me to say who comes to work here."

"I'll tell Plenty to fetch her when he goes for the mouse traps. You'll not get any help from that little snit upstairs. Godamighty! I've never seen such a worthless, contrary female. She's not worth the powder it would take to blow her up."

"There are a lot of men who would not agree with you."

"That's true. But most of them are after a quick release for the moment," he said bluntly, and watched the color come up to cover her cheeks.

Smith reached out a finger and looped a strand of hair over her ear. His warm fingertip touched her cheek. Something inside Willa began to melt, spreading warmth through her from the point of his touch.

"Do you like that . . . doctor?" Smith was scarcely aware the thought was spoken aloud. He drank in the sight of her. She was so pretty, so soft, so sweet, so far above him, that he had no right to even look at her.

"He's . . . nice. He seemed to know what he's about." She held her breath waiting for his fingers to move against her cheek again. To her disappointment, he dropped his hand to his side and stepped toward the door.

"I'd better get Plenty started so he can get back by dark. Inez will come around by the road. She'll not be here until morning."

"Smith—" Willa watched him turn toward her. Against the light she couldn't see the expression on his face and she wanted to. "There's a small bed in one of the rooms. May I put it in Maud's room to sleep on?"

He took a step toward her. "Why?"

"I'm a light sleeper. I'll hear her if she needs me."

"If it's what you want, Charlie and I will move it. I was going to suggest that Inez clean one of the rooms for you."

"Thank you. I'd feel better if I stayed close to Mrs. East-wood."

"Suit yourself," he said briskly and walked out.

The doctor listened intently while Willa told him what Smith had said about Maud having fits.

"I suspected it when I saw that her jaw teeth are ground down to the gums. When you found her on the floor, had she voided her urine?"

Willa nodded. "And . . . her bowels."

"Epileptic fits begin in early life, rarely after the age of twenty years. If I didn't know that she has had them for years, I might suspect that she has either a brain tumor, brain syphilis, or hardening of the cerebral blood vessels. Heredity is believed to play an important role as a cause."

"Oh, the poor thing—"

"I'll talk to her and find out how often the seizures occur. Evidently they are not as severe as some, or she would be dead. Plenty of rest, regular meals and no excitement is about all I can recommend. Bromide of soda or potash have been used, but these drugs stupefy the nervous system and may do more damage than good."

Dr. Hendricks reluctantly left the coziness of the kitchen. He had enjoyed the conversation. Willa Hammer was a well-read, sensible woman. He had been able to discuss symptoms and treatments with her as he had done with Bertha.

Standing on the lower step, he looked around at the decay of a once beautiful home and shook his head sadly. Such waste. The place gave him a chill. It was completely unlike the Mathews home where he had stayed last night. Four miserable rooms, but brimming with laughter and love.

At the top of the stairs, Dr. Hendricks looked back once more. Where did Smith Bowman fit in all this? He was a strange man. His eyes had practically devoured Miss Hammer. And he'd had the feeling the man wanted to punch him in the nose.

Whether he would admit it or not, the doctor thought as he opened the door to Maud's room, Bowman was in love with the woman. The question was—how did she feel about him?

CHAPTER
* 19 *

Willa finished changing Maud's bed. She straightened, her hand unconsciously going to the small of her back and the ache that plagued her.

It had not been an easy night.

After dark the previous night Willa had heard a crew of men ride in. They had greeted Billy and Smith in loud boisterous voices as they had unsaddled their horses and turned them into the corral. There had been lights in the bunkhouse and later she had heard someone playing a guitar. This morning a crew had ridden out again.

Maud had continued her verbal abuse, spitting obscenities, cursing Smith, ordering Willa out of the house. She had convinced herself that Willa was in a conspircy with Smith to kill her. Willa had sat beside Maud's bed a good portion of the night, talking to her, trying to keep her mind off her pain.

In the final hours before dawn, Willa's patience had come to an end.

"If Smith wanted to kill you why did he send for the doctor?" she asked, standing and staring down at the

woman's pale face. "All we would have to do, Mrs. Eastwood, is go off and leave you. You would lie here and die
an agonizing death. We are trying to help you until you're
back on your feet and can take care of yourself. Now, I'm
getting tired of your slurs on my character, your coarse,
unladylike language and your railing about Smith trying to
kill you when I know it is not true. If it doesn't stop, I'll
remove myself from your presence, shut the door, and leave
this house. The choice is yours."

After that Maud had been almost subdued, and one time
she had even called Willa by name and asked her for a drink
of water.

This morning Willa had brought warm water for her to
wash her face and hands, then a plate of flapjacks with butter
and honey.

"I'll ask one of the men to make a little table to sit across
your lap so you'll be more comfortable when you eat," Willa
said cheerfully.

Maud snorted. "'Bout all you'll get them to make for me
is a coffin."

"You'll not need that for a good long time if I can help it."

"What was all that rumpus I heard this mornin'?" Maud
asked after Willa had given her the quinine powder the doctor
had prescribed.

"Oh, that was Charlie and Jo Bell. He brought his sister's
trunk to her room. She was bawling him out about something.
Those two get along like a dog and a cat."

"Why'd they come here?"

"For a visit. Their father was killed back at the stage
station. His name was Gilbert Frank. I suppose you've heard
of him?"

"He was no good. Oliver said he went through Regina's
money in nothin' flat. Who killed him? Not that it matters."

"Another gambler. Mr. Frank accused him of cheating. I

doubt if Jo Bell will stay here very long. She's a town girl.
Charlie is different. He's a fine boy, Mrs. Eastwood. He
wants to be a cowboy. You'd like him if you got to know
him.''

''I'd do no such thin','' she fumed. ''I want 'em gone from
here. I don't like her none a'tall. I woke up 'n' she was in
here . . . lookin' at me. She's got a evil eye.''

Why the sly old thing. She had been playing possum.

''She's a year older than her brother. Charlie is a good
worker. He'll earn his keep and hers while they're here.''

''I ain't got no say 'bout what goes on outside this house.
Smith and that whiskered old buzzard do just what they please
and don't tell me nothin'. Inside is mine. I don't like that
black-haired witch. She hates me. I could tell.''

Willa had seen Smith when she had opened Maud's door
to let Buddy out. He had been coming from the water closet
at the end of the hall with a wire cage containing two dead
rats. She had hurriedly shut the door and had waited until she
was sure that he had left the house before she had gone
downstairs.

Inez drove into the yard in a two-wheeled cart pulled by a
donkey. Her black hair was streaked with gray, her face
round, and her body immense. She jumped down, agile as a
young girl. Smith went to meet her.

''How do, Smith?''

''Hello, Inez. How's my best girl?''

''Go on with ya, ya horny rooster.'' She swung her arm.
The blow that landed on Smith's chest would have felled a
smaller man. ''How's that white-haired old coot that hangs
'round here? He ain't been to town for a while.''

''He'll be glad to know you've missed him.''

''I ain't said I missed *him*.''

"I was away for a few weeks. He had to stick around here."

"Jeez, Smith, I was plumb bumfazzled when that mud-ugly, bowlegged Injun brought me the paper. Hell, I ain't never had no letter before. Good thin' my sister's boy could read writin'. I'd a been settin' there yet a'lookin' at it."

"It's like I said in the letter. I'll be obliged if you'll help out here for a while. Mrs. Eastwood fell and broke her leg, and—"

"Well, now, ain't that a lick? Can't say I'm sorry."

"Hush up, Inez, and listen." Smith led the donkey over to the water tank. Inez walked beside him.

From the kitchen window Willa saw Smith talking to the heavy-set woman. She wore a loose white shirt over a full dark skirt, short enough to expose thick ankles and beaded moccasins. Her hair was tied at the nape of her neck with a wide red ribbon. She laughed occasionally. Smith's mouth spread in a wide grin, and he flung an arm across the woman's shoulders as they walked toward the house.

Willa was pouring water over the soiled bedclothes when Smith and Inez came into the kitchen. The woman's loud pleasant voice filled the room.

"Golly-bill. I never 'spected to step foot inside this place. It's grander than what I thought." Her eyes swept the kitchen. "Whoo . . . ee! There's ever'thin' there is to do with, ain't they?"

"Inez, this is Miss Hammer. She'll take care of Mrs. Eastwood if you'll help her out with the other chores."

"Howdy." The hand that enveloped Willa's was big as a man's and just as rough. The woman's eyes were large and midnight black. They were smiling, friendly eyes.

"Hello." Willa liked the woman immediately. "I've never been in such a place as this, either."

Smith was backing toward the door. "Billy will get you what you need to cook meals, Inez. I've got work to do."

"Don't ya be worryin' 'bout a thin', boy. Me 'n' Miss Hammer'll do just fine."

"—Please. Call me Willa."

"Willa. Ain't that a pretty name. And ain't ya a pretty little jigger. Ain't she, Smith? Huh, Smith?" Inez turned to look at him when he didn't answer. "Well, I'll be a flop-eared mule!"

Smith was looking at Willa and she was looking at the caster set on the table as if she expected it to take wings and fly.

"Lord-a-mercy!" Inez chortled. "Smith's a-lookin' calf-eyed at a woman. 'Tis 'bout time. I was startin' to think ya didn't have all the right parts."

Although shocked by Inez's blunt words, Willa couldn't keep her eyes from going to Smith. His mouth was tight, and beneath his suntanned skin, his face was ruddy.

"You talk too much, Inez."

"Yore right 'bout that. Go on with ya. If yore wantin' me to get anythin' done, I got to be gettin' to it."

Smith's eyes clung to Willa for a long moment, then he backed out the door. She had a strong urge to go to the door and watch him cross the yard, but her feet felt glued to the floor.

"He's a damn good man," Inez said belligerently as if she expected Willa to argue with her.

"Have you known him long?"

"Since he was 'bout the size of a fence post."

"He carries a lot of anger around inside him."

"Ha!" The snorted word was the only comment Inez made.

Willa was amazed at how fast the cheerful woman took over the kitchen. By mid-afternoon, she had not only washed the soiled bedclothes and hung them on a line to dry, but she also had a pot of chili simmering on the stove and bread dough set aside to rise, and she had knocked down the cobwebs in the hallway and swept down the walls.

Maud was angry when Willa told her that a woman had come out from Buffalo to help.

"Get her outta my house," she yelled. "I got to keep things nice for when Fanny comes."

"We need her, Mrs. Eastwood. I can't cook your meals, wash the bedclothes and spend time in here with you. She'll not bother anything. I promise."

"*He* had no right to bring her here. Fanny will come. She'll take care of me." Tears flooded Maud's eyes and ran down her cheeks.

"I'll take care of you until Fanny gets here. Don't worry. You'll not be alone. I'm going to sleep in here every night, like I did last night." To Willa's surprise, Maud reached out a bony hand and clasped hers.

While Maud napped, Willa washed herself and changed into another of Starr's dresses. She hated wearing the woman's clothing and longed for things of her own. After brushing and recoiling her hair, she piled her arms with bedclothes from the bureau drawers and went down to the kitchen.

"These things haven't been washed in six years, Inez, and they smell musty. Shall I hang them on the line to air before we make up a bed for you?"

"I'll hang 'em out. Sit 'n' rest yourself a spell while ya can." Inez snatched the bedclothes from Willa's hands and was out the door before she could protest. When she came back, she spoke as if she hadn't left the room. "Yore runnin' yoreself ragged. Smith said ya was usin' yoreself up, so sit right down. I'll brin' ya a glass a buttermilk. He said ya was partial to it."

"You're not to wait on me, Inez. I'm here to work same as you." Willa spoke the last words to an empty room. She sank down in the chair thinking that Smith had been saying quite a bit. She wondered if he had prepared Inez for Jo Bell. Willa didn't get the chance to ask her.

Looking fresh and beautiful in a white dress with a blue ribbon in her black curls, Jo Bell came quietly into the room, paused and looked around. Inez stared at her. Jo Bell lifted her chin and stared back.

"Charlie said we had a maid."

Willa stood. "Inez, this is Jo Bell Frank, Mrs. Eastwood's niece. Inez isn't a maid, Jo Bell—"

"The chamber pot in my room needs emptying," Jo Bell announced, looking at the older woman with her dark brows raised in an intimidating fashion.

"Zat so?" Inez tilted her head and put her hands on her ample hips. "Then empty it, yore . . . graciousness."

Willa watched silently as the shock on Jo Bell's face turned to anger, and she steeled herself for the unpleasantness that was bound to come.

"Who do you think yore talkin' to? Ya'll do as yore told or get out. I'm next of kin here."

"Horse-hockey!" Inez snorted. "Yore just a snot-nosed kid! I ain't carin' 'bout what kin yore next to."

"I'll not stand for a servant talkin' to me like that."

Inez laughed. "I don't give a whoop 'n' a holler what ya'll stand for."

"Damn ya to hell," Jo Bell screamed.

"Don't ya be cussin' at me, girl." The tone of Inez's voice changed from amusement to anger. "I'll back-hand ya cross the mouth. I'm thinkin' it's what ya've been needin'." Inez raised her hand as if to slap the girl.

Willa held her breath.

"Ya just wait, ya . . . fat . . . old tub a lard! Ya just wait. I'll get even with ya and that . . . slut, too." Jo Bell wheeled and pointed her finger in Willa's face before she ran from the room.

Willa could hear her running up the steps and followed to

see if she went into Mrs. Eastwood's room. She didn't. She went into her own room and slammed the door.

"Well, if she ain't a hat full?" Inez said from behind Willa. "Smith said she was a pissant. He said she didn't have no more sense than a cross-eyed mule. He didn't mis-put it a dang bit. I swear to goodness. I come to within a whisker of slappin' her jaws."

"She was unreasonable before, but since her father died, she's ten times worse. Inez," Willa turned and looked the woman straight in the eyes. "I don't want her in Mrs. Eastwood's room when I'm not there. I'll be grateful if you'll help me watch."

"Hummm . . . course, honey. Do ya think she'll hurt the old gal?"

"I don't know. Maybe I should lock Mrs. Eastwood's room when I go out."

It was not yet dark.

Smith turned away from the corral and looked toward the lighted windows of the house. He had never expected to see anyone other than Maud in the house again. It made him think of other times he had stood alone and lonely and stared at the lighted windows, wanting desperately to be welcomed inside.

Tonight he had eaten his fill of Inez's chili, drunk his coffee and gone outside. Willa had not come down to supper. Jo Bell had stayed in her room, thank God, and Charlie had chosen to eat with the men in the bunkhouse. Sitting at the table with Inez, Smith had eaten his first meal in Oliver's house.

Inez had told him about her encounter with Jo Bell.

"Will ya fire me if I slap that girl's mouth shut?" she had asked teasingly.

"Hell, no. I'll give you a raise." Smith knew Inez well enough to know it wouldn't come to that unless the girl struck her, and that wasn't likely.

The sound of a running horse interrupted Smith's thoughts. He stepped away from the corral gate and looked toward the trail coming from the southwest. As soon as he got a glimpse of the rider, he knew it was Sant, and he was coming on fast. No one sat a horse like Sant Rudy.

"That you, Smith?"

"Hell, yes."

"Open the gate. We're driving in six of the sightliest mares you ever did see." He wheeled his horse, rode back a way, then turned to ride on one side of the lead mare. Another horseman rode on the other side, boxing her in. A rider at the rear drove the herd, and within minutes they were inside the heavy pole corral, circling, whinnying, kicking at the barrier separating them from freedom.

"Well, old hoss!" Smith slammed the gate shut and turned to the man stepping down from his horse. They clasped hands and jerked each other about.

Although Sant was older than Smith by twenty years, he did not show his age in his movements or reactions. He was still rangy and stood well over six feet tall. He was hawk-nosed and butt-jawed. His dark reddish hair showed no gray. There were two things about Sant that people noticed when they met him for the first time. His eyes were light gray, clear and so cold-looking that they had been likened to the ice feathering the edge of a mountain stream after a heavy frost. A fearsome scar on his right cheek ran from the corner of his eye to his jawbone, the relic of a bone-deep furrow slashed by the claws of a mammoth grizzly, a grizzly that Smith had killed to save Sant's life. The whitish scar stood out against Sant's weathered skin. Neither wind nor sun had darkened it.

"Glad to see you, Sant. Damn glad."

"You ain't got no better lookin' while I was gone."

Smith laughed. "I guess you think you did. Hellfire, you smell like a wet goat."

"Bathing never was top of my list. What 'a you think of the mares?"

"You didn't steal them from the silver lobo, did you?" Smith asked jokingly.

"That we did."

"No!" Smith whistled between his teeth, showing his surprise and appreciation.

"The silver lobo was off fighting a couple of interlopers who were trying to take some of his mares. This group was lagging—they're heavy with foal. God, he was mad when he got our scent. He made a pass or two and was primed to fight. It was all we could do to stay outta his way and hold the mares inside a rope corral with a rope halter on them."

"I'm surprised he gave up."

"He caught a sniff of something. Probably a panther. He was off like a shot. Never thought I'd be grateful to a panther. He saved our bacon. The sonofabitch was trying his damnedest to kill us." Sant turned to the men who were stepping down from their horses and spoke to the older of the two men. "Cliff, come meet my partner, Smith Bowman. This here's Cliff Rice; he's buying work stock for the railroad crews."

After the two men shook hands, Smith glanced at the other man Sant had failed to introduce. He was loosening the cinch on his saddle.

"Billy's been saving you some supper. He said you'd be in today. Come on in and put your feet under the table."

"I take horse now." Plenty Mad crowded between the two tall men and took the lead rope from Sant's hand. "You stand, you gab, you don't care horse tired, damn you."

Sant laughed. "That crazy Indian will never change. Be

careful with that horse, you ugly little fart," he called. "Are you sure you know which end to feed?"

"I know end that shits. I feed other end. Damn you kiss my ass. I ain't crazy. Plenty Mad one smart Injun. It's damn dry up north. Big fire come like big herd a buffer. You crazy or you listen to Plenty Mad."

"What's he talking about?"

"He's got a bug in his bonnet. He thinks there'll be a fire because it's dry. He been haranguing me about it ever since I got back."

"He's right about it being dry in the upper Bighorns. Been plenty of rain south. Elk are coming down to feed. Grass in our canyon is knee-high. What's going on with old Maud? The place is lit up like she was having a ball."

While they waited for Rice and the other man to take care of their horses, Smith told Sant about Jo Bell and Charlie. He mentioned Willa as a woman traveling with them. He told about finding Maud with a broken leg, getting the doctor out to set it and hiring Willa to take care of her.

"The house hasn't been touched in six years. Mice and rats were taking over. Caught two rats last night. They had come up the pipes into that inside privy Oliver put in. I sent Plenty Mad to fetch Inez. She's got a handle on things."

"Now ain't that rich? Old Maud's hamstrung and has to let a *low-life* like Inez do for her." Sant laughed a dry humorless laugh. "Bet she's fit to be tied."

Inside the cookshack, Smith introduced Charlie to Sant, Rice and to the younger man Rice called Vince, who sank down in a chair at the end of the table and watched and listened.

Rice was a gray-haired man, stocky and solid. The other man was no more than twenty, whip-lash thin, and wound tighter than a watch spring. He was a good-looking boy with sandy hair and blue eyes. The skin was broken under a dark bruise on his right cheekbone. When he ate, he chewed on the left side. He kept his eyes on his plate and did not contribute to the conversation.

"Cliff made a offer on forty head of mules." Sant made the announcement between mouthfuls of biscuit covered with gravy.

"Did you take it?" Smith asked.

"Yup."

"It'll be a job cutting them out."

"I'll get me a crew of Cheyenne—"

"—Shit!" The word came from Vince at the end of the table. Sant continued to talk as if he hadn't been interrupted.

"—from the camp down on Casper Creek. Talked to 'em on my way up here."

"I never saw the like of that silver lobo," Cliff said. "That's a horse and a half."

"He is that," Smith's green eyes shone with enthusiasm. "We've been watching him for years. He's got a lead mare that's a sight to behold, too. She's silver gray with a white-star blaze on her forehead. Her long mane and tail shine like gold in the sunlight."

"I'm surprised that every horse hunter in the country isn't out there trying to catch them." Cliff held his cup out for more coffee when Billy brought the pot to the table.

"That stallion or his lead mare must not be caught or harmed in any way. The man that attempts it will get his ass full of lead. *Any* man," Sant repeated and looked down the table to where Vince's head was bent over his plate.

"Folks in these parts, even the Indians, leave them be," Smith explained. "The silver lobo's selective in his choice of mates. Who knows but someday he might produce an outstanding breed. His offspring now are fast and durable and can be broken if caught young. The silver lobo would die before he would surrender to captivity."

"The right breeder would pay a pile of money for a horse like that," Cliff said.

Not liking the way the conversation was going, Sant pushed back his chair and got to his feet.

"It pains me to do so, but I'll take to the water tank and wash off the odor of my honest labor."

"Don't do it on my account. You can sleep in the barn." Smith grinned and threw him a hunk of yellow lye soap he snatched from the wash bench. "Make yourselves to home, fellows. I'd better follow that old boy and see that he don't drown. He's not used to water."

In a room above a saloon in Buffalo, George Fuller lay face down across the bed. The day after Smith Bowman had shot him, he had parted company with Abel Coyle and headed for town and old Doc Goodman, hoping the old man would be sober enough to help him. On arriving, he was told that the old doctor had died but that a new city doctor had an office above the bank.

George made his way painfully up the steps alongside the building. After telling the doctor he had been creased by a stray bullet, he had endured the agony of having threads from his britches picked out of the wound and having it cleaned with a solution of alcohol. He lied again when he told the doctor he had been kicked in the crotch by a horse and asked him if any permanent damage had been done to his manly parts.

"Only time will tell," the doctor said after a careful scrutiny of the injured area.

The statement did nothing to lessen George's fear that he would never again know the pleasure a whore could give him. He vowed that someday soon he would make Smith Bowman pay for what he had done. He thanked God that Coyle had gone on to Sheridan, for he would have been sure to spread the story of his humiliation. Come to think on it, he'd get even with that son-of-a-bitch too.

George rolled off the bed and went to the window. He'd been here three days, going out only to get a bottle of whiskey and food to bring back to the room because it was too painful to sit down in a restaurant and eat.

The town consisted of a double row of weather-beaten, false-fronted buildings, some of which had never been painted. Most of the scattered dwellings were of stone and log. A few houses had been built of sawed lumber as was the two-story hotel. A stone building, square and solid, was identified by the sign: BUFFALO BANK.

George watched the activity on the street. It was dusk and a few lights had been lit to dispel the gloom. Two women in short, low-necked dresses crossed the street and went though the bat-wing doors of the saloon. The shouts of welcome and male laughter drifted into the open window.

One of the women had black hair and reminded George of the Frank girl. Not that he needed a reminder. She had been constantly in his thoughts. The first sight of her had aroused him so much that his flesh had instantly become hard and painful. She had been hot for him too. He could tell by the way she had looked at him out of the corners of her magnificent eyes.

He knew now that he had scared her the day he had tried to pull her off the wagon. He would not make that mistake again, but he would have her. He was more determined than ever now. If any woman would bring his member back to life, it would be that black-haired, violet-eyed vixen.

As soon as he could ride, he was heading for Eastwood Ranch.

CHAPTER

* 20 *

The object of George Fuller's thoughts was also looking out the window.

Jo Bell watched the activity around the barn and the bunkhouse as she had been doing for the last two days. At dusk three men had arrived driving a herd of horses. She saw Smith greet one of them as if he were an old friend and discounted him as being one she would approach to help her.

She turned her attention to the other two men. Both wore range clothes. One had gray hair, rounded shoulders and was thick in the middle. The other man was young, but not as young or as awkward as Charlie. His hat was black, flat-crowned, and held beneath his jaw by a loose thong. His vest was of black cowhide and he wore a tied-down gun. Moreover the man Smith had greeted so warmly was ignoring him, which could mean that he was an outsider without connections here at the ranch.

Jo Bell fingered the rings and the watch she had taken from the room across from Maud's. Charlie had refused to give her the money her father had left, but what she had found was worth far more. Papa had said that she and Charlie were the only blood kin Uncle Oliver had and that he would be sure to see that they were provided for in his will. She didn't really consider taking the rings and watch to be stealing. They were hers by right.

She wouldn't dwell on the right or wrong of it now. Uncle Oliver was gone, and that old woman across the hall wasn't going to last long. Maybe even tonight she would have one of her fits and pass on. Lord, she hoped so. She had listened outside the kitchen door and heard the doctor and Willa talking about Aunt Maud's fits. It wasn't fair that that nasty old woman would have all this when she had nothing.

She began to fantasize what she would do when the ranch was hers. She'd sell it, of course, buy a nice big house in town, and hire servants to wait on her. It would be just as Papa had planned. Papa! Why'd he have to go and get himself killed? With him here it would have been so easy.

As soon as the men went into the lighted cookshack, Jo Bell cautiously opened the door and tiptoed down the hall. She paused to listen at the door to Maud's room and heard Willa talking to her aunt. At the bottom of the stairs she paused again to listen. All was quiet. She scurried down the hall to the big double doors and opened one just wide enough to allow her to slip out. She stepped out onto the veranda and quietly closed the door behind her.

Smith was mistaken if he thought he could keep her shut up in that room. The thought of getting even with him was never far from her mind. Damn his hide! She would find Fuller and tell him to kill Smith. He would do it, too. Papa had told her she had the *power* to make men so crazy about her they would climb to the moon if she asked them to. Jo Bell giggled happily, then sobered. Papa hadn't told her how to handle men like Smith. *Why didn't you, Papa? Why didn't you?*

Keeping to the shadows, she worked her way around the

house and across the open space between it and the ranch buildings. In the shadow of the bunkhouse she moved along the wall to the cookshack and peered in the window. The men were seated at a long table. She could see their faces clearly.

The young man had a bruise and cut on his face, but he was still as handsome as she knew he would be. He had a wild, reckless look about him that made Jo Bell's heart skip a beat. His eyes flicked past the window as he turned an icy gaze on the man with reddish hair. He must be the one Smith had greeted like a long, lost friend. Jo Bell ducked down. Charlie had turned his head toward the window. She waited and held her breath. If her brother had seen her, he would be sure to come outside and stir up a fuss.

A minute passed. Jo Bell sighed with relief. She had to find a place where she could watch and wait for a chance to talk to the man with the cut cheek. Running lightly across the yard, she sank down on the ground beneath a growth of sumac that ran along the fence. She had a view of the cookshack as well as the bunkhouse door.

She hadn't been there long when Smith's friend came out and then Smith. They went around the corner toward the cabin set back behind the buildings. Charlie had told her that Smith and Billy Coe lived there. It wasn't a very big house, certainly not something she would be interested in living in. Built of logs, it had a peaked roof that overhung in front supported by two heavy posts. It was like any number of crude homesteads they had passed on their way here.

The gray-haired man came out, lit a cigarette and sat down on the bench in front of the bunkhouse. A few minutes later the young man joined him. Jo Bell could see Charlie helping Billy clean up after the meal. The men on the bench talked in low tones. Jo Bell could just hear the murmur of their voices. She hoped and prayed the young man wouldn't go inside. When the old man stood, dropped his cigarette butt and ground it out with his heel, she held her breath for fear the other man would follow

He didn't. He sat there and lit another cigarette. The lights went out in the cookshack, and she saw Charlie pass the window in the bunkhouse. Billy had probably gone out the back to the cabin he shared with Smith. Jo Bell was trying to decide if it was safe to cross the yard and ask the man to walk away from the house with her so that she could speak privately with him. While she was trying to make up her mind, he stood, tossed his cigarette and, to her astonishment, crossed the yard and came directly to her

Jo Bell rose on shaking legs. "How did ya know I was here?"

"I saw you looking in the window and spotted that white dress the minute I came outside. Why are you sneakin' around out here?"

"I ain't sneakin' I want to talk to you—where nobody'll see us."

"Why?"

"Cause   I want ya to help me get away from here."

"Why?" he asked again.

"Smith Bowman is keepin' me here and I want to leave."

"Are you his woman?"

"No! I'm not anybody's woman   yet. Are ya comin to talk to me or not? If Smith or Charlie sees me, I'll have to go back in."

"I never could refuse a pretty girl."

"I am pretty Papa said I was."

He took her arm and urged her down the row of sumac to the end, lifted her over the fence and followed. They backtracked to a dense clump that shielded them from the house and the ranch buildings.

"No one will see us here but an owl or two. What's on your mind?"

"My name is Jo Bell Frank. I've got to get to Sheridan and see a lawyer or a judge or somebody "

"You're the boy's sister?"

"Charlie? Yes. We came to visit my uncle, but he died before we got here. His wife, our Aunt Maud, is awful sick. When she dies, this ranch will be ours. There ain't no blood kin anywhere but us. That's why I got to see a lawyer " She heard his indrawn breath whistle through his teeth and was encouraged to go on. "I think this ranch is worth a lot of money, don't you?"

"Bowman foreman here?"

"I guess so. He makes me stay in the house. He said I'd cause t-trouble with the m-men." Jo Bell let her voice tremble. "I don't know why he's so m-mean unless he's plannin' on gettin' Uncle Oliver's ranch for hiss-self "

"What does your brother say about this?"

"Charlie's fifteen. He don't k-know anythin' Will you h-help m-me?" Jo Bell sniffed prettily

"Don't cry, pretty little thing. I'm thinking on it."

"What's yore n-name?" She swayed toward him.

"Vince. Vince Lee."

"Oh, Vince, I   just don't know what I'm goin' to do. I'm just   scared all the time."

"What do you want to do, honey?" She was so close he could smell the heat of her body

"Go to Sheridan 'n' find somebody to h-help me. Charlie took my money, but I've got these." She put her hand in her pocket and pulled out two gold rings and a diamond-studded railroad watch. "You can have one of the rings if you take me to Sheridan."

Vince struck a match and glanced at what she held in her hand. Then his eyes went to her face and he drew in a deep breath. He slowly blew out the match. He'd never seen such eyes. She was the prettiest woman he'd seen in all his born days. Gawdamighty!

"Maybe I want more than a ring," he said softly.

"Do you want both rings?" He shook his head. "Then what in tarnation do you want?"

"Well—" he hesitated. "We could start with a kiss."

"A kiss?" She looked at him stupidly for a moment. Then she laughed. "Oh, is that all?" She slipped the rings and the watch back in her pocket and moved her hands up his chest to clasp them behind his neck. "I like to kiss. I haven't done it much though."

Her warm lips reached and found his. She melted against him as if she didn't have a bone in her body. In the circle of his arms and hearing the heavy beat of his heart, she was conscious of a change in his breathing. It quickened. She was having just the effect on him her papa had said she would.

She made to pull her mouth from his. But his hand at the back of her head held her until she decided she didn't want to pull away even if her papa had said for her not to give too much too soon. She liked kissing. Her arms tightened about his neck and she allowed his tongue to enter her mouth. His hand moved down her back and pulled her tight into the vee of his crotch. He began to kiss her savagely and thoroughly She arched against him, not understanding the strange new emotions he had awakened in her body. She was only conscious that she wanted more.

Somewhere in the back of her mind she thought, *so this is how it feels*? This was the power her papa had said she had. Without knowing why or what she was doing, she moved against the hardness that had sprung up between them and was pressing against her belly.

"Christ," Vince muttered when he pulled his mouth away

from hers and looked down at her ''You're hotter'n a cow-town on Saturday night.''

''Does that mean you like to kiss me?''

''Yeah—''

''I like kissin' you too, Vince.''

''G-gawd,'' he groaned. ''Where'n hell did you come from?''

Jo Bell laughed happily ''It's where I'm goin' that matters.''

''G-gawd,'' he gasped again. ''I thought you said you hadn't kissed much.''

''I haven't. Papa told me what to do.''

''Your Papa? Hellfire! What kind a papa did you have?''

''The best papa in the world.'' she said staunchly.

''You . . . didn't . . . with . . . him?''

''No!'' She tried to push him away, but he held her ''No,'' she said again. ''But he told me . . . things.''

''All right, all right. Just be easy, be easy,'' he crooned as if he were soothing a skittish horse.

''I've not done more than . . . kiss. Ya'll not take advantage of me, will ya, Vince?''

''Course not,'' he scoffed. *Where in the world had this hot little thing come from?* She was a dream, a mirage, as sweet as angel's breath.

''Have you done *it* with a lot of women, Vince?'' she asked and let her tongue roam over his lips. ''Papa did. He said a real man would do it ever chance he got. He said that nice girls like me would only do *it* with one man and that I wasn't to give it away. Papa always had a woman along to give him comfort.''

Lord, what was he going to do? If he threw her to the ground and did what he wanted so desperately to do, she might scream and yell rape. If that happened there'd be hell for breakfast.

"Gawdamighty!"

Vince was in agony from holding back. It had been weeks since he'd been with a woman. He had visited his first whorehouse at fourteen. Since then he had been in hundreds of brothels all the way from Texas to California, and he had never seen a prettier woman or one who had fired him up so fast. Was it the plain talk coming out of such a beautiful mouth and innocent-looking face? He knew as sure as his name was Vince Lee that if he did to her what his body was screaming for him to do, he'd not leave Eastwood Ranch alive.

"All right . . . what did you say your name was?" He dropped his arms and moved away from her, breathing deeply in an effort to calm himself.

"Jo Bell."

"Jo Bell," he repeated. "The problem is this—if I took you away from here, and they caught up with us, they'd hang me."

"Not if I leave Charlie a letter sayin' we eloped to get married."

"Married?" The wheels began to turn in Vince's head. *Married to a woman who owned a ranch like this!* Good Lord! All he'd ever had was a horse, a gun, and a few dollars to last until the next job.

Vince was silent for so long that Jo Bell became worried.

"You wouldn't have to marry me if you didn't want to." She spoke in a small sad voice, leaned close to him so that her hair tickled his nose, and blew her warm breath on his throat. The palms of her hands moved up and down his arms. He trembled and pushed his hardness against her She wanted to laugh. It worked just like her papa had said it would.

"Course, I'd want to," he said quickly and squeezed her upper arms so tight that she winced. "You'll need a horse—"

"I got one. That sorrel with the black mane and tail is mine. Papa said he was worth a lot."

Vince jerked her to him, lifted her, and whirled her around. He had ridden with hard luck all his life. Now in the space of thirty minutes his luck had changed.

"Sit down here on the grass, darlin' We've got plans to make. I'm leaving in the morning, but I'll be back. Get your letter ready and pack only enough to tie behind your saddle. When you see a circle of stones beside the outhouse door, meet me right here."

"Oh, Vince! I'm a'thinkin' I love you!"

His grin was so wide it hurt the cut on his jaw

Smith and Sant sat in the cowhide chairs on the cabin porch and waited for Billy to join them. In as few words as possible Smith told Sant about his trip to Denver to see Fanny

"She wants nothing more to do with Maud. She's cut her out of her life completely I can't help but feel a little sorry for the old woman. Fanny put out the story that her folks sold their land and cattle for cash money and headed for Europe where they planned to live in style. The ship sank in a storm and all were lost, leaving her a poor little orphan."

"For Gawdsake! Who in their right mind would believe a cock-and-bull story like that?"

"Her in-laws, the Brockfords, swallowed it hook, line and sinker They're high-society folks in Denver Fanny was so anxious to see the last of me that she was even halfway decent for a change.'

"I bet."

"I couldn't tell old Maud the truth, so I told her Fanny had gone to London. It was the first place I thought of that was far enough away "

Smith told Sant about meeting the Franks and Willa at the stage station and the events that followed.

"It was lucky for old Maud they came when they did. She took it pretty hard when I told her Fanny wasn't coming. My guess is that it brought on one of her fits and she fell and broke her leg."

"I'd hate takin' care of her. With two good legs she's meaner than a cow with her teat caught in the fence. Tied to the bed she must be a ring-tailed tooter."

Smith paused and built a smoke. He didn't want to talk to his friend about Willa and that was the direction the conversation was headed. Willa with her big sad eyes, the proud tilt of her chin, the sweetness of— Lordy, he had to stop thinking about her . .

"Did you have a run-in with that kid with Rice? I see he's marked up some."

"You might say that. Damn fool. I caught him with his gunsight on the silver lobo's mare and let him have it with the butt of my rifle. He claimed he could crease her down the spinal nerve and stun her long enough to tie her up."

"The bastard. Most of those shots either miss or kill."

"I knocked him down. Before he got up he understood what would happen to him if that lobo or the mare were harmed. Corner him and he's like a rattlesnake. He fancies himself quite handy with a gun."

"Did he draw on you?"

"Started to. He ain't as fast as you was at fourteen."

"Remember when Oliver caught you teaching me the fast draw?" Smith chuckled.

"Yeah. He stormed and raved about it for a while. 'Teach him to fight with his fists like a man.' I can still hear him. 'Smith ain't going to be no gunfighter.' "

"I miss him still, Sant."

"Yeah, well, that's the way of it. We can't live forever Get the guitar and play me a tune. I been hankerin' for music "

Sant leaned back against the wall, his hands stacked behind his head. This place was the nearest thing to a home he'd had for as long as he could remember Smith was the nearest thing to the son he'd never had. For several years after Oliver died Smith had grieved, drunk and brawled continuously More than once Sant had had to step in to keep him from killing someone or from being killed.

Two years ago Sant had found a grassy meadow within the walls of a canyon. A clear stream of water came down the side of the mountain. He and Smith had filed on the land, driven a herd of wild horses and mules into the canyon, and built a pole and brush fence across the narrow opening. It was from this herd that they would cut out the forty head of mules for Cliff Rice.

"I bought new strings while I was in Denver." Smith came out and sat down on a bench. "I put them on the other night." He plucked at the strings and twisted a key. "I'll never forget the day you rode in with this guitar in a gunny sack. You'd come all the way from Sheridan in a raging blizzard—had ice on your whiskers and were about frozen to the horse. It was the day before Christmas."

"Yeah. I was wore out and wanted to sleep. You plunked on that damn thing till I threatened to get up and bust it."

"I've sure had a lot of pleasure out of this guitar, Sant. I don't reckon I ever thanked you properly."

"Shitfire. Ya thanked me till I was blue in the face. Now stop yawkin' and play *Red River Valley*."

Willa debated with herself for a long time before she finally relented and gave Maud a few drops of laudanum. The doctor

had said to wait a couple of days. She had waited a day and a half. The hours Maud had spent in pain had taxed her severely and she badly needed rest. Both of them did.

When she was sure her patient was sleeping soundly, Willa left the room, taking Buddy with her. She locked the door, put the key in her pocket and glanced toward Jo Bell's room. As far as she knew the girl had been there all evening. Willa had eaten supper with Maud, knowing that Inez was expecting Smith. She had no desire to face him in such close proximity until she had settled a few things in her mind—the main one being why he had the power to make her almost mindless in his presence.

A light shone from under the door of the small room at the bottom of the stairs that Inez was using. Willa went through the darkened kitchen and out onto the back porch.

It felt so good to be alone in the quiet night. A half moon rode high in a sky studded with a million stars. The creaking of the wooden windmill was a pleasant sound. Even Buddy was content. He dropped to the porch floor and lay with his head on his paws.

Then from somewhere behind the bunkhouse someone began to play a guitar. She had heard the music several nights ago but only faintly. Tonight it had a strange compelling quality, and was hauntingly beautiful. Willa could not define its particular magic. She only knew that it gave her goose pimples. It drew her as the Pied Piper of Hamelin in the Browning poem had compelled the children to follow him.

She moved down the path to the fence that separated the house and the barnyard, irresistibly drawn by the sweet, clear sound. Buddy got up and walked along beside her. She felt her heart still. A spell of enchantment engulfed her as if the lilting notes clinging to the evening air were coming from another world. The tune was *Home Sweet Home*, but it was

played with such expertise that Willa was almost stunned by the beauty of it.

She paused at the end of the bunkhouse when the music stopped. Then she heard someone singing in a low and whispery voice as if he were singing to himself.

> Oh, bury me not—on the lone prairie,
>   These words came low and mournfully,
> From the pallid lips of a youth who lay,
>   On his dying bed at the close of day.

The singer finished the song and sang another and another. The music continued after the singer stopped singing. She didn't know much about music, but she did know that whoever was playing the guitar was a gifted musician and that he loved playing the instrument. The music washed over Willa in a soothing wave, drowning out her awareness of time and place.

Buddy growled, drawing Willa's attention to him. The dog stood on stiffened legs looking into the pitch-black darkness between the cabin and the bunkhouse. A vicious snarl came from his throat and the hair stood up on his back.

"Come on, Buddy, let's go." Willa pulled on the hair at the back of the dog's neck, but he refused to budge. "Buddy . . . come on."

The dog's answer was a loud, excited bark followed by a savage growl.

"Willa!" Smith's voice—and he was coming toward her—running. "Willa," he said again when he reached her. "What's Buddy fussing about?"

"I don't know. He saw something there behind the bunkhouse. I'm sorry we disturbed you. I . . . just came out for a while and I heard the music—"

"Stay here," he said and gently pushed her up against the wall. "I'll see what it is."

Willa felt like a child caught eavesdropping. More than anything she wanted to run for the house.

"Howdy, ma'am. What's the to-do 'bout?" Billy's voice came out of the darkness first, then came Billy.

Embarrassment caused Willa to stammer. "I . . . don't know. Smith went to s-see."

"Ya was welcome to come over. I knew ya was here. Reckon Smith did, too."

Willa's mouth formed a startled "O" before she spoke. "You did?"

Billy chuckled. "Yup. Ya get used to shaders and shapes of thin's. Ya showed light again the wall. Figured t'was you. The little filly'd not stood still so long."

"Oh, my. I'm sorry I was enjoyin' the music."

"Plays right pretty, don't he?"

"I heard someone playing the other night."

"Sant has a cravin' for guitar music."

Smith came out of the darkness as silent as a ghost.

"Find a fox after the chickens?" Billy asked.

"No. I thought it might be the silver lobo after the mares Sant brought in. It could a been a skunk, or a possum." He squatted on his heels and rubbed Buddy's head affectionately "You're a damn good dog. Do you know that? You didn't run off to chase whatever it was you saw You stayed to protect your lady "

Buddy whined and licked Smith's hand.

"Thin's goin' good up at the house?" Billy asked.

"I think so. Inez is a big help. Tonight I had to give Mrs. Eastwood a few drops of laudanum to keep her from thrashing around. She needs rest."

"Her givin' ya a peck a trouble?"

"She's right mouthy at times." Willa laughed softly "But she's been quite decent since I called her bluff and threatened to leave."

"Guess she ain't wantin' ya to do that now Night to ya, ma'am. Best I get back. Sant took off like a turpentined cat when the dog barked. Most likely he'll come back spinnin' some tall tale 'bout how he run off a grizzly 'stead of a little bitty old possom."

"I'm sorry for the disruption, Billy."

"Don't bother yore pretty head 'bout that. Reckon Smith ain't sorry a'tall."

"Go on to bed, you old goat. I'll be back as soon as I walk Willa up to the house."

"You don't have to do—"

"—Yes, I do."

Smith took her elbow in a firm grip and guided her back past the cookshack and along the yard fence. Willa knew it had been foolish to lurk in the shadows and was afraid to guess what Smith must be thinking. Instead she simply allowed herself to feel his hand on her arm, guiding her along the dark path.

At the porch she stepped upon the first step and turned to him. His hand slid down her arm and clasped hers. Their faces were level.

"It was you . . playing the guitar." Her voice was soft and little puffs of warm breath caressed his mouth. "It was beautiful."

Smith shuffled his feet, but couldn't take his eyes from her face. "Any music sounds good when it's all there is."

"No. You like to play, don't you? Did you teach yourself?"

"Yeah. Sant got me a book so I could learn the chords."

"You play the tunes by ear."

"I guess you'd say that."

"I enjoyed it. There in the darkness it seemed to me that the music was coming from some enchanted land. Do you think that's silly?"

"Maybe a little."

"Did you know I was there? Billy said you did."

"Yeah."

"I'm sorry—"

"—Don't say that again. You've said it four times."

"I have not!"

"You have. I don't want you to be sorry you came out."

"I'm not sorry I came out. I'm sorry Buddy interrupted you."

"I'm not. It gave me an excuse to come over to you." For a long time his green gaze was locked with hers and she was scarcely aware that she spoke.

"You needed an excuse?"

"Yeah." He tilted his head and took a deep breath of air into his lungs.

"Why, for heaven's sake?"

"Cause you scare the hell out of me."

A look of bewilderment came over her face. Then she laughed—softly.

"You're joshing me. You're twice as strong as I am— even with a skillet in my hand."

His face was still grave, and even in the semi-darkness she could see that his eyes held a tenderness.

"Oh, Smith—"

"Yeah. Crazy, isn't it?"

"No . . ."

"I think it is."

Her gaze dropped to his mouth and her heart seemed to stall before it settled into a pounding rhythm. Her hands were on his shoulders and she was unaware of how they had got there.

His arms circled her waist.

Helplessly she watched as his mouth formed her name.

He drew her against him.

His lips touched her cheek, and she knew they were coming to meet hers. Slowly, deliberately, his mouth covered hers, pressing gently at first while he guided her arms up and around his neck and then wrapped her in his. She leaned into his kiss as it deepened and floated on a sea of sensuality where everything was gently given and gently received. The touch of his tongue at the corner of her mouth was persuasive rather than demanding. She parted her lips and gave herself up to the waves of emotion crashing over her.

Smith moved his face back from hers and looked at her. Her breath came quick and cool on his lips made wet by her kiss.

"Willa . . sweetheart . . . I shouldn't have done that, but God help me, I can't help myself."

She was aware that his pulse was racing as wildly as hers. His face hovered over hers for several seconds. Then the soft utterance that came from his throat might have been disgust with himself when, at her invitation, his mouth came down across hers. She met the fervor of his passion with unrestrained response. Her mind whirled and her nerves became acutely sensitized. She pressed herself against him, her arms holding him with surprising strength. His hand had moved up to the nape of her neck, and his fingers threaded into the hair that tumbled there. He tore his mouth from hers and buried it against her cheek.

"Here I am, holding you, kissing you. I must be out of my mind." His voice was ragged with an obvious effort to control his breathing.

Tears filled Willa's eyes—the result of nerves strung taut and disappointment over his obvious regret at having shared himself with her for that brief moment.

"Then why did you do it?"

"I wanted to. I wanted to so damn bad it was killing me." He moved his lips across her face and into the hair at her temples. His arms were still around her, his hand on the small of her back. "I don't like this feeling I have for you," he whispered in her hair, and she wasn't quite sure she had heard correctly

"What kind of feeling? Like? Dislike?"

"Like. More than like."

"You don't want to like me?"

"I should get the hell away from you before it's too late."

"Why? I'll not make any demands on you."

The flat of his hand moved down to the taut swell of her hips and pulled her to him with urgent force. Had she not been adrift in a sea of emotions, she would have felt the hardness of his desire pressing into the softness of her belly

"Tell me I'm a worthless no-good cowardly drunk."

"No!" she said fiercely "I'll never tell you that, and I wouldn't believe it if a million people swore to it on their mother's graves." Her arms tightened about his neck.

"You said it once. And you were right."

"Don't remind me of that." Her voice was impatient and there was an undertone of desperation. "You may not want to like *me*, but I like *you*. I can't help it. I may even *love* you! So there! Does that make you feel better?"

When he made no reply, Willa wrenched herself from his arms and stumbled into the house. She closed the door so quickly that she left Buddy on the other side. Tears of frustration ran down her cheeks.

CHAPTER

* 21 *

W illa's eyes feasted on the panorama stretching out before her. From Maud's window she could see forest-covered slopes giving way to grassy plains and gently rolling hills. In the distance the sky was edged with purple mountains. The last three days had been cloudy with the promise of rain that didn't come. But today there was a soft quality to the afternoon sunlight as it filtered through the clouds.

She loved this land: the space, the clean, uncluttered landscape, the sharp pine-scented air.

"What 'er ya lookin' at, girl?"

"The land." Willa answered absently "It's a beautiful land."

"I wish I could see it."

"You will, Mrs. Eastwood." Willa came to the side of the bed. "You should be able to sit in a chair soon. We'll put one here by the window and Inez and I will carry you to it."

"Poot!" Maud's mouth closed like a trap after she snorted the word. "I ain't havin' *her* doin' for me."

"I can't lift you by myself. I'd hurt your leg."

264

"Then I'll just stay here." There was an unmistakable stubbornness in the set of her face.

Willa laughed. "You'd best be careful. I might get the idea you like me."

"Well, I don't."

Willa was sure she saw a twinkle in Maud's eyes before she turned them away.

"Yes, you do. You're too ornery to admit it. Ah, listen— the clock is striking. Isn't that a beautiful sound?"

"I never told ya to fix my clock."

"You were asleep and I couldn't ask you. I'll go down and stop it if you don't want to hear it strike."

"Leave it be. What's done is done."

"Would you like for me to get you a nice cold drink of buttermilk?"

"Why? Ya wantin' to get outta here?"

"Partly. I need to visit the outhouse."

"Go on then. But I ain't wantin' none of that damn buttermilk."

"Are you saving room for another piece of Inez's choke-cherry pie? I told her to save some for your supper."

"I didn't like it. Too sour."

"Why didn't you tell me? We could have put more sugar on it. I'll go now. When I come back I'll read to you if you like."

"I ain't carin' if you do or not."

Willa smiled as she rounded the end of the bed. She knew Maud was enjoying James Fenimore Cooper's tales of Leatherstocking. She had seen interest in her eyes. At first she had been angry and accused her of *stealing* Oliver's books and vowed she would not listen. But after the first chapter, she had said no more about it.

Willa paused in the doorway It was getting hard to think of an excuse to close the door when she left the room. Billy was sure they had gotten rid of the rats and the holes where they had come in had been plugged.

It disturbed her the way Jo Bell crept about the house, not speaking to her or to Inez, but giving them sly looks as if she knew a great secret. The girl was up to something and Willa wanted to be sure it had nothing to do with Maud.

"Don't be shuttin' the door. Ya hear? I want to hear what's goin' on in *my* house."

"A mouse might come in."

"Hellfire. I've shot bears in my day. Why'd I be scared of a mouse?"

"Ring the bell if you want anything. It's there on the table."

"Damn cowbell hurts my ears," Maud grumbled.

Willa had to smile. Maud was feeling better.

Downstairs, she found Inez in the parlor struggling to push back the heavy draperies that covered the windows. A cloud of dust floated in the air.

"Beats me why anybody'd want the winders all covered up thisaway. There's enough cloth here to cover a lodge pole teepee and have some left over. Ain't decent to waste all this cloth just lettin' it hang here shuttin' out the outdoors."

Willa silently agreed with Inez that it was a waste to cover the beautiful view of the mountains.

"Will you keep an eye on Mrs. Eastwood's door while I go to the outhouse? She didn't want me to close it."

"Sure, honey. Get on out there and do yore business. I was goin' to take bed clothes up anyhow. It'll take me a while to get 'em in the chest. Got to fold 'em just right, y'know." Her eyelid drooped in a knowing wink.

"I'm glad you're here, Inez. I'm so glad," Willa said softly and squeezed the woman's arm when she passed her. "I don't know if I could bear it if not for you."

"Go on with ya before ya mess yore drawers." Flustered

because of the compliment, Inez's voice boomed in the quiet house.

Willa paused on the porch and looked off toward the bunkhouse and the corrals. Smith had been gone for a week. The morning after she had left him on the porch, Charlie had come to tell them that Sant Rudy had left to hire the Indians who would help round up and break the mules he and Smith had sold to the railroad. Charlie was going with Smith and the drovers to drive cattle down from the upper range. Sant would join them later.

"Smith said I've got the makin's of a real cowhand. He's givin' me a trained cow horse to ride—one he trained his self. I'm ridin' with Boomy. He's kinda foreman under Smith. Smith says Boomy's got more know-all 'bout cows than anybody he knows. Smith says Sant hates cows." Charlie had been so excited that the words had tumbled out of his mouth. Willa had smiled.

"I'm glad you're going, Charlie, but be careful."

"Smith says I'm ready to take on a man's job."

Smith says. Charlie thought what Smith didn't know wasn't worth knowing. Willa tried to shut off the powerful physical memory of Smith's arms around her, his lips against hers. Each time she thought of it the same breathless feeling arose in her.

Impatient with herself for dreaming of the impossible, she stepped out into the bright sunlight and hurried down the path. When she reached the privy, she saw that the board nailed to the side to keep the door shut was up. Someone was inside. She turned to retreat up the path but was stopped by Jo Bell's voice.

"I said, are ya wantin' to use the outhouse?"

Jo Bell's hair was held back with a blue ribbon and the neckline of the blue checked dress she wore had been lowered to show the tops of her breasts. She wore lip paint and a pair of Starr's dangling earrings. Since Smith had left the ranch, she had dressed as if she were the lady of the manor.

"Why else would I be here?" Willa said brusquely.

Willa moved past her and into the privy, pulled the door shut with a bang and latched it. She held her breath through the seconds of silence that followed. She heard Jo Bell laugh. The girl had moved over close to the door

"Bet ya a pretty ya don't know where Smith's gone to. Ya think he's out workin' with the hands, but he ain't."

Willa swallowed the tightness in her throat and remained silent.

"He come back half-sloshed and went off again. Billy sent the Indian to fetch him, but it wasn't no use. He'd got him a whore and a stash of whiskey and said he wasn't comin' back till both him and the jug was drained dry. Papa said a real honest-to-God whiskey sot would get a cravin' for whiskey and whores. Nothin' short of a bullet in the head'll get that notion out once it's in there."

He had come back and left again.

Willa shut her eyes tightly against an unwanted surge of hot tears. The kisses they had shared had meant nothing to him! Nothing deep and lasting. It was evident that Smith Bowman had no need for the love, enduring love, of a woman. All he wanted was whiskey and a whore. The pain of knowing that was fresh and sharp and hurt like hell! What did she expect from a man like that, for heaven's sake? He had said that he didn't want to *like* her. *Like* had to come before love. Didn't it?

Her face burned with shame. Demoralizing as it was, she loved him and had told him so. It was insane that she could be in love with a man who was a fall-down drunk, who wallowed with whores and who was completely ruthless. Yet, she had seen another side of him, a sweet and gentle side. That was the side she had fallen in love with. Mrs. Eastwood had called him a murderer. Had he really killed her husband? She seemed to be so sure and Smith hadn't denied it.

Pain stabbed her heart. How she both loved and hated the man for the feelings he stirred in her! She felt absolutely wanton when she was with him. Perhaps Mrs. Eastwood had a perfectly good reason for hating Smith. But Willa was sure that Smith had no intentions of harming the woman.

"Reckon I'd better go on and get outta the sun." Jo Bell's voice barged in to break up her thoughts. "I swan to goodness. I found two freckles on my nose this mornin'. Papa'd have a fit if he knew about it."

With a satisfied smirk on her face, Jo Bell ran the toe of her shoe over the small circle of stones beside the outhouse door, then walked leisurely up the path to the house, swinging her hips in the way Starr had said was sure to tantalize any man watching her.

Standing close against a tree on the slope behind the ranch house, George Fuller studied the lay of the land through his spy glass. All around him were trees and brush. He had arrived at the place that morning after hearing in a saloon in Buffalo that the Eastwood hands were driving their cattle down from the upper range. He figured Smith Bowman would be away ramrodding the drive and he'd have a chance to talk to the girl. But first he needed to know how many men had been left at the ranch. So far he had only seen a squat, bow-legged Indian, a white-haired old man and a fat, black-haired woman—none of whom would give him any trouble.

He longed for a glimpse of the girl who had been in his thoughts for weeks. Just when he was about to lower the glass to rest his eyes, he saw a flash of blue on the porch. *It was her.* He adjusted the glass with eager fingers and whistled through his teeth. God, she was a beauty. He felt the same thrill he had experienced the first time he had seen her, standing by her pa's grave. Watching her walk down the path to the privy ignited a fire in his guts and his manhood began to swell.

George wanted to shout for joy. Bowman hadn't ruined *it!* It was coming back to life.

Holding his breath and scarcely batting his eyes, he watched Jo Bell until she disappeared inside the outhouse. He let a big puff of air out of his lungs, lowered the glass, rubbed his eyes, and lifted the glass again. The blond bitch who had bit him came off the porch and headed for the privy He kept the glass on the door. The black-haired beauty came out, talked to the blond, and went up the path switching her little tail as if she knew he was watching. George laughed out loud.

His plan was to wait until dark. The girl would use the privy again before bedtime. He knew that if he could talk to her alone, she would come with him. If not, he would take her anyway and sooner or later she would accept him.

Behind George and to the right, the trail dipped down through the trees to the creek. He turned, scanned the trail, and swore. Two riders were leisurely walking their horses down the trail toward the creek crossing. One was hatless. The sun shone on his light hair Even without the glass, he knew the blond was Smith Bowman. The other man was older and wore a high-crowned Texas-style hat with a rolled brim.

An idea popped into George's mind. If he moved down the slope nearer to where he had tied his horse and hid himself in the brush, he'd have a clear shot at Bowman. Not knowing where the shot come from, the other man would break and run. It would be as easy as falling off a log. He had never back-shot a man, but after what Bowman had done to him, the bastard would get what was coming to him.

Running bent over to keep out of sight, he quickly found

the spot that would give him a view of the crossing. He checked his weapon and settled down to wait.

The rocky trail turned north and ran alongside the south fork of Clear Creek. Riding side by side, Smith and Sant followed a wagon path that skirted the huge boulders fringing the mountains.

There had been days of hard labor driving the longhorns from the burned up pastures in the north to the grasses down in Crazy Woman Canyon.

"I never want to see another dad-blasted longhorn as long as I live." Sant looped the reins around the saddle horn and reached in his pocket for the makings of a cigarette. "What Oliver saw in them is beyond me. Never was a more ornery critter put on God's earth than that bag of hide and bones."

"They're tough animals. When Oliver got the start for the herd, most Wyoming ranchers were getting herds from Texas. We'll round up this bunch this fall, sell them, and get us a start of beef cattle." Smith held out his hand for the tobacco and papers. "Charlie did good, didn't he? He wanted to stay with the drovers."

"From what I saw, he did. Boomy'll look after him. He'll have some rough edges when he gets back."

"Why don't you take him with you when you go down to break the mules?"

"Nope. I ain't takin' no kid to raise. I only come back to get me a chuck wagon and a couple a hands. Boomy'll be here in a day or two. I'll take the Kirk boys. They got some Indian blood. They'll hit it off with the Cheyenne better than most."

They rode through tall pines and scatterings of birch and aspen along the slope. The trail they followed wound down to a brawling, swift-running stream about a half mile from the ranch buildings. Willows skirted the banks, and a trout leaped in a pool formed by a rock slide.

Smith stepped from the saddle. While the horses were drinking, he allowed himself the luxury of thinking about Willa. A week ago, when he had set out on the drive, he had vowed not to take a drink of whiskey and not to think about her. He was surprised at how easy it was to get along without the whiskey, but not thinking about Willa was the hardest thing he'd ever tried to do.

In spite of the heat and the dust or how tired and irritated he was at the stubborn, cantankerous longhorn cattle, the image of her face floated across his mind. The last words she had spoken to him echoed in his ears when he lay down to sleep. *I may even love you. So there!*

The beat of his heart quickened. He would see her tonight. He had a perfect excuse. It wouldn't look right to Inez if he didn't go to the house to see if things were going all right.

Smith was so wrapped in his own thoughts that he failed to notice that up the stream a pebble dislodged from the bank and fell with a tiny splash in the water.

Sant, squatting to drink, noticed. Then he noticed other things. There were no brown thrashers darting about and no yellow warblers among the willows. He got slowly to his feet, glanced at Smith, and saw that he was staring into the water, unaware.

In his own mind Sant was sure that someone was watching from the brush upstream. Smith's horse was between them and whoever it was. Sant casually moved his hand down his side to his holster and freed his gun butt.

"Smith . . ." Sant spoke Smith's name to get his attention. "Smith—"

Smith didn't seem to hear. He bent, picked up a stone and tossed it in the stream.

"Psst . . . Smith, dammit to hell—"

Smith turned his head. "Yeah—"

It was then that Sant's eye caught a tiny bit of blue color

among the brush where no such color should be. An instant later the loud sound of a rifle shot echoed down the ravine. Smith was knocked off his feet and into the water. His horse shied. The next shot creased the horse's fetlock, causing him to rear, leap into the stream and dash for the other side. Another shot took the hat from Sant's head.

Sant darted behind his horse and poured shots into the place where he had seen the color. Then he heard the sound of scurrying in the dry brush. He holstered his gun, grabbed Smith under the arms and pulled him out of the water. Blood poured from a wound on the side of his head, but he was conscious.

"Lucky ya turned yore head, boy. Ya pert near got it blowed off. Don't look deep, but yore bleedin' like a stuck hog."

"My . . leg—"

"Damn. The bullet that creased your horse went in yore leg. Looks like it's still in there. Ain't nothin' we can do 'bout it now. Here, tie this around yore leg to shut off the bleedin'." Sant whipped off his neckerchief. "I'm goin' after that back-shootin' son-of-a-bitch!"

Without waiting for Smith to reply, he mounted and put spurs to his horse, and the animal leaped up the bank. Sant turned the horse sharply when he saw movement and swept down through the woods at a rapid gallop. As he rode, he lifted his rifle, guiding the horse with his knees. When he was within firing distance of the rider, he took careful aim.

The rifle spoke.

The horse went down.

The man hit the ground, rolled to his feet and dived into the rocks at the edge of the trees.

A string of obscenities burst from Sant. It went against the grain to kill a horse, any horse, even one carrying a murdering bushwhacker. Sant swerved his horse in time to escape a bullet that clipped the leaves above his horse's head. A tide of fierce but controllable anger swelled within him. He hated nothing more than a dirty coward who would hide and wait to ambush a man.

Sant jumped from his horse, dropped the reins to ground-tie the animal, and darted into the woods. Once there he thought of his spurs. Kneeling down, he unfastened them from his boots and hung them over a low branch. He wanted no jingling to give his presence away. Years of fighting and hunting beside the Sioux had taught him a thing or two about woods fighting. There wasn't the slightest doubt in Sant's mind that he would find the man and kill him. Like a shadow he moved among the trees. All his senses focused on the hunt.

In the end it was so easy to locate the man crouched behind the boulder that Sant wanted to laugh. The damn fool was just sitting there watching the trail and waiting for him to appear so he could shoot him. Sant came up behind him and was within a few yards before he spoke.

"Stand up and turn around, ya yellow-bellied buzzard bait. I want to know who ya are before I kill ya."

Shock kept Fuller still for several seconds. Then he leaned his rifle against the rocks and, careful to keep his hands in sight, stood and looked into the barrel of Sant's Smith and Wesson.

"Who are ya?" Sant said again.

"Who wants to know?"

"The man who's goin' to splatter yore brains all over them there rocks ya was hidin' behind." Without taking his eyes off the man, Sant spit.

"Bowman had it comin'."

"Yore a low-down back-shooter. Ya didn't have the guts to face him like a man."

"What's your stake in this?"

"What'a ya think? Ya stupid clabber-head. Ya shot my partner and ruint a damn good hat."

The man stared across the short space like a man in a trance. He was trapped and faced a fight to the death. He had never thought it would turn out this way He might win, but there was something about this battle-scarred old timber wolf that told him he wouldn't.

Suddenly life was sweet and he wanted to prolong it.

"Mind tellin' me who you are?"

"Sant Rudy I reckon a man's got a right to know who kills him."

"Then you'd better know, too. I'm Fuller "

"Howdy "

"Are you givin' me a chance?"

"Why, course," Sant said gently and shoved his gun into the holster "I'd not kill a rattlesnake without givin' it a chance to coil up."

Fuller stared at the other man for a long moment, his face expressionless. His mistake had been in thinking that the old man would break and run. He'd killed Bowman. That's what he'd set out to do. He'd put the second bullet in him to make sure. Damned old man had nicked his leg with a bullet when he fired into the bushes. Maybe he should've stayed and shot it out with him then and there.

Well, hell, no use putting it off any longer It had to come sooner or later. George dropped into a half crouch, his lips curled back from his teeth, his protruding eyes made brighter with mingled rage and fear His hand clawed for his gun.

In the quiet woods a gun boomed like a crash of thunder George Fuller was thrown back against the rocks and crashed into his rifle, and both slid down into the dirt. His gun had not cleared his holster

Calmly, Sant walked over and looked down at him. There

was a strained, foolish expression on George's face as if he couldn't believe what had happened to him. Sant had aimed for his forehead but had shot him through the eye.

"Shit!" he said and spat on the ground beside the dead man's head. "Reckon I'm gettin' old. Missed twice today "

CHAPTER
* 22 *

The well water was fresh, cool and sweet.

After drinking deeply, Willa hung the dipper on the post beside the pump. It was good to be out in the sunshine. She wished that she were free to walk into the foothills behind the ranch, to smell the pines and pick the wildflowers that bloomed on the grassy slopes. If she could be alone for a while to listen to the bird songs, it would rest her mind.

Maud was asleep, Jo Bell in her room. For the moment, at least, she had a few minutes to do whatever she wanted to do. She would visit with Billy. She liked the old man. He had not only a wealth of wisdom to impart, but a sense of humor. At times he even poked fun at himself.

Willa saw the riders when she was about half way to the cookshack. There was *one* rider and he was pulling something behind his horse, she realized on closer scrunity. The other horse was riderless. Then it dawned upon her that it was Smith's horse following along behind one of those Indian carriers called a travois, and a man was lying on it.

Was Smith so drunk he couldn't stay in the saddle? Had he drunk himself senseless as he had done at the stage station and his friend was bringing him home? What a waste of a human being. A wave of shame washed over her. Shame for the secret dreams she had harbored of making a life with this miserable excuse for a man.

She stood perfectly still as the horse pulling the travois neared. Then she saw a blond head with a bloody rag tied around it. Breath left her and a knot of fear and dread formed in her stomach. He was not only drunk, he was hurt, too. Her heart began to beat furiously and she shook as if she were standing naked in a snowstorm. After a moment of hesitation, she lifted her skirts and began to run. Billy was coming out of the cookshack by the time she reached it. Both of them hurried to meet the rider.

"What's happened? What's happened to Smith?" Billy demanded in a voice made high by his concern.

Sant stopped the horse. "Caught a couple a bullets down by the creek crossin'"

"Bad?"

"I ain't knowin' yet." Sant's dark eyes rested intently on the woman who pushed herself in front of Billy to look down at Smith.

"Then what'er ya lollygaggin' fer? Get on down to the house so we can take a look see."

Willa's heart dropped like a rock. Smith looked so young, so pale, so helpless. Blood covered his shirt and the leg of his britches. She tried hard to recall Jo Bell's words so she could whip up her resentment against him, but her mind was completely out of circuit.

Unexpectedly, her vision blurred. She tried to blink away the moisture and failed miserably. She looked up at the man who had turned in the saddle to look down at her, knowing perfectly well he could see her tears. In the back of her throat she made a choking sound, and her voice was shaken loose.

"He's lost   a lot of blood. You've got to get him in a bed. If he should go into shock get some honey or sugar water down him and keep him warm."

"Yes, ma'am."

Sant turned the horse toward the cabin behind the bunkhouse. Willa stood motionless until Billy nudged her arm.

"The boy said ya was handy at nursing. I'd be much obliged if ya'll turn a hand to help."

"He's not a boy He's a grown man."

"I be knowin' that." Billy looked at her strangely "Are ya helpin' or not?" Worry made him speak harshly

"I've not had much experience with gunshot wounds, but I'll do what I can."

She walked along beside the travois as it bumped over the rough ground. Jo Bell's hateful words kept pounding in her ears. *He's got a jug and a whore stashed somewheres He ain't comin' till him and the jug is drained*

"Plenty!" Billy shouted. "Plenty Mad! Get yore worthless hide out here 'n' get Smith's horse. Gal-damn that ugly bowlegged cuss! He ain't never 'round when ya need him. Plenty Mad!"

"God the damn hell, Billy Why you yellin'?" The Indian crawled through the corral bars. When he saw Smith, he came to look down at him. "What you on that travois for, Smith?" Plenty Mad bent over and peered at Smith as if he expected him to answer "You dead, Smith?"

"Of course he's not dead. Any fool could see that," Willa said angrily

"How I know he not dead? He not move." The Indian looked her up and down with his hands on his hips. "Silly white squaw talk, talk, talk," he muttered.

Willa didn't hear him. Her heart was working like a runaway windmill. Now was not the time to panic, she told herself sternly. She must remember everything she had ever heard about tending gunshot wounds.

Willa stayed beside Smith, her eyes on his face, until the horse pulled the travois under the porch roof of the cabin. She held the door open and stood back while Sant and Billy, straining under Smith's weight, carried him inside and placed him on a bunk built against the wall. Willa was vaguely aware that the cabin was neat and dim and cool. Other than that, she was unaware of anything but Smith.

Gasping for breath, Billy straightened after pulling off Smith's boots.

"Ma'am, there's a teakettle a hot water on the stove in the cookhouse and clean rags in the cupboard by the wash bench. If ya'll fetch 'em, me and Sant'll take off his britches so we can get a look at his leg. 'Pears to be just above his knee. Bullet still in there, ain't it, Sant?"

"Yeah. The cut on his head ain't bad. Bullet parted his hair some. Ain't deep. Bled a lot. He helped get his self on the travois before he passed out."

Relieved by Sant's words about the head wound, Willa went to get the water and the bandages. *Passed out* So he *was* drunk. She had to get away from this place, from him, before she did something foolish. As soon as she convinced Maud that Inez could take care of her, she and Jo Bell would go to Sheridan. Maybe they could be gone before Charlie got back. Once there, Jo Bell would go her own way and she would go hers, putting all this behind her.

A glimpse of Inez hanging the heavy draperies on the line reminded Willa that she had the key to Maud's room in her pocket. She ran out the door, the bundle of rags in her arms.

"Inez," she called. "Smith's been shot. Here's the key to Mrs. Eastwood's room. Stay with her See that Jo Bell stays out of the room. I'm afraid of what she might do. Maybe she would only aggravate her, but I can't take the chance she might hurt her. She's got this notion that the ranch would be hers and Charlie's if something happened to Mrs. Eastwood.''

"Smith shot? Blessed Virgin! Who shot him? Is it bad?''

"I don't know who shot him or how bad." Willa couldn't bring herself to tell Inez that he'd been away for days drinking and . . . whoring.

"Poor Smith." Inez shook her head sadly. "That boy's had a cat on his back since Mr. Eastwood was killed. Don't worry, honey, I'll look after Maud and see that little hussy don't bother her none. Go on. Do what ya can for the boy.''

"Thank you.''

Why did they keep calling him a boy? He was a man, for Godsake, a man who was responsible for his actions the same as any other man.

Sant met Willa at the door of Smith's house and took the teakettle from her hand. They had removed Smith's clothes and covered him with a sheet from his hairless chest down to the ragged wound in his leg. The bullet had left a raw, red, ugly hole that was still oozing blood. Think of what has to be done, she told herself sternly. Think of that and only that.

"Besides these bandages, we'll need boiling water to rinse the knife we must use to get the bullet out, something to use as disinfectant—vinegar or whiskey, and ointment if you have some. The teakettle water will do for us to wash our hands in. I brought lye soap.''

Billy began pulling things out of a cabinet. He placed a bottle of whiskey, tweezers and pincers on a table that he drew up close to the bunk.

"We got some of that Lambert listerine. Old saw-bones from Buffalo left it here.''

Willa's eyes met the old man's. "You've done this before.''

"When I had to. I ain't good at it."

"I may not be good either. Shouldn't we send for the doctor?"

"Be tomorry before he got here," Sant said. "Bullet'd be all festered in by that time. Reckon we ort to get on with it before he comes to. It's gonna hurt like hell."

Willa scrubbed her hands, a procedure a doctor had told her was essential when working on an open wound. Without having to be told, Billy washed his hands. When Sant brought a pan of boiling water, they scalded the tweezers, pincers and a sharp knife.

After washing away the blood, Willa discovered the almost spent bullet had gone through the fleshy part of Smith's leg and had almost come out the back. If she made a small cut on the back of his thigh she could reach the bullet without probing the wound. She told this to Billy, and he gently rolled Smith onto his side, being careful to keep his privates covered.

With the knife in her hand, she hesitated. She wasn't sure she could cut into his flesh. As she hesitated, Billy's gnarled hand came down on her shoulder

"Ya wantin' me to do it?"

"No." She ground her teeth together. "I started it; I'll finish."

"Ya be a good lassie. Smith'll be thankin' ya."

"I don't want his thanks," she said grimly. "I don't want anything from him."

She was thankful that Smith didn't flinch when she made the incision. She reached in with the pincers, pulled out the bullet, and dropped it on the table. After she swabbed the cut with listerine, she soaked a pad and placed it over the wound.

Billy eased Smith onto his back.

With the tweezers Willa picked out fragments of cloth from the jagged hole and disinfected the lacerated flesh. Smith didn't move or make a sound even when she put in the stitches to hold the flesh together.

"Smith'll be happy we didn't waste good whiskey," she said, and dabbed at the crease on the side of his head with an antiseptic-soaked cloth.

"Yup. He be known to take a drink or two."

"A drink or two?" The strain of working over him had stretched Willa's nerves as tight as a fiddle string. Her voice was harsh. "More likely a whole bottle or two."

"Yup. He done that too, but not lately."

"Not lately." She looked at Billy with cold disdain. "What do you call lately? The last hour or two? Are you saying that he *hasn't* been shacked up with a . . . a loose woman for a week and that he *hasn't* drunk himself into a stupor? Did she get tired of him . . . pawing her . . . and shoot him?" Pride and only pride kept Willa from crying and throwing something against the wall.

"What in tarnation are ya talkin' 'bout?"

"I merely wanted to know who shot him. But I'm sorry I asked. It's no business of mine," she said briskly, dropping the bloody rag in the wash basin. "Absolutely no business of mine."

"I'm a knowin' that, but I'm tellin' ya anyhow cause I'm a thinkin' ya got thin's back-sackered, girl. Feller named George Fuller bushwacked him and Sant down by the creek. Sant trailed 'im and killed 'im. He's takin' the buckboard and bringin' him in to the marshal at Buffalo."

"Fuller? Oh—" Willa's eyes sought Smith's face. Her hands stilled; one was resting on the top of his head, the other held the cloth she was using to wash the blood out of his hair.

"Sant said Smith'd tangled with him over you women folk."

"But . . . I'm the one who bit him. Smith wasn't even there."

"He found his camp and kicked the sh . . . stuffin's out of him. Then he shot him in the butt for shootin' yore dog."

"When did this happen?"

"Before ya got here, I reckon."

"He never said anything to me about seeing Fuller again."

"Don't surprise me none a'tall." Billy picked up the wash basin. "I'll fetch ya some clean water."

The light from the window shone on Smith' face. He looked so tired and pale beneath several day's growth of whiskers. His lashes were long and gold-tipped. His brows curved in a high arch. Willa ran her fingertip lightly over one of them, then moved it away guiltily.

"Do you think I want to love you?" The words came on a breath of a whisper. "I don't! You would give me nothing but pain, and I've had enough of that to last a lifetime." She choked back the sobs as she thought of the long, lonely future that lay before her.

Billy returned and set the wash basin on the table within easy reach. He stood back and watched Willa clip Smith's hair so she could smear ointment along the cut on his head.

"When do you reckon he'll come to? He's been out a long time."

"I don't know if he passed out because of the whiskey or loss of blood—"

"Because of whiskey? Ya keep harpin' on that. Are ya one of them prohibition woman goin' round bustin' up saloons and preachin' hell-fire and brimstone?"

"I am not," she said staunchly, turning to glare at him. "I believe that liquor has its place if it's not misused. It has a certain medicinal value. It's also addictive. Some men and some women, I might add, can't leave it alone."

"Ya think Smith's one of them, and he passed out 'cause of whiskey? Far as I know he ain't had any since he come back."

"Of course he hasn't." She wanted to shout but controlled her voice with effort. "He's been unconscious."

"Let's me and ya get a thin' or two straight, missy. Ya think he's drunk *now*?"

"I don't think anything. As I said before it's none of my business if he drinks himself into a stupor. I'm just trying to help another human being."

"I'm gettin' yore meanin' clear as a bell. I'm a tellin' ya Smith ain't been off on no drinkin' spree. He's been herdin' a pack a ornery steers for a week."

"He came back—"

"If'n he did I didn't see him."

"You sent the Indian to get him—"

"I ain't sent that clabber-head nowhere."

"—It was no use. He wouldn't come. He was with a woman who . . . sells her services."

"That's pure sh . . . horse-hockey!"

Willa's throat filled up as the truth hit her. Billy would have no reason to lie—to try to hide Smith's . . . activities from her. A wave of pure joy washed over her, followed quickly by self-condemnation. She had been so gullible, so easily convinced by Jo Bell's spiteful words that Smith was a despicable degenerate. Oh, she had known about the drinking; she had seen that with her own eyes, but it was the other that had hurt so damn bad. Tears she could not control rolled down her cheeks. She tried to turn her face away, but Billy's hands on her shoulders turned her toward him.

"I'm not knowin' much 'bout women folk, but I know one don't cry lessen' she's feelin' bad 'bout somethin'. If yore thinkin' Smith'll die, there ain't much danger of it less he gets blood poison."

"I thought . . . someone told me that he'd come back and left to meet a . . . woman and get drunk."

"It ain't so. But why'er ya feelin' bad? Ain't ya glad, lass?"

"I'm tired and discouraged, but mostly I'm ashamed. I was duped into thinking the worst about him."

"Reckon it was that gal. Smith said she was pure poison—"

"She's that all right. I've never met anyone like her."

"Ya've had ya a hard time, ain't ya? Charlie told how ya happened to be with the Franks. Smith's had a hard time too, but he's a tryin' to make the best of it." She leaned her forehead against Billy's shoulder for an instant. "I know fer a fact Smith ain't been drunk since ya been here. I ain't sayin' he didn't use to do that some. More'n some. The boy had a load to carry that'd break a weaker man."

"Thank you for telling me that, Billy." Willa pulled away. "We've got to watch him. He may go into shock. It worries me that he hasn't regained consciousness."

"If he'd a'been drunk, lass, ya'd a knowed. He'd a smelled like he been wallerin' in a hog trough."

"Smith dead yet?"

Willa and Billy turned to see Plenty Mad. His face was covered with gray ashes. He had smeared something black on his nose and had tied black feathers to the braids on each side of his face.

"No, ya blasted dog-eatin' jackass!" Billy's voice thundered in the quiet room.

"Why you get all mad, Billy? Plenty Mad ready for death ceremony. I sing songs of friend Smith's courage in battle and hunt for the big buffer."

"Get yore tail out before I kick it out!"

"Ahhh . ." Plenty clamped his hands over his ears. "You make me not to hear with loud voice."

Willa looked down to see if the shouts had disturbed Smith. His eyes were open and he was looking at her

"You're . . . awake," she whispered breathlessly. "You're awake," she repeated as if she couldn't believe it. "How do you feel?"

"I'm thirsty—"

"He's awake, Billy. And he's thirsty." Willa's voice had a smile in it.

"Well, dog my cats. Howdy, boy." Billy came to the bed with Plenty Mad close at his heels.

"You ain't goin' to be dead, Smith?" Plenty asked, jabbing an elbow in Billy's ribs to push him aside.

"Don't know yet. I see you're ready for it." Smith moved his head slightly and grimaced.

"Plenty Mad looks plenty damn good, huh, Smith? Dance all night for good friend. Plenty Mad ready to build good, high scaffold."

"It's good of you, but don't trouble yourself." Smith closed his eyes wearily.

"No trouble. No plenty damn trouble. No wolves get to friend Smith. Plenty Mad build damn fine scaffold." He slapped away Billy's hand on his shoulder. "Stop pushin', Billy. Stop hell damn pushin'."

"Then get out, ya gal-durned dumb-head. Get out before I throw ya out."

"Kiss my damn hell ass, Billy. You make me plenty damn mad. I tell spirits make you plenty damn sick. Hair fall out, teeth rot, manroot fall off." He made a breaking gesture with his two hands. "You see. You see plenty damn quick."

"Horse-hockey!"

"I go, Smith, or I skin Billy like jackrabbit. Don't worry, friend Smith. You die, Plenty Mad make plenty big to-do. Give friend Smith plenty good send-off."

"That's comforting to know. Thanks a lot." Smith spoke with his eyes closed.

Growling like a bear with a sore tail, Billy grabbed up the water bucket and followed the Indian out.

"Here's some water," Willa said. "Can you drink or would you rather I spoon some into your mouth?"

"I'll drink."

She put her hand under his head to lift it. He drank thirstily, emptying the glass.

"I thought I was seeing things when I saw you standing there."

"Do you know where you are?" she asked as she gently lowered his head to the pillow.

"Sure. My head's clear as a bell. It's strange having you in my house, but good too."

"I . . well . . Billy asked me to help. I'll have to be getting back—"

"Don't go." He reached for her hand, turned her palm to his and interlaced his fingers between hers. "How bad am I?"

"You've got a new part in your hair—over your ear. A bullet went through your leg, but missed the bone. I'd say you're in pretty good shape."

"Then why am I so weak? I can hardly keep my eyes open."

"You lost a lot of blood. I was worried you'd go into shock. You still could. You must stay still and stay warm."

"It was Fuller. If I'd known it was him Sant went after, I'd not have worried so much while he was gone. That back-shooter didn't stand a chance against Sant."

"Billy said you went to Fuller's camp that night."

"Billy talks too much."

"You shot him."

"Yeah. I wouldn't have, but he shot your dog."

Willa looked down at their two hands. His fingers were squeezing hers so tightly that they were almost numb. She could feel his eyes on her face and, not ready to meet his direct gaze, she looked toward the window.

"Look at me." His quiet words dropped into the stillness.

There was a strange quietness about him. They looked at each other for a long while. His eyes were like clear green pools of mountain water. *They were beautiful*. Into her clouded mind drifted the thought that she had never seen such beautiful eyes on a man, but then she had never looked into a man's eyes as she was looking into Smith's.

She didn't know what to say. He lifted her hand to his chest and clasped it in both of his.

"I tried not to think about you while I was gone." His voice dropped to a whisper. "But it was no use." His eyes moved to her mouth and lingered before lifting to stare intently into hers. "I dreamed about kissing you."

Willa saw deep tension in his face and something she hadn't seen before. She wasn't sure if it was a hunger for something or if it was a pleading for understanding. She took a deep breath that quivered her lips. Her eyes softened and caressed his face.

He watched in fascination as her eyes smiled warmly into his. The look warmed him to his very soul, and a trembling joy came over him.

"While I was on that damn bumpy travois, I thought of you. I tried my level best to stay awake until I got here so I could see you." His voice was low but vibrated with emotion.

"I saw Sant bring you in."

She tried to smile while the fingers of her free hand poked strands of hair into the knot at the nape of her neck. He lay there, his eyes glued to her face.

"You're even prettier than I remembered."

She responded to the tug of his hand and sank down on the bunk beside him.

"That bullet must have damaged your eyesight—"

"You're tired. You have blue circles under your eyes. Are you getting enough sleep?"

"Of course. I've not given Mrs. Eastwood laudanum for several days. Inez is a big help. And . . . I like her. She makes the best pie. Even Mrs. Eastwood—" Her words trailed when she realized he was watching the movement of her mouth but not hearing a word she said.

"Will you kiss me again?"

She swallowed. It took her a full thirty seconds for the import of his words to take root in her mind. She shook her head.

"No. No, we shouldn't—"

"I've thought about it for a week. I'll not ask for more." The low, husky whisper came to her ears.

She stared into his eyes and then, as if mesmerized, she lowered her head, placed her lips on his and pressed gently. His cheeks were rough, his lips soft, yet firm and gentle as they moved beneath hers. Willa closed her eyes. Her heart was racing, thundering in her ears as his hand moved to the nape of her neck and his fingers spread into her hair. He took only what she offered voluntarily and didn't try to hold her when her mouth moved away from his.

His hand moved slowly over her shoulder and down her arm as if reluctant to lose contact with her. Time assumed a dreamlike quality as they looked at each other. As his eyes searched her face, a wave of helplessness came over her. He had become everything to her. She had never really understood the magnetism between a woman and a man before. It was both wonderful and devastating.

Finally it was Willa who broke the silence.

"I should go see about Mrs. Eastwood."

"I wish you didn't have to."

"So . . . do I—"

"You'll come back?"

"When I can."

"There's something about you that's . . . peaceful."

"Well . . . I'm certainly not a threat to anyone." She laughed nervously. "I really must go—"

"Before you go— I want to tell you that I'm sorry if I hurt you the other night."

"You didn't." She shook her head in denial.

"Yes, I did. I could tell. Some of the things I said didn't come out the way I wanted them to." He flattened her hand on his chest. His skin was warm beneath her palm. She could feel the steady beat of his heart and her fingertips pressed in an unconscious effort to keep that life-sustaining part of him safe.

"That happens . . . sometimes."

"I've never cared whether anyone liked me or not . . . until I met you." He expelled a heavy breath, but his eyes never wavered from hers. "Then it purely scared hell out of me when I discovered you had invaded every dream I had and how much I longed to hear you say what you said—about *maybe* loving me."

Willa was deeply affected by his words. They hung in the air between them. He lay there watching her with anxious eyes. She didn't know that she was crying until she felt the tears running down her cheeks.

"Don't cry. Please don't cry. If you didn't mean it, I'll understand." He spoke as if his throat were raw.

Fighting to regain her composure, she wiped her cheeks with the heel of her hand.

His eyes took on a questioning look as she groped for words.

"I won't deny that I feel something for you. But I realize that nothing can come of it. We wouldn't be compatible at all, and in time we would despise each other. Love can't last where there is no respect." She couldn't bear to look into his face. She lowered her chin and looked down at the hand that lay in her lap.

"Having someone to . . . to look out for you isn't enough?"

"Not for me. I'm sorry."

"I wish it could be . . . different."

"So do I."

"I can't change what I am. I can't go back and undo what's been done. I have to live with it or . . . blow my brains out."

"Did you kill Mr. Eastwood? Is that what you have to live with?"

"Yes."

"And Mrs. Eastwood is justified in hating you."

"Yes."

Willa looked into his eyes. His chilling answers to her questions pierced her heart like a shard of ice. Her spine sagged. Her brain was full of turmoil. It was as if her heart had been pounded into a pulp and her mangled emotions heaped on top. She pulled her hand from beneath his and stood.

"I must go."

"I'm sorry I'm not the man you want me to be." Shadows of pain clouded his eyes.

"I could say the same. It wouldn't matter to some women that you drink yourself senseless and that you killed a man who had been your benefactor and friend, but it matters to me." Lines of bitterness etched her face.

"Will you come back?"

"No," she said on her way to the door.

Smith watched her leave and closed his eyes wearily. What the hell could he have said but the truth.

An agony of despair washed over him. The pain in his leg was not to be compared to the pain in his heart. He felt once again like the lost, frightened boy who had stood alone on the bank of the river so many years ago.

CHAPTER

* 23 *

*I*nez opened the bedroom door to see if Maud was still asleep.

She wasn't.

"I heard ya unlock the door," Maud demanded as Inez came into the room. "Why'd ya lock me in here for? Where's Willa?"

"The girl needs a minute to herself once in a while. She locked the door and gave me the key. She was 'fraid you'd jump up and run off."

"Yore lyin'. She knows I can't get outta this bed."

"Guess she thought ya'd get on a broomstick and fly out the winder. Ya bein' such a ornery witch and all."

"Where's she at? I'm payin' her wages to tend me."

"Horse-hockey! Smith's payin' her wages."

"You'd not talk to me like that if I was on my feet."

"If ya was on yore feet, a team a mules couldn't a dragged me in here. I brung ya some fresh water."

"I don't want no damn water. Smith brought ya here to pester me, and I want ya outta my house."

"I'm not carin' what you want. I'm here, and there ain't nothin' ya can do."

"Get out!" Maud shouted. "Ya ain't nothin' but low-down white trash."

"Hold on just a gol-durned minute. Who'er you callin' low-down white trash, Maud Putney? Before ya married Oliver Eastwood ya was just as poor and down-and-out as anybody I ever knowed. So hush yore mouth. Hear?"

Maud lifted her head and shoulders up off the bed and shouted. "Don't ya talk to me that way."

"I'll talk to ya the same as ya talk to me. Ya was always mouthy. Ya've got worse in yore old age. Now ya can scream and holler all ya want, but I ain't takin' no shit off ya. I've knowed ya since ya was ass high to a duck. Course when ya married rich, ya didn't know us down and outters no more. Ya forgot how it was to live in a dugout and eat tater peelin's like the rest of us done one time or other."

"I ain't forgettin' ya was the brat of a whore," Maud said nastily. "Ever'body knowed what your ma was. None of the Sawyers ever amounted to a hill a beans."

"Yeah, my ma was a whore. She worked to feed us kids. Yore old man stole coal from the railroad and peddled it for whiskey money. His kids would'a starved if that old whore hadn't brought in grub now and then."

"That's a lie!"

"It ain't and ya know it. I ain't holdin' it against ya, Maud. Ya warn't so bad till ya married Carl Holt. Guess him beatin' the tar outta ya ever'day turned ya mean. Can't say I blamed ya fer that. I'd a cold-cocked that bastard with a stick a stove wood. Ya fell outta a bucket a shit when Carl died and into a bed a roses when Oliver Eastwood married ya. I ain't never figured how ya managed that."

"Ya was jealous. All of ya was."

"How'd ya know that? Yore nose was so high in the air

it's a pure wonder ya didn't drown when it rained. Well, I'm here to tell ya, ya ain't no better'n me. Not even as good. I got friends that'd come a runnin' if I needed 'em. What'a ya got, Maud?''

"I got the finest place in the country, damn you."

"Ya got this big old house that's goin' downhill faster than a goose shitting apple seeds, and that's all. Nobody gives a goddamn about ya. Not even yore own kid. She's livin' high on the hog in Denver, ain't she? Why ain't ya been to see her, Maud? No invite?''

"Shut yore m-mouth!'' Maud choked back a sob.

"Take a good look at what ya got, Maud. Ya'd be in a hell of a mess if Billy and Smith pulled foot and left ya sittin' out here on the prairie by yoreself.''

Inez set the glass pitcher down on the bureau with a thump, turned with her hands on her hips and glared at the woman lying on the bed. Tears streamed from Maud's tightly closed eyes and ran down her wrinkled cheeks. The hands that lay at her side were knotted into fists.

"I ain't wantin' to say them mean words, but ya had 'em comin'. Ya turned yore back on yore friends a long time ago and treated us like dirt. We wasn't good enough no more. The air's clear now, Maud. Stop yore bawlin','' Inez said gruffly. "Ya ain't no better or worse than anybody else.''

Inez looked down at Maud and remembered the slim young girl with the laughing dark eyes who had wanted so much. She had changed drastically after she married Carl Holt and moved out on his homestead. She had come to town a few times, but after she had one of her swooning spells in the general store, she had never been back.

Folks were shocked to hear that she had married Oliver Eastwood, a friendly, generous man who mixed easily with the town folk. He had built this house, but as far as Inez knew, only a few people from Buffalo had seen the inside of it.

"Are ya goin' to lay there feelin' sorry for yoreself, or do ya want this water?"

Maud looked up. "I ain't no good, Inez. Guess I never was. I tried so hard to be somebody."

"I'm thinkin' ya tried too hard, Maud. Ya tried so hard all the softness in ya just flattened out. I ain't sayin' Carl wouldn't'a turned me mean, or havin' all this wouldn't'a turned me snooty. Guess what I'm tryin' to say is—what's done's done. Pull in yore horns and be decent."

"Oh, God. I've been so lonesome." Maud covered her face with her hands.

"It's been yore own makin', but it ain't too late to change." Inez pulled up a chair and sat down. "It's real pretty up here with all the nice fixin's." She looked around the room. "I swear to goodness. Ya've even got yore own heatin' stove for winter."

"Fanny ain't comin' back, Inez." Maud's voice held resignation.

"How'd ya know that? She'll be back sometime—"

"No. She's shamed of me. Never wanted me to come visit at that fancy school."

"Well now, that makes no sense a'tall. I'd bet my last dollar that this house is right up there with the grandest in the state."

Maud was silent for a long while before she spoke. She seemed to be carefully studying the ceiling above her bed.

"Where do you live, Inez?"

"With my sister. Ya remember Yolinda."

"Was she the one with the big gap between her teeth?"

"Yeah. She's got a bigger one now. Hardly got no teeth a'tall."

"I heard somewhere you'd married."

"Yeah. Pud Snodgrass. But I branded the seat of his britches with my foot years back. I ain't makin' a livin' for no bastard too lazy to turn a hand."

"Pud was a good ball-player."

"That and gettin' under a loose skirt was all he was good at. I tell ya, Maud, I wasn't sorry to see the back of him. Last I heard he'd pulled foot for Californy."

"Time's gone by fast."

"Ya know what I got to thinkin' 'bout the other day? Remember when we was kids and that skinny, sissyfied school teacher took us on a trip to the woods to teach us 'bout flowers and birds and stuff like that? We caught us some red ants in a whiskey bottle and Jobe Tasser, who was the meanest kid that ever lived, slipped the neck of the bottle down the back of the teacher's britches."

Maud began to laugh. "I'd forgot 'bout that."

"In no time a'tall that feller was dancin' Yankee Doodle. When he took off for the creek like a cat with his tail on fire, us kids piled in the wagon and beat it for town."

"I remember when Ralph Volk put a dead frog in his coffee—"

"—And a dead rat in his coat pocket." Inez doubled over laughing. "Remember when Carl drove a nail up through the seat of his chair? When he sat on it, he came up fightin' mad. Carl laughed so hard he fell off the bench. I think he got a whippin' for that."

"Was probably the last whippin' he got," Maud said solemnly.

"One mornin' old sissy britches went to get the books out of the drawer and found a big old rattler curled up in there. He took off like a scalded cat. Lord-a-mercy! He fairly flew outta that schoolhouse and never come back."

"We never did learn how to read and write good, did we?" Maud said regretfully.

"It's grand to have somebody to talk to about old times, ain't it, Maud?"

"It's been a long time since I seen anybody that knowed me back then." After a pause she asked, "Why'd Willa lock the door?"

"She don't want that young gal, that Jo Bell, comin' in here botherin' ya. That's the God's truth."

"She was here lookin' at me one day when I woke up. Why'er they lettin' her stay here?"

"She don't have no place else to go, leastways that's what Willa said. That gal fairly needs her butt blistered the way she carries on." A broad smile spread across Inez's face. "She's plumb put out with Smith 'cause he don't pay her no mind."

"Smith! Ha! Don't mention that rotten piece a trash to me after what he done."

"Ya just ain't got no forgiveness in ya a'tall, have ya?" Inez said with disgust. "I'll say this once, Maud. Nobody feels more sorry 'bout what happened to Mr. Eastwood than Smith."

"Then why is he tryin' to kill me?"

"Kill ya?" Inez screeched. "Bullshit! Yore crazy as a bedbug if yore thinkin' that. He's worked his ass into the ground to keep this place goin' for ya."

"He thinks it'll be his when I'm gone, but he ain't gettin' nothin'. Fanny'll come back when there ain't nothin' here for her to be shamed of."

"Land sakes. What'd ya do without him here to run things? Why he stays and puts up with ya for is beyond me, Maud."

"I don't need him to run things. I told him a hundred times to get out, but he won't. He hangs around drinkin' and whorin and stealin' me blind."

"Ya ain't goin' to make me believe bad thin's 'bout Smith. Yeah, he drinks some, but he does good thin's for folks too."

"Ya don't know him like I do." Maud drank from the glass on the table beside the bed.

"And I'm thinkin' ya don't know him a'tall."

"I know as much as I want to know."

"Pretty day, ain't it?" Inez said pointedly to change the subject.

"It's been a long time since I was outside on a pretty day," Maud answered, seemingly willing to drop the subject of Smith.

"When yore fit again, we'll go lookin' for some berry bushes and make us a cobbler."

"You make a good choke-cherry pie, Inez."

"Yore right as rain 'bout that. I make 'em for the Palace Restaurant in Buffalo. Folks come from miles 'round to eat my pie. Now the secret to makin' good pie is the lard. I never use meat fat for crust."

Willa let herself quietly into the kitchen. She was hurt and confused. The shock of hearing Smith admit to the killing of Mr. Eastwood was evaporating now, but deep tremors of unease still chased through her body. She felt as limp as a pile of wet laundry.

Jo Bell had lied about Smith coming back from the cattle drive and leaving again for a week of debauchery. This time he was innocent of the accusation, but what about the next time?

Knowing the kind of man he was, how could she be so desperately in love with him? *Because you can't help yourself!* her heart cried.

Willa squeezed her eyes shut. Her heart constricted painfully and she struggled to keep the sobs from breaking loose.

She couldn't afford to let go. She had contracted to care for Mrs. Eastwood. After that obligation was fulfilled, she would have time to indulge in self-pity.

On her way up the stairs, Willa's mind ground to a halt as she heard a sound coming from the room behind the library. It was the room Mr. Eastwood had used for an office. She paused at the door to listen and heard the muffled sound again. Could a rat or a squirrel have gotten into the room? If so it could be gnawing at all those wonderful leather-bound ledgers piled atop his desk. She hurried back through the kitchen and called softly to Buddy, who was lying on the porch.

With the dog beside her, Willa hurried back to the office door and listened. When she heard the sound again, she flung open the door.

"Get that rat!"

With an angry growl, Buddy leaped into the room.

Jo Bell let out a yell of surprise and quickly closed the drawer she had been rummaging through.

"What are you doing in here? You're a guest, Jo Bell. You have no right to go through your aunt's things."

"It ain't no business of yours what I do. 'Sides, they're as much mine as hers."

"That isn't true. I'll not stand by and see you prowl through things that don't belong to you."

"I suppose you'll sic that old dog on me."

"No. I can handle you without Buddy's help."

Jo Bell flounced out of the room and started up the stairs. Willa closed the door. The girl turned and looked down at her.

"What'll ya do when Smith dies? Ya won't have nobody to back ya."

"Smith isn't going to die. So you can forget that."

"I ain't a forgettin' it," she said smugly. "And you better

not forget it either." She turned and went swiftly up the stairs.

Something in the girl's attitude caused Willa's stomach to stir restlessly. She had given in too easily. Jo Bell loved a yelling match like a dog loved a bone. There was a glint in her eyes that hadn't been there before. It was an "I-know-something-you-don't-know" expression.

It suddenly occurred to Willa that Jo Bell had said, "*when* Smith dies," not "*if* Smith dies." Had she known that George Fuller was going to ambush him? No. She couldn't have known that. She may have overheard Sant and Billy talking about Sant taking the buckboard to bring in the body. Whatever Jo Bell had in mind, she would have to act alone. As far as Willa knew there wasn't a person on the ranch that would do her bidding.

The loud ticking of the clock that stood at the end of the hall caught her attention. She watched the brass pendulum swing back and forth. How quickly goes the time. It seemed only a short while ago that she was a little girl sitting between her mother and Papa Igor on the seat of the caravan. The sky was blue, the breeze warm. And the birds sang merrily in the trees.

Time had suddenly turned the little girl into a woman. Her mother and Papa Igor were gone. Today she wasn't sure that she was strong enough to cope with life on her own, but try she must. As Smith had said, there was no turning back the clock.

The sound of laughter reached her before she reached Maud's open door. Surprised, Willa slowed her steps.

"Now ain't that a lick? I swear, Maud, I never knowed old man Keith was a brother to Banker Caffery. Lord, wouldn't Marge Caffery bust a gut if that old drunk showed up at one of her fancy doin's? Ha! Ha!"

"He wasn't but half-brother. But guess blood's blood no matter how little or how much. Marge Caffery's eyes bugged when she saw this house. She wasn't snooty to me then; she was fallin' all over herself a bowin' and scrapin'. But I just looked down my nose at 'er like she was nothin'."

"Doggit! I'd a like to a seen ya take her down a notch or two."

Willa hung in the door not believing what she was seeing. Inez, with a dishpan full of apples in her lap, sat in the rocking chair, her feet up on the side of the bed. She was peeling the apples and Maud, propped up with pillows, was slicing them into another pan.

"Hello, ladies."

"Ladies? Hear that, Maud?" Inez chortled. "I ain't been called that in a coon's age. How's Smith?"

"He's going to be all right."

"I figured he was or we'd heard. Me'n Maud's been talkin' over old times."

"You never said you knew Mrs. Eastwood."

"Never knowed a *Mrs. Eastwood*. But I sure as hell knowed Maud Putney. We went to school together. What there was of it, huh, Maud?"

"Who'd Smith get in a wrangle with?" Maud asked abruptly.

"No wrangle. According to Billy, a man named Fuller ambushed him and Mr. Rudy at the creek crossing."

"He ought a shot his blasted head off," Maud grumbled and shoved the pan of apple slices off her lap.

"I'll swear, Maud, that's downright mean." Full of bluster, Inez's feet hit the floor and she stood.

"If he'd done to ya what he done to me, ya wouldn't be . . . ya wouldn't be—"

Maud stopped speaking in mid-sentence. Her face paled and her entire body assumed a condition of extreme rigidity.

Willa rushed to the side of the bed, knowing that Maud was having one of the seizures the doctor had talked about. The rigidity lasted for only ten of fifteen seconds, but to Willa and the startled Inez it seemed an hour.

What followed was small quivering movements which involved her whole body. Her arms, shoulders and head twitched, and saliva ran from her mouth. Her face appeared swollen and had a purplish cast.

"What'n hell is wrong with her?" Inez blurted.

"Hold her broken leg so she can't move it," Willa said calmly. "She's having a convulsion. There, there, it'll be over in a minute," she crooned more for Inez's benefit than Maud's.

"Lordy mercy. I ain't never seen anything like it."

"The doctor said that she's probably had seizures all her life. I'm sure it's why she's spent so much time alone. She's been made to feel ashamed."

The convulsions did not last more than a minute or two. Their violence then decreased. Maud's breathing became near normal and her face less livid. Finally she drew a deep sigh and fell into a sound sleep.

"It's over." Willa placed Maud's hands at her side and covered her with the sheet.

"Was she a havin' one of her fits?" Jo Bell asked from the doorway. Willa looked up to see her lounging there, her shoulder against the doorjamb.

"She's had a convulsion. It's a mild form of epilepsy."

"I ain't carin' what they call it. Is she dyin'?"

"Of course not. People live a long time with epilepsy."

"Oh, shoot! Why can't that mean old cow die? She ain't no use to anybody."

"More use than ya are!" The words burst from Inez and she started for the door.

Jo Bell saw immediately the anger her words had provoked

in both Willa and Inez. She ran down the hall to her room. Once inside, she slammed the door.

"Did ya hear that?" Inez demanded. Then before Willa could answer, "I ain't never heard the like. She's a bad one. The devil's right in her."

Willa was beyond being shocked by the hateful words that spewed from Jo Bell's mouth.

"At times I'm sure she's . . . dangerous." Willa spoke with a worried frown on her face. "I've been thinking that since I found her here in the room. I've been afraid to leave Mrs. Eastwood alone when she's in the house."

"Well," Inez said stoutly, "I can handle that feisty little flip-flapper, but about Maud—will she be all right?"

"She's worn out and will sleep for a good long while. We must be careful how we act when she wakes up. I'll mention that she had a seizure and we'll act as if people have them every day, that it was nothing unusual at all. We must never use the word 'fit' or make her feel ashamed."

"It just plumb scared the waddin' outta me. We'd had us a good visit, that is after we'd gnawed on each other for a while. Maud ain't had it all roses. Her first man was as ornery a critter as God ever made, and I'm a'thinkin' that girl of her'n took after her pa." Inez waddled to the door.

"Thank you. The two of us must keep a close watch on Mrs. Eastwood. Inez, you've done her a world of good. I don't know what you said to her, but I'm glad you said it."

"It was jist plain talkin' I done. Times is a feller's got to put the cards on the table." She stacked the pans one atop the other and settled them on her hip. "These here apples is turnin' brown. I'd best get on down and get some water on 'em. Ya comin' down?"

"In a little while."

Willa closed the door to the bedroom, then sat down in the rocker and looked out the window. She was glad that Inez had broken through the thick barrier of bitterness that surrounded Maud. Perhaps, now, the woman had a chance for some happiness.

But as for herself, she realized now, love, happiness and contentment were not in her future. She felt sick inside, sick with guilt for wanting Smith, sick with the anxiety caused by Jo Bell, and sick with worry about her future.

CHAPTER

* 24 *

J o Bell could scarcely contain her excitement as darkness approached. She had rolled what she thought she would need in a bundle and tied it with a sash from one of her old dresses. The rest of her things were locked in her trunk.

Standing at the window, she could see part of the bunkhouse, the barn and corrals. There was no sign of Vince, not that she expected one. She was glad that Charlie was away and that he had left their horse. The note she had written to her brother was on the bureau.

Vince had promised he would be back as soon as he collected his pay from the mule buyer. And this morning the ring of stones had been in place beside the outhouse door.

Too bad, Jo Bell thought now, that whoever shot Smith hadn't done a better job. Arrogant, uppity trash was what he was. He'd be sorry for the way he treated her. He wouldn't be so smart when this place belonged to her, and it surely would. After all, she was the eldest of Oliver's sister's children, and the brightest. Charlie didn't have enough gumption to know which end of him was up.

Her papa had saved the letters that had been written by her

Uncle Oliver, and she had found letters in Oliver's desk that had been sent to him by her mother. What more proof did she need? The letters were in the bundle she would take with her to Sheridan, along with the rings and the gold watch and the money she had discovered during her latest search of Uncle Oliver's room, more than a *hundred dollars* in gold pieces. It was all hers. She didn't plan to share it with Vince. She would let him think that the rings and the watch were all she had.

Jo Bell's thoughts went to Smith. He was looking out for the old woman. There must be something in it for him. If the two of them were out of the way, there would be no stumbling block at all to getting control of this place. With the money she could get for it, she thought with a feeling of elation, she could even buy a fancy town house on Jackson Square in New Orleans. She sighed and indulged herself in dreams of the kind of life her papa had planned for her.

Jo Bell had given a lot of thought to Vince Lee during the past week. She knew he was handsome even though she hadn't seen him close up in the light of day. He had trembled like a leaf in the wind when she had kissed him and rubbed her breasts against him during the time they had sat on the ground behind the bushes and talked far into the night. After telling him about their trip from Louisiana and that she and her brother were the only living blood relatives of Oliver Eastwood, she had let him kiss her and even let him put his hand inside the neck of her dress, but that was as far as she'd let him go.

She had enjoyed using the power she had over him. But he was poor. All he owned was his horse, saddle and gun. Her papa would call him piss-poor. In order to get him to do what she wanted him to do, she would let him kiss her and might even do *it* with him, but she'd not marry him. No sirree. Papa had said for her to set her sights high and that's what she was going to do. She was going to marry a *rich* man.

The clock downstairs struck ten. Jo Bell moved from the window to the bed and picked up her coat, a scarf for her head, and the bundle. The lamp had been put out long ago so that her eyes would become accustomed to the darkness. She opened her door without making a sound and stepped out into the hall. Only the faint creaking of the floorboards told of her passing. She hurried down the stairs and let herself out onto the front veranda. Going quickly to the end, she saw the shadow of a man, and jumped into Vince Lee's arms.

"Thought you'd never come," he whispered and kissed her passionately. "I wondered if I'd dreamed you."

"Ya didn't, sweet boy. I'm here." Jo Bell wrapped her arm about his neck and kissed him back with an open mouth. She pushed her breasts against him, moaned softly, and gently bit the tongue that slipped between her lips. He backed her against the side of the house and ground his hardness against her. She waited until he began to tremble violently, then pushed him away.

"Not now, sugar—"

"Little tease," he whispered, breathing hard. "You make me horny as hell."

"We got lots a time for *that*. We gotta get away from here first. Guess what?" she said, straightening her dress. "Somebody shot Smith."

"Who?"

"Don't know. I thought it might'a been you. I was hopin' it was you."

"It wasn't me. I came in last night, laid the stones, and then beat it back up to the hills."

"I wish they'd a killed him. He ain't no good for nothin' but causin' us a heap a trouble."

"Has he bothered you?" Vince asked sternly.

"He would've, honey, but . . . I held him off." Jo Bell sniffed prettily. "Vince, sugar, there ain't nobody here but Smith, a old man and a crazy Indian. Maybe we ought to get rid of Smith now. He'll not be easy to handle later."

"What do you mean, sweetheart?"

"He's down in the bed. Got shot in the leg. We could wait for the old man to leave and we could   we could . ."

"Kill him?"

"Would it be so hard?"

The moonlight shone on her upturned face. She was the prettiest woman Vince had ever seen. He hadn't been able to think of anything but her since the night he met her. Surely she wasn't asking him to shoot an unarmed man who was already down.

"Honey . . . I couldn't—"

"P-please—"

"You don't mean that, honey. It could get us into a peck of trouble. Once this place is yours, we'll have the right to run him off. If he don't go, I'll call him out."

"And   shoot him?"

"If I have to. I've not run up against anybody yet who's slicker than me with a gun."

"You'd do that for me?"

"I'd do anything for you. Come on and point out your horse so I can saddle him. We don't want the sheriff out hunting us for horse-stealin'."

"Smith can be plumb mean, sugar—" Jo Bell insisted.

"Don't worry. I'll handle him when the time comes."

"Is it a long way to Sheridan? Can we find it in the dark?" she asked as she walked along beside him.

"We'll go to Buffalo tonight and take the stage in the morning." He flung an arm about her shoulders. "You scared of the dark, honey? Don't be. I'll take care of you."

Willa was sitting in the rocking chair in Maud's room when she heard the creaking of the floorboard in the hall. She opened the door of Maud's room in time to see Jo Bell, her coat over one arm, a bundle in the other, going down the stairs. Anxious to know what the girl was up to, she slipped out the door and watched as Jo Bell let herself out onto the veranda and softly closed the door.

With Buddy beside her, Willa moved quietly down the stairs to Inez's room and rapped on the door.

"Yeah?"

Willa opened the door. "Are you asleep?"

"Not now. Somethin' wrong? Has Maud—?"

"No, nothing like that. Would you mind staying with Mrs. Eastwood while I go out for a while?"

"Has Smith took a bad turn?"

"Not that I know of, but—"

"Run on and see 'bout him. I'll go up and stretch out on yore cot. Is Maud still sleepin'?"

"Yes, but after her attack today, I didn't want to leave her alone."

"Take yore time, I'm a light sleeper. I'll hear Maud if she wants somethin'."

Willa went through the dark kitchen, feeling her way along the table to the door. She had let her hair down earlier in the evening, and now she wished she had something to tie it back with. Having nothing, she looped it behind her ears and let it fall down her back.

It was strange, but she had been thinking about what to do about Jo Bell when she had heard the noise. Surely the girl would not be foolish enough to leave the ranch in the middle of the night—unless she had someone to go with her. But who?

Willa paused on the porch to listen. Her eyes probed the darkness and saw nothing unusual. Buddy's eyes and ears were better than hers. She looked at him. He was calmly waiting. She patted his head and together they went down the walk to the gate and headed for Smith's house.

How could she rouse Billy without waking Smith? She paused beside the bunkhouse where she had stood the night she heard Smith playing the guitar. Buddy stood close beside her. The house was dark, as she had expected it to be at this time of night. Uncertain as to what to do next, Willa suddenly realized that she was on a fool's errand. How could she and Billy stop a foolish girl like Jo Bell from doing what she was bent on doing? And why should they?

She leaned to touch Buddy's head to let him know she was going back. The dog was moving away from her toward Smith's house, his tail swishing back and forth in a happy greeting.

"Buddy," she hissed. "Come back."

The dog continued on. Willa ran a few steps to grab onto his neck fur and drag him back.

"Willa. Over here—" Smith's low voice came out of the darkness.

She stopped in her tracks. "Smith?"

"I'm here   by the house."

On a bench beside the door, his injured leg extended out in front of him, Smith was scratching Buddy behind the ears when she reached him. The dog was delighted to see him. His wagging tail shook his entire body and little whines of pleasure came from his throat.

"What in the world are you doing out of bed?" she whispered urgently

"Shhh   sit down." He reached for her arm and pulled her down onto the bench beside him.

"I can't believe you're out here. You were shot only this morning, lost a lot of blood and passed out. You'll get a fever—"

"You'd care?" The question was accompanied by the gentle squeeze of his fingers on her arm.

"What a stupid thing to say! Of course, I'd care."

"Plenty brought me a crutch we had lying around and helped me get out here. I didn't strain your stitches so nothing popped loose."

"You don't even have on a shirt." There was exasperation in her tone.

"I didn't have time to get one. Were you worried about me? Is that why you came out?" he asked hopefully.

"No. I knew Billy would take care of you. I came to tell him Jo Bell is up to something—" she whispered.

"Why didn't you come to tell me?" He looped his arm over her shoulders so his lips could reach her ear.

"Because you're in no condition to do anything. I think Jo Bell's leaving."

"I know. Plenty told me."

"You know? What are you going to do?"

"Nothing. Plenty is watching to see they take only the sorrel Charlie rode in on."

"She'll get lost out there." Then, "You said *they* "

"She's hooked up with a young kid who was here with the buyer for the railroad. He's come back for her."

"How do you know that?"

"Plenty Mad. He sees in the dark like an owl. He spotted a horse back behind the corrals and recognized it as the one belonging to the kid. Then he found him hunkered down by the veranda. He figured he was waiting for Jo Bell because he had seen them together the night before the men rode out. He's watching them now."

"For goodness sake. Doesn't Jo Bell have sense enough to know it isn't safe to go off with a strange man?"

Smith was silent for a few seconds. "You did," he said softly

"Well, yes, but that was different."

"How different? It was dark then, too."

"Yes, but you were . . you were— It was different and you know it."

"Sshh . . . listen— Buddy, stay here," he said when Buddy stiffened and a low growl came from the dog's throat.

"I don't hear anything—" Then she heard the faint sound of horse hooves on soft ground. "Now I do," she whispered.

"They're gone," Smith said after a few minutes of silence. "That fool kid will regret this night. The girl's trouble. I hope he comes to his senses before she gets him killed."

"Do you think she'll be back?" Smith's arm was still around her. Her shoulder, hip and thigh were pressed firmly to him. She was reluctant to move.

"If things go her way she won't."

"Charlie will be worried. He takes his responsibility seriously."

"He's got to cut her loose. Sooner or later she'll get him mixed up in something he can't handle."

Smith turned his face. It was just inches from hers. She could feel his warm breath on her mouth. She strove to close her heart against the thrill of being close to his warm body and inhaling the very presence of him. When she was with him, his magnetism drew every speck of logic from her mind and all that mattered in the world was her own desperate need to belong wholly to him and to have him belong wholly to her.

"Ah . . . you . . . should have on a shirt."

"I'm not cold." He lifted her hand and placed her palm against his chest. "See—"

His skin was warm, but she felt the quivering of his flesh.

"You're trembling—"

"Not from the cold."

"Then weakness. Did you have a good supper?"

"Billy poked everything he could find down me."

"I shouldn't have come here, Smith. If I had any brains I'd run back to the house as fast as my legs would carry me."

"Please don't be sorry " His fingers moved to push strands of hair from her cheek and loop them over her ear "I hoped you'd come back."

"I'm . . . just begging for more hurt."

"I'd die before I'd hurt you or let anyone else hurt you."

"There are different kinds of hurt."

"I know Oh, God! I know " His fingertips caressed her cheek, then moved to her hair "Remember when I dried your hair with my shirt?"

"I remember "

"We were alone in the dark. I felt like I was in another world—a calm, peaceful world where there was only you and me. I feel that every time I'm with you."

Slowly, giving her plenty of opportunity to move away, he lowered his lips onto hers. He kissed her with slow deliberation. His lips caressed her mouth gently, sweetly, for a long time, being careful not to scratch her face with his whiskers. When he drew back to look into her eyes, they were haunted and dark with despair.

"Oh, Smith . . . I don't understand myself We're wrong for each other."

"I know. I can't forgive myself; how can I expect you or anyone else to forgive me."

The agony in his voice touched her heart in a way his words could not have done. She pulled her hand from beneath his and cupped his cheek. She could feel the pull of his whiskers against her palm, his lips against her thumb.

"We can't turn back the clock. You said that."

"Once in a lifetime, during one small speck in time, you get a chance to have everything you ever dreamed of having.

If you grab for it and miss it, you've lost your chance. I grabbed, I missed, I know what I've lost." He turned his lips into her palm.

For a moment Willa couldn't speak. Her voice was a pathetic croak when she spoke at last. "I don't know what to say."

"You don't have to say anything," he said tiredly. "I just wanted you to know. Having you know how I feel is like a bond between us."

"You're a sweet, sensitive man like Papa Igor. He was small and deformed, but he, too, could say beautiful words."

"I've never talked to anyone the way I talk to you."

"You've talked to others through your beautiful music."

They were so involved in each other that they failed to hear Buddy growl as Plenty Mad came around the side of the house.

"Hey, Smith. I boil that hell damn dog in pot someday."

The Indian came to stand in front of them with his hands on his hips. Willa would have moved away, but Smith's arm held her to him.

"Buddy is a different kind of dog, Plenty. He only growls at people he likes. He likes you."

"That so?" Plenty Mad cocked his head to the side and looked down at Buddy. "Hell damn. Plenty Mad not know 'bout different dog. Me see now. He mighty fine dog."

"Did they take the sorrel and Charlie's saddle?"

"They take. Make noise like herd of buffer," Plenty Mad said with disgust. "Silly damn white squaw talk, talk, talk." He drew his hand in a knife-like gesture across his throat. "You need help from Plenty Mad, Smith?" He looked pointedly at Willa.

"No, but thanks—"

"You need help, you call Plenty Mad. Silly damn white squaw too skinny to help big man like friend Smith."

Willa could feel the chuckle in Smith's chest, but no sound came until he spoke.

"I've got the crutch, but I'll call if I need you, Plenty."

They didn't speak for a long while after the Indian left. Willa knew that she should go back to the house, but she was reluctant to move when she felt his hand press her head to his shoulder and his cheek against her hair.

"Stay a while longer," he whispered and brushed her forehead with his lips.

Time had no meaning. They sat quietly together, neither intruding on the other's thoughts as they enjoyed the simple pleasure of being close. With her, Smith felt a peace he hadn't known since that unforgettable day. With her, he no longer felt so lonely inside.

"Tell me about yourself, Smith. You know all about me."

"What do you want to know?" She felt him tense.

"The usual. Where you were born and if you were a mean little kid."

He chuckled, and she realized it was with relief.

"I was born on a farm in Tennessee. We were dirt-poor, but we got along until a spring flood along the Mississippi claimed our land and a new channel was born. My pa— Are you going?" he asked quickly when Willa moved away from him and stood.

"No. I want to hear it all, every little bit, but I'm going to get something to put around you. You've got goosebumps."

"On a rack inside the door—"

She was back with a flannel shirt within seconds and draped it about his shoulders. He gathered her tenderly into his arms, and held her against his naked chest. She could feel the wild beating of his heart.

"You scared me half to death when you got up. I thought you were leaving me," he said against her hair after he had wrapped the shirt around her.

"Deep down I know I shouldn't be here, but God help me, I can't help myself "

He kissed her mouth, her cheeks, her eyes. "I never dreamed a woman could be like you. I'm scared, sweetheart, so damn scared of all those tomorrows without you."

"Tell me," she whispered, kissing the rough line of his jaw. "Start over and tell me about Tennessee, about when you were a boy, about coming west. I want to know. Don't leave out anything."

"As I said, the river took our farm. Ma had lived in one place all her life. She had never been more than fifty miles from home. She couldn't imagine the distance. Pa and I were excited over the trip, but Ma and my little sister hated it. We crossed into Arkansas and came up though Missouri. We stopped for a couple months in Iowa so Pa could work, then again in Nebraska. Every time Ma wanted to stay Pa had dreams of land and cattle."

He told how he had walked alongside the wagon, about how the wolves had attacked and killed his dog. Nevertheless, he had had a feeling for the land, a feeling of coming home. He had looked ahead to the purple mountains and vowed he would live here all the days of his life. He didn't know then that the days of his mother, father and sister were soon to end.

Smith talked unemotionally about losing his family—it had been so long ago. He spoke of being alone, hungry and scared, of waking one morning to the smell of bacon frying and his meeting with Billy and Oliver.

"I cried, but they didn't make me feel ashamed of crying. My pa had told me that *men* don't cry, and I expected a dressing-down, but none came. Oliver said, 'Cry, son, you've earned it.' "

"He must have been a very understanding man."

"He was. He and Billy became my family. I was closer to

them than I ever was to my own pa. Not that my pa didn't care for his family, but he didn't waste words, especially words of praise. In fact he seldom talked to me. Oliver and I talked about everything. He and Billy taught me practically everything I know because I never had much schooling before I came here. I care a lot for that old man in there," Smith said huskily, gesturing toward the door behind them.

"And he cares for you."

"I was gone from here for a couple of years. It was Billy's idea that I light out on my own. He said that he and Oliver would always be here if I needed them and that I needed to see more of life than was here on the ranch. He was right. I had to learn a few things the hard way, but I got by Billy thought that without me here, Maud might settle down and life would be easier for Oliver She resented me from the day Billy and Oliver brought me here."

"Why would she resent a little boy?"

"Billy said she was jealous. She didn't like Oliver spending time with either of us. Billy and Oliver had been together for a long time. Years back they were partners in a gold mine in Colorado. When they got enough money together for a bit of land, Oliver came here to the Bighorns to make the purchase and Billy stayed to work the mine until they could sell it. By the time he got here, Oliver was married to Maud."

"Mrs. Eastwood doesn't appear to have much in common with a man like Mr. Eastwood."

"The best Billy and I can figure out is that she found him dying on the prairie, took him to her homestead and saved his life. Oliver was strong on paying his obligations."

"Then . . . Billy owns part of the ranch."

"Billy owns all of it. Oliver left his half to Billy with the provision that Maud have the house and the things that she needs for as long as she lives."

"Does Mrs. Eastwood know?"

"The lawyer tried to tell her, but when he said the house was hers, she didn't hear another word he said."

"Why do you stay on here?"

"I'll not leave Billy. He's like a father to me. And I'm obliged to do what I can for Old Maud. Without us she'd be alone. Her only child has turned her back on her. Fanny understood Oliver's will and knows there's nothing here for her."

"That's a shame. What will happen to the house when Mrs. Eastwood's gone?"

"It'll sit there until it falls down. Billy will never live in it."

"And you?"

"Never!"

Smith's hand moved up and down her arm. She adjusted the shirt to cover his shoulders, then buried her hand beneath his arm, her palm against his ribs. His hard cheek rested against the softness of her hair. He had told her a lot about himself, but he had stopped short of telling her the most important of all—*how and why he had killed Oliver Eastwood*.

Willa's moment of happiness began to slip away from her. Would she grow old alone with only memories of this brief interlude? Would she never see him when his blond hair was as white as Billy's or when lines fanned out from his green eyes? Would she never know the joy of mating with him and bearing his children?

Right now, at this moment, she knew she was not strong enough to live her life without him unless what he had done was so repulsive to her that it would kill her love for him. With that in mind, she lifted her head to look at him, her eyes full of love. The unasked question hung in the silence between them.

For a long, quiet moment they gazed at each other.

"I know what you want to know. Don't asked me to tell you   now." He watched her face with anxious eyes, and through them she sensed the mental agony he was suffering. His hand moved to her hair and, gently clutching a handful, brought it to his mouth.

"I've no right to question you—"

"You don't understand, my love." His whispered words caressed her cheek. "I'm a selfish bastard trying to prolong this sweet moment. I want you more than I've ever wanted anything. You came into my life so unexpectedly, and from the first you made me feel things I never thought I would feel. I never felt shame like I did the day you came to the barn and saw me lying in the stall. That's why I was so angry." He accented his words with tender kisses. "Let me hold you for a little while longer, feel your softness, and smell your sweet body." The raw pain in his voice brought sobs to her throat.

"Oh, Smith," she whispered. "All I can say is that I never dreamed I'd fall so desperately in love with a man, that I wouldn't care who or what he was. There's so much sweetness in you that I want to pull you into my heart, hold you there and keep you safe from hurt."

He closed his eyes tightly, unable to bear the pain in hers or let her see the moisture in his. The mouth he sought was sweetly parted, her breath warm and moist. Holding her close against him, he could feel her heart pounding heavily against his breast as she kissed him with fiery sweetness. His hand moved behind her head and held her lips to his. They whispered to each other, mouth to mouth, sharing breath and soft, sweet kisses.

"I love you." Her voice was the softest of whispers.

"I've never heard those words before." His arms tightened around her as if she were about to be snatched away from him. "And I've never said them until now. I . . . love you, too."

"They're not hard to say when you mean them."

"I should have said them to Billy and Oliver. You . . . unlocked something in me."

"I'm glad. Oh, Smith, I can't give you up . . . now."

A groan of anguish left his throat. "Kiss me again, love—"

From the doorway, Billy could see that the couple on the bench were wrapped in each other's arms. The dog lay at their feet.

Things were looking good. The lass was pure hickory and she'd got under the boy's thick hide, that was certain. With a little luck he would see him settled right here on this ranch before he passed on. Not that he planned to go anytime soon, Billy corrected his thoughts quickly.

"It's a'goin' to work out jist dandy, Ollie," he mumbled. "Ya'd like the lass. She ain't no namby-pamby. She'll tell him how the cow ate the cabbage, but she'll give him a heap of love too. I'm a thinkin' it's what he's been hurtin' for."

With a smile on his whiskered face and a feeling of thankfulness in his heart, Billy crossed the room and went back to bed.

CHAPTER
* 25 *

The days marched slowly by without Willa exchanging a word with Smith. She was determined that he make the first move if he wished to see her alone. It worried her that not once during the time they had spent in front of his house had he spoken of their sharing their future together. After three days and four sleepless nights, uncertainty was eating her up inside.

Billy came to the house each morning to bring the milk and to visit with Inez. Through him Willa learned that Smith's wound was healing.

"What he needs is a bowl of my chili," Inez said, dipping the cream off the milk she had brought up from the cellar. "I'll make that boy a custard pie, is what I'll do."

"That *boy*? How 'bout this here *man*?" Billy asked.

"Man? Hell, I don't see no man. See a whiskered old goat sitting at my table."

One morning Billy announced casually that Smith was itching to start breaking in the mares Sant had brought in.

"Surely he's got more sense than to get on a wild horse

before that wound is completely healed." Willa's reply was swift and stern.

"Reckon ya oughta go tell him, lass. He ain't goin' to pay me no mind. I can talk till I'm blue in the face and he'll do just as he pleases. Always has."

Willa would have believed him if she hadn't turned her head just in time to see him wink at Inez.

Jo Bell's departure had eased the tension in the house, and Maud's mood had lightened considerably. She now welcomed Inez's company even though most of the time was spent in an argument that usually ended in a shouting match. They discussed in detail the lives of everyone within a hundred miles of Buffalo. Inez would tell her that she was as crazy as her old man, and Maud would reply that Inez could never make a living as her mother had done because she was too fat for a man to find what he was looking for

In spite of this, Maud's disposition was improving rapidly When she talked of coming downstairs so that she could see what a *mess* Inez had made of her kitchen, her eyes twinkled.

Both women enjoyed listening to Willa read to them, which she did each afternoon. Later she would hear them arguing about what they thought would happen next in the story.

A crew of men rode in one evening. Charlie and Sant were among them. Willa saw them from the kitchen window and braced herself to tell Charlie that his sister had left the ranch. She didn't have long to wait, because as soon as he had taken care of his horse, he came to the house. She met him at the door

"Charlie!" Willa gave him a brief hug and watched his young face turn fiery red. "It seems as if you've been gone forever."

"Yeah." He grinned broadly. "I was goin' to clean up before I come up, but—"

"—I'm glad you didn't. How did it go?"

"Great! I got teased a lot. Reckon I had it comin' 'cause I was so green."

"That was to be expected." Willa smiled fondly at him.

"Yeah. 'Cause I was new, I gathered firewood for the cook and rode drag—that's behind the herd where the dust is. Trailin' steers is hard work. Boomy say there ain't a critter born meaner than a Texas longhorn. He says some of them come up to a thousand pounds."

"That big? My goodness, you could have been hurt."

"I did all right. Well . . . the fellers did save my bacon a time or two." He laughed, pleased over her concern. "The horse Smith give me to ride was smarter than me. Boomy said that when Smith was my age he was trail boss."

"Now you're a real cowboy. Charlie, I'm proud of you."

"This is the life for me. I ain't ever goin' to do nothin' else. Ya work hard all day and at night ya sit around a fire and listen to the fellers lie to each other." His young face was creased in smiles, then suddenly he was the serious Charlie she knew. "Pa wouldn't understand—"

"Thank heavens, we don't have to like the things our parents liked, Charlie. My mother loved boiled turnips. Ugh!"

"Yeah. Boomy's pa was a preacher and Boomy can cuss louder and longer than anybody."

"Maybe he does take after his father in a way—preachers can *talk* louder and longer than anybody." They both laughed, then Willa said seriously. "Jo Bell is gone, Charlie. She left four nights ago with the young man who was here with the mule buyer."

"She went off with that Lee feller?" A puzzled look came over his young face.

"They must have made plans for him to come back for her. She left a note in her room saying they were going to be married. I don't believe it, Charlie. You know how she was always talking about marrying a rich man."

"Damn her! Damn her to hell! Why'd she go off like that for? She always ruins things for me."

"I know you feel responsible for her, but there comes a time when you must let go. If she ruins things for you here, it's because you let her."

"But she ain't got no sense. She'll get herself in a peck a trouble."

"She'll not welcome your interference."

"I ain't carin' 'bout that." He went to the door. "I'll have to go and see 'bout her. Ain't no tellin' what that feller'll do to her."

"Charlie! Wait. Please don't—"

"I won't go off half-cocked. Don't worry."

"Talk to Smith and Sant first."

"Sant said Fuller bushwacked him and Smith. It was because of Jo Bell. I know it was."

"Let her go. She'll find a place for herself." Willa followed Charlie out onto the porch.

"She'll end up in a whorehouse is what she'll do. Or . . . dead. I promised Ma—"

"—Your mother wouldn't want you to give up doing what you want to do to ride herd on Jo Bell for the rest of your life."

Charlie stepped off the porch, turned and looked back. The sad expression in his eyes made Willa want to cry.

"Dammit! Sant was goin' to take me with him to get the mules he sold to the railroad."

"Go with Sant. Jo Bell will come back."

"I can't, Miss Willa. I just can't."

Charlie walked slowly away, his shoulders slumped, his head down. Willa thought it one of the saddest things she had ever seen—the death of a young boy's dreams.

* * *

"I saw that damn kid in Buffalo." Sant fished in his shirt pocket for makings and began to build a smoke. "He ducked out of sight when he spotted me."

Smith sat at the table in the cookshack; his coffee cup, freshly filled, was before him.

"The crazy kid fell for a pretty face and a hot little tail. In her letter she says they're running off to get married, but hell, she's just using him. Billy, this coffee tastes like dishwater."

"I had to clean the pot. It ain't been cleaned for a month— was half full of grounds. It'll be all right again in a day or two." Billy shoved wood in the cookstove and slammed the fire door shut. "I ain't sorry to see the back of her. She sure was a feisty little split-tail."

"She's got it in her head that because she's kin to Oliver she's got a claim here."

"She'll whistle Dixie!" Billy exclaimed and banged an iron skillet down on the range.

Sant laughed. "Boomy sent the extra hands back a day or two early thinkin' you'd need 'em. He's goin' to drive everythin' across Crazy Woman, then he'll be in. He says Charlie took to drivin' cows like a duck to water."

"His sister rode off on the sorrel. Charlie'll feel bad about losing that horse." Smith's hands curled around his coffee cup.

"He beat it up to the house as soon as he unsaddled. Reckon the kid's moonin' over Miss Willa?" Sant saw a scowl darken Smith's features. It took Sant only seconds to realize that Smith was jealous. Shitfire! The boy had fallen tail over tea kettle for pretty little Miss Willa.

"He knows by now that his sister has flown the coop," Smith said after a pause. The words had no more than left his mouth when Charlie stepped in and hung his hat on the peg.

"Howdy, Smith. Howdy, Billy."

"Howdy yoreself," Billy said. "Want coffee? Smith's a bitchin' 'bout it, but he ain't a'turnin' it down."

"No. But thanks just the same." He looked first at Smith, then at Sant. "My sister jist up and left with a itchy-fingered, wet-eared drifter. I jist can't figure why she'd do it."

"Women get funny notions." Sant's voice broke the silence that followed.

"Smith, will ya give me the loan of a horse? I'll write ya out a bill of sale for our mules to hold till I get back."

"You planning on going somewhere?"

"To find Jo Bell. I promised my ma I'd look after her."

"My guess is that they went to Sheridan. There's not much for a girl like Jo Bell in Buffalo."

"I thought of that." What Charlie didn't say was that he was sure his sister had gone to Sheridan to see if she had some rights to Uncle Oliver's property.

"If you wait until my leg heals a little, I'll go with you."

"Thanks, but I'd best get after her before she gets herself raped or . . . killed. I ain't askin' for no help. Except . maybe on how to get there."

"I been a'needin' to get up to Sheridan," Sant said, blowing smoke out through his nostrils. "I ain't hankerin' to make the trip all by my own self so I'll just mosey on up there with you."

Charlie looked at him with a blank stare. "But ya said ya had to get back to Horseshoe Canyon."

"Naw . . . them Sioux know more 'bout breakin' mules than I'll ever know. It'll give 'em another week to whip 'em in shape for drivin'."

"Ya ain't goin' now just cause I'm goin'?"

"—Hell," Billy chortled. "I ain't never knowed Sant to do a blasted thin' fer anybody. Stubborn as a mule and ain't half as smart is what he is."

"Ain't ya puttin' that kinda strong, old man?" The front legs of Sant's chair hit the floor and he leaned over to flip his cigarette butt out the door.

"Who ya callin' *old*? Ya ain't no spring chicken yoreself."

"I'll be glad for your company, Sant."

"We'd better be leavin' at daybreak."

Smith was playing the guitar.

Willa heard it the instant she stepped outside the door and remembered what Billy had said about Sant craving music. She sank down on the edge of the porch, and Buddy, with a deep sigh, flopped down beside her. The wide open sky was studded with stars that seemed only an arm's length away.

She strained her ears to hear every note. It warmed her and made her proud that the man she loved could make such beautiful music. All too soon it was over and there was silence. She sat quietly, her fingers fondling Buddy's ears.

Love is the understanding and acceptance of imperfection.

Willa's fingers stilled. Had Papa Igor spoken to her? It was ridiculous, but she was sure she had heard his voice.

Real love means standing arm in arm with your man against the world.

Was she crazy? A voice in her head was talking to her.

It's knowing that you're one body, one mind. Faith and trust in each other is what matters.

Willa sat quietly. As the words took root in her mind, the voice spoke again.

How insignificant the question of who makes the first move.

Her heart felt as if it would soar right out of her breast. Smith had said that once in a lifetime you get a chance to have everything you ever dreamed of having, and if you grabbed and missed, you'd lost your chance. She was going to grab and she wasn't going to miss.

Willa stood quickly and walked toward the gate. She would tell him that nothing mattered except that she loved him and wanted to spend the rest of her life with him.

Smith was there—on the other side of the gate.

"I couldn't stay away any longer," he said.

She opened the gate and went to him.

"I was coming to tell you that there's nothing in the world more important to me than you, Smith Bowman. I love you and will spend my life with you if you want me."

"If I want you? Oh, love, I want you so bad it's eating the heart out of me." His voice was a hoarse whisper—then she was in his arms.

Smith's heart was drumming so hard he could barely breath; he was too stunned with happiness to say a word. His arms squeezed her more tightly, his mouth searched for hers and covered it hungrily. She was so small, so soft, so sweet that he was almost afraid of breaking her. But he sensed that she felt the same urgency that he did.

At last he was able to whisper her name, and, muffled against his mouth, her own hoarse whisper reached him.

"My darling, my beloved, I'll spend a lifetime making up for all the hurt you've suffered."

Her arms were around his neck and the unreal softness of her breasts and her belly pressed against him.

"It's been the longest three days of my life," he said in a strange, thickened voice. His mouth was at the corner of hers, then slid up to close over it.

"I was waiting for you—hoping you'd come."

Her mouth quivered weakly under the persuasion of his kiss. The searching movement parted her lips, and he began sensuously exploring the inside of her mouth with his tongue. A melting heat began in the pit of her belly. The hungry coaxing movements of his mouth were sending signals to the very core of her femininity.

"Your leg—you should sit down," she said when Smith lifted his lips.

"Come with me to a place I know." His lips hovered fractionally above hers.

Her answer was to loop her arm about his waist and walk along beside him.

"Inez and Maud are playing cards. They don't need me."

"I do. I need you like I never dreamed I'd need anyone."

Smith stopped at the clothesline and removed one of the heavy draperies Inez had hung out to air.

"What are you doin'? Oh, Smith, you shouldn't. These are imported draperies. They cost a lot of money."

He answered with a laugh of pure happiness. With one arm wrapped around her and the thick tapestry drapery over the other, he guided her toward the grove north of the house. On a soft bed of pine needles, he spread the expensive cloth, sank down and pulled her down beside him.

Buddy, standing a few feet away, tipped his head to the side and wondered why he had not received as much as a pat on the head from his new friend. He dropped down, sighed and rested his head on his paws. He would take a little nap, with one eye open, of course, until they decided to notice him.

"I wish I could take you back to that warm pool," Smith said, holding out his arms. She moved into them and was locked in a gentle, tender embrace.

"We'll go there—someday." Releasing a deep and trembling sigh, she raised her lips to receive his kiss. All was peace. She was home.

The kiss was long and tender. Afterward, Smith lay down and pillowed her head on his shoulder. For a long while, they lay there, awed into silence by the miracle of their feelings for one another. Soon they were sharing whispered confidences.

"I never knew that love made you feel light and fluttery inside."

"I didn't know it would feel like someone was twisting a knife in your guts."

"—And make you say and do foolish things."

"Like what?"

"Like the day I lit into you at the stage station. I'd never done that before."

"I deserved it. I was a perfect jackass."

"I must have loved you then. It made me angry that I thought you handsome." She giggled.

"I smelled like a wet goat."

"—And you were cross as a bear."

"My head felt like it had been shot out of a cannon."

"But you shaved before you came to the station room."

"Yeah. I was ashamed of how I'd looked and what I'd said."

"Ordinarily, do you like buttermilk?"

"Love it."

There were short periods of silence, but they continued to hold onto each other as if they were two lost souls being buffeted by a fierce wind.

"I feel like some part of me that I didn't know about has come to life." Smith turned on his side to face her. Their lips met in joint seeking. His hands roamed over her, caressing every inch of her back and sides. One hand shaped itself over her breast, the other flattened against her buttocks and held her tightly against him.

"I can touch you and kiss you anytime I want to," she said with a breathless laugh.

"I'll never get enough."

"Oh, I hope not!"

Her mouth was warm and sweet. She parted her lips and accepted the wanderings of his.

"I don't deserve you," he whispered, placing light feathery kisses on her face.

"Yes, you do. And I deserve you, darling. The sweetest, dearest, most wonderful man in the world loves me. I must have done something right that caused God to bring you to me."

"Oh, God, sweetheart. I'm not any of those things. I've caroused, brawled, and raised my share of hell. And I've even—"

"Shhh . . ." Her fingers covered his lips. "I'll hear nothing bad about the man who is going to be the father of my children. We're going to have the family that neither one of us has ever had." She kissed his mouth again and again. "Oh, darling, just think. We'll grow old together!"

The pins had come out of her hair. She lifted her head to look into his face and the blond locks fell down over the hand that was slipping inside her bodice to caress her breast.

"How could I have doubted for one minute that you were anything but good and sweet and honorable."

"Don't say that, sweetheart. You don't know—"

"I know *you*. I feel in my heart"—she pressed his palm against her breast—"that I know everything about you." She brought her lips to his and kissed him with such sweetness that he felt a great swell of joy wash over him.

"Willa. My sweet Willa—" The words came from him in a tormented whisper. "It's going to be hard waiting to make you mine."

"—And you mine," she whispered, her eyes shining like the stars overhead. "Smith, darling . . . we don't have to wait. You're my mate for life . . . in my heart."

"Sweetheart!" He felt a tremor run through him as if the earth they were lying on were shaking.

"Have I shocked you?" Her voice came against lips that

were tormenting hers. An insidious primitive desire was growing in both of them.

"We can't . . . I want to tell you before we—" His voice trembled. It was Smith that drew back.

"I *don't* want to know before. This is my way of saying that I love you, trust you, believe in you with all my heart. Some day when we're old and gray and sitting in our chairs before the fire, you can tell me about every day of your life, but not now."

"You'd give yourself to me . . . here?"

"I'll not be *giving* anything. We'll be sharing."

"Oh, God! It purely scares hell out of me to think that I may never have found you."

"I know of no better place for a man and a woman to consummate their love than here on God's earth beneath a blanket of stars."

Smith felt moisture fill his eyes. Here in his arms was a treasure he would cherish until the end of his days. Her hands were at the buttons on his shirt. She opened it wide and snuggled against his bare chest. Smith's head was spinning, and he thought before reality slipped farther away that he must be gentle with her—something he'd never had to think about before.

"Do you want me to take off my dress?" She spoke with her mouth against his flesh.

"Do you . . . want to?"

"Yes. Yes, I do. It's so big it'll come off over my head." Willa moved out of his arms and sat up. "It isn't my dress," she said as she untied the sash. "I don't even own a dress," she went on nervously. "I've nothing of my own."

"You've got me," he said quietly.

"Then I'm the richest woman in the world."

He watched as she removed the dress. Beneath it she wore

a chemise, also much too large for her slender form. The straps slipped from her arms as she let the garment fall to her waist. Her shoulders and pink-tipped breasts gleamed in the moonlight. Smith drew in a ragged breath and a small sound came from his throat at the sight of her round, firm breasts.

She was so open, so honest, so . . . beautiful.

"Willa, love, you're so pretty," he whispered and reached for her.

Her arms slid up to encircle his neck and she pressed her breasts to his chest. Her mouth was soft and sweetly giving against his. He sank down on his back, bringing her with him. She stretched out beside him, her cheek against his shoulder. While they kissed, his hands softly stroked her back and hips.

"You're my love," he whispered.

"You'll have to show me what to do."

"Loving like this is new to me, too." His rough calloused fingers found her nipple and stroked it. He felt a tremor go through her. She reached for his lips and kissed him with a hunger that both surprised and thrilled him.

"Are you going to take off your britches?"

"In a minute," he said when he could get his breath. "I don't want to scare you."

"I won't be scared. I felt it against me when you sat me in front of you on the horse. At first I wasn't sure what it was." She giggled against his cheek. "But I knew what it was the night you kissed me on the porch."

Smith chuckled. "It's something I find hard to control. It happens when I'm with you." He moved away from her, and in a moment he was back, spreading her dress and his shirt over them.

"Are you cold?"

"No. I'll be careful of your leg—" she said when she felt the bandage against her.

"But . . . not too careful. Oh, love"—he gathered her to him, slipped his hand under the loose chemise, cupped her bottom and pressed her mound tightly against his hip—"you feel so good!"

"You too."

Her palm moved down over his stomach and slid beneath his extended sex. Smith caught his breath sharply and waited as it settled on the back of her hand. Slowly she turned her hand and her fingers closed around him. He ground his teeth and tightened his buttocks. His desire for her was a deep pain gnawing his vitals. His large hand stroked her flat belly and down through crisp hair and into her moist depth. He whispered words of love, their meaning lost to her as he kissed her soft breasts, her shoulders and neck.

"I don't want to be rough," he breathed desperately. "My sweet love . . . I can't wait much longer!"

"Don't . . . wait—"

He turned her gently, moved over her and sought entrance. He filled her completely with one deep thrust. The pain-pleasure was so intense that she cried out his name.

"Oh, my God! I've hurt you," he moaned and tried to withdraw. Her frantic hands on his buttocks kept him from leaving her.

"No! We fit, darling. We fit perfectly."

She arched to fit herself more completely with his throbbing maleness. He probed urgently, increasing the pulsing rhythm to an unbearable tempo that brought her nearer and nearer to the fulfillment her body sought. Suddenly she felt deep, thrilling spasms of exquisite pleasure, and from somewhere she heard Smith's soft, triumphant cry.

Willa became aware that her hands were clasping Smith's tight buttocks, his hair on her cheek as he rested face-down. He was still huge and deep inside her, but the waves of frenzied pleasure that had ripped through her were subsiding.

Now she felt a burning desire to comfort and pleasure him. She moved her hands over his back and turned her lips to his cheek. His heart was still thundering against hers. And finally when he eased over onto his side, he took her with him, reluctant to part from her.

Covered with the skirt of her dress, they lay face to face, her soft belly tight against his hard one. They kissed for a long time, as if it were the first time they had kissed, as if there couldn't be anything beyond a kiss.

"Hello, wife," he said against her mouth.

"Hello, dearest husband."

"Someone's watching us."

"No! Who?"

"Buddy." He laughed deep in his throat.

"You . . . tease! You scared me."

"I want to see this in the daylight." He had a handful of firm breast.

"Tomorrow I'll not wear a shirtwaist." She giggled and nipped his chin.

"You'd better, or I'll swat your butt," he growled. "These are mine." His lips nuzzled the soft flesh in his hand.

"Yes, darling, all yours."

They kissed, while learning each other with their hands.

"Your skin is so smooth—"

"Yours is soft."

She wiggled her hand down between them, amazed to discover how completely they were joined. Her brilliantly alive eyes laughed up at him. Her face was damp and covered with a happy smile.

A little noise came from his throat, and he began to move his hips rapidly as gentleness gave way to greed. His need was a tumultuous pressure in his groin. His movements became frenzied. She urged him on with wild abandon, giving her love with unbridled recklessness, wanting to give . . . give.

She drew him deeper and deeper into her as if she could hold him to her forever, chaining him to her with bonds of warm flesh.

Finally her own body splintered and fell apart. During her shuddering convulsions he poured his stream of life into her, his heart pounding violently in that final moment of fulfillment. She held him with all her strength while violent tremors continued to rock his powerful body. Then she heard hoarsely whispered words in her ear.

"I feel as if I have come home after a long, lonely journey through the Badlands." Slowly he pulled himself out of her, sighed deeply and placed his blond head on her breasts.

She lay quiet and stroked the damp hair from his brow. Love for him filled her heart. She delighted in the sensation of his warm body pressed close to hers, the weight of his head on her breast, and reached for his discarded shirt to cover his back. Never had she felt so complete.

They were enclosed in their own private world. Time disappeared as if by magic. Willa relished the night breeze swirling over them like a caress. She gazed up at the sky. Tonight the stars were brilliant against a velvet background. The moon looked as if someone had hung it just over the treetops.

A thought entered Willa's mind and she began to laugh. Smith lifted his head from her breast, leaned over her and kissed the smile on her lips.

"What was so funny all of a sudden?"

"It's nothing, darling. I was just wondering what Maud would say if she knew what we've been doing on her expensive drapery."

CHAPTER

* 26 *

Jo Bell stomped out of the lawyer's office, slammed the door behind her, and marched down the boardwalk. Vince moved away from the wall where he had been leaning and hurried to catch up with her.

"What's the matter, honey? What'd the man say?"

"He laughed is what he done. Laughed! Uncle Oliver only owned half of the ranch and he left it to that old Billy Whiskers. Smith'll get it all when old Billy dies. It ain't fair!" she wailed.

"And ya can't get none of it even if you're next of kin?"

"The way that ugly old fart put it, I've got as much chance as it snowin' in hell."

"That ain't much chance, hon. But it ain't the end of the world."

"It is too!"

"I've got a little money left."

"I got a dollar or two," she lied.

"I got eight. If we're careful till I can get a job we'll be all right."

"Shut up! Just shut up. I got to think." Jo Bell walked

338

alongside the young cowboy, her head down, a mutinous look on her face. At the double doors that opened into the lobby of the hotel, she said crossly, "Bye, Vince."

"Bye?" He put his hand on her shoulder and turned her to face him.

When she saw the puzzled look on his face, she dimpled sweetly "Bye for now, I mean. I'm tired and got to think 'bout thin's."

His face relaxed. "All right, hon. I'll come back after you've rested. Don't worry your pretty little head. We'll get by "

Jo Bell forced herself to stand still while his hands caressed her shoulders.

"Yore sweet, Vince. I don't know what I'd do without ya."

"Go on now and rest. I'll be back and we'll decide what we're goin' to do."

As soon as she turned away from him the smile left her face. It wouldn't do to get rid of him now, she thought. Although she still had the rings, the watch and the money, she might have use for him later She straightened her shoulders, lifted her chin as her papa had taught her to do and entered the hotel.

The interior was dim compared to the bright sunlight outside. Jo Bell didn't see the woman who rose from the deep leather chair in the middle of the lobby

"As I live and breathe—Jo Bell Frank."

Jo Bell spun around. That voice! It sounded like—

"Starr! Oh, Starr!"

"I was sure it was you I was hearing about—black curls, violet eyes and very beautiful."

The redheaded woman was fashionably attired in a tight-fitting green taffeta dress. A small green hat was perched on top of her high-piled curls. A folded parasol hung from a loop over her waist. Jo Bell flew across the room and wrapped her arms around Starr's waist.

"Whoa now, honey You'll mess my fine dress."

"You look like a regular   lady. Oh, Starr, I knew you were pretty, but dressed like this you're . you're just the prettiest thin' I ever did see."

Starr laughed softly and threw her arm across Jo Bell's shoulders.

"That wouldn't have anything to do with the fact you're glad to see me, would it?"

"No! How did you find me?"

"'Twas easy. After you dined at the Chicago Restaurant last night, every man in town was dying to meet you." Her laugh was light. "When I heard the pretty girl's name was Jo Bell, I started looking for you. I figured your papa would stay at the best hotel in town."

"Papa's dead. A mean man shot him at a stage station. Charlie and I went on to Uncle Oliver's, but he's dead, too."

"Gil was bound to get it sooner or later Bet he was cheating at cards."

"The man said he was, but I don't believe it."

"Charlie with you?"

"No. I'm by myself."

"Who was the cowboy you ate dinner with?"

"His name is Vince. He just . . . brought me here."

"Then he's got no hold on you?"

"No! Lord no. I'm goin' to marry a *rich* man."

"Good. I'll help you find one. Come, let me show you something."

Starr took Jo Bell by the hand and led her to the door and out onto the hotel veranda.

"See that new building down on the corner? Read the sign. STARR PALACE. That's mine. Remember the freighter I rode away with? Well, he came into some money, then got himself shot.'' Starr didn't mention that the money had originally belonged to someone else. "I own the fanciest saloon in town.''

"Ya own it? All by yoreself?''

"Sure do. It's mine, all mine. How about coming to work for me?''

"What would I do?''

"Sing. The men will go crazy over you.''

"But . . . I don't sing very good.''

Starr laughed. "They'll not even notice. All you have to do is look at 'em and smile. They'll drown in their beer.''

Jo Bell clapped her hands. "I always wanted to be on the stage. I'll work hard, Starr. I truly will.''

"Just do what comes naturally, kid. You'll be a sensation.''

Jo Bell clapped her hands again. "I'll love that!''

"It's settled then. Get your things and let's get out of here.''

A week later when Charlie and Sant rode into town, Vince Lee was one of the first people they saw. He was at the livery saddling his horse. He looked up as Charlie dismounted, then put his knee against the horse's side to tighten the cinch.

"Where's my sister?'' Charlie demanded.

Vince looked up again. His eyes moved to Sant, who was sliding from the saddle.

"Try Starr Palace.'' Vince turned his back, picked up his saddle bags, flung them over the horse and tied them down.

"What'a ya done to her?''

"Nothin'. I brought her here. It's what she wanted.''

"If ya've ruint her, I'll kill ya.''

"Big talk," Vince muttered.

"I mean it," Charlie said and almost choked on the words. "She's just a dumb . . . girl."

Vince turned to face Charlie, his hands at his sides. "Let me tell you somethin' about your sister, kid. She can take care of herself. I'll admit I was taken in by her pretty face, but believe me that's all she's got—a pretty face. She's a selfish bitch! She wants no part of me. I'm lucky to find that out now. She's the kind that'll eat a man alive."

"Ya got no right to be sayin' that."

"I think I have. She played me for the fool I am. I never touched your sister. Not that I didn't want to, mind ya. She can make a man forget everything except the urge to get between her legs. I may not amount to much to some folks' way of thinking"—he glanced at Sant—"but I ain't never forced myself on a woman."

"Ya aimed to just ride off and leave her?"

"My money's gone and if I don't work, I don't eat."

"Well, guess I can't blame ya none. Where'd ya say she was?"

"Starr Palace. It's the new saloon up the street."

"Well," Charlie said again. "I'm obliged to ya for lookin' out for her till I could get here."

Vince shook his head in disbelief and glanced at Sant.

"If you're wantin' a job, mosey on down to where we penned the mules." Sant spoke around the cigarette in his mouth. "I'll be needin' a extra hand."

"You mean it?" Vince looked surprised.

"Said it, didn't I? Me and Charlie'll be along."

"I'm obliged. But if you don't mind, I'll hang around and ride back with you."

"Suit yoreself."

Sant followed Charlie down the street and through the swinging bat-wing doors of the Starr Palace. Sparkling chandeliers hung from the ceiling. The long bar had a brass foot-rail and behind it was an array of mirrors and bawdy paintings. The place was crowded with businessmen in black serge suits, drovers, gamblers, drifters, and railroad workers. They had all came to see and to hear the beauty known as "The Darlin' of Sheridan."

On the well-lighted stage, a girl in a pink dress decorated with lace and ribbons sat in a swing—the ropes of which were entwined with flowers. Her short dress exposed long slender legs, the low neckline showed a goodly amount of her bosom. Satin streamers trailed as she swung gently back and forth and sang in a low, husky voice.

> In Scarlet town where I was born
> There was a fair maid dwelling.
> Made every youth cry well away,
> Her name was—Barbara Allen.

The huge room was deathly still while Jo Bell sang the sad song. Anyone who dared whisper or shuffle his feet was quickly hushed. The card players ceased to play, their eyes riveted on the girl. Men at the bar held their drinks in their hands. Starr stood on the stairs looking down at the scene with a smile on her face.

The song ended. Jo Bell slipped from the swing, bowed and threw kisses. The roar from the audience fairly shook the rafters. She came to the edge of the stage and was immediately swept up in the arms of a young drover, who carried her to the middle of the room where she was placed on a table. Her face was flushed with excitement. She smiled and clapped her hands, her eyes sweeping across the faces of the men, who gazed at her adoringly and continued to cheer

At first Jo Bell didn't see the young boy pushing and shoving his way through the men who crowded around her

When she recognized him, the smile left her face, her mouth turned down at the corners and she stamped her foot angrily.

"Jo Bell! Get off that table and stop makin' a show of yoreself," Charlie demanded. "They can see yore legs clear up past yore knees."

A few of the men around him snickered, others turned to look at the boy.

"Hear me, Jo Bell? Get down off there right now!" Charlie reached up to grab her hand.

"Hold on here, youngster " A big man in a black serge suit threw his arm out to push Charlie back. "Ain't nobody touchin' our little darlin' "

"She's *my* sister, ya big clabber-head." Charlie looked up to see Jo Bell shaking her head. "Get off there, Jo Bell. Yore shamin' yoreself."

"How about it, little lady? Ya want me to turn this kid inside out and hang him out to dry?" The man in the suit caught Charlie by the nape of the neck.

"I ain't carin', sugar," Jo Bell said in a breathless voice. "I ain't never seen him before."

"Jo Bell," Charlie yelled. "I'm warnin' ya. Straighten up and act right, or   or   I'll wash my hands of ya."

For an answer, Jo Bell bent over, put her thumbs in her ears, wiggled her fingers and stuck out her tongue. The men hooted and ogled her exposed bosom as her dress fell away Two big cowhands grabbed Charlie under the arms and lifted him off his feet. As they headed for the door, Sant stepped in front of them.

"Put him down."

"Ya wantin' some of the same, old man?"

"Put him down . . . easy." Sant's hand hovered over the gun on his hip.

"Hey, now. Be careful, old man. There ain't but one of ya and there's two of us."

"There's two of us too." Vince's voice came from behind Sant. "I'll take the one on the left, Sant. I'm thinkin' he figgers he's pretty fast."

"Well, looky here. Ain't this the cowboy we threw outta here the other night for botherin' our little darlin'?"

"Damned if it ain't. Reckon we didn't learn him nothin' a'tall." The cowboy's voice was loud in the sudden hush.

"You've got another chance," Vince said. "Make your move."

"Put the boy down." Starr's voice filled the quiet room. "I'll have no rough stuff in my place." She stepped in front of the cowboys.

"If it's what ya want, ma'am." The men set Charlie on his feet and backed away.

"Go on back to where you came from, Charlie. This is what Jo Bell wants," Starr said kindly.

"This ain't what Ma had in mind for her, or Pa either."

"They're dead, she isn't," Starr said cruelly. "Stay here and I'll get you some money—for the kindness your pa showed me."

"Ya paid him by sleepin' with him. I don't want yore damn money. What I wanted was for my sister to be decent and if she ain't goin' to, then she's goin' to have to do without me."

"She'll be all right. I'll look after her "

"And turn her into a whore like you," Charlie spat.

Starr laughed. "You'll soon find out, if you haven't already, that a good whore is an important part of a man's life. Stay and listen to your sister sing again. When she sings *I'm Only a Bird in a Gilded Cage*, the crowd goes wild."

"I ain't wantin' to hear or see any kin of mine actin' like a slut." Without as much as a glance at his sister, who was still standing on the table, Charlie shoved open the bat-wing doors and left the saloon. Vince followed.

"It's better to cut the tie completely." Starr looked at Sant and recognized him for the man he was—a tough old timber wolf who had been over the mountain and around the bend.

"Yeah. The girl's a born whore—like you." Sant dropped his cigarette on the floor and stepped on it before he nudged Starr beneath the chin with his knuckles.

"You said it right, old hoss. Come back—anytime." Starr's laugh followed Sant out the door and across the porch to the street.

When Willa told Maud that she and Smith were going to marry, the woman was so angry Willa feared she would have another convulsion.

"What'd ya say? Yore goin' to . . . goin' to marry that slick-handed, murderin' bastard?" Maud raised up in the bed, her eyes wild, her face distorted with hate and disbelief. "Ya know what he done."

"I love him."

"Love? Godamighty," she swore. "Ya ain't got the brains of a pissant if ya—"

"—That's enough, Mrs. Eastwood. My private life is none of your business."

Willa's sharp words had no effect on Maud.

"I was wrong 'bout ya. Wrong as I could be. Yore lookin' for the main chance. Just like him. Yore likin' what ya see here and thinkin' that sneakin' shithead'll get it for ya."

Willa was stunned by the intensity of the attack, but not so much that she didn't feel a hot flash of anger boil up inside her and spill out in harsh words.

"Just stop right there!" she shouted. "You're a selfish, hateful old woman who hasn't an ounce of compassion in your miserable body."

"He took everythin' from me," Maud yelled and burst

into tears. "He shined up to Oliver till Oliver was with him more'n me. Then 'stead of helpin' him, he killed him. Damn him. He killed him!"

"I know that. He had to have a . . . reason—"

"—He courted ya, jist to get ya away from me."

"He did no such thing. Smith is a good man. He stayed here, took your abuse and looked after you. And he loves me." Willa had to shout to make herself heard over Maud's sobs. "And I love him. Do you hear? I love him!"

"Get outta my house, ya   . hussy! Get out and don't ever come back. Hear?"

"Gladly, Mrs. Eastwood. I'll leave you to wallow in self-pity, to hold onto your grudges, and to place the blame for your lonely existence on everyone but yourself."

Willa went through the door just as a glass crashed into the doorjamb by her head. She was too angry to realize what she had done until she was halfway down the stairs. Then she was horrified. What if she had upset Maud to the extent the woman had another convulsion? Willa hurried down the stairs to the kitchen.

"Inez! Inez!"

Inez pulled her hands from the dishwater and dried them on her apron.

"You told her, huh? I could hear her yellin' all the way down here."

"She's very upset. She could have another convulsion. Will you go stay with her?"

"'Course. You go on out and cool off yourself. I swan, there's times I think Maud's got horse shit for brains."

Willa walked out onto the porch and wrapped an arm about a post and leaned her head against it. Life was not easy. Maud's hatred for Smith did not in any way diminish her own love for him. She saw him in the corral talking to a group of men who were mounted and ready to ride out. His sun-bleached hair was wind-tousled. Some men seldom took their hats off; Smith seldom wore one. Her heart swelled with love and pride.

The men rode out. Smith closed the gate behind them, waved to her and came toward the house. It had been three days since they had first made love to each other. Willa had hugged her happiness close, telling only Inez—until today. She dreaded telling Smith of Maud's reaction. But—she had been ordered out of the house. She couldn't very well stay where she was not welcome.

Smith's eyes held hers as he approached. "What's wrong?"

"Why do you think something's wrong?"

"I can tell." He put his hands on her waist, drew her to him and kissed her hard on the lips.

"Smith! We shouldn't . . . right out here where everyone can see."

"The only ones to see are Billy and Plenty. They won't be shocked."

"Mrs. Eastwood ordered me out of the house." Willa wrapped her arms around his waist and leaned her cheek against his shoulder.

"Was she having one of her temper fits, or did she mean it?"

"She meant it. I told her about us."

Smith was silent for a moment. "That's just a sample of what to expect if you marry me."

Willa lifted her head and looked into his face. "*If* I marry you? Have you changed your mind about wanting me?"

"You may change yours."

"I don't care what Maud or anyone else says or thinks. It won't change my opinion of you one bit. I'm just wondering where I'll stay until we can marry."

"You'll stay with me. Billy will move into the bunkhouse.

We've already talked about it. But first there's something I must do.''

"What?" Willa's heartbeat quickened with sudden fear as she realized his voice was different; full of resignation and something more: weariness.

"Can you get away for a few hours?"

"Of course. I'm no longer employed here. Remember?"

"I want to take you somewhere." Smith took her hand and led her toward the barn. His hand held hers tightly. She could feel the tenseness in him. At the door he stopped and, without looking at her, said, "Wait here. I'll be right back."

As Willa waited the lump in her throat became larger. She had the feeling that her entire future would be decided within the next few hours. When she was sure she was going to burst into tears, Smith came out of the barn leading two saddled horses.

"The mare is Billy's. She's gentle. She'd have to be for him to ride her."

Smith boosted Willa into the saddle, waited while she struggled to get her skirt down over her knees, and adjusted the stirrups.

"Where's Pete?" Willa asked when Smith had settled into the saddle on a handsome buckskin with a black mane and tail.

"In the corral. I was afraid he'd get excited around that mare you're riding."

Willa was nervous at first. It had been a long time since she had ridden a horse. But as the gentle mare moved along beside the buckskin and they left the ranch to head in a westerly direction, her confidence grew. The terrain that opened before them was a succession of valleys divided by ridges crested with pines, their slopes dotted with clumps of aspen.

Smith was quiet. He was tense. It was evident in his stiffness as he sat in the saddle and in the way he held the reins, his hands on the pommel. Willa wondered what was on his mind and where he was taking her.

The horses splashed across a stream and climbed the bank on the other side. The sweep of the magnificent valley glistened in the afternoon sun. Willa's eyes drank in the beauty of the landscape. Smith headed for the far side of the valley where the land rose to meet a granite bluff from which a stream of water flowed, feeding the creek below. A breeze drifted down from the mountains and waved the lush, green grasses alive with small birds whirring up from under the feet of the horses. It was all so very peaceful.

On a rise, high enough for a full view of the valley, Smith stopped the horses.

"This is the most beautiful place I've ever seen," Willa said in an awed, hushed voice, her eyes glowing.

"I think so too." Smith stepped down from his horse, tied the reins to a low branch and came to help her down.

"Is this what you wanted to show me?"

"Uh-huh. Billy and I own this land. Someday we want to build a house here."

Willa's heart was suddenly filled with dread. *He and Billy. He hadn't included her.*

"It's a lovely site," she managed to say without crying.

"Willa—" Smith took her shoulders in his two hands and turned her to face him. "I can't go on like this much longer— living on the brink, not knowing when I'll be pushed over the edge."

"What do you mean?"

"I'm midway between heaven and hell. I've got to know which it will be." His voice shook in spite of his desperate attempt to control it.

"Oh, Smith—" She wrapped her arms about his waist even though he was trying to hold her away from him.

"I've got to tell you how it . . . happened. You've got a right to know before you marry me."

"Then tell me. I want to share the burden with you," she whispered, her lips against his cheek.

Smith took a rolled blanket from behind his saddle, spread it on the grass beneath an oak tree, and motioned for her to sit down.

"Are you going to sit with me?"

"In a minute," he said and walked behind her where she couldn't see him. "Oliver loved this land and he loved those damned longhorns. They're mean and unpredictable. If one gets so weak he can't stand and has to be helped up, he'll immediately attack his benefactor." Willa heard Smith strike a match and smelled the smoke from his cigarette.

"I wish to God we'd never left the ranch that day to drive that wild bunch out of the timber," he said wearily.

Willa waited, apprehension holding her motionless.

CHAPTER

* 27 *

Oliver, Smith and a cowhand, Gary Base, left the ranch that spring morning and headed northwest into the Bighorn Mountains with enough provisions to last several days. Base had come through the area on his way from Medicine Wheel and told Oliver about seeing a small herd of Eastwood cattle in a primitive area high in the mountains. Knowing they would be gaunt from wintering there, Oliver decided to drive them down to the valley grass so they would fatten for the fall roundup.

Toward evening, after sighting a couple of steers on a rugged mountainside, the men camped in a draw sheltered from the chilly April wind by a thick stand of pine trees. The next morning, in the dim light, they rose and stretched themselves. Oliver loved being in the mountains and was anxious to begin the drive. They ate a hearty breakfast because they knew they would have a rough day getting the wild longhorns bunched so they could drive them down the rugged slope.

Smith admitted to Oliver that he felt uneasy about rounding up steers that had grown wild and primitive after several years in the wilds. Longhorn cattle were a mixture of big oxen and the smaller fighting cattle from Mexico and they did not easily submit to the domination of man.

"Horse apples," Oliver snorted good-naturedly, dismissing the danger. "We'll go around and get above them."

The year before Smith had signed on to drive a herd of Texas longhorns from the Red River to Fort Dodge. The beasts had been hell to drive even on the prairie. They had the strength and stamina to run for miles, and if the notion struck them, they were quick to turn and attack. Cattle in a bunch observed a hierarchy based on strength, vigor, aggressiveness, and set of horn. Smith had learned that strays, even an old cow, many times a grandmother, could be as dangerous as a young bull.

"If we get this bunch trail-broken, I'll be mighty surprised," Smith said. "Some of them will weigh a thousand pounds and will have to tilt their blasted horns to get through the trees. They're not going to want to go down that slope."

Oliver laughed. "You're acting like an old man, boy."

"Maybe so, but I know what they can do. Be extra careful."

Gary Base didn't have much to say. He listened to the talk between Smith and the boss. He would rather have stayed at the ranch. He hadn't had any experience driving half-wild cattle, but if Mr. Eastwood thought they could do it, he'd give it a try. He was a competent cowhand, well-liked, self-assured about ordinary things, and always broke. Now he wished he hadn't told the boss about seeing the damn strays.

It was almost noon when they reached the highpoint. Oliver counted ten head of cattle on the rocky slope below.

"There may be more farther on down that I can't see," he said. "Let's start with these and maybe we'll gather more on the way down. Spread out. I'll take the left flank."

"I'll take it," Smith said when he saw the rugged terrain.

"Base and I will ride swing. Make plenty of racket and maybe we'll scare them on down to where the going is easier."

When Smith started down the slope, all his thoughts were concerned with the task at hand. He picked his way down through the natural obstacles and saw a wrinklehorn steer that appeared to be mostly bones. The steer's tailbone was a peak in the rear and deep hollows showed between his ribs and hipbone. His walk was a swinging stride that caused his dewlap to sway like a pendulum of a clock. He seemed calm enough to make a lead steer and moved on down the slope when Smith slapped his hat against his thigh and yelled.

Smith was still apprehensive. He wiped the sweat from his brow with the kerchief he pulled from around his neck. He moved his horse out of the trees and onto a shelf where he could view the landscape and pick an easier route. This steep terrain was hard on his horse. He saw movement to the right. Oliver was headed toward a clearing below and directly in his path was a big steer.

The longhorn's coat was not merely shaggy but rough, patchy, coarse: he was still shedding his winter hair. It was the color of sandstone and limestone with highlights and shadows of spotted moss. He was fierce-looking and alert to Oliver's approach.

From this point Smith lost sight of Oliver for a minute or two. Then he appeared out of the trees seeming to be unaware of the steer. Something about the way the animal stood, his big head sagged far out ahead of his narrow hump, his back legs spread, caused Smith to want to shout a warning to Oliver. He reached back to slip his hat under the strap on his saddle, keeping his eye on the longhorn.

Suddenly, so fast that it was hard to believe what was happening, the beast charged Oliver's horse. The frightened animal reared. Oliver fought to control it, but he was finally thrown to the ground and the horse bolted out of the clearing.

Smith put the spurs to his own horse while dragging his rifle from the scabbard. He sped recklessly down through the trees, trying to get a clear shot at the beast that was charging the man on the ground. Oliver was dazed and trying to get to his feet. Smith fired, grazing the top of the steer's back.

The enraged beast attacked Oliver with a vengeance.

Smith came out of the trees to see Oliver on the ground being gored by one of the animal's long horns. He fired again, hitting the animal in the neck, but it continued to attack with horns and hooves. A horn pierced Oliver again and again, at times lifting him off the ground. The steer turned to face Smith with Oliver impaled on one of its horns. Smith jumped from his horse and steadied the rifle for another shot. The beast shook his head, confused by Oliver's screams—screams that would stay with Smith for the rest of his life.

Dear God! He couldn't shoot with Oliver still impaled on the horn. The beast could fall on Oliver and crush him. He had to shoot, he had no choice. He aimed carefully before he pulled the trigger and shot the animal between the eyes. It staggered and lowered its head. Oliver's body slipped off the horn. And just as Smith had feared, the steer fell on top of him.

By the time Smith reached Oliver, his heart was pounding like a runaway train. Oliver was still conscious and screaming with pain. Smith tried to push the dead animal off him, knowing it was impossible for the beast must weigh somewhere near eighteen hundred pounds. He yelled to Gary Base as the young cowboy rode in.

"Tie a rope to the horns. Pull the head up so I can pull Oliver out from under him."

"God no, boy! Leave me be—" Oliver gasped.

"Do it," Smith shouted when Base hesitated.

Agonizing minutes later Smith managed to drag the injured man clear of the dead animal. It was only then that he could see the extent of Oliver's injuries. The horns had ripped into his stomach from his ribcage to his groin, both legs appeared to be broken as well as his arms. Smith pulled aside the torn shirt and tried to push the intestines back into the gaping hole.

Gary took one look at the stomach wound and ran into the brush to vomit.

"We'll make a travois and get you down to the doctor." Smith's voice shook. He was scarcely aware of what he was saying as he frantically tried to hold the jagged edges of the wound together.

"Nooo . . . don't move me. Oh, God, my guts are on fire!" Oliver's mouth worked to keep from screaming. "Help me, Smith, I can't stand . . . it. Oh, Jesus . . . Sm . . . ith—"

"Base!" Smith shouted. "Start making a travois."

"No! I'll not—God, help me!"

"Yes, you will! We'll get you down."

"It's more . . . than twenty m-miles." Racked with pain, Oliver rolled his head. It was the only part of him he could move. Blood trickled out the corner of his mouth and whimpers came from his throat. "I know what . . . this means. So do you."

"Don't give up. Just hold on. I'll get a blanket."

"Don't go," Oliver begged when Smith stood. "Stay with m-me." Smith knelt down again. "Look after Maud. She's not quite right in the h-head—"

"I'll look after her."

"I owe her my life."

"Don't worry. I'll take care of her."

"Stay with Billy. You're all he has—"

"I will. You know I will."

"There's something else you can do for me."

"Anything, Oliver. Anything."

"Put your gun in my hand."

Smith's mouth hung open and a blast of fear caused him

to tremble violently when he realized what Oliver was asking him to do.

"I . . . can't—"

Oliver's eyes were pleading. "Let me die with some dignity, for God's sake."

"I can't," Smith repeated, his eyes filling with tears.

Oliver rolled his head. The veins stood out on his neck and he struggled to choke off the screams that filled his throat.

"My guts are spilling out. Don't let me die screaming—"

"Don't ask me to do this—"

"Please, boy. I've loved you like my own— Dear God, I . . . I can't stand it much l-longer."

Through tears Smith looked at his dear friend's tortured features. Oliver was in the worst kind of agony. He had known from the first glimpse that the man who had been like a father to him was mortally wounded.

Could he refuse him this last request and save him hours of excruciating pain?

Slowly Smith pulled the six-gun from the holster, flipped off the safety and tried to placed it in Oliver's hand, but Oliver's forearm was broken, his wrist limp. His other hand was badly crushed.

"I can't lift it, son. Help me—"

"I've not told you what being with you all these years has meant to me." Smith's throat was full of sobs, tears rolled down his cheeks.

"I knew without having to be told." Oliver's eyes were bright, his breath shallow. "Now you have a chance to repay me. It'll be quick. I'll thank you with my last breath."

"I can't—"

"Yes, you can. When it's over, take me home to Eastwood and bury me on that little rise behind the ranch."

The gun had slipped from Oliver's fingers. Smith picked it up. It was slick with Oliver's blood.

"Do it, son."

Smith placed the end of the barrel against Oliver's temple.

"Thank you," Oliver murmured and closed his eyes.

Smith turned his face away and pulled the trigger. The sound of the shot reverberated in Smith's head. He dropped the gun and buried his face in his hands.

"Godamighty! What'd ya do?" Base shouted. "Jesus! Ya killed him."

Smith stood to walk away.

Base grabbed his shoulder. "Ya killed him!" he repeated shrilly.

"Get away from me!" Smith yelled at the top of his lungs. "Get the hell away from me!"

"Murderer!"

The word had scarely left Base's mouth before Smith's fist flattened his lips against his teeth. The young cowboy was knocked off his feet. Smith staggered into the grove, wrapped his arms around a tree, and pressed his tear-drenched face against the rough bark. He knew that from that moment on, his life would never be the same.

Halfway through the telling Smith had sat down on the blanket, but he had kept his back to Willa. She crept up close to him and put her arms around him. The tears on her face wet his shirt.

"Oh, darling! What a brave, unselfish thing to do. You poor, poor man, you've been grieving all these years—" Willa moved around to kneel in front of him and put her arms around him.

"Life was hell," he said against her neck. "Until I met you."

"You were afraid I'd not understand?"

"I was afraid you'd despise me—as Maud does."

"No! A couple of years ago I saw a man go out of his mind with pain. He chewed his tongue and tried to tear out his eyes. It was so terrible that it's haunted me. Oliver was brave to want to end it quickly. I'm sure he didn't realize what it would do to you."

"Only Billy and Sant knew how badly Oliver was wounded. They dressed him for the burial." Smith pulled her onto his lap. "Gary Base came down and told his story. The news spread like wildfire. Billy tried to tell folks that Oliver couldn't have lived. They chose not to believe him." A deep sigh shook him. "Sometimes I wake up in the night and see Oliver's broken body and his eyes—pleading with me."

"Darling, I love you more because you had the courage to do what you did." Willa's voice choked on a sob. "Mr. Eastwood couldn't have lived more than a few hours even if he had been in a doctor's office. What you did saved him from what he feared. He didn't want to die a pile of broken flesh and bones, screaming until the last breath left him."

Smith's eyes glinted like green fire and the strength of his fingers brought physical pain when he gripped her shoulders.

"You're . . . not just saying that?"

Willa shook her head vigorously. Great gulps of tears tore up from her throat and shuddered through her. She cried for the lonely man who carried the burden of having had to kill his friend and benefactor. She cried with relief because now the way was cleared for them to share a life together.

"Don't cry for me, dear love." Smith cradled her in his arms and tilted her chin so that he could place soft kisses on her tear-stained face. "I love you." He said the words simply and looked deeply into her eyes.

"I love you too." Her voice was husky from crying. She clung to him. "No more lonely nights for either of us. From now on, I'll be with you."

Smith cupped her face with his palm and moved his mouth

over hers with incredible lightness. He felt as if a boulder had been rolled off his chest and his heart was soaring on a cloud of happiness. There was more love welling up in the eyes of this woman that he had ever hoped to see. He looked into her eyes with a lifetime of love and longing in his.

"I had resigned myself to a damned lousy life. After this glimpse of heaven, I'll never let you go. I can stand old Maud's hatred and other folks' scorn as long as you're with me."

"Just try to get rid of me." Her whispered words came against his lips. She lifted her head and smiled through her tears, and then settled her mouth on his for a long tender moment.

His reaction startled her. He rolled with her in his arms until she was flat on her back and he was leaning over her. She saw the love in his eyes and knew that she was one of the lucky ones—she was truly loved and cherished.

"It would kill me to lose you." His voice was thick with emotion. "I love everything about you—your spunk, your pride, your beautiful face, your warm, lovely eyes. I'm going to look into them when our bodies are joined and try to tell you how much I love you."

His lips kissed away her tears. He opened the front of her dress and worshiped her breasts with his fingertips and his lips. It was so much sweeter than before. Willa lay with lids half closed while the stroking of his hands on her skin sent waves of pleasure up and down her spine.

He was gentle and sweet and she welcomed his intrusion into her body with eyes open, looking into the green depths of his. She heard the low murmur of love words between kisses, and then she was beyond hearing, beyond everything, except feeling.

The last rays of the sun crept across their entwined bodies. Smith pulled her skirt down over her legs, propped himself up on an elbow and looked down at her. Her fingers traced the lines at the corners of his smiling eyes and delved into the corners of his tilted lips before reaching to encircle him with her arms and caress the smooth skin of his back.

"Tomorrow I'll send Plenty to fetch the preacher, unless you'd rather ride into Buffalo to be married."

"Will Billy want to be there when we say our vows?"

"I'm sure he would. He's been telling me what a fool I was for not snatching you up."

"Then it's settled. I never thought I'd be married in a patched dress that belongs to a woman of ill repute."

"You can cut a hole in one of Maud's expensive draperies and wear it poncho style."

Tangled in each other's arms and legs, they rolled on the blanket and laughed.

"I'd like to stay here forever," she murmured after a kiss that seemed to last forever.

"You will. We'll build our house on this very spot."

"When?"

"Next spring. Will you mind sharing it with Billy?"

"Of course not! But what about Mrs. Eastwood?"

"I'm hoping Inez will stay on. She's the only person I know who can get along with her."

His lips found the tip of Willa's nose, then nuzzled her neck. "I like the feel of your breasts against my chest," he rasped in an agonized masculine need.

"I like it, too," she whispered.

"You make me happy and . . . hungry for you," he said and laughed. "If it wasn't getting late, I'd have you again, but as it is, it'll be dark by the time we get back to the ranch." He pulled the top of her dress together and buttoned it.

CHAPTER

* 28 *

Willa and Smith lingered so long that it was dark by the time they reached the creek crossing. Smith took the reins of the mare Willa was riding and cautioned her to duck the low branches. In a happy state of mind, she watched Smith, aware each time he turned to look at her. They came out of the dense pine forest and Smith stopped the horses.

"I smell smoke. Could be a forest fire. If it is, Plenty Mad will be happy. He's been predicting one."

Worry began to nag at Smith. A forest fire was something everyone dreaded. It was too dark to see smoke, but he sure as hell could smell it.

"Are you up to a little faster pace, honey?"

"I'll hold on."

"Yell if we get to going too fast."

Smith put his horse into a trot and the mare followed. Willa pressed her feet firmly in the stirrups and held onto the saddle horn. Still it was a jarring ride. She concentrated so hard on staying in the saddle that she didn't see what Smith saw until he shouted.

"My God! The house is on fire!"

When the reality of what he said took root, Willa gasped, "Mrs. Eastwood! Give me the reins and go. I'll be all right."

Smith did not hesitate. "Hold on. The mare will bring you to the barn."

The mare didn't want Smith's horse to run off and leave her. Willa held tightly to the reins until she settled into a pace she could handle. With her eyes on the flames coming from the roof of the big house, her heart pounding with fear, it seemed forever before she was close enough to see Inez, Billy and Plenty Mad, buckets in their hands, standing helplessly in the yard.

"Where's Smith?" Willa shouted the instant her feet were on the ground. She could see flames shooting higher than the tallest tree.

Billy turned and looked at her, an awful strained look on his face. "In there," he said.

"No! Oh, God, no!"

Maud had been in a temper since Willa had told her she was going to marry Smith. Inez had tried to reason with her but to no avail. She had cried, cussed, and sworn to kill Smith if ever she got her hands on a gun.

"He took Oliver from me long before he killed him," she shrieked and knocked a glass from Inez's hand. "He run Fanny off, and he worked it around so he gets Willa away from me. Get out, ya fat old sow. I don't need ya. I don't need anybody!"

"I'm going," Inez said crossly, "But if you have one of your fits, Maud, you'll have it by yoreself, because, by damn, I don't have to take yore shit."

"Get out! Get out!"

Maud didn't have a convulsion, but she didn't care if she

did. All her life she had taken leavings. Once again something she wanted was being taken away from her. It wasn't fair. She had liked the girl and the girl had liked her. They could have lived here together. It would have been like having Fanny home again . . . only better because Fanny was hateful at times and Willa was never mean or out of sorts. Damn Smith! He had turned her against her.

As the day worn on Maud's resentment increased to include Inez. She kowtowed to him just like everyone else. Inez didn't believe her when she told her that Smith had killed Oliver. She thought Inez was her friend. They had known each other for a long time.

By suppertime Maud was so worked up she refused the meal when Inez brought it to her.

"For crying out loud!" Inez snorted. "I even went and made bread pudding 'cause you like it so much."

"I ain't wantin' it." Maud's face was set in stubborn lines.

"Ya need a hairbrush on yore bottom, Maud Holt."

"Maud Eastwood, and don't ya forget it."

"Yore a mean, selfish old woman. That girl's done everthin' she could for you and you're puttin' a damper on her weddin' a good man."

"Good! Ha! It ain't no business of yores nohow. Ya just work here. Go tell that whiskered old billy-goat to send for the doctor. I'll have him find me a *decent* woman."

Inez hooted. "Shit, Maud, you'd not know a *decent* woman if she waved her butt in yore face."

"Get out!" Maud shouted.

"I'm goin'. I'll take the puddin' down to Billy. Want me to light the lamp?"

"Light it, and don't ya take nothin' down to Billy. Hear?"

"Billy sent up the raisins and the cinnamon for the puddin'. I'm takin' it to him. I don't give a hoot if ya like it or not."

Inez glanced at Maud's scowling face. The ornery old biddy was not going to back down.

After Inez left, Maud lay for a long while with her bony hands clasped over her stomach. She wished she hadn't told Inez to light the lamp. What did she need a light for? All she could see was three walls. With the light off she could see only what she wanted to see and remember what she wanted to remember. She liked to recall the days when she was young, when she and Carl would race their horses across the prairie—before Carl turned mean.

Maud rolled to her side and stretched to reach the lamp. It was a good six inches from her fingertips. She grasped the two spindly legs of the table to pull it closer to the bed. It moved an inch or two. She pulled harder, the table tilted and the lamp began to slide off.

"Shit!" she said and tried to right the table, but it was too late. The lamp crashed to the floor.

Suddenly fire was running across the kerosene-soaked carpet to the window curtains and spreading to the papered walls. Maud's mind went blank and she stared at it stupidly. When she came to realize what was happening, she screamed.

"Help! He . . lp!" she cried, but she could scarcely hear her own voice over the roar of the fire. Oh, God, she'd be cooked alive. "Inez!" she screamed, even though she knew that Inez had gone down to the cabin behind the bunkhouse.

She threw the feather pillows on the floor and, scarcely feeling the pain, she flung herself off the bed. Maud screamed again when her leg hit the floor and she rolled off the pillows and onto her stomach.

"Dear Jesus, don't let me die like this. He . . . lp! Someone . . . help!"

Hysterical with fear, she dug her elbows into the floor and slowly and painfully dragged herself toward the door. The fire was spreading rapidly, already racing across the ceiling. It reached the bureau. The other lamp burst into flames, but Maud was unaware of it. *She had reached the door to find it shut!* She whimpered with pain and fear. After several tries she managed to reach the doorknob and open the door a crack. It was enough to allow her fingers to slip through and she pulled it back.

Suction from the open doorway drew the swirling, leaping flames. They swept to the hall ceiling and danced rapidly down the hallway, reaching hungrily down the walls to the floor. From there the fire spread throughout the upper floor of the house like water from behind a dam that had burst.

"Smi . . . th!" Gasping for breath, Maud pulled herself down the hall toward the stairs. He had always been there when she needed him. Where was he now? "Smi . . . th, help m-me."

Maud prayed that she wouldn't swoon or have one of her fits. By keeping her face close to the floor she could breath easier. "Smith will come," she told herself aloud. "Smith will come. God, help me get to the stairway."

Maud had almost reached the top of the stairs when she thought she heard someone call her name.

"Maud!"

She listened. The hoarse shout came again.

"Maud!"

It was Smith. He had come.

"Here," she croaked, her throat filling with sobs. She lifted her face and peered through the smoke. Her eyes burned and watered. "Hurry! Hurry!"

"Keep calling so I can find you."

"He . . . re! By . . . in . . . the . . . hall! Sm . . . ith! Sm . . . ith!"

It seemed as if an eternity passed before Smith hunkered down beside her.

"I got to drag you to the stairs so I can get you on my back."

Without waiting for her to reply, Smith took her hands and dragged her to where he could go down a few steps and hoist her upon his back. He threw a wet blanket over both of them and began the slow journey down the stairs with Maud's arms clasped tightly around his neck. Flames reached for them with hungry fingers. Smith moved as fast as he dared, knowing that their only chance was to go through the hall and out the front door. If the ceiling burned through, they would be trapped. He had come in through the kitchen, but now that part of the house was feeding the ravenous fire.

Coughing, choking, with Maud on his back, Smith burst out of the roaring inferno and stumbled across the veranda and down the steps. He sucked the outside air into his grateful lungs and staggered away from the house.

"He's out! Thank God!" Willa's frantic voice reached him.

Someone pulled the wet blanket off them and he knelt so that Billy and Plenty could lift Maud off his back. Then Willa was in his arms, her hands running over him from his singed face down his arms to his hands.

"Are you all right? I was so . . . scared. Are you all right?"

"I'm fine, sweetheart."

"Are you sure?"

"I'm sure. Let Inez see to Maud. The rest of us had better get wet blankets or sacks and try to keep this fire from spreading to the grove."

It was after midnight. The Eastwood mansion was a pile of smoldering embers. It had been back-breaking work to keep the fire from spreading to the grove. From there it would have leaped to the forested hillside and Plenty Mad would have had his forest fire. Maud had been carried to the cabin behind the bunkhouse. She was in terrible pain, but before she would take the few drops of laudanum Billy had prepared for her, she insisted on seeing Smith.

He came to the bed and looked down at her. Billy, Willa and Inez stood back out of the lamplight, not knowing what to expect from this meeting.

"Ya saved my life."

"Ah, I don't know. You might have crawled down those steps."

"Ya come and ya didn't have to." Tears filled her eyes and rolled down her cheeks. "If ya'd wanted me dead you'd'a left me there."

Smith shifted his feet, plainly uncomfortable. "You don't have to bawl about it," he growled.

"I'm tryin' . . . to say thanks. And that . . . I'm sorry—"

To Smith's utter amazement, she reached for his hand and grasped it tightly.

"It's all right," he said and looked away from her.

"I knew in my heart that what you did . . . was right for Oliver, but I didn't want to believe it. I'm . . . mean and stubborn—"

"I can't argue that."

"I'll . . . try to change. Inez made me see . . . what I am. I've been so lonesome."

"Yeah . . . well— Let Billy give you that laudanum. Plenty's going to Buffalo tomorrow to fetch the preacher. Willa and I are getting married. He'll fetch the doctor too."

"Can I be at the weddin'? I ain't never been to but my own."

"It's all right with me if it's all right with Willa."

"What'll I do now, Smith? I ain't got a home."

"Of course you have. You got this one. It ain't fancy like

the big house, but you'll be taken care of.'' Maud began to cry. Smith slipped his hand from hers and looked around for Inez. "You'd better do what you can for her. She must be hurting in places she didn't know she had.''

Smith and Willa went outside and sat down on the bench. He put his arms around her and they clung to each other. All that mattered to Willa was that he was safe, holding her as she was holding him.

"I remember how terrified I was the night the crowd set fire to the house in Hublett. But it was nothing compared to how scared I was tonight when you were in that burning house.'' Willa's palm cupped his face and she kissed his smoke-blackened cheek.

"I'm glad the house is gone. Can you understand that? I think Oliver would rather it burn down than to sit there and decay.''

"Did what Mrs. Eastwood said surprise you?'' Willa asked, after they had exchanged a kiss.

"Sure did. In all the years I've been here she's never said two decent words to me.''

"Why did you go in after her? You risked your life.''

"I don't know. I didn't stop to think about it. She's a human being. She was helpless. Lord, I'm tired.''

"We'd better find a bed and get some sleep or we'll miss the wedding tomorrow.''

"How about bedding down in the haymow?''

"I'm smoky and dirty.''

"So am I. We'll bathe in the morning.''

Smith struck a match and lit a lantern. Arm in arm they went to the barn. He held the light so Willa could see to climb the ladder to the loft.

"What you doin', Smith?'' Plenty Mad came out of one of the stalls at the far end of the barn. "Damn plenty good fire, huh, Smith? Roar like herd of buffer. I say that. Plenty

Mad say fire come. Nobody pay no attention to Plenty Mad. Plenty smoke, plenty hot fire, huh, Smith?''

"We were lucky it didn't spread to the grove. It would have taken everything.''

"I say to Billy fire would come. He say I crazy Indian. I tell Billy he can hell damn kiss my ass—''

"Watch your language, Plenty,'' Smith cautioned.

"How you watch language, Smith? Can't see language. God hell damn, you gettin' crazy like Billy?''

"Stop grumbling, Plenty, and hold the lantern. Blow it out when I get up the ladder.''

"Damn hell,'' Plenty Mad grumbled. "What you goin' up there for, huh, Smith?''

"I'm going to sleep up there.''

"With silly damn white squaw?''

"Yeah, with silly damn white squaw. Now blow out the lantern and go to bed.''

"Things plenty damn bad here, Smith. Big fire, Billy say Plenty Mad crazy Indian, boss sleepin' in the hay with silly damn white squaw.''

"Yeah. Things are plenty bad.'' Smith climbed up into the haymow, took Willa's hand and led her to a far corner. They sank down into the soft hay.

"I heard what Plenty said.'' Willa giggled happily and snuggled into Smith's arms.

"About boss sleeping with silly damn white squaw? He was wrong. Boss isn't going to sleep for a while. He's going to love silly damn white squaw and tell her how much his life has changed since she came into it and make her forget the first time she saw him sleeping in the hay.''

"Silly damn white squaw has a few things to say herself. But you'd better get on with the loving; it'll be morning soon and she's getting married.''

EPILOGUE

On the porch of their new home Willa held her first-born, William Oliver Bowman. The tow-haired child was the spitting image of his green-eyed father. She hugged her son to her and turned when the screen door slammed behind her.

"Give him to me. He's getting too big for you to carry" Smith lifted the boy from her arms.

Little Billy squealed and threw his chubby arms around his father's neck.

"Ride, Papa, ride."

"Not now, rascal." Smith put his mouth against his son's neck and made loud popping sounds. The child went into spasms of giggles. "Go in and see if Grandpa'll give you a cookie." He set the child gently on his feet and steadied him until he got his balance.

Willa watched Smith and his son. How different he was from the sullen man she had known only a few years ago. Smiles came easily to his face now, and a hundred times a day his eyes would catch hers and hold for a second or two. They were one in mind and spirit and needed no words to communicate with each other. However, they talked about everything, knew everything about each other. Smith had known she was pregnant with little Billy almost as soon as she had. It was the same now. Their second child would be born during the Christmas season.

Strangely, now that Smith was at peace with himself over Oliver's death, the community accepted him. Today he and Willa were hosting a July Fourth celebration for neighboring ranchers and friends from Buffalo. There would be dinner "on the ground," horse racing and bronco busting. Smith had prepared contests for the kids and had sent to Sheridan for fireworks.

Willa was so happy that, at times, it scared her. Sometimes in the night she would awaken afraid that it was all a dream and reach for her husband, whose arms always welcomed her. Her love for the man she had married grew each and every day. He was her life and she was his.

Billy came out of the house with his "grandchild" in his arms. He was delighted with the boy and spoiled him shamefully. Little Billy had a mouthful of cookie and another in his hand.

"Ain't they comin' yet?" Billy asked. "Inez is goin' to make chili. If she keeps on a foolin' 'round she won't have time."

"They'll be along." Smith moved over behind Willa, put his arms around her and pulled her back against him. "Tired?" he murmured in her ear.

"Heavens no. I'm just barely pregnant," she whispered, her face turned up to his.

"Silly damn white squaw won't admit she's tired until she's worn out." His hand caressed her barely rounded stomach, his lips nuzzled the side of her face.

Contented, Willa leaned on her husband and looked across

the valley of gently waving grasses and watched for the buggy bringing Maud and Inez for the day. They came to the ranch as often as the weather permitted. Maud and Inez spoiled little Billy, too, but no more than his doting father did.

Smith and Maud said very little to each other when they were together, but there was no animosity between them. After the fire Maud's leg had had to be reset and now she had difficulty getting around. Still, there was a visible change in the woman. She had gained weight and at times was pleasant company. During the past year, she had suffered only one of her convulsions. Inez appeared to be happy in her present situation. She went to Buffalo to visit her family but she and Maud spent holidays with Willa and Smith.

Boomy had moved into the bunkhouse on Eastwood Ranch and was in charge of that end of the ranching operation. The longhorns were gone and white-faced cattle grazed on the land. A huge hole had been dug and the charred remains of the big house pushed into it and covered.

Plenty Mad still grumbled, quarreled with Billy, and threatened to leave, but as soon as the barn on the new place was ready, he moved in. He no longer called Willa "silly damn white squaw." He called her Smith's Squaw and declared that on the night of the fire he had told the *spirits* to help boss man make plenty fat papoose. After little Billy was born he took full credit, much to old Billy's disgust.

Jo Bell and Starr moved on out West when a buyer came along to buy Starr Palace. The greenhorn didn't realize until it was too late that it was Jo Bell who brought the customers to the saloon.

Sant had built a cabin on the land he and Smith owned and Smith was almost convinced that Sant's wandering days were over. He had taken it upon himself to teach Vince Lee and Charlie about the wild horse herds. Vince had settled down to being a good hand. They were now working to start a strain of horses using the offspring of the silver lobo and his lead mare.

Although Charlie insisted on sleeping in the bunkhouse, he was considered by Willa, Smith and Billy to be one of the family. He never mentioned his sister anymore, but sometimes he thought about her—singing, with all those men cheering her on. *If that's what makes her happy*, he'd tell himself as he fell asleep to dream about the purple mountains and the thundering steers and the people who made him happy.

A great sigh shuddered though Willa. She leaned back against her husband and watched the road where a dust cloud trailed the approaching buggy. She tilted her head and sought his eyes. They were soft with amber lights, his mouth smiling, his face free of care.

"I'm the luckiest woman in the world."

"I love you, Mrs. Bowman."

"I know." Her lips were not quite steady when he kissed them.

Willa rested against him, feeling the pump of his heart against her back. Her own heart surged.

She was wrapped in love.